An Unexpected Caliph

An Unexpected Caliph

Steven Derfler

ISBN: Softcover 978-1-4836-6506-1
Ebook 978-1-4836-6507-8

This is a work of fiction. Names, characters, places and incidents either are the product of the author's imagination or are used fictitiously, and any resemblance to any actual persons, living or dead, events, or locales is entirely coincidental.

This book was printed in the United States of America.

Rev. date: 07/11/2013

To order additional copies of this book, contact:
Xlibris Corporation
1-888-795-4274
www.Xlibris.com
Orders@Xlibris.com
119371

Contents

DEDICATION

The history of the human experience is merely "half a history". The world of archaeology puts "flesh onto the bones" of the ancient past, and allows the "what ifs" to often become realities. But all too often biases and prejudices against minority communities prevent the acceptance of their significant contribution to the nations that they called 'home'.

This work explores these very real possibilities.

Thank you to my friends and colleagues for their support and assistance in this great adventure.

Special thanks with love to my wife and daughter for sharing a love of this part of the world and experiencing it with me.

SD

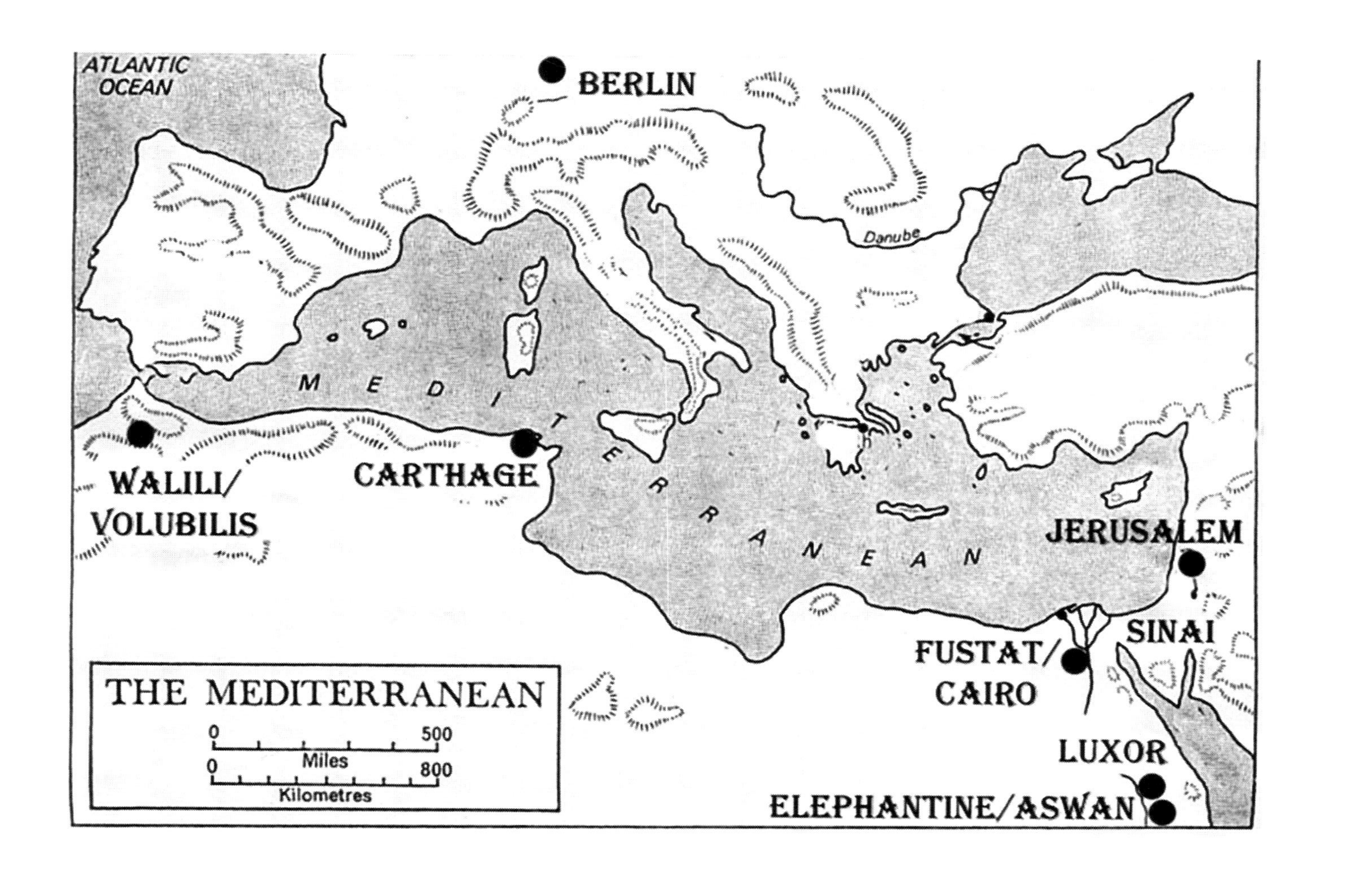
ATLANTIC OCEAN
BERLIN
Danube
MEDITERRANEAN
WALILI/
VOLUBILIS
CARTHAGE
JERUSALEM
SINAI
FUSTAT/
CAIRO
LUXOR
ELEPHANTINE/ASWAN
THE MEDITERRANEAN
0
500
Miles
0
800
Kilometres

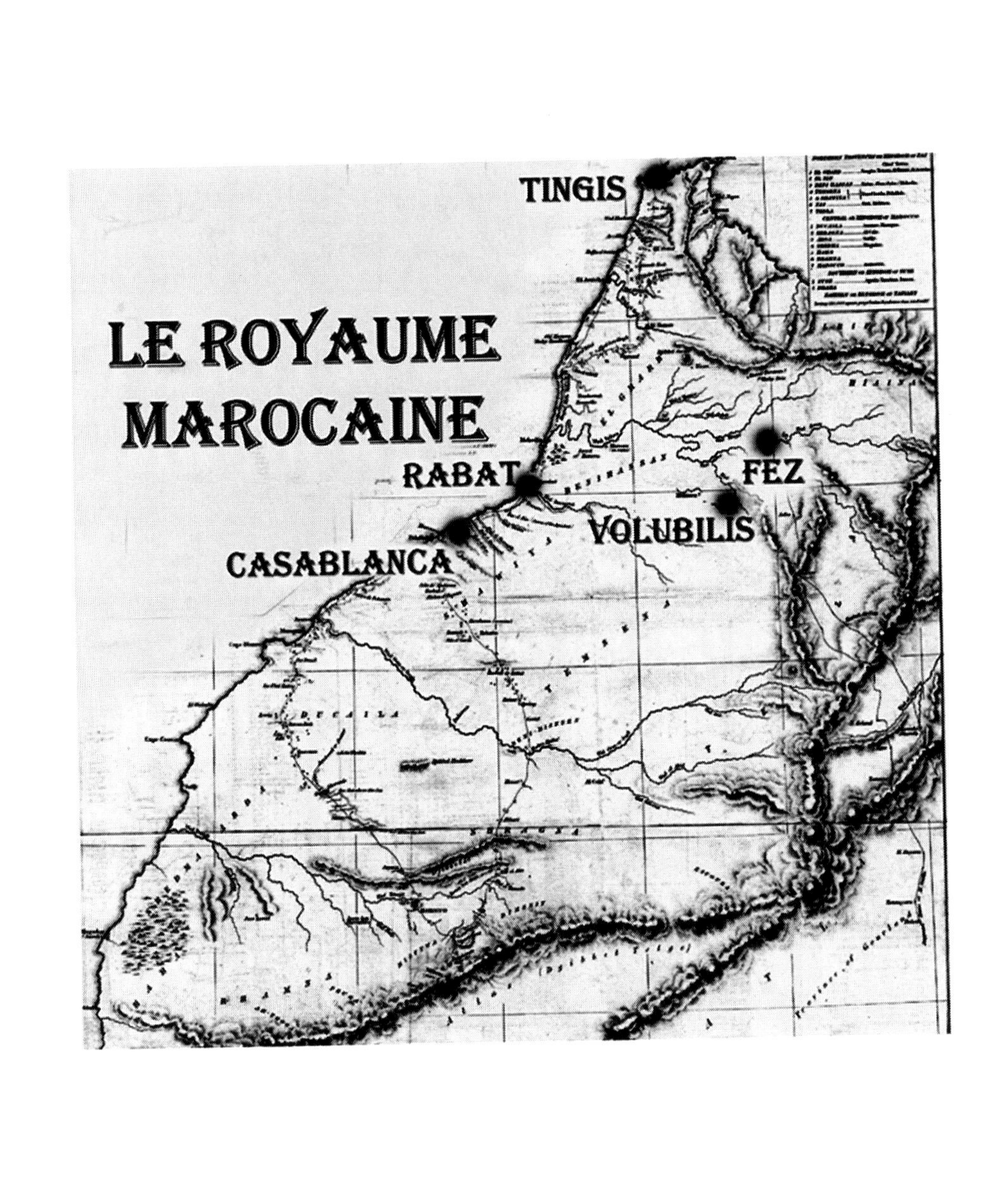
LE ROYAUME
MAROCAINE
TINGIS
RABAT
FEZ
VOLUBILIS
CASABLANCA

PROLOGUE

Tingis, 525 BCE . . .

HE STOOD PATIENTLY in the wings, just inside the crease of the heavy woven drapery that ringed the throne room apse. The men of his family had stood here for generations, serving their leader with a passion that only working in anonymity affords. After all, how would the empire react if they knew who the chief advisor to the monarch really was.

The king was weary, decline and devastation weighed heavily on this descendant of the once mighty Phoenician Empire. The days of glory, the days of economic boom and political security, results of a military superiority along the North African coastline for centuries, seemed to be coming to an end. The Carthaginians were on the rise, and, more importantly, on the move as they sought to extend their control westward to the great sea that stretched beyond the strait that separated Iberia from Africa. The founders of his Phoenician world centuries earlier felt that the narrow passage, where the two continents, like tentative lovers, almost kissed was so important for control of the region that they established a military outpost and religious shrine there in Gorham's Cave to establish a spiritual link that would allow them to ally themselves favorably with the local community.

There was no formal name for this expanse of water; the Greeks actually thought that it was an enormous river that encircled the world. It wouldn't be known as 'the Atlantic' for another century or so, when the Greek historian Herodotus would name it 'Atlantis Thalassa', the Sea of Atlas.

Regardless of its name, settlement along it eastern shoreline on the western coast of Africa was a worthy goal for its economic benefit, and the Carthaginians were trying to make the most of it. Their tremendous advantage over the descendants of Phoenicia was that, due to the remote African location, the Phoenician colonies never got a hold of the new technology of iron. They were still using bronze as the metal of choice. Carthage, on the other hand, integrated iron technology and proved their superiority via technology on the battlefield. Another benefit for Carthage came with the use of the horse. Although introduced into Egypt by the Hyksos as early as 1700 BCE, their use spread more slowly to the west – but of course coming first to Carthage before Tingitana. It wouldn't be until around 300 BCE that horses were used in caravans across the continent.

Tingis, on the cusp of the Great Sea, as the advisor's ancestors called it in the Taanach, the Hebrew Bible, was the first to feel the heat of the army from Carthage. Larache, Sale and Asileh, further southwest and directly on the great sea coast, wouldn't be far behind.

However, the most important thing that was uppermost in the king's thoughts was the protection of his family. He adored his wife and children, and the administration of his realm was directly linked to their well-being and security. What was good for his family out of necessity would translate into what was good for the monarchy. The Advisor, as he was called, knew this, and many times thought that the king's attitude on life closely reflected that of his own faith and culture. He would like to think that his own background played a major role in shaping the king's outlook on the world. That was why he continued, even in this most difficult time, to remain close to someone that he also considered a friend and ally – not just 'an employer'.

And for this, he would sacrifice his chance at escape and freedom. Eventually, in return, the king would grant him extraordinary power as the world collapsed around them, culminating in the rise to the throne of an unlikely king, known as the Agella in the ancient Berber tongue, many generations and cultural changes later.

* * *

Tingis buzzed with an expectant air, but not a good one. One could almost imagine looking to the east and seeing the vast dust clouds of 30,000 feet marching westward across the North African desert. The army of the Carthaginians was swallowing everything in its path. The name that spread in advance of their columns was the one that the Greeks had assigned to all foreigners – "barbaroi". Although the implication was there, that these non-Greek societies were uncivilized and uncultured, the word would not come to be so demeaning 'officially' for many centuries to come.

Civilians were hastily finding ways to flee southward, where they hope that protection could be afforded. Chaos reigned. The streets immediately adjacent to the city gates were clogged and traffic was at a standstill. Tempers flared as usually mild, friendly citizens of the port city assumed a moblike, escape-at-all-costs mentality. Families were torn asunder, children wrenched from the grasp of their parents because of the incessant pushing and shoving to get out the gate and onto the road to the countryside. More than one person suffered broken limbs that then precluded a flight to supposed freedom.

The king looked down from one of the palace towers and a tear rolled down his cheek. He could envision the end now as he saw neighbor fighting neighbor, rather than coalesce around his standard to defend their freedoms. He summoned The Advisor for it was now time to set in motion actions that would preserve the memory of his legacy.

"You are well aware of the circumstances that have led to what we face today. Together we have struggled to do the best that we could for our people, our land. I know what you're thinking – 'you have done the utmost given the circumstances my Lord'. But have I? Have I done absolutely everything that was humanly possible. The only real truth that I am cognizant of right now is that your family has served mine, and our people, selflessly, how do you say it in your ancient tongue? 'L'dor v'dor' – from generation to generation."

The Advisor remained mute, absorbing all that his king said with a resigned attitude; sensing the imminent defeat at hand and the ultimate indignity that awaited his ruler. He silently steeled himself for the end as well. Who said it best, 'all will turn out fine in the end; and if it isn't fine, then it isn't the end'. He thought a moment, and decided that he had no clue as to who said it. But he no longer cared if he couldn't give his king the answers that he sought – things were too far gone. But then, the next words from the mouth of the king stunned him.

"As my devoted advisor, descendant of the greatness that was once an admirable People of the Book, I have a final request that I hope you will embrace. Take this scroll, but don't read it until you and your family have safely fled. My last request is . . . ."

The captain of the royal guard burst in. "Your highness, outlying scouts have reported the Carthaginians approaching Abyla just east. You must hurry if you are to escape."

The king stood his ground. "I will defend my land with honor and dignity. Lead me to the eastern battlement and we can prepare our defenses together." And to the Advisor he simply said, "Go now with your family and serve me well by obeying my wishes." And he was off.

I

Casablanca . . . . the present

FROM THE DROWSY, never-never land of "not quite asleep yet not quite awake" state of overnight international air travel, I first sensed, rather than felt, the final approach to the airport. A subtle shift in the monotonous drone of the turbines, the slight downward pitch of the cabin, and then the obvious . . . . cabin lights came up with a shocking intensity and chimes announced the coming automated message . . . .

"Ladies and gentlemen, *madames et messieurs*, we have begun our final approach into Mohamed V International Airport, please return your tray tables and seatbacks into their upright and locked position. We'll be on the ground shortly."

It was a relatively smooth landing, after a reasonably uneventful flight – twin puffs of Saharan dust rising only a split second apart from the tarmac of Morocco's modern air gateway to the world accompanied the sudden roar of reverse thrust as the airliner quickly slowed to a crawl. After all, no longer did the *casbah* serve as the terminus of grueling desert travel across North Africa. Yet after 6 ½ hours it was enough to jar one out of the netherworld of international air travel. I began to focus upon grounded matters, such as collecting the scatterings of air travel comforts deemed necessary for long overseas travel – books, air pillows, IPod (and of course my "air guitar" to go along with the IPod).

And then, after only a few moments delay adjacent to the jetway, the 'whooosh' of the sealed doorway, allowing the first jet-fueled whiff of Casablanca, and the smiling, sun-darkened faces of Royal Air Maroc's ground crew welcoming you to *their* kingdom. Quietly I pondered the differences in style and attitude of airport personnel in dealing with their "clientele" as I stiffly struggled along several hundred meters of quiet, rubber-cupped concourse floor. I also thought about the events that drew me to this wonderfully strange kingdom.

The adventures surrounding the statue fragment of a previously "unknown" pharaoh still shook me to the core. As they say, there's nothing like a good chase through the streets of Cairo, down into the Sinai and across to Jerusalem to get the juices flowing. Throw in an old-fashioned earthquake and it would be enough for anyone to say "ENOUGH!" But that's the nature of this part of the world that I've learned to accept . . . . to a degree.

So what do I do for a little bit of R 'n R? Of course, go back to the insanity that is the chaos of the Middle East. Yet, I rationalize, Morocco is the most civil of all North African countries; having dealt with cultural and religious diversity as well as anyone could under the circumstances, even Bogart.

So why was I really here? Still chasing archaeological windmills I suppose. There had been rumors of forgotten tribes of Jews that had made their way across the Maghreb centuries ago, settling down in the Atlas Mountains in relative obscurity for a couple of hundred years – tolerated and generally forgotten or left alone by Romans and Berber tribes until the advent of Islam. Some felt that theirs was a story that could shed light on the nature of Israel in Africa so to speak. No, I wasn't referring to the Israelis in 1973 crossing Suez under the capable military leadership of Arik Sharon (who subsequently would prove incapable of fathoming the Israeli political process). I am referring to the Israelite captivity as one group of many during the heyday of Egypt's New Kingdom, their subsequent release and Exodus wanderings.

But did all of them head "back East", as followers of Charleton Heston? According to these legends, many did not – proceeding westward ho; along the North African coast through Libya, Tunisia, and Algeria on to the region of Morocco. The stories, the adventures, the myths of these people seemed to hold keys that would allow the doors of clarity to swing wide open – gaining access to puzzle pieces still missing.

* * *

I left the baggage carousel and re-entered the blinding light of the North African sun, and before my eyes could adjust was embraced in a professional wrestler's bear-hug of a greeting.

"*Saba el-kheir, Habibi, comment ca-va*?" was followed by a rapid-fire kiss on the left-then-right-then-left cheek again. My friend and colleague Omar gushed with joy, a combination of Arab and French – a passionate and sometimes dangerous mélange.

A hand-rolled cigarette in the left, my bag in the right, he steered me in the direction of his 17 year-old Peugeot 504; a car that was as immaculate as his carefully knotted tie. Old habits die hard in this part of the world, and Omar's habits would eventually die the hardest of all. His was a combination of all of the World War II stereotypes of a native Casablancan; not too Arab and perhaps a little too much French. Claude Rains had nothing over him to say the least. However, Omar was able to pull this off with little difficulty.

There was one more aspect of Omar that I neglected, his "*British-isms*". In spite of everything French that he loved, his linguistic passion was "the King's own". Peter O'Toole couldn't fly the flag more.

"I've taken the liberty of booking you at the Hyatt, after all, it is the home of your favorite bar . . ."

I remembered it well. And who wouldn't, if they'd seen the movie. Bogart and Bergmann would be right at home under the enormous teak and brass paddle-fans, sitting in the huge caned chairs, drinking and talking and listening to the old, slightly out-of-kilter upright . . . But then, what would they make of the larger-than-life stills from the movie set adorning the walls in the wide open spaces between brass sconces? I pulled shut the door and sat back with closed eyes . . . too tired to think. Omar, although impatient almost to the point of no return, grudgingly acceded to my wishes and drove on in silence.

A squeal of brakes, a heavy-handed horn, and some *very colorful* language, brought me back to this world with a jolt. The 45 km went by in what seemed like just a moment, for I had slept the entire distance from the airport to the outskirts of the city. We were just entering the international district, where foreigners had decided to build, on the southern edge of the city. A riot of color assailed me, flowers of every hue and variety grew in abundance. Stucco boundary walls that protected ambassadorial residences and private baronial estates dripped with the whites, reds and purples of Bougainvillea. The boulevard was lined with Royal Palms. A serene sense of calm and order permeated the atmosphere.

As we turned onto the Corniche, the small island that was the city's namesake appeared to our left, a couple of hundred meters out into the Atlantic. The Casa Blanca, the White House, was actually the tomb of a Muslim holy man, a *sheikh*, that pre-dated the mid-9th century founding of the modern city. From that point on, the image of the city radically shifted, to that of any other North African metropolis; dingy, dilapidated, dismal – yet dynamic – in its own way. The streets and alleys suddenly became congested with throngs of people singular of purpose, to be done with their chores, their errands, their work, before a brutal North African sun conspired with a Sirocco Wind to suck the life out of living beings foolish enough to be caught out of doors after noon-day prayers. It was for good reason that the concept of mid-day siesta extended all around the Mediterranean Rim.

Here's the thing about arriving in Casa. You're still a relatively weary traveler upon arrival, but the African day has just begun. As I am a baby-boomer approaching his mid-life crisis, the idea of second wind does not come as second nature any longer. I no longer need to feign weariness and jet-lag to try to get some quiet time alone – I just need to be truthful. I as much as told Omar that.

"But *Habibi*," came the expected protest. "It's been much too long since we all last saw you here. You must come to the shop and see lovely Martine, she constantly asks about you." I remembered his daughter, a kind girl for whom Omar would love to arrange a marriage, *to me!* I had successfully put him off during our last visit a couple of years ago, but now I could use the best excuse in the entire universe; an excuse that he could grudgingly accept.

"By the way, Omar, you know, with the jet-lag and all, I totally forgot to mention the most important thing that has happened since we last met. I have fallen, inextricably into the web of a most wonderful woman; a scholar, an athlete, a beauty of such charm and grace . . . ."

"*Halas!* Enough already . . . ." came as an almost inaudible sigh of resignation. "I get the picture, mon ami, you don't have to create a fiction . . . ."

I silently scolded myself. "My brother, were it not so, I would be honored to court the fair Martine. But I must tell you, my heart has truly been won by a dear, sweet woman named Kati Ben Yair. God has smiled kindly on both of us . . . ." I took his hand in friendship and with the other pulled out a dog-eared and creased photo of the assistant curator of Jerusalem's Rockefeller Museum. My heart warmed as he looked at the photo and involuntarily drew in a breath. He then smiled.

"Ah well, *Ma'alesh.* What's done is done, I see through your eyes into your heart, and I see the same view via hers. All the best. She *will* have to visit Casa, and soon. After all, as a new member of our extended family . . . ." He blind-sided me with his bear-hug again. As I felt that I had breathed my last breath, I knew that all was right. Yet who to find for Martine?

I wondered where Eitan, my Israeli 'brother', was . . . . or for that matter my other 'Egyptian brother', Sobhy. *Now that* would be a match, I smiled inwardly.

* * *

The cool, crisp air of the glass and chrome lobby of the Hyatt was a welcome relief after the Peugeot's balky, clammy air conditioning. The beaded sweat cooled so rapidly as to send an involuntary shudder down my backside. Omar, always unflappable wherever he was, seemed to adapt instantly to the climatic change with little or no visible sign of discomfort. He ambled over to The American Bar, a cigarette already well on its way to its last few puffs even before he slouched down into one of the blood-red leather and brass-studded settees that lined the walls.

I, on the other hand, found that the catnap on the ride in merely sped up the process of jet-lagged fatigue, rather than ameliorated it. The smooth check-in became a faint footnote to the already long day as I wearily plopped down beside my friend.

"So, *mon ami*, are the rumors floating amongst my colleagues true? Did you *really* burn down the Cairo Museum because you lost a handful of *Shesh Besh* games due to inept rolling of the dice?"

Omar's laugh began as a rumble deep within the chasm of his torso, welling up and out as a freight train careening along a downhill slope. Quickly, and somewhat frighteningly, it turned into a dry hacking that only a quick shot of liquid could quell. He took out his starched linen handkerchief, wiped his eyes, then his mouth, and gave a feeble smile of apology. My look of concern must have alarmed him as well, as he hurriedly took a deep breath and resumed what I now discerned as a false bravado. He shrugged it off, but behind those penetrating eyes was something else, the look of a man struggling to face his own mortality. Omar smiled again at his recollection of the Egyptian events. Yet I saw in his eyes a quizzical, searching look that belied his attempt at humor.

"You know, there are a few people here upset with the stories that came out of *El Kahireh*, in spite of all efforts to hush it up."

I sat back, reluctant to draw my long time companion into a closed chapter.

"Let's just say that the toll of the earthquake was of a magnitude that was greater in scale than any of us could ever imagine." I knew that statement wouldn't mollify him in the least, but that it would suffice for now.

"But you know, I'm here now, ready to dive into the mysteries of our ancestors with total focus . . . if you'd only put out that foul-smelling stick and talk to me . . . ."

* * *

Traditional scholarship had widely assumed that a Jewish presence in North Africa came about as a result of the Hellenization process in the 3rd and 2nd centuries BCE, with Greek Jews migrating west in search of fortune. After all, the Ptolemaic Greek Empire of Egypt was well known for its tolerance, if not outright support, of "its Jews" as solid citizens. And the literary and archaeological evidence fully bore this out. The Jewish communities from Alexandria to Aswan enjoyed all the creature comforts of the mid-to-upper classes of this society, well integrated into its everyday structure. That is, until the Islamic revolution.

The incomplete picture of the foundations of the "*Sephardim*", the North African, Arab, Jews, was not helped by either archaeology or historical analysis for decades. This was in part due to the intransigence of emerging Arab states in the 20th century with regard to anything "Jewish" or even remotely connected with the State of Israel; in part due to sparse discoveries that could shed light on this subject.

Even the Jews of North Africa seemed to be content with taking pride in a 22 century old tradition, rather than be curious about their true, earlier origins. I suspected that something else came into play, though. For decades, at least since the rise of political Zionism, they were in fear of their lives, or at best their homes and livelihoods, should they "rock the boat" and attempt to delve into the past with abandon, in search of the lost chords that signaled the opening stanza of their sojourn in the *Maghreb*, the North African coast. After all, why jeopardize a healthy, prosperous existence in a country that accepted them, just for a few extra generations and substantive link to Israel, viewed with an irrational hatred by Arab regimes. Yes, I understood, although it was painful.

After all, here in Morocco, over a quarter of a million Jews, an integral part of the kingdom socially, politically, economically, found themselves "on the road again" with the declaration of the Jewish State in 1948.

Omar came from a family that could legitimately trace its roots back to the 12th century, during the rule of the *Almohads*. They were of mountain-Berber stock, and had suffered at the hands of the "lowlanders" of Morocco, those living along the coastal plains of both the Atlantic Ocean and the Mediterranean Sea, for centuries. The *Almohads* unified, rose up and established a kingdom that stretched from Cap Spartel, at the confluence of these great bodies of water, all the way along the North African coast to the vast desert of Libya. In addition, they would cross the Straits of Jebel Tarik and enter Iberia. In 1148 these North Africans would conquer the famed city of Cordoba.

However, their own suffering gave rise to their creation of an Islamic kingdom that relied on a strict fundamentalist Islamic doctrine. Any and all under their rule who were of a different path were subject to intense scrutiny, and often forced to adapt to this rigid faith . . . or die.

Those Jews who stayed were either converted or killed. They were called a wide variety of names by their overlords. One large group in Morocco was the *Anusim* (Hebrew) `the coerced'. They were Jews who were converted to Islam by force. It was also applied to their descendants. Many of them continued to practice Judaism in secret.

It would be at this time that one of Judaism's greatest philosophers and religious leaders, Moses ben Maimon, Maimonides, would come into direct contact with this dynasty. Born in the Iberian Peninsula, his family would be forced to flee rather than convert to Islam or be killed. After ten years of wandering, the family would end up in Morocco.

From 1159-1165 his presence graced the city of Fez, where he studied at the University of *Al-Karaouine*. During this time, he composed his acclaimed commentary on the *Mishnah* which he completed around 1168. His spiritual presence affected all in Fez, including Islamic scholars. Yet this wouldn't prevent another forced migration, eventually ending up in Egypt.

In order to escape from the 'inevitable conversion or death', Maimonides would first flee to the Holy Land, and then eventually settle in Fustat, Egypt; now today Old Cairo.

Omar's family apparently fell into the category of *Anusim*, and took a veneer of Islam as a 'cover story' until the mid 13th century. At that time, the *Almohads* were overthrown by a new dynasty, the *Merinids*. They seemed to look with favor upon the remnant of the Jewish community, and offered preferential treatment.

At this time, Omar's family celebrated a low-key 'coming-out' and resumed a modest, yet circumspect, life as Jews. This 'under-the-radar' approach allowed them to survive and become well respected members of their community. But they always kept an eye out, the proverbial glance over the shoulder now embedded as a character trait from one generation to the next.

* * *

Protocol, and friendship, insisted that I sit and drink a cup of 'mud', that thick and potent cup of Arabic coffee laced with cardamom. This was in spite of my obvious weary state.

"I have long wondered at my ancestors' status under the kings of Morocco prior to their going into hiding," he told me. "Who were they before, how did they manage to survive? And I'm not just referring to my immediate family, but all Jews in the *Maghreb*. Some information has trickled up to us . . ."

I interrupted, perhaps in part due to my tiredness, in part due to my, at times, nitpicking nature when it comes to linguistic 'correctness'.

"You mean 'trickle down' don't you?" I teased. "Gravity prevents 'trickling up'!"

I realized how difficult English idioms (or idiots) could be, but couldn't resist. To me, the irregularities of English can confound even native speakers. Take, for instance, the verb 'to be'. It's more irregular than a circus fire-eater's bowels! One of the biggest scams in English is the conjugation of this verb. Where in the world did 'go, went and have gone' come from? Shouldn't the natural progression be 'go, goed, and have goed'? Anyway . . . . I let him go on.

"Well, after long hours in the General Library and Archives, on the campus of Muhammad V University in Rabat, I found some interesting tidbits. As you know, it is *the* national library, with holdings of 600,000 volumes."

He started to slip into his 'tour guide' mode – for that was a part-time job for him as well.

"But it wasn't those everyday volumes, but the 1,600 ancient manuscripts in Arabic that drew me to the archive room. A couple of them mentioned 'Jewish Berber tribes' and it got me to wondering.

The Muslim conquest of North Africa west of Egypt began in the late 7th century. One of the most famous episodes, or myths, of resistance to the conquerors is the story of the *Kahina* ("priestess/sorcerer"). According to Ibn Khaldun and earlier Muslim historians, the Kahina was the leader of what may have been Judaized Berber tribes in the Jerawa and Aures Mountains who fought long and valiantly before succumbing. The mythical *Kahina* has since been adopted as a symbol, in turn, by French colonialists, Algerian nationalists, Jewish nationalists, and 'Berber – backers', while also winning the grudging respect of Muslim Arab historians . . ."

I couldn't resist . . .

"You mean carpet pads?" I clearly was 'punch-drunk' with travel-related weariness. "I'm going to bed, see you at dinner".

* * *

The few short hours went by all too soon. The faint call of the *muezzin* gently brought me back to consciousness. It was at this moment that I *could* have created a formula for fomenting a future international incident.

As everyone familiar with Islam knows, the world is an enormous cartwheel when it comes to the Islamic direction of prayer. Around 624, after Mohamed and his followers, the *Umma,* were unceremoniously evicted from the city of Mecca because of their monotheistic zeal, the community would emigrate and set up shop in the city of Medina, about 160 km away. They were welcomed in the community with open arms, and quickly built the oldest existing mosque in the world, The Prophet's Mosque. Mohamed, after initially guiding his followers to pray in the direction of Jerusalem, the 'hometown' of monotheism, found that his emotional and spiritual ties to the city of his revelation were stronger than The Holy, *al Quds* in Arabic. He soon rescinded his order and made Mecca the hub of the Islamic 'wheel'.

As a result, every Moslem in the world orients his or her prayer in the direction of Mecca. Mosques would follow that premise as well, with the *Qibla,* the directional wall facing Mecca, containing the precise prayer niche, or *Mithrab,* that showed the way to the holy city.

For travelers, modern amenities can be very generic. A Hyatt is a Hyatt is a Hyatt anywhere in the world. It is exactly this conformity that gives aid and comfort to those on long journeys – a sense of 'having been there'.

However, this doesn't bode well for the Moslem journeyer, and confusion can easily reign. After all, as one of Islam's five pillars, prayer is an essential for the devout adherent to the faith. In a foreign city, in the dark of night or within a heavily draped room, who will know where Mecca lies over the horizon.

The answer in the region was to glue "Mecca finders", small stickers with an image of the *Ka'aba* in the Great Mosque, with an arrow pointing in the direction of prayer. This would allow the guest to unroll his or her prayer mat in the direction of the city and pray with complete confidence.

Unless, of course, I had succeeded in my foggy-minded quest for order. At times I can be a bit anal about neatness and 'regularity'. As I slowly roused my sleep-deprived body from its uneasy unconscious state, I glanced at the nightstand and saw what I imagined was a small coaster. It was a bit cockeyed on the table. My ingrained sense of order commanded my hand to straighten out this piece of cardboard and neatly align it with a corner. I discovered that *it was tightly glued down!* As I rubbed my eyes, I suddenly realized that it indeed was a Mecca finder! God forbid that I should have actually unpeeled it, and re-placed it in the wrong direction! Moslem occupants in the room following my stay would have unknowingly prayed in the wrong direction!

Religious crisis diverted, I quickly showered and headed down to meet my friend.

* * *

Meals in the Mideast and North Africa are a sensory overload. The sights, the aromas, and above all, the tastes of the region are simply out of this world. And when it's on a twenty-five foot long buffet table, well, perhaps that's why the native garb is the *djellabah*, the loosely flowing male gown that hides nearly all the sins of overindulgence!

I found Omar pacing impatiently by the Maitre D's podium, the ubiquitous cigarette dangling in his left hand. Apparently he hadn't eaten for, oh, three hours, and it clearly was his feeding time. And he let me know it. I needed to get the last word in before entering the dining room.

"You know, this hotel has a non-smoking policy in the dining room; it *is* universally accepted now." I glared mockingly at him.

"But *mon ami*, there's nothing like a smoke and snifter of cognac after a meal."

"This is *before* . . ." I wasn't allowed to continue.

"*Ma'alesh*, this is Maroc," he replied.

I caved – sometimes there's no fighting Moroccan logic, especially in three languages.

I immediately knew that it was a mistake to sit down for a grand meal if I really wanted to 'sync' my body by the next morning. But I crumble like aged Feta when it comes to a well prepared *tagine* meal. Slow-cooked lamb in a succulent apricot sauce, over a bed of couscous and asparagus spears is heavenly. We sat back and relished the thought of sweet, minty tea and *Halwa dyal Makina*, the tubular Moroccan pastry that was injected with a rich chocolate crème, that we could see on the waiter's tray as he approached us, gracefully weaving between tables at a breakneck speed. I wondered if both the tray and waiter would remain upright by the time they got to us.

"Looks like Adrian Peterson of the Vikings", as I pointed at him.

"*Qui est ce*?" "Who's that?" came from behind the linen napkin as Omar wiped the last bit of juice from his chin.

"O, no one other than one of the greatest football running backs of the new century."

"You mean like David Beckham?"

I forgot what continent I was on. "Never mind, it's time to loosen our belts a notch". Although full, we still attacked the plate with gusto.

Between sojourns back to the buffet, we explored avenues of inquiry into this fascinating notion of rediscovering ancient community interaction. As Omar pondered the glory of the dessert table, I wracked my brain to come up with a coherent plan. To me, the most logical approach would be to more fully explore the great collection of ancient secular and Jewish texts from Egypt.

"I think that we need to go to some of the original sources to see exactly what the ancients knew pertaining to the tribal and spiritual history of the *Maghreb*. Maybe it's time to return to Egypt."

I looked at Omar. If I were to 'Google' the definition of 'double-take', his photo would have graced the article.

"After all that you went through in *Misr*", he had used the Arabic term for the country, "I would have thought that a *vacance* from that land would continue to be in order." He shook his head slowly, but a piece of baklava still made its way into his mouth with nary a crumb lost on his shirtfront.

"I know, I know, but as you say, *ma'alesh,* it's the most straightforward solution – at least at this time.

Omar went on, "In that case, perhaps I'll join you, for it's been a while since I last visited Fustat and the Ben Ezra." Using the ancient name for Cairo, he was referring to the ancient synagogue in the Coptic Quarter and the documents in the *Genizeh,* or storage facility.

In Judaism then, as now, sacred texts of all sorts were considered, well, sacred. As a result, in this instance, one of the major tenets of Judaism, that of being caretakers of and responsible for, the world, fell by the wayside. *Tikkun Olam,* "repairing the world", meant being stewards of the planet in every way. So today this would obviously include 'going green'. However it was not extended to sacred texts. There's no recycling of paper and re-using resources. For one never knew where the material would be sent and how it would be re-constituted.

When a Jewish text became worn out, damaged, torn or otherwise unreadable, it would be symbolically "buried" with all respect and dignity. In the ancient world, at times, the damaged material would actually be buried. The term that would be used in Hebrew was *Genizeh,* "storage room", coming from the root meaning "to hide". However, the practice soon was extended to nearly all documents with a Jewish context. The reason for this was that nearly all personal and secular letters and legal contracts could open with an invocation of God.

According to both the *Books of Kings and Chronicles* in the Hebrew Bible, in the 7th century BCE the King, Josiah, would institute this concept in order to preserve the Ark from being captured, and it would then extend to all sacred writings. The *Talmud*, Jewish commentary ascribed to between 200-500 CE, (Tractate Shabbat 115a) directs that holy writings require a "genizah". So clearly there is ancient precedent.

However, my friend was mistaken as to which ancient sources I was talking about.

"*YOU* can visit Old Cairo at your leisure. *I* was thinking of the wonderful collection of Aramaic papyri from Elephantine. Many are housed at the Egyptian Museum, and we'll just have to proceed from there. I think that my friend Sobhy's reputation has been sufficiently rehabilitated that there should be absolutely no problem with the SCA. In fact, with the way that things eventually all turned out, I should have lots of *proteksia* with the powers that be. In fact, *they* should be the ones turning to me to solve other mysteries because of the track record."

Utter disbelief first flashed across Omar's face, then his enormous, crooked smile lent audio to his visual and he laughed aloud. "You're right, in spite of the *pflabunged* comedy of errors, all turned out for the best!"

I turned back to him, "And *where* did you pick up Yiddish all of a sudden?" I was amazed. He had used the word for "screw-up" in that amalgam of Hebrew and German with a flair.

"Al-khrite al-khreddy, ve vill proceed mit der plan!" Once again, the master of linguistic butchery had me rolling on the floor. In spite of the fact that Morocco was far removed from the central European world of Ashkenazic Jewry, he had the Yiddish/English accent down pat. My grandmother would have fully understood, and twisted my ear for laughing at what *she* would have heard as impeccable English!

All of this was well and good, but first we needed to get re-acquainted with the foundation in Morocco as we all knew it. This meant heading north and inland to Fez.

* * *

The sun burned the early morning mist away, as I walked down the half-flight from the restaurant to the lobby and corner entry. My travel bag slung over the shoulder, I heard, rather than saw, Omar's approach down Avenue *Moulay Hassan I*. The wheezing and belching of smoke made the car somewhat indistinguishable from the dozens of other similarly maintained personal vehicles going to work as the day began. The same held true as he lay on the horn to grab my attention – the cacophony of sound reminded me of Cairo. The Peugeot pulled into the porticoed driveway. I waved away the doorman as I approached the vehicle. His chagrined look indicated that he knew that no tip was coming. Omar's car looked like it was on fire inside. The grayish-white smoke of at least a dozen already-smoked *Gitanes* filled the interior; as attested to by the overflowing ashtray I saw as I tried to strap myself in. The extender seemed to be stuck on the "child-size" position as I locked up. "Tight" wasn't the right word – how about "crushing"? Coupled with the foul air, I just knew that the ride was going to be a disaster.

"How can you possibly drive like this? Can you even see where you're going?" I cranked down the window as fast as humanly possible given the age of the mechanism. I then reached around to the passenger-side rear window and lowered that pane as well.

"Don' worry, *habibi*, once we're on the A3 to Rabat the breeze will blow away the remnants and, by the way, I don't smoke while on the highway – too much chance for an accident."

"At the rate that you're going, we'll be dead long before . . . ." and I left it at that.

Soon we left the chaotic Casablancan streets and hit the highway north to the imperial city of Rabat. The city today is the political capital of the Kingdom. The older, ancient city, *Salé*, sat astride the *Bou Regreg* River, and served to protect the river trade that emptied out into the Atlantic Ocean. Its location gave it its name from the Berber, *Asla*, and meaning 'rock'. The bastardization of that tongue would lead to '*Salê*'. The first settlement seems to have been one of the westernmost Phoenician colonies on record during the 7th century BCE. The Romans called the place *Sala Colonia*, part of their province of *Mauritania Tingitane*. Pliny the Elder mentions it (as a desert town infested with elephants!). The Vandals captured the area in the 5th century CE and left behind a number of blonde, blue-eyed Berbers. The Arabs of the 7th century CE kept the old name and believed it derived from "*Sala*", the son of Ham, and son of Noah. Their lore said that *Salé* was the first city ever built by the Berbers.

In spite of the fact that it was a mere 250 km distance, the road congestion eventually put us on the outskirts by midday. The bottled water had run out an hour earlier, so we opted to break for lunch and a bit of rest before moving on. We swung off the main thoroughfare and headed for the *Chellah* Necropolis. It is a lovely place to rest, grab a bite, and take note of a couple of thousand years of history as well.

Approaching the southeastern side of Rabat, nearing the *Chellah*, the traffic thickened considerably and slowed to a crawl. As we pulled up to the car park, the unbelievably beautiful sounds of a jazz composition wafted through the air. Omar smacked his forehead with an open palm.

"I totally forgot . . . all this month is '*Jazz au Chellah*', an annual jazz festival that's been around for nearly a dozen years! Just our luck . . . ." he said.

I looked at him with delight. "You're absolutely right. *It is* just our luck. We needed a break, and now it's with some really great music!" Music was still an integral part of my life.

We walked over to the stone and mud brick entry, nearly 1000 years old, bought entry tickets and proceeded into the compound. The area teemed with people, bringing renewed life to the ancient fortress complex in a way that it hadn't seen for a long while. The festive occasion lifted our spirits. Street vendors and food carts lined the stone-covered paths. Children darted in and about the Roman-era ruins. And even the storks in their enormous nests, built on the tops of ancient minarets from the ruins of the 12th century *Almohad* mosque, seemed to enjoy the rebirth. On the ground, the somewhat kitschy water sellers in their flamboyant costumes and wide-brimmed hats now felt right at home – and young and old stood in line to get their photos taken (of course, in the process leaving the customary *dirham* tip). It was truly a delightful experience, one that fortified us to help continue the rest of the journey to Fez.

As we reluctantly bid farewell to the *Chellah*, we worked our way across the Avenue Hassan II to the N6 that merged into the A2 expressway. It would be another 170 km to Fez, and most likely a mid-evening arrival. It's a good thing that we booked space ahead of time as the A's a feeder road, the N6, wended its way through rich farm land. This was much the same way that country roads criss-crossed the U.S. in the 1960s before Eisenhower mandated the interstate highway system. Think Route 66, and you're on your way to get your kicks. Huge stands of cork trees lined the route and it seemed that this part of the world was yet to be touched by the 21st century. With the wind blowing through the open window of the Peugeot, I closed my eyes and remembered the stories that my father told me about a different age – when the world lost its innocence and America took on the responsibility of being a world power.

However, when he did reminisce, some of the stories were wonderful tales of the past when an American had his eyes opened to the world. The authenticity of his adventures was at times interwoven with what sounded like "exaggerated inventiveness" as I would put it kindly.

Omar glanced over at me. "Hey, *Amriki!* You're supposed to keep me awake!" He punched my bicep. "Talk to me *mon ami* before we have a train wreck even though there's no train."

I rubbed my shoulder, then my eyes, and told him one of my father's stories. "You know the old man was all over North Africa during the war", I began. He was acquainted to a degree with my background. "Well, after landing at *Sidi Slimane*, his unit was barracked with a British garrison in Fez. It was actually the foundation for the Nouvelle Ville that would spring up outside the walled city following the war. It was located along the southern bank of the *Oued el Adhan* – but still within walking distance of Fez el Bali. It was safe, secure by then, for Rommel was light years away to the east. So Allied soldiers were free to roam about the town, and mix with the locals. As he put it much later, 'Bogie had nothing on him and his buddies.'"

Omar stared at me longer than was comfortable. After all, he *still* was driving. And the N6 was chocked full of tractors and wagons now that we were well on the road inland. And apparently he watched too much of the Golf Channel in his spare time.

"Your father played golf very poorly in Fez then?" he innocently (?) asked. Usually I could read his face like a *Classics Illustrated*, it was that animated. But now, I wasn't quite sure.

"I was referring to the movie, *idiote!*" I said with a smile. Suddenly his grin was wider than the roadway.

"I was just pulling your arm pretty good there!" he laughed. I'd been had. And now I knew it. But at least I could get one last shot, although somewhat anemic, at him and his butchered English idiom.

"I hope that you meant 'leg'." I continued with the story and he settled in behind the wheel with a refreshed look on his face.

II

North Africa, 1942 . . .

HE WAS A combat engineer with the 36th Brigade. His unit had landed in 1942 at the *Sidi Slimane* Air Field in the area, to serve as support for the Algerian Campaign, called Operation Torch. They would then go on in support of the Tunisian Campaign which would effectively force the Axis out of Africa. At that time, the North Africans were ecstatically delighted that the Allies had landed. They had endured the arrogant incompetence of the Italians and the insufferable haughtiness of the Germans of Rommel's famed *AfrikaKorps.* The oppressiveness of Axis superiority weighed even more heavily on them than the Sub-Saharan desert climate. The naïve, fresh-faced youth of America were welcomed with open arms. But the horrors of desert warfare would soon harden them. Even to his dying day, it was still a sore spot with my father.

There was basically only one hard and fast rule for the soldiers. Remember that they were the guests in Morocco, and try to act accordingly. Although set in the *Maghreb,* Arabic Africa, Morocco had suffered at the hands of European colonialists for centuries. Part of that 'suffering' involved the westernization of the people – and not necessarily the good portions of the west. Speakeasies abounded, and when the allies landed, spread their offerings to include not only alcohol and gambling, but members of the opposite sex. This didn't refer necessarily to call girls or 'escorts', but more often than not hostesses and dance partners in the public venues.

Many of these were located in converted *riads,* or courtyard houses that were typical in this part of the world. The streets of any *medina,* or walled city, were narrow, alley-like affairs that were often only a few feet wide. All buildings directly fronted the paved way, making for dark, airless corridors. In addition, at night these poorly lit, noisy paths were not the safest places to be even for longtime residents, until the advent of electricity. So houses were designed with all of these criteria in mind. There were really no windows on the ground-floor buildings – a matter of security. After all, a window is an easy access point for anyone who really wants to get in. So the buildings were patterned after the age-old *megaron*-style defensive structure; a series of rooms that surrounded a central court.

As you entered the heavy wood-and-bronze-barred doorway you passed between two rooms, a distance of perhaps five m. or so. The hall was dark and uninviting to say the least. But suddenly you entered into an enormous space of light and air, quiet except for the soft burbling of a central fountain. The sounds of the city were left far behind, as an Eden-like atmosphere enveloped you. Rooms with folding wooden door panels were left wide open to the court to allow in air and light. The same held true for the upper storeys – many times reaching four or even five floors. But they did have windows facing the street to allow greater circulation. However the trade-off was usually the street sounds that encroached on the rooms from the latticed windows.

Remember, this is an Arabic land, where ostensibly the honor of a woman was protected. Moslem women were not to be seen unveiled in public after reaching the age of puberty. More often than not, they were not expected to take part in everyday city life after marriage. It must have been tremendously stifling for them to sit at home day-in and day-out. The upper floor windows were their only glimpse onto the vibrant life of the *medina*. The architectural compromise that would allow women to see, but yet not be seen, was a wooden screen called a *mushrabiyya*. This would allow limited light and air into the chamber, but prevent anyone from street level from seeing into the room and perhaps catching a glimpse of someone looking out. The carved elegance of these panels can still be seen today in hundreds of *riads*.

During one of these evening outings, several of the soldiers, including my father, happened upon one such converted house, where they heard music drifting out of the doorway. They entered into the *Riad du Soleil* to have a couple of beers and relax. By all accounts, the evening was turning out to be festive, yet not overly raucous. A few 'modern' Moroccan women dared to dress in western clothing and go to enjoy jazz and the opportunity to mingle with the foreigners. Apparently this didn't sit very well with their male relatives, traditionalists who were very anti-western in spite of their liberation at Allied hands. To top it off, some of these Moroccan men actually sided with their former occupiers, the Vichy French Nazi sympathizers, because, perversely, their strict regimentation of occupied Moroccan life sort of fell in line with traditional Islamic doctrines. These extended not only to women but to any of the minorities within the realm, like Moroccan

Jews. After all, in spite of being people of the book, they were still infidels in the eyes of the faithful; and therefore subject to treatment as second-class citizens in spite of their ancient pedigree.

The GIs seemed to be totally enjoying themselves. The word 'totally' should be stressed, because they were *totally* oblivious to the fact that several Moroccan men at the battered, zinc-topped bar were *totally* focused on the American soldiers and the young Moroccan women sharing a table with them. It would turn out that they were brothers of the girls, and on strict orders from their fathers, the patriarchs of the family, that no harm should befall the young ladies. Now, there are many interpretations of the word 'harm'. To the GIs, acting with an extraordinary amount of chivalry for young, western, military men out to blow off steam from being cooped up on a military base, they were acting with a tremendous sense of decorum, albeit in a somewhat inebriated state. There had been no risqué language, no subtle-or not so subtle – hints at inappropriate behavior; just some 'good ole boys' out to enjoy the evening and perhaps, if lucky, get a peck on the cheek.

To those at the bar, even the mere presence of the girls in the converted *riad* was enough to infuriate them, and as an extension, their fathers as well. So they bided their time, waiting for the right moment. However, they knew full well that 'the moment' should not be in the bar – the military police constantly patrolled the *medina* and were all too aware of establishments that were frequented by the troops. Barkeeps had sawed-off shotguns or the North African equivalent of a baseball bat, and a police whistle on a cord around their necks. The unwritten rule that was understood by all was that it was legit to swing or shoot first, and then blow the whistle for military intervention. More often than not, this didn't bode well for instigators.

As curfew approached (and yes, there was one that was strictly enforced the next morning) the GIs bade farewell to the girls, and the establishment, and began to weave their somewhat drunk, yet happy, way back to the barracks. None noticed the leather-jacketed men trailing a dozen or so meters behind. At that moment, my father noted that he left his forage cap back at the *riad.* He told the others to go on ahead, and that he would catch up in a few minutes. He found the cap right where he had left it, gave the bartender a *dirham* as a tip of thanks that it still was there, and hurried along the narrow alleyway in search of his buddies.

In the meantime, the other men saw that the one GI had split from the others. This gave them precisely the edge that they needed. They turned into a side street and waited for him to re-emerge from the *Soleil,* a solitary target. Once he did, they let him pass and then started to tail him. One of the rougher men sprinted around a corner and disappeared from view. Remember, the narrow passages are dim even in the midday due to the height of the buildings on either side of the pavement and the claustrophobic width. At night, the smallest of paths had no light at all. My father quickly lost his way and the men following sensed an opening. As they say, he 'heard the footsteps' getting closer and closer, but didn't yet see them. He quickened his pace, they quickened theirs. It seemed that they were comfortable in the spacing, since they knew precisely where they were – a great advantage. Suddenly someone whistled from a doorway up ahead. It was the presumed leader of the pack who had earlier broken away to set the ambush. One of those trailing answered with a whistle of his own. My father sobered very quickly at this point. Fear will do that to you. He gauged where the forward sound had come from, took off his boots, and swiftly ducked into a narrow lane. He then ran as if his life depended on it (and to hear him retell the story, it *probably did!*). Stockinged-feet made no measurable sound on the pavement, and he fled from them, apparently, successfully.

Once the Arab group met up with the leader who was in front, and found no one in between them, their anger grew. To save face, they couldn't simply leave, they needed to find this soldier and, through him, teach all the foreigners a lesson. The men dispersed and began to search all the alleys and avenues in that part of the *medina*. After all, they knew the quarter like the backs of their hands – they grew up here.

As the GI rushed through the side streets, they perceptibly narrowed more and more til he found himself on a lane just about a meter and a half wide. Twenty or so meters on the path dead-ended at a plain, nondescript wooden door. In the darkness, from the faint look and feel, it seemed centuries old. My father felt trapped and panic began to set in. By now, he was stone-cold sober and scared to death. He ran his hands over the rough, scarred surface. Tiny splinters embedded in his palms as he sought the door handle. He found a fairly large iron bolt that seemed to shriek at the sky as he threw it back along the heavily rusted channel. He was sure that the others had heard it as well. He pushed the door in a couple of feet, slipped through the entry and then heaved the door shut with all his might.

As soon as he did this, he threw the deadbolt back along the track, and then swung it down into a locking position. Given the weight and heft of the iron bolt and the thick, forged channel, he was sure that no one could break into the place that he found refuge. But where exactly was he?

The darkness was pierced with a faint glow, coming from a miniscule lamp suspended from the ceiling at the far end of a room. It flickered, indicating that in it was some kind of candle or wicked oil lamp. The light afforded absolutely no help in clarifying the interior space. One couldn't even make out any furnishings, as the darkness swallowed everything beyond a one or two meter distance away from the tin metal cage. The only thing to do was to curl up in a corner, try to get some rest, and wait things out til the morning – all the while hoping that whoever was in pursuit had lost the trail and given up.

Outside, in the passages along the *medina's* periphery, the brothers of the young women from the bar had indeed lost the trail. But they doggedly kept up the pretense of the search, in part to assuage their guilt at having 'failed' to protect their sisters, in part to save face the next day when asked by their friends if they in fact had beaten the *anglisi* to a pulp. To many Moroccans, there was no difference in the nationalities of the foreign soldiers, they simply opted for the easy answer to all the woes of North Africa and the Middle East – 'blame it on the British'. The funny thing, though, was that all too often, as a matter of course, most of the time, the phrase fit!

The fellas quietly tried several doors, and finding them locked tight against the night, finally called it quits and went home – all the while discussing amongst themselves the concocted story about 'capture, retribution and annihilation'. One even smashed his knuckles in feigned outrage against the wall, bloodying his hand. By morning, the scabbed over areas would lend credence to their recounting of the night. And, although their sisters would feign anger and frustration at the barbaric and antiquated approach to the world, would secretly be proud and pleased. They too would find the old ways hard to shake in this uncertain mid-twentieth century war.

* * *

Dawn breaks quickly in North Africa, and the sun burns through the early morning mist with a swift vengeance – preparing to sear those caught out of doors after eleven in the morning. The idea of 'pm siesta' is well suited for the entire Mediterranean rim, not just the southern European shore.

My father was roused from his rough, fitful couple of hours of uneasy rest by the *Adhan,* the Islamic call to prayer, echoing from the *minarets* of a dozen mosques that were within earshot. It can be a beautiful, haunting sound, soaring and reverberating across rooftops and courtyards throughout the closed city – designed to awaken the faithful to a prayerful start of the day. However, given the Doppler effect, and the split-second difference in starting times by the various *muezzins,* or 'callers to prayer', it becomes a cacophony of sound that, to the Moslems, is a slight irritant; but to others unfamiliar, a nightmarishly bruising bucket of cold water in the face of someone lost in dreamland. Having been in the North African theatre of combat for a few months, the shock factor was not as intense with 'greenies' just off the transport ship, but it nevertheless startled him.

He rubbed his eyes, spat out the remnants of the aftermath of the night before into his handkerchief, and scrubbed his index finger across his teeth and gums. He patted down his tunic pockets and found half a stick of Wrigley's wedged in the fold of the battle blouse. The sweet, pepperminty flavor exploded in his mouth and refreshed him. Feeling half-human again, he set out to explore where he ended up, wondering in passing if anyone *from either side* was out looking for him. Cautiously leaving the small vestibule and going up a half-flight of stairs, rounding a corner, he noted the weak, pre-dawn light struggling to find its way into the building from tiny windows set very high along the outside walls. They almost seemed to be an afterthought of the architect. Shapes began to materialize in the lessening dark. Within a few minutes, the room was dimly lit and he was shocked to identify it. It was a Jewish synagogue! But which one?

My father methodically moved around the perimeter of what was the prayer hall and discovered a wall plaque. He could fluently read the words, although his Hebrew was the 'prayer-reading' kind. This form of Jewish education was typical of Diaspora Judaism of the 19th and early 20th centuries. Hebrew was a language of faith, sacred, holy; and not a language of the modern world. (Remember, the State of Israel had not yet come into existence, and therefore modern Hebrew as a national tongue was yet unknown.) 'Thank God for my limited French', he thought to himself. For the plaque was bi-lingual. It was a dedicatory inscription serving to honor recent past presidents of the congregation. He was stunned when he followed with his finger; tracing the words. He had found his way into the *Aben Danan* Synagogue; the oldest existing synagogue in Fez! He knew a little of it, and was awestruck.

Fez was an incredibly cosmopolitan city when the *Aben Danan* was first built. Jews had lived in Fez for nearly 1000 years. In fact, legend has it that Fez was a small, nondescript Jewish tribal village when King *Idriss II* incorporated the city at the start of the 9th century. He then invited the Jews to live there side by side with their Arab brethren. Although, as a devout Moslem, *Idriss* restricted the freedom of Fez's Jews, he did create an economic environment that still allowed them not only to survive but thrive. It was the home of Maimonides in the 12th century.

No one is quite sure exactly when the building was erected – but the consensus is that it was some time in the mid-17th century. Certainly not the largest, *Aben Danan* did apparently have a vibrant congregation; which attested to its longevity that far surpassed many of the larger, more prosperous houses of prayer in the *Mellah*, or Jewish Quarter. The current building reminded one of an older dowager princess who had seen better days, yet still retained an air of elegance and dignity. The high ceiling was supported by beautifully painted wooden beams. Dozens of ancient silver and bronze oil lamps hung by chains; secured to the beams. The décor of the columns and woodwork was faded and chipped in spots, yet you could tell that it originally was of a robin's-egg blue. Along one wall, reached by two steps of beautiful green and white ceramic tile, was the location of the *Bamah* where the service was conducted. Adjacent to it, also on the same raised platform, were seats that most likely were reserved for the more important (read 'wealthier') members of the congregation. Directly across from here was the *Aron Kodesh*, 'the Ark of the Law', where the Torah scrolls were kept. The elegant wooden niche was surrounded by extraordinarily lovely plaster Arabesque latticework imagery; the faded blues, yellows and whites now muted.

As my father looked around, a warm sense of connectivity enveloped him. The longevity of this often persecuted community instilled a sense of pride, dignity that was a hallmark of the Jewish people for millennia. He noted a staircase and headed for it. As he glanced back at the hall, he caught sight of the dim light that he saw upon first arriving – it was the *Ner Tamid,* the 'eternal flame' that burned endlessly in every synagogue around the world; representing the spark of creation as described in the Hebrew narrative. He climbed the stairs to the Women's Gallery, for in traditional Judaism men and women prayed separately. This was especially true with the traditional Sephardic, or Arabic speaking Jews from North Africa throughout the eastern Mediterranean basin. But the real reason was to look out one of the small windows down to street level and ensure that life had resumed its normal hubbub in the medina, so that he could hurry back to the barracks and try to explain away his absence. The coast seemed clear, the early morning rush of men to work and women to the random open air markets had that urgent sense of normalcy associated with the controlled chaos of Fez in the morning. He went downstairs, put on his boots, straightened his somewhat disheveled uniform, and strode out the synagogue as if he had just left the *Shaharit* morning prayer service and was departing for work.

Suddenly he stopped and turned around. He reentered the synagogue and retraced his steps through the vestibule. He found what he was looking for. Adjacent to the arch that led into the prayer hall was a small wooden box. The once sharp corners were now rounded smooth by countless hands that had gently caressed it as their fingers sought out the slot carved out of the hinged lid. My father followed the same routine, as he dropped a ten dirham note through the slit, all the while reading the faded Hebrew letters painted there – *Tzedakah,* 'charity'. He gave a silent blessing for his incredible good fortune that saw him through the night. *Now* he could go on his way in good conscience. The sun seemed brighter as he exited the second time . . . .

III

Fez, the present . . .

BY NOW, OMAR was thoroughly 'into' the story, listening and hanging on every word. I had never really told anyone about the stories that my father related to me regarding his escapades in 'the big one' as he himself called it. What really intrigued me was a renewed look of admiration and respect that he threw me every so often on the way to his glance at the passenger's side view mirror to check traffic from that angle.

"You never told me the extent to which our parents might have interacted a generation ago" he said. "My father's family came from Fez, and they worshipped at *Aben Danan.* If in fact your father met some of the congregants during his stay, he may very well have met my father! The coincidence is not just probable, but most likely possible. He was the *Gabbai*, the sexton, for many years."

He promised to ask him what years his tenure of office ran. In addition, he would also ask his father if there were any strange occurrences in the synagogue or within the community during the war years. Now, *I* was intrigued as well.

The time had truly flown by during my story-telling, as we were already well past the *Sidi Allal el Bahraoui* Junction and now speeding down the A2 Highway. As a matter of fact, the exit sign for *Khemisset*, only 110 km from Fez, was just ahead. We decided that the exit to *Meknes*, another 45 km on, would be a good place to get petrol, stretch our legs, and get something to drink before the final push into Fez.

By now it was late afternoon. Omar was forced to angle the rear-view mirror away from his face as the setting sun produced a glare that could bring on a migraine-sized headache if allowed to keep boring into his eyes. But once we would get into the low, undulating hills of the *Meknes* area, the dipping sun would have no impact. The benzene station was just ahead. I looked forward to getting out and limbering up.

We pulled up to the pumps at an *Afriquia* Oasis Café, one of over four hundred in Morocco. Talk about a monopoly. I pumped from the '96' reservoir while Omar inserted his Eurocard from *Banque Morocaine.*

"Hey dude, check the oil and give a *spritz* to the windshield?" I asked in my best SoCal accent. "Like waddaya say man?" I laughed at the non-plussed look that he gave me like, "What the fuck?" He threw up his arms in resignation.

"Sometimes I have absolutely no idea what you're talking about!" Shook his head, finished the screen transaction, and set off for the rest stop to . . . . take a . . . . rest. I followed after, chuckling.

In the Oasis, we got a couple of *bocadillos,* Spanish-style Moroccan sandwiches. I ordered the baguette with tuna and mixed salad, while Omar opted for *schwarma,* sliced lamb with a yoghurt-dill sauce. We washed it down with a couple of Fantas before making the final push to Fez. It would be an evening arrival by now.

* * *

Lights on, we exited the highway and made our way toward the north side of the old city. Because of some well-earned *proteksia* after many previous journeys here,. I was able to secure a room at the incredible *Palais Jamai,* within the city walls by the ancient gate of *Bab Guissa.* Now part of the Sofitel Hotel conglomerate, it originally began life as a palace constructed for *Jamai,* the grand vizier of the Sultan *Moulay el-Hassan.* In 1879, *Jamai* asked his sultan for a favor, to have a palace built for him in the magnificent city of Fez. The Sultan complied with his wish, and the rambling, elegantly garish manse accommodated *Jamai's* family, servants, Harem and guests with a cultured ease. Nearly every room in the original palace afforded breathtaking views over the medina. A lush Andalusian-style garden surrounded the building, designed to give it the utmost in security, seclusion and serenity. The palace was converted into a hotel in the 1930's.

Located in the part of Fez known as *Fez el Bali,* or 'Old Fez', it served as the original capital of the *Idrissid* Dynasty of the 8th Century. The city would be made a World Heritage Site of UNESCO in 1981. Its counterpart was *Fez el Jedid,* or 'New Fez'. It is extraordinarily difficult for anyone from the 'New World' to conceive of the idea of a 'new' city that was founded around 1270, but there you have it. Nearly five hundred years after the initial founding of Fez.

New Fez was a planned city, built by the *Merinid* Dynasty. It took only 3 years to build and was finished by 1273. The walled city became a safe haven for the Dynasty from its enemies. In the 14th century, the *Mellah,* or Jewish Quarter, was built just to the west, also within the city walls.

We registered, went to our respective rooms, freshened up and met in the garden prior to going for dinner. So the main question was, "which cuisine reigns supreme". Okay, so that's straight from Alton Braun's mouth to your ears on Iron Chef America. But in Fez, it was a legitimate and very deep question. As Omar descended the stairs and made his way through the foliage to my bench, I asked him.

"You know, I'm wide open when it comes to food, but probably am more prone to Moroccan tonight. But I will leave it up to you . . . since you're buying!" I grinned widely like the Chesire cat. His mouth dropped open, oh, about a metre or so. I could see him about to explode and blubber something inappropriate. I quickly cut him off with a laugh. "Just kidding *habibi,* I just wanted to get your juices flowing for dinner!" He paused, took a deep breath, and realized that this time *he'd* been had.

"Well, um, it should be a joint decision. We can skip the French and 'go native'", he said. "But wait, *I am native,* you can adapt . . . I'm already here", he chuckled. "I know just the place that's quite close, right inside *Bab Guissa.* We can eat traditional Moroccan Arabic or indulge in their specialty, food of the *Gnaoua,* relatives of the *Tuareg,* the 'Blue men' of the desert."

"Wait, I think that I know what you're referring to, but you certainly don't mean those strange guys on stage who paint themselves blue and specialize in percussion?"

Now it was his time to laugh. "The *Gnaoua* are often referred to as "blue men" because of the bright indigo dyes that they use on both their *djellabahs* and even their skin. This gave them a sense of fierceness that caused people to flee from them in panic."

I was really on the edge of confused now. "I thought that *Gnaoua* was a term used by 'true Arabs' in alluding to what they saw as the 'dumb-as-a-rock' intellect of the native North African tribespeople when they encountered them. I thought that it literally meant "deaf and dumb", a really insulting view. To me, illiterate does not mean lack of smarts."

"*Stana Schwayeh,* relax *mon ami,* of course you're right. But then, I'm right as well." He just had to toss that aside in. I just shook my head and told him to lead on, Abu MacDuff.

We ended up going to *al Firdaous* Restaurant on *Rue Zenjfor.* It certainly lived up to its name, "Paradise". A 15th century *riad,* the food was exquisitely done, a blend of both Arabic and *Gnaoua* cuisine (can I say that, even though it's not French? Well, sure). We shared both lamb and chicken *tagines,* meals prepared in specially created ceramic vessels, called *Tagines.* They are heavy, shallow bowls with a high-rising cone-shaped lid. The genius who designed these vessels knew what he or she was doing. They are made to go into the *tannur,* the oven, and bake the meal right inside. The conical lid is shaped so that the condensation from the vegetables, rice and meat then drips back down onto the savory mix, keeping it succulent. Once cooked, the lid is left in the kitchen and the large, flat bowl is the serving container brought to the table. In essence, the meal becomes a rich, thick rice-based stew that is quickly sopped up with *pita,* the generic flatbread of the Middle East and North Africa.

Before we were served, reclining on puff-cushions adjacent to a low, round, acid-etched brass table, we were entertained by traditional music from both traditions. The 'full' orchestra would set the stage for the approaching dance entertainment, the belly dancer. The rhythms of the Mideast and Africa are enticing, hypnotizing, and extraordinarily sensual. Usually the largest section of the 'orchestra' was percussion and drums; with tribal traditions and variations adding and crescendo-ing until, at times, they overpower the rest of the instruments.

The long, drawn-out note from the violin served as the prelude to get people settled in. Suddenly, the drum section, the *doumbeks* and finger drums, brought the beat to a pulsating consistency that got everyone tapping their fingers on the brass tabletops. They were joined by the *Oud,* the multi-stringed lute, and the *rebaba,* the single-stringed Bedouin instrument. From the distant corner, out of sight, the clash of bronze castanets reverberated along with the beat, and all eyes turned toward the darkened doorway.

Often perceived as a 'veiled temptress', the belly dancer began to pirouette her way onto the makeshift stage platform in the center of the room. All eyes followed her, entranced. And those with the most rapt attention were the women. Were they 'checking out' the competition? No, the greatest critics of belly-dance were Arabic women themselves. For belly dancing is not seen as a seductive means of cheap thrills, but rather a sensual dance designed to show grace, agility and rhythm in extraordinary ways. In the Mideast, there is no 'belly' that is exposed. Rather, due to the true nature of this form of entertainment, the women are actually modestly dressed – wearing body stockings that cover them so no actual flesh outside of arms and legs is exposed.

After a couple of numbers designed for her, she took a break. Other dancers came to the stage, folklorists of a sort, both men and women performing traditional tribal and village dances that told a story – not unlike a Hawaiian hula. Wooden sword sticks, walking sticks, brightly woven Nubian-style baskets all served as props for these lively performances. They were as well received as the belly-dancer herself.

When she returned in a different costume, there seemed to be a subtle change amongst the audience. Well versed in the musical routine, the patrons were aware that, at some time in this set, she would dance her way through the crowd of diners and pick one or two to join her onstage. She wouldn't discriminate – she could pick either a man or a woman, or both. As she eyed the crowd and they eyed her expectantly, I gave a very subtle flick of the wrist toward my colleague. She winked, got the message, and began to slowly weave her way between tables. As she passed each one, there were almost audible sighs of relief *or* anguish – guilt at either having been bypassed *or* reluctantly passed over. (And to think that they weren't even Jewish!).

With a feigned, perplexed look on her face, as if trying to decide who to choose, she navigated the tables and headed toward us.

"You're in for it now," Omar laughed. "She's gunning for you *habibi!*" Little did he know . . .

* * *

The next morning I got an early, and rude, wake-up call.

"I'm never going to let you forget this." It was all too apparent that Omar had yet to light his first *Gitane,* or even really clear his throat from overnight congestion as he growled at me through the handset. "Meet me in the restaurant in fifteen or you'll really be sorry. And by the way, you're paying."

Before I could reply he had already disconnected. I knew then that I'd better hurry and rolled out of bed and into the luxurious shower. I made it with two minutes to go.

Omar was almost back to normal, he was impeccably dressed, as always. In between his fingers was the nearly omnipresent cigarette, as always. There was a smile a meter wide, as *almost* always, depending on whether the first two morning rites of passage had been accomplished. As they say in this part of the world, *praise Allah* that equilibrium had been restored in the life of my Moroccan colleague.

I was tempted to remind him of the previous evening's added 'entertainment', but decided that it could wait. After all, nobody wants to be reminded of the circumstances surrounding the evening's 'entertainment'.

* * *

After the belly-dance show, on Wikipedia, when one looked up the word 'embarrassment', Omar's picture on stage with the dancer would accompany the article. He had always talked about how difficult it was for him to find a solidly fitting pair of shoes, because he needed two left ones! I had just 'poo-pooed' it as false modesty because he was a graceful man . . . out on the street. Suddenly it was painfully (for him, delightfully wicked for me) apparent that on the dance floor he was as elegant as Sesame Street's Big Bird. The dancer approached the table and gently, almost seductively, drew the thin veil over his shoulders and around his face. The crowd roared with delight, urging her on. She obliged. Shocked, he was dragged up on stage, with a red blush quickly traveling up his neck to his face.

This was especially irritating for him because he truly thought that the dancer was coming for me.

Cameras flashed, the emcee announced, in three languages, that a new star had been born, and my friend resigned himself to his fate. He shuffled and awkwardly spun in time with the pulsating beat. The crowd clapped and roared its approval. With his hands above his head, clapping with the beat, he made his way back to the table. He took a bow, to the applause of everyone, including the belly dancer and orchestra. When his back was to me for a moment, I surreptitiously slipped some *dirham* into the palm of the dancer. She smiled at me, and, for just a moment, I melted a bit.

"What are *you* grinning about?" Omar had turned back to me at the table. In spite of his feigned anger, he really had a great time – pleased that she had 'chosen' him over me. I coughed into my napkin, hiding my face, while I composed myself. The rest of the evening was uneventfully pleasant and we ambled back to the *Palais Jamai* just before midnight.

* * *

Over the incredibly 'over-the-top' buffet breakfast, and potent, thick Moroccan coffee, we charted our course for the day. We'd take a trip to the Roman city of *Volubilis,* which had some of the most substantial evidence of the early Jewish community of Morocco. The sad thing about the ancient world, all too often the evidence of ancient societies is only seen in their death, not their life. In other words, cemeteries 'speak' to us more loudly in many instances than the communities that they served. *Volubilis* was no different, and this is what we set out to examine.

We loaded up with many bottles of *Sidi Ali* mineral water, some dried fruit and, of course, for Omar, a carton of *Gitanes,* and made sure that the Peugeot's tank was full. Omar later confided in me that it was always a guessing game because the gauge was unreliable – *m'zroob,* 'screwed up'. As a result, he always had a jerrycan of petrol in the trunk as a precaution. I didn't say a word, but the word *mecanician,* auto mechanic, did come to mind. Barring any mishaps, it should take about an hour to the ancient Roman ruins.

We headed almost due west from Fez on the N4/N6 road, past some of the most fertile land in the country. Vast fields of wheat, barley and 'alfa-alfa' were testimony to the fact that Morocco has long been referred to as 'the breadbasket' of southern Europe. But even more importantly, both the climate and land were suitable for orchards and olive groves. We were in the heart of Morocco's olive production industry. In fact, since the site's abandonment centuries ago, many of its outlying areas were 'taken over' by olive groves. Farmers used centuries-old technology here, not burdened by the rush of the 21st century. Because of this, the size of the plots of land, and the land ownership itself, was limited in acreage.

The upside was that huge conglomerates didn't dominate the business end of the agricultural industry here. It was all quite refreshing a concept actually. Farmers helped farmers, neighbors supported neighbors – a time-honored tradition. However, there were cooperatives that allowed these small-time entrepreneurs to unify and 'lobby' for better prices.

From *Zagota* Junction we turned south on the N13, a narrow one and one-half lane (or two lane if you're an optimist) road that would pass *Volubilis* on the way to *Meknes*, one of the four Imperial Cities. Now, farm equipment rivaled vehicles for dominance on the roadway. Several times we needed to wait, impatiently I might add, for oncoming traffic to thin before swinging out and passing tractor-wagon combos that seemed to move slower than the many pedestrians that walked the berm. As a 'city boy' all his life, Omar grew impatient at the change of pace, tapping both his index fingers on the leather-wrapped steering wheel. I noticed that the precise place that he was tapping was almost completely worn through the leather. Apparently he had done this quite often – you could almost see his fingerprints embedded in the thinned material.

"Here, relax *habibi*." I shook out a *Gitane* from its crush-proof box and pushed in the dashboard lighter. I knew that I'd regret the smoke, but also knew that I'd regret it even more if he did something rash to speed our journey and we ended in the ditch.

"*Merci, mon ami*, I appreciate the thought. But it'll be a cold day in the Sahara if I try to light my 'addiction' from the car – lighter. It hasn't worked for some time." He smiled and withdrew his battered bic from his shirt pocket. A flick of the bic and he inhaled deeply. It seemed that even the one drag calmed him, and the incessant drumming slowed, then stopped altogether in a couple of minutes. I sat back, a bit calmer myself, and we made our leisurely way to our rendezvous with the western end of the Roman Empire. Before entering the site, we stopped at the kiosk by the entry to be fortified by a couple of *falafel*, chips, and Fanta before setting out on our exploration.

Volubilis was the ancient capital of the province of *Mauretania*. It was founded in the 3rd century BCE, and became a major outpost of the western limit of the Roman Empire in Africa; with many elegant buildings. Extensive remains of these survive on the archaeological site. *Volubilis* was later briefly to become the capital of *Idris I*, founder of the *Idrisid* dynasty, who is buried at nearby *Moulay Idris*.

During the expansion of the Roman Empire, the son of King *Juba I* (okay, wait for it . . .) *Juba II* (surprise!) was sent to Rome where he would be educated. International intrigue sets the table now. He would be married off to an orphaned princess who was now a ward of the Senate. Her name was *Cleopatra Selene*, the daughter of "Elizabethus Taylorus and Ricardus Burtonus" – of course meaning *Cleopatra VII* and Marc Antony. Augustus Caesar appointed him to be King of *Mauretania* on behalf of Rome. In spite of the fact that he made his capital in Algeria, *Volubilis* was perhaps his most prosperous city. This all came to a screeching halt in the next generation, as the corrupt and decadent *Caligula* would murder *Juba's* son, *Ptolemy*, in 40 CE. *Mauretania* would cease to exist as an independent entity.

Apparently, long after its abandonment, the site would suffer from the 1755 Lisboa earthquake. I mentioned this to Omar, and he was sufficiently intrigued to suggest a demitasse of *Ahawa masboot*, the thick, sweet Arabic brew favored by a majority in this part of the world. He suggested that I break out my Samsung tablet and make the internet connection to find out more. According to a Wikipedia article that I found (I know, they're sometimes unreliable *but just how politicized* can a 250 year old earthquake get? I trusted this one).

I read aloud to him, 'The 1755 Lisbon earthquake, also known as the Great Lisbon Earthquake, occurred in the Kingdom of Portugal on Saturday, 1 November 1755, at around 9:40 am.'

"And exactly how do we know that it was precisely at that time," he asked.

I scrolled down to the first footnote. "Apparently there were plenty of eye-witness accounts that were published, after all, it was the 18th century . . . . of this era! The scholar was able to dig up . . ." A bark of laughter interrupted my reading. After it dawned on me as well, I joined in. A few moments later I continued.

"As I said, Bello *uncovered* evidence by rummaging through old copies of the *Gazeta de Lisboa* in the National Archives and noted that tremendous fires engulfed the city, but the safes of the Royal Exchequer and many of the private citizens were recovered when the flames died out. In addition, numerous hand-written accounts in the years following were preserved in the royal archives. I continued to read from the article. 'Seismologists today estimate the Lisbon earthquake had a magnitude in the range 8.5 – 9.0 on the moment magnitude scale with an epicenter in the Atlantic Ocean about 200 km (120 mi) west-southwest of Cape St. Vincent.'"

"Look at this map that accompanies the article." I showed him the graphic of what the scientists called the most likely fault-line. "It runs jaggedly across the Atlantic, rises northeast toward Lisbon, and then plunges southeast just off the coast of Morocco north of Rabat. It then rises again to the northeast, passing just north of Fez toward the Med. Wow, *Volubilis* is only a few kliks south of the fault-line. No wonder the ruins fell into ruin . . . again."

We entered the site, a part of UNESCO's World Heritage List since 1997. No matter how many times one visits, the awe, wonder and splendor of Roman engineering and art boggles the mind. Once again, we were not disappointed.

We walked up the path, through breeches in the ancient city wall, and past the oil presses that lay on the periphery of the town, and topped the gentle ascent to the Basilica to find the site spread out before us. Due to the flat nature of the terrain that the city found itself on, the ruins seemed to go on forever. In fact, measured at about forty-two hectares, or in the neighborhood of one hundred acres, it *is* an enormous city given its age. One could visualize the vibrancy of the city, as a model of Roman engineering and efficiency. It was laid out on the Hippodamic city plan of blocks of houses, *insulae*, that shared common walls and were surrounded by streets that met at right angles one to another. Marking the forum and the heart of the city was an open air plaza, where 'high street' and 'main street' would meet. However, the Romans would feel more comfortable if the signs indicated the *Decumanus* (the major east/west thoroughfare) and the *Cardo* (its north/south counterpart). In the finest engineering tradition, the streets had drains built beneath them to carry away excess water, and curbing stones on their flanks to prevent any added water from running from the street into the shops and houses that were merely a step away.

We walked on and paused at the House of the Four Seasons. No, not for Franki Valli, but so named due to the stunningly beautiful mosaic work discovered in the rooms. The *triclinium*, or dining room, had a wonderful 1st century CE mosaic that had medallions on the four corners. Each had a portrait of a woman who was identified as one of the seasons of the year. Their faces were a testament to timeless elegance and beauty.

I remarked that they were quite similar to the 'Mona Lisa of the Galilee' discovered at *Sepphoris* in Israel. It too, was a statement about unsurpassed beauty and grace that transcended time. "The one thing that I can't quite get my head around is the attitude of the Ministry of Culture regarding the preservation of archaeological sites. Here you have the magnificence of *Volubilis*, and the extraordinary architectural art associated with the Roman city, yet weeds and overgrowth seem to dominate. Where is the protection and preservation of such a national treasure?"

My colleague simply shrugged his shoulders. "*Ma'alesh*" was his all-too-familiar-in-the-Arab-world reply. "There are too many other pressing needs" was not even a half-hearted response. The government is rife with incompetent, nepotistic employees who haven't a clue as to what their jobs are. They are hired through family ties and located in jobs that will guarantee tenure. The head of the academic section of ancient sites within Culture isn't an archaeologist – he isn't even an academic. How do you say it, he pushes 'parchment'!"

It was close enough, I knew what he was saying. But I continued to press him. "But left out in the open such as we see here, doesn't the ancient site run the risk of disintegration and destruction from nature, not to mention the thousands of tourists annually. After all, something may be wonderfully protected for millennia under the ground, but once exposed to the elements, can disintegrate faster than a sand castle at high tide."

He shook his head. "*Ma'alesh*" and pulled out another *Gitane*.

"Consider the Solar Boat at *Giza*. It's the oldest, largest, intact boat in the world, at around *4500 years old. But since its excavation in 1954 had deteriorated more in the last half-century* due to exposure to the modern air pollution and human 'side-effects' of sweat and carbon dioxide than in the first 45 centuries. The potential is the same here . . ."

"But this is stone, *mon ami*, not wood." It was a weak response.

"Okay, granted, but go back to the *Sepphoris* mosaic. The image is also of natural colored stone of different varieties. However, the Israeli Dept. of Antiquities and Museums decided that, due to its remote location, the cost of protection would be too high. Not so much as protection from standard elements like rain and sun, but the site itself is in an earthquake prone region. Any minor tremor could split the mosaic floor. It's really an identical situation here at *Volubilis*. After all, don't forget Lisbon." It was more a smile of regret that I gave him rather than pleasure.

"So, what did the Israelis do?"

"It was an incredible feat, not unlike the work that the Supreme Council of Antiquities did with the Solar Boat. The Israelis, after fully excavating and recording the floor, with nearly one and one-half million stone *tesserae*, in 28 colors, decided to move it to a new home, a new outdoor 'building', on the grounds of the Israel Museum in Jerusalem. First, the preservationists glued a canvas 'backing' on the top of the mosaic surface. They slowly would undercut the entire mosaic floor. Thank God for the Romans – the concrete foundation that the mosaic was set into was over 10 cm thick. The archaeologists then gently rolled the floor/foundation onto an enormous wooden spindle, not unlike a telephone line drum, that was over 2 m diameter. This enormous girth prevented cracking. All the while they sprayed a fixative to further secure the floor. Then, when all rolled, they loaded it by crane onto a flatbed to transport at a blazing speed of 20 kph to the new home on the plaza of the museum. Today, hundreds of thousands have ready, and centralized, access to this incredible work of art – protected from the elements by a fiberglass canopy.

Omar gazed wistfully at the Four Seasons. He knew that the Israeli way was right. "Well, our Israeli cousins certainly do know how to do the proper thing. We still have a long way to go to take ownership of our heritage and protect it – rather than simply set up an entry booth and take tickets. In their defense, and I don't do it often, the site is *so* large that wouldn't moving all the floors be at odds with the purpose of archaeological sites, their preservation and visitation by the public?" He had a good point.

"Just a thought, but why not simply create the same type of fiberglass canopy over each major mosaic-floored room, and leaving them on-site. Therefore, the ambience in association with context is still there." I didn't want to push too hard, his Moroccan sense of national identity so closely tied to the monarchy ran deeply, powerfully.

He smiled in agreement, noting that I hadn't bruised too much the ego of the government that he supported. But I hadn't heard him, I was enveloped by the warm fog of remembrance of the last time I saw the Mona Lisa . . .

We continued on past the House of Columns, and I paused. Omar glanced inquiringly at me. I explained the reason, and it was due to the discovery of the Lisbon earthquake information.

"I want you to see this, for it really explains why *Volubilis* last so long as a Roman city in spite of the fact that it sat in the earthquake zone. Just look at the columns of the peristyle that surrounds the central fountain. What do you see?"

Apparently his eye for women didn't extend to archaeology and architecture. He hemmed and hawed for a moment, and then – "I see really meticulously carved spiral-fluted columns sitting on square stone bases. Am I missing something?"

"Take it all in, look carefully *ya hamar*!" He knew that it was a term of endearment, but still looked a bit defensive. "How is the column constructed? Is it monolithic, or what? How many pieces are there? Don't just look, but see."

He still didn't seem to get it. Not wanting to waste any more time, I gave up and told him. "Look at the seam of the column base and the column itself. Now do you see the genius of Roman engineering? No, I thought so. Deeply embedded in the seam is a two cm thick slab of lead. LEAD! Do you get it now? Remember about the earthquakes, the faultlines, the 'shake, rattle and roll' of Bill Haley and the Comets?"

"*Na'am*, what are you saying?" I guess that one of the Lost Boys had just stood next to me. He was totally out to sea, or out to lunch, or out to somewhere.

"Faultlines, *habibi*, faultlines. With the constant, minor tremors that persisted in the region, the Romans were innovative. They put a padding of lead between the column bases and columns themselves, so that when a minor tremblor hit, the lead would absorb the shockwave, the column would 'settle' into the soft lead, and the building would suffer no damage structurally. Such brilliance and ingenuity is one of the reasons why the empire lasted so long."

I saw the look of an 'a-ha' moment light up his face. He smiled a congratulatory smile, all the while praising his 'Roman Moroccan' ancestors. I know that we all love to co-opt greatness from time to time, but in North Africa it seemed to be a regional pastime.

Suddenly I heard a bit of shouting a couple of hundred meters away. It didn't seem associated with a tour group that was wandering through the residential area, but rather along the periphery of the site, by the northern limit, near the city wall and the gate that led to the ancient port city of *Tingis*.

IV

Tingis, 525 BCE . . . .

THE ADVISOR KNELT before the king, the Agella, and was overcome with sadness. The empire was collapsing around him, and his friend, the king, seemed Hades-bent on going to the netherworld, taking as many Carthaginians as he possibly could before himself succumbing. But what could the king wish to tell him? The king's hoarse voice shook him from his reverie.

". . . my last request is for you to become heir to my throne. You have shown your wisdom and knowledge, you have shown the wisdom and knowledge handed down by your people. We will all be dead by morn, but you have a chance to escape and rebuild this land using your wits and ingenuity. But don't let on who you really are, for, even though it may be deceitful, in the end the empire will survive and thrive via your talent. I will supply you with whatever you may need, provided that you and your escort can carry it with due haste. YOU MUST ESCAPE TINGIS and head back east. Mix with your people in Misr, bide your time, establish your persona within the ancient community there."

The loyal servant was stunned. He never assumed that a request such as this would ever be made of him. The look on his face was one that the king had seen when riding in his chariot in the countryside at night. Although he thoroughly enjoyed the freedom of feeling the wind blowing across his face, and rare moments of limited solitude, he still had a body guard with him – a loyal palace soldier. The soldier would brandish a torch that cast a faint light on the path so that the vehicle could maneuver along the rutted road with little danger of a crash. On occasion, a dama gazelle would be crossing the track, and it would freeze in the glow of the torch. Its eyes would glimmer lustrously, but the look would be one of apprehension. THAT was the look that the king saw on the Advisor's face. He knew that he needed to allay his fears.

"My friend, I have been planning this for a year or so, ever since we rebuked the Carthaginian envoy's overtures 'at peace'. I knew that we'd go down fighting, but also knew that our people would look upon any of my descendants who survived and fled as 'traitors'. So a 'new lineage' of my family, distant relatives in far off Libya, have been 'discovered' a generation ago. I have had carefully prepared documents created, attesting to this, that have been artificially aged and dated to the last century. How, you might ask? The papyrus scrolls that were written were first steeped in goat urine and buried in the desert for a couple of months. Then they were singe-ed by fire, lending an air of antiquity. In addition, I have prepared a special royal signet ring that fits you perfectly, and have filled a purse with enough gold and jewels to get you and your family members discretely situated far from here. Now, go with your God and gird yourself for the extraordinary trials that lay ahead. But in the end, you, or your descendants will return in triumph to rule our ancient land again. Just don't forget me, and our bond."

The Advisor's eyes filled, and tears stained his tunic. But he endured all this in silence, with the utmost respect for his king and protector. He knew that protest would simply delay the inevitable. So he kissed the king on both cheeks in a an enormous embrace, something that he NEVER would have done before, and turned and fled the hall; not daring to look back as the king hurried off to join his royal guard in defending to the last man.

The sounds of preparation for battle, the clanging of weapons being readied and the shouting of commands being executed were the last that the Advisor and his family heard as they exited the Sale Gate. For they knew it was safest to leave via the southwest and make a broad circle around the city counterclockwise to bypass the approaching army. From there, they could make the mad dash across the desert to the security of Egypt and the safety of the Jewish community there.

V

Volubilis, the present . . .

WE MADE OUR way to the ancient city perimeter and discovered an archaeological crew excavating a handful of squares. I recognized *Hassan Aboulafia* of the Moroccan *Institut National des Sciences de l'Archéologie et du Patrimoine.* He was in his trademark khaki workshirt emblazoned in French with the inscription, "*une carrière archéologues est en ruines*"; which roughly translates into 'an archaeologist's career lies in ruins'. When Omar saw the logo, he burst out laughing. It was so genuine, so loud, that nearly everyone on the field crew stopped what they were doing and looked up.

We walked over and introduced ourselves. I told him of my appreciation for what he was doing, and my jealousy over his coup in getting the Moroccan government to begin to re-excavate *Volubilis* after so many years lying dormant. In way of an answer, he told his crew to take a break, and he then broke out the teapot and starting brewing for us.

As he described the work going on in the five m squares of the excavation, I marveled at the use of modern technology. The voluminous amounts of paperwork associated with any dig for over a century seemed to be gone. The locus diaries where the archaeologists recorded on a daily basis what occurred in each locus, or three-dimensional unit of excavation, were gone. As were the daily basket lists, wall cards, etc. Although I myself hadn't been in the field for only half a dozen years, I felt ancient and out of date.

The replacement for all of this paperwork was the tablet. No, not the yellow-paged, lined notebook of school days (or law firms) gone past; but the wonderful, 'wi-fied' electronic marvels that were now all the rage in the real world. 'Apps' were now in existence that tapped into electronic data-bases that in a previous age could only be found in museums and university libraries. Other programs contained all of the forms that prior to this decade needed to be meticulously filled in and then copied so that two records were in play should one be damaged or destroyed accidentally. I looked on with envy as the archaeological crew sat back and tapped data entries with great prowess. To them, it was effortless. In addition, with laser-guided transits, computer generated imaging was much more precise and easier to manage as well. The team surveyor most likely knew more about computers than architecture in this modern day and age. However, as I thought back to previous excavations that I had been a part of in Israel, I recalled the vast storehouse of knowledge that was in the mind of the chief surveyor/architect in Tel Aviv University's Institute of Archaeology. *Shmulik* was truly the archaeologist's archaeologist – although you should never call him that to his face! He could look at what seemed to be a pile of stones and evoke the probable history and context in a way that only years of experience could ever allow. (Try that on for size with your tablet, I thought)

Another way that I was thoroughly 'blown away' by the use of modern technology was via the digital imaging. Yes, I was familiar with using digital cameras. In fact, we began to switch several years ago. In the AF Era, (that's analog film era) you often ran the risk of not capturing an incredible image due to improper lighting, exposure, or even having enough film on hand. For that reason, archaeological photographers needed to do a few things to ensure that the record was accurate, safe, secure and preserved for posterity. After all, archaeology is a deconstructive business. In order to get to earlier, more ancient material, you need to remove the latest layers of occupation-hence the deconstruction. If things aren't properly recorded and documented, they are lost forever.

So 'in the olden days', photographer's would need to bracket their images, over and under F-stops, over and under shutter speeds, so that the excavation was ensured of a good, viable picture. In addition, many excavations would need to go to the expense of setting up a darkroom to have the images available in timely fashion; you couldn't continue to excavate until you had exhaustively recorded and documented the material brought to light.

But there's another reason for the need for recorded accuracy. Archaeologists are human, and prone to some of the more basic human traits like stubbornness and ego-boosting vanity. Therefore, without the irrefutable facts, its one person's word against another – when you physically break the connection with the earth, then the recorded data is all that you have left.

The modern archaeologist can digitally shoot an image and instantly view it. If it isn't to standards, or doesn't capture the essence quite right, it can be instantly dumped and reshot with no loss of time for the digging process. This has proven to be an incredible boon to the archaeological method in terms of time and cost savings. I still remain in awe of this technology.

* * *

Aboulafia asked about what brought us out to *Volubilis,* aside from its archaeological value. Omar glanced over, uncertain as to how to respond. I gave a slight nod of assent, and he launched into the whole 'such a diverse nation we have in Morocco spiel' as a prelude to understanding the origins of the Jewish tribes and community of the kingdom. Over sweet mint tea he explained the yawning gaps in our knowledge, and the desire to fill them in. I chimed in.

"It has always been known that many ancient Israelites made their way unintentionally to Egypt, according to the biblical narrative; and that there is substantial circumstantial evidence for their enslavement by the Egyptians. Both more importantly, the external evidence, such as the Tale of *SInuhe,* also seems to support this theory."

"I'm not really familiar with this story. Fill me in" *Aboulafia* said as he refilled our glasses and tossed in a sprig of fresh mint.

"In spite of the fact that some scholars simply don't believe that *Sinuhe* was a real Egyptian diplomat of the Middle Kingdom, around the 19th century BCE, the setting rings true to all scholars. Some call the author the 'Shakespeare of his day '. *Sinuhe* is a diplomat who travels with an Egyptian prince, *Senwosret I,* into the western desert. After the death of Pharaoh *Amenemhet,* he overhears certain conversations and, as a result, finds that he must flee into *Retenu,* the land of Canaan." I took a sip, sighed with content, and went on.

"The tale then goes on to describe *Sinuhe's* life and many feel that it has a tremendous kinship with the biblical narrative of Joseph. *Sinuhe* the Egyptian flees to Canaan and becomes a member of the ruling elite, marrying and settling down, before being reunited with his Egyptian family. The parallels to the age of Abraham and Sara, Isaac, Rebekah, Jacob, Leah and Rachel are uncanny. The similarity to the Joseph narrative is astounding in its presentation."

I chimed in now. "Everyone has been under the assumption that the Israelites eventually returned to the Promised Land with Moses after the Exodus. And yet everyone is okay with the proven fact that there was a substantial Jewish population in Roman Morocco in the 1st century BCE. But when did they get here? Is there any information about that? That is the nature of our quest. Rumors of Jewish Berber tribes abound, but the evidence? That's what we hope to discover, and previously excavated evidence from the site indicates a tie."

Now he was intrigued. *Aboulafia* agreed to give us a visitor's pass into the archives and storerooms of the archaeology museums in Fez and Rabat, as well as have one of his assistants let us into the storage facilities of the site itself. We were free to 'rut about' and see what there was.

* * *

By now, the sun was well on its way into its western descent, and we gave ourselves at maximum one hour in the on-site storage facility before returning to Fez. We approached the storage area on the site perimeter and showed the guard the visitor pass. He barely glanced at it and referred us to the *qablan*, or foreman, of the area. He was responsible for recording and documenting artifact entry into the large trucking containers that had been pressed into service for storage due to their strength and security. There were three of them, and we randomly chose one since there was apparently no rhyme or reason to the location of objects in storage. It was haphazard at best. It reminded me of the Cairo Museum's behind-the-scenes store rooms and an earlier adventure that was more than exciting.

The roster of artifactual evidence from *Volubilis* was incredible. Some of the finest Roman-era ceramics, Eastern *Sigillata* Ware, from any site in North Africa was stacked on metal racks six shelves high. Each piece was accurately labeled as to site location, etc, but randomly stored. At least one bit of good news hit us – the container was partitioned off according to material; stone, ceramic, metal, glass, etc. Not that it really helped us since we hadn't a clue as to what we were looking for.

Forty-five minutes sped by, with nothing to show of it. I was tempted to call it quits, chalk it up to the ubiquitous "*ma'alesh*" that was the answer to everything in the Arabic world. Yet the eternal optimist, Omar, wanted to give it a bit more. We stepped outside for some fresh air and a bottle of water, and for Omar, a smoke.

"It's a frustrating mess in there," I said. "The haphazard storage – there could be incredible treasures worth their weight in . . . *anything* . . . that no one is aware of. I don't envy *Aboulafia* and the work needed to sort out the chaos in there."

"We call it *tohu-bohu* from the French for 'pandemonium'." Omar replied.

"I like it – *tohu-bohu* it is!" We sat back and rested a while before returning to the task for one last shot before exiting for Fez.

"You know, as you have said in the past *mon ami*, the description of the life of the city can often be found in its 'death'. How about we ask the *qablan* where the Roman cemetery gravestones are located; for that is where the reports indicated that there were stones engraved in Hebrew, attesting to the Jewish community members."

I said that it was a brilliant idea, and, laughing, told him I was glad that *I* thought of it! Feigning anger, he flicked his cigarette butt at me and began to charge. He wrapped me in that signature bear-hug of his, giving his best 'rebel yell' all the while.

"*Halas, bas, ya-hamar!*" Laughing and struggling to catch your breath don't go hand in hand. He put me down also laughing, and wheezing from the effort. The foreman came running around the corner, alarmed at the sound of 'wild animals' as he would later put it to his workmen. Discovering the two of us just horsing around, he sadly shook his head and muttered something about the craziness of archaeologists and their apparent disconnect with reality. I called after him, inquiring as to where the tombstones could be found. He returned, locked up the container that we had been in, and led us to the third down the line. He unlocked it, still shaking his head, and told us to call him when we were done.

There were maybe a dozen intact Roman-style stelae, and fragments of maybe twenty or more stones. Most were badly eroded, their surfaces either worn smooth by wind or water action, or pitted as a result of wind-borne sand or stone particles scouring the surface that faced the prevailing breeze for centuries. Some had been cleaned, while others were covered in debris.

"Just look at those encrustations," I said, gently rubbing one of the stones to see the extent of accumulation.

"You know I don't eat shellfish, and what are you talking about?" Apparently the English word was unknown to Omar.

"Never mind," I sighed. "Some of the stela inscriptions are only covered in a lens of dirt so they're easy to clear off. Help me try to find any that may shed some light on what we're looking for – and beware of the 'crustaceans' – those lobster claws can really pinch down hard!" I laughed.

I sort of regretted saying it, for the horrified look on Omar's face was a bit embarrassing; but well worth it! I'd at last gotten in the last word. 'One small step for man . . . '

The 15 minutes we'd allocated turned into 45. We peeked out the container and saw the sun approaching the horizon and heard the *qablan* call out to us from his shack/office that we'd just another twenty before he would close up and go for evening prayer. I came to the next to last row of stones and discovered two stelae in Hebrew said to be companions to the two in the Fez Museum, attesting to the Jewish presence during the first century of this era. It memorialized a woman named '*Tiziri*'. It seemed to be a dialectic derivative from the Babylonian word meaning 'beginning'. Also from that word came the first month of the Hebrew calendar, *Tishrei*. Here was yet another tangible link to the Jewish community that 'headed west' like all pioneers (okay, that may have been a real stretch!).

The other was only a mere fragment, also in Hebrew. I faintly traced the cursive lettering and realized that it was the fragment described by the Moroccan Jewish scholar Haim Zafrani. After moving to the University of Paris, he published a book about the early Jews of Morocco before death in 2004. The name on the tombstone had been totally worn away, but the next line below was preserved – 'descended from *ben Itshaq* of *Syene*'. Our first tie to the east, and Egypt, was now 'set in stone' as they say. *Syene* was the ancient Egyptian name for the Island of Elephantine, in the Nile opposite Aswan. And there was a Jewish community there as early as the late 6th-5th centuries BCE! Our excitement grew.

Lying next to it was another stone, yet this one was a mystery, at least to me. It was not a stela in the Roman-era sense of the word. Rather, it was a small, somewhat nondescript tablet of stone that was incised with an unrecognizable language. I thought that if we could catch a member of the archaeology team before they left for the day we might get a quick answer and be on our way.

A French archaeologist by the name of Marie-Claire was also their linguist. She joined us a few minutes later on her way out of the compound. We were fortunate in that she had seen that stone before but didn't think much about it. She also assured the *qablan* that she would take responsibility for locking up. We watched that 'happy camper' head to a nearby mosque to ritually prepare for the evening service.

"It is unique from the sense of its language and therefore its age." She said. "The language is called *Tifinagh*, a script that is the derivative of ancient *Punic*. It has been deciphered because of the discovery decades ago of a couple of bi-lingual inscriptions found in Tunisia. Modern *Berber*, *Tuareg* dialects come from this source."

"So what kind of dates are we looking at?" I was starting to get a good feeling about this.

"I could easily place it as early as 5th century BCE', she replied. "Here's a rough translation of this particular tombstone."

I couldn't help it but started to chuckle. Both Omar and Marie-Claire looked at me like I'd finally, really lost it. And it's a good thing that I kept what I was thinking to myself or they would have had me locked up. ("As the stone mason began to chisel the inscription on the marker, he innocently asked the family members present, 'what do you want on your tombstone?' One of them answered, 'pepperoni and mushroom'." See, only an American could possibly appreciate that, so I remained silent – but with the grin on my face.)

She went on, "The name on this marker is *Amanai*. It is a common *Tuareg* word used for 'attendant of god'. Most scholarship assumes that it is derived from origins to the east; namely, the chief deity of the Egyptians, *Amon*."

This really set the wheels turning. Now the smile was legitimate, and I could see the same notion percolating in Omar's head as well. We had two links to the east that pre-dated the Romans and even the Greeks by centuries. We thanked her profusely and got back to the Peugeot that had been waiting patiently for us. The ride back to Fez was a lot shorter than it had been coming out.

The plaintive call of the *muezzin* called the faithful to prayer as the set finally set behind us on our way to a late dinner and bed. I needed to make travel plans to get back to Egypt and the archives of the Cairo Museum. The new Director for Excavation in Sinai for the Supreme Council of Antiquities would be happy to take time out to come to the city victorious to reconnect. I would call *Sobhy* from the *Palais Jamai* after I knew the flight I'd be on.

* * *

Early in the morning, Omar and I decided to take breakfast outside the hotel on the way to a local office of a travel agency that he had worked with. Luckily, it was not far from the hotel, but still inside the *medina*. We ambled through the narrow streets and alleys to *al Fassia* Restaurant, a typical hole-in-the-wall place; but one packed with local residents. If it was good enough for the residents of *Fez el Bali* then it certainly was good enough for us. Fava beans, *falafel*, *humus*, pickled salad and thick, rich coffee fortified us. From there, we wended our way to the office of Sunset Sahara Travel. But it would not be without a bit of adventure.

As we slowly sauntered along the alleyway, we kept one eye on the road and one eye on all the shops, for its amazing what one can find in the *souk*, or marketplace. There's everything from sheep to nuts as they sort of say. Omar was looking for a ceremonial *shabria*, a short Bedouin dagger, for his nephew's 21st birthday. He assured me that he would make sure that if the blade wasn't already dulled, he would 'desharpen' it for the young man. After all, it was to be only ceremonial.

However, in North Africa and the Mid East, eye contact is truly the kiss of death. And beware, that unsuspecting visitor to the *souk* who was not prepared, or didn't heed, the advice given to all before entering the warren of shops. Don't stop, don't smile, don't even engage the shopkeeper unless you really want to buy an item. By the way, this also applied to Moroccans from other cities. One could always tell a local Moroccan, as one could always tell a *Casablancan* in Fez. Each city had its own attitude that it imbued in its residents, and 'foreigners' could be spotted from dozens of meters away. Omar tried his best at flying under *Fezzi* radar, but it didn't work. He was pulled into a metalwork shop faster than I could grab his arm to prevent entry. He was hooked, and all I could do was follow and shake my head.

One hour, three cups of mint tea, and one *shabria* with a mother-of-pearl and sycamore wood box thrown in on the side, and Omar's wallet lightened by many *dirham*, we continued on our way. Yet there were other surprises still in store. We passed a rug factory, and I shielded my colleague's eyes like the blinders on a horse. I whispered that we shouldn't have another day to waste before making plans for *el Cahireh*, Cairo. He agreed, but the childish pout on his face said that he wasn't happy about it.

We walked on another twenty meters or so, and suddenly heard the cry "*Balak, balak!*" from almost immediately behind us. It was too late. Omar had seen what was coming from the corner of his eye and ducked before he could say one word. I, on the other hand, didn't, and got squarely smacked in the back by a form of 'flying carpet'. This one flew only a meter and a half off the ground, and was on the back of a donkey!

The streets and alleys are so narrow in *Fez el Bali*, old Fez, that the only vehicular traffic is either small push/pull carts or two-wheelers pulled by pack animals. But a majority of the residents simply use their animals as beasts of burden with no cart at all. The wonderful rugs that are one several major handicrafts that Fez is noted for are transported out of the *medina* on donkey-back; but not fastened on the back of the animal lengthwise. So the carpet is draped over the critter at a 90-degree angle and *across* nearly the entire width of the passage! Hence the cry of '*Balak*', which in essence means, 'get @#$%@ out of my way!' So Omar ducks, and I get 'doinked' in the back by a non-flying carpet. I fell to my knees and the oriental rug 'sailed' past me at an altitude of 1.4 m. As I watched it proceed down the lane, creating more havoc, I brushed dirt off the knees of my pants, my ego bruised more than my body. And guess who's laughing the last laugh at this juncture – the guy leaning against the wall smoking a *Gitane*.

At this juncture, I silently said to hell with the time schedule and opted to enjoy the stroll through the city to the agency office. On the way, I decided to stop at one of Fez's four famed tanneries, *Chuara* Tannery. It has been around for nearly 900 years.

As we turned down the alley to the tannery, we were stopped by a young lad. Fez has an unwritten law in the *medina* – to keep young boys out of trouble on the streets, they are 'hired' by people to serve as *proteksia*. In essence then, people are extorted to some degree and everyone eventually walks away a bit lighter in the pocket but safe and secure – until the following day when it might start all over again. Our 'security guard' escorted us to the entry, brandishing a smile and swagger that he hoped others would envy. The *bakshish* that we settled upon apparently was more than enough. At the doorway that led directly to a flight of stairs, he gave us both a sprig of mint. It was designed to serve as a primitive air filter; we would definitely need it in a few moments.

We ascended the ancient staircase to a series of storage and showroom chambers that overlooked the open-air dyeing facility. The limestone stairs were well-worn, cupped in the middle from countless feet that had used them for over a millennium. As we rose, the faint 'aroma' of the tannery grew stronger and stronger. By the time we reached the third floor the mint was an absolute necessity.

But the view was worth it. A small balcony looked out over an immense array of fired clay vats, adjacent to several drying platforms A dozen workers scurried about, carrying tanned hides from the sun-drenched dryers to the vats, filled with every color in the rainbow. Other laborers in hip-boots waded in the dyes; they themselves covered more often than not in their particular hue.

It was truly a 'Kodak moment', and we relished the break in the hectic schedule. The midday *adhan*, the call to prayer, roused us from our reverie. We returned to street level and made our way to the travel agency. Omar felt that he couldn't leave Morocco at that time in spite of the fact that he so very wanted to go to Egypt. So I booked a coach seat on a RAM flight for the next day. The Peugeot sat waiting patiently for us in the car park of the *Palais Jamai*. The return drive to Casablanca was uneventful, albeit smoky – in spite of the rolled down windows.

I was dropped under the portico and re-checked in at the Hyatt. Omar accompanied me into the lobby for just a moment. Before ascending the lift to my room, I got 'the treatment' again – the bear hug of an embrace. Some day he'll squeeze the life out of me, I'm sure. But meanwhile . . .

"*Bon voyage mon ami*," he said, with a hint of regret. I knew that he really wanted to go, but he did have a group to escort in two days – the timing just wasn't right. We both hated it when work got in the way of what we loved to do. "I'll be waiting here at Mo Vth to pick you up when you return with all the answers. Don't come back without them," he laughed as he waved. I turned toward the bank of elevators.

I'm not good at goodbyes, or 'adios-es', or 'see you arounds' or *any* type of departure farewell. I hate to leave friends at any juncture. *'Why can't they all just live in one place'* I thought. The best exit that I know is that of Patrick McGoohan in "The Prisoner". Not many people remember that quirky, cutting-edge-for-its-day British show of the late 60s. It had its cult following though and I was a thoroughly faithful member of the cult. In fact, I even had the entire series on VHS (yes, it was *that* old!). So how did good old Number Six 'carry on"?

It was a simple three-fingered salute as one walked away, stating – "Be seeing you!"

VI

To Cairo and beyond . . . .

THE FLIGHT TO Cairo was uneventful, as usual; *Royal Air Maroc* did its admirable job of getting travelers from here to there. As they always say, 'any flight that you walk away from is a good flight'. In general, it's usually better to say a silent prayer with a third world country's national airlines, but RAM is an exception. In many of the more advanced almost-to-the-first world country states, such as Morocco and Egypt, the 'national' airlines take tremendous pride in their version of representing their nation on an international level. The planes are very well maintained, the crew tremendously well-schooled in their jobs, and both the planes and crews fastidious in their presentation to the public. To them, they are *the face* of their nation in the international community, and it's their job to 'fly the flag' properly.

Long gone are the old days of air travel on these carriers. I remember back in the 80s when I first flew to Morocco. The RAM crews consisted of swashbuckling, somewhat boastful and arrogant male flight attendants who thought that they were *Allah's* gift to the passengers on their flight. They even had the *chutzpah* (can I say that in this context?) to have tailored uniforms that had shoulder boards with stripes on them *as if* they were cockpit crew! The handsome, chiseled, swarthy look of these male Moroccan 'models' sent palpitations through many a female passenger. "But did they know their jobs as air safety officers?" you might ask. I'd never had the need to question, or make use of, their trained IATA knowledge. But as far as I knew, the airline's record was nearly flawless and better than the vast majority. These stewards would joke and carry out the onboard service with a casual informality that, provided they did know what they were doing in an emergency, was quite refreshing and made the flight tolerable. At one point, a cabin attendant even asked what someone wished to drink, and then proceeded to *roll* the can of pop down the aisle a few rows to the passenger. Everyone laughed, applauded, and had their fears of flying allayed by this – and it worked, provided in the back of everyone's mind these "airshow" entertainers knew when and how to be serious.

But, as I said, those days are long gone; in part due to the extremely touchy nature of air travel and international terror in the skies. Now, although the casualness is gone, the informal, yet professional attitude of RAM attendants, now male and female, still allows for an enjoyable flight.

The flight took slightly longer than the norm, also in part due to the current situation. The Arab Spring had begun a transition to "summer", with very little yet to be resolved. However, one aspect of the sweeping changes that was clear was that the strongman of Libya, *Ghaddafi*, was dead and buried, and his despotic rule brought to an end in one of the more violent overthrows in the region. But this didn't mean instantaneous peace and prosperity. The Provisional Libyan Government was rife with its own form of corruption, deeply divided and fragmented, with constant sporadic outbursts of violence of daily concern scattered across the landscape. The result was that the vast majority of flights criss-crossing North Africa east-west or vice versa would opt out of Libyan airspace lest a stray missile track them. It wasn't too far out of the way, flying over 'the *Med*', but it still was a bit of deviation.

I tracked the sea to my left, and the *Sahara* to my right, as we began a long, slow descent into *Heliopolis*. That's part of the beauty of a flight over uninhabited areas. The descents can be very gradual – none of this take off and take-up steeply to let urban dwellers get their beauty sleep; or the reverse, come screaming down sharply to the tarmac below.

As we angled back south once we crossed the Libyan/Egyptian border, we were flying low enough to see such sites as *Siwa* Oasis and *El Alamein* of World War II fame. I closed my eyes and once again thoughts of my father's North African adventure intruded.

VII

1942 . . . Somewhere in the North African Desert . . . .

ORDERS WERE ORDERS, he thought. But the high command in North Africa had more important things to do than track than a wayward corporal. There was an exciting, unknown international experience waiting for a young man from South Philly who's main vision of the Mideast and North Africa was via Rudy Valentino. Or so he thought. After his somewhat harrowing experience in the back alleys of Fez, he had vowed to toe the line for the rest of his sojourn as part of the North Africa Campaign, unless of course the end came early with a 'toes up and toe tag'. That thought certainly wasn't uppermost in his mind as he re-read the flimsy that was given to him by his NCO.

Report to AFHQ Cairo, 1st Inf. Div. under command of Brig. Gen. T. Roosevelt, Jr.
Secure MATC space and proceed to Div. HQ

Maj. J.D. McKay

The one thing that he noted, with some pleasure, was that there was no *arrival date* entered on the orders that were cut for him. Being the adventurous soul that he was, he took it to mean 'whenever you get here' – so he planned on making the most of it wherever possible. That is, he planned this as long as he was able to stay out of the way of trouble. The Military Air Transport Command was a real SNAFU, according to all the GIs involved in Operation Torch. It was an acronym for, 'Situation Normal, All #@#%ed Up'. Some said that they didn't know their ass from a weather balloon sent aloft. Regardless, he was ordered to make his way to the nearest facility and proceed to Egypt.

Sometimes, logical thinking isn't, well, logical. My father decided that since Cairo was to the east, it made absolutely no sense to backtrack to the west, to get to the east. There was no airfield in Fez to speak of. Rather, it was a small strip of beaten earth, designed for light spotter planes and small 'sand hoppers' for high-ranking military personnel. No transport pilot in his right mind would try to land there.

The nearest major air facility was the *Anfa* Airfield outside Casablanca. Originally used by the Vichy French, the Allies appropriated it after the occupation and would continue to use it as a military base and main cargo hub for MATC until the early 1950s.

It also would eventually be the spot, in 1942, where Capitain Louis Renault would finally give Rick his letters of transit, telling him that it was the start 'of a beautiful friendship'. Of course, Rick gave them to Ilsa and her husband, Victor Lazlo, at the last moment. They would then board a flight out of the mist and fog on the way to freedom. There's nothing like big-screen romance . . . . 'but just remember this, a kiss is just a kiss . . .' unless it's with Ingrid Bergmann.

So logic dictated that, as long as you were always moving east, you were progressing toward the terminus of your orders – Cairo. It would take two days of being bounced from one office to another before he was able to secure a spot on a convoy headed towards Oujda, about fifteen km from the Algerian border – *to the east*! If asked, it was clear 'progress' en route to Cairo. Several hours on a dirt track, often bouncing dangerously close to the steel struts supporting the canvas cover, were enough to shake anyone's *baitsim,* as his father would have said in Yiddish. This journey was often brought to a screeching halt by radio chatter that warned of Axis air patrols. In spite of the fact that they were well behind Allied lines, random German Storch spotter planes did venture out to try to gain intelligence on troop movements. When these warnings came, the convoy would quickly seek out a *wadi* adjacent to the track, scatter the trucks, and then hastily cover them with scrub brush and netting to hide them from view. Word was that this tactic worked . . . some of the time.

These infrequent alarms, and false alarms, made the normal several hour journey a two day stroll. It taxed the already frayed nerves of the convoy commander, as well as the 'desert rats' who were a part of the troop movement. Evening of the second day saw the faint bluish blackout lights of the desert outpost shimmer in the distance. Everyone breathed a sigh of relief and looked forward to some warm grub and at least enough cool water to shave and bathe.

*   *   *

As Homer would have put it a continent away, the 'rosy fingered dawn' broke over the North African desert, tinting the desert a pinkish amber color. But none of the soldiers saw it, as they had finally bivouacked around three in the morning, fighting the chill of the sand dunes. In the desert, the hot, dry climate cools rapidly, with nothing to 'store' the heat of the day it radiates off at a rapid pace – leaving one to awaken to a briskness that can be unexpected. It wouldn't be until eight or so that the soldiers began to stir. My father took his tin mess kit to the large tent that served as the camp dining facility, and sat down to a plate of slop, washed down by a cup of mud. The quiet allowed him to chart his course. The base's soldiers had already eaten and gotten started on their daily routine a couple of hours earlier. He decided to explore Oujda before heading to the MATC Quonset hut adjacent to the airfield.

Located about fifteen *kliks* from the Algerian frontier, and sixty south of the Med, it really was a pimple on the ass of the *Sahara.* The early desert oasis community enlarged by the Arab conquest of the general, *Naqba ibn Nafi,* in the 7th century gave rise to a town in the 10th century of this era. It served the caravan route that led across the desert from Alexandria, Egypt to *Sale* in Morocco. But as a result of this, the town suffered greatly from time to time – a result of Berber raids on the outpost. The architectural simplicity of the mudbrick *casbah,* or fortress, was still the core of the community, in spite of French colonial modernization. The two and three storey structures effectively blocked the sun from hitting the narrow lanes that they fronted. And, although cast in shadow for the entire day save the couple of hours flanking high noon, the streets were cool and comfortable. In addition, the thick mudbrick walls served as wonderful insulators as well, keeping the interiors of the buildings at a close-to constant temperature year 'round.

As he walked through the alleyways, kids swarmed around like flies. And flies swarmed around them . . . like flies. One of the few troubles with having a close-quartered *casbah* was its lack of airflow. The gentle breezes that kicked up in the desert around midday never quite made it into the community, so the still air allowed flies to 'fly' with impunity. And they always sought out moisture as well; meaning that if you didn't keep moving, they would congregate around the mouth and eyes. Desert dwellers seemed 'programmed' to be able to overcome this irritation, the foreigners not so much.

In addition, the oddity of paler, westernized faces was a source of intrigue and mystery to the Arab children. So the soldiers were forever under their scrutiny. They also seemed to be healthier, fatter, better fed than the local population so the kids were constantly asking for handouts of all sorts; especially food. The more permanently garrisoned troops were aware of this and always prepared when they entered into the town; passers-through not so much.

My father's supply of Wrigley's quickly ran out, and regrettably the kids that got a stick were soon set upon by the others less fortunate. It was a hard lesson to learn, as he disappeared into a small tea shop to escape for a few moments. From there, he went directly out and to the airfield to see what might be available – understanding that he was in no hurry to get to Cairo.

He discovered that all of the direct transport flights to Cairo were totally booked with fighting units and cargo. When told this, the OOD (Officer of the day) saw the briefest of grins flit across his face. He thought it odd, but then, this was in the heart of the African desert and stranger things had happened. *Maybe it was a mild form of sunstroke,* was one thought. It passed quickly, as he began to chart a path east . . . eventually . . . for my father.

A small cargo transport was due to take off for *Tafroui* Airfield outside of *Oran,* Algeria, in a few hours, and my father got 'booked' on it. So he went back to base, got his duffel, and returned to sit it out on a hard stone bench til the plane was readied.

As the heat of day approached, and the Douglas C-53 Skytrooper, the newest iteration of an incredible aviation workhorse, was readied, the meteorological officer came to the tarmac with some very 'iffy' news. A front was moving in, bringing with it a sirocco wind that jeopardized all flights out of *Tafroui* and west North Africa for what might be several days. Once again, that faint smile crossed the lips of my father. *Another delay to Cairo . . . what do the Arabs say, 'ma'alesh'; too, terribly bad.*

But in this instance, as bad luck would have it, the flight took off in front of the front, and he made it out in the nick of time for the short hop into Algeria. Who knew, though, if the weather would hold. As the plane began its approach to *Tafroui,* the sky started to close in. At first, the plane was buffeted by the wind. Then, the closer to the ground they came, blinding particles of sand caught up in the *sirocco* blasted the airship. The pilots, although some of the best that the Army Air Wing had to offer, fought the ever-increasing intensity of the rising sandstorm. The pair of Pratt and Whitney R-1830s strained against the wind and sand. The pilots' main fear was that of air filter failure, getting clogged with the sandy grit from the desert floor. With no margin for error, their straining eyes caught site of the wind-socks that flanked the edge of the tarmac, and, after bouncing once, then twice, allowed gravity to overtake them and they rolled to a halt near the Quonset hut that served as operational HQ. *It was a damned good thing that the patent on gravity had expired,* thought the second officer as he cut the throttles. *I didn't have enough change in my pocket to pay the royalty.*

As soon as all the aircrew and troopers alit, the airfield was engulfed in a zero-visibility situation that ceased all operation. At ground level, the wind scaled back to only a few knots, and my father suddenly realized that all the French Foreign Legion movies that he had seen in the cinema before the war were patently untrue. Sandstorms on the ground were not howling, raging entities. Rather, they were far worse, and longer lasting. Sand that had been picked up and carried aloft by strong, initial winds, now found itself in the grip of a slow-moving front. The sand particles were suspended in air, with an eerie relative stillness that enveloped everything in a dim, choking cloud. You couldn't see past your arm, and needed a cloth over your nose and mouth in order to breathe – but with shallow breaths. This all-encompassing soup could last suspended in the air for days, weeks, til a fresh front pushed it away.

Inside wasn't much better. Remember, the buildings constructed at the airfield were temporary at best, ramshackle at worst. The architects who designed them and the engineers who built them used specs that seemed to be created by the famous WW II cartoon character, 'Kilroy'. Well, if Kilroy 'had been here', as the graffiti universally proclaimed, he would have found sand creeping in from every seam, getting into every nook and cranny, and filling orifices that the common soldier never even knew that he had. The next several days made those in the battened down base *wish* that they were anywhere else . . . including the Libyan front.

* * *

The morning of the third day dawned bright, clear, with the promise of an intense sun and overwhelmingly hot temperatures. But nobody complained. For the first time in over 70 hours GIs, aircrews and ground support personnel, ventured outdoors. Immediately, sand was swept, surfaces washed down, and life began to return to the insanity that was a military base during wartime. Since any movement in North Africa had been suspended during the *hamseen*, as the Arabs called it, flight plans and rosters were created in a very laid back and haphazard fashion. No one took notice of the fact that my father seemed to always get his place pushed way back in line to get to Cairo. He'd show up at the airbase, sign in to the MATC on call sheet, and proceed to tell the sergeant first class at the desk that he had reported as ordered. He then slipped a pack of good old Lucky Strike unfiltered surreptitiously in the noncoms battle blouse and headed out the door. Clearly, the exploration of *Oran* wasn't quite completed. Unfortunately, it only took one day for the 'nickel tour' to be completed – there simply wasn't anything there in 1942.

On one hand, with a heavy heart, my father resigned himself to the fact that Cairo was now an inevitability. But on the other, he grew increasingly excited at the prospect seeing that magical city, getting out to Giza and the Pyramids, and maybe sailing on the Nile.

The following day, he reported as usual to the desk sergeant. But after signing in, and the sarge looked expectantly for the smokes, but this time got none. My father quietly moved his duffel to the bench adjacent to the swinging door that led directly to apron where the transports sat. The glum duty officer did his duty, *sans* cigs, and within five hours another Douglas Skytrooper winged its way to the Nile Valley, and, *el Kahireh*, the City Victorious.

VIII

Cairo . . . the present

THE RAM FLIGHT gently descended through the high layer of clouds, and the extraordinary site of the *Giza* Plateau could be seen out both sides of the 757. The only ancient wonder of the world left standing, the pyramids of IVth Dynasty Egypt have stood in mute testimony for over 4500 years – a tribute to the ingenuity, and perhaps folly, of the human experience in its quest for immortality. Having been a student of archaeology Yes, no matter for how long, and no matter how many 'letters' are after your name, we're always 'students'. I fondly remember my father telling me that 'when you stop learning, you're dead'. That remains one of my credos as well. Continuous, lifelong learning is not a luxury, but a necessity.

I could hear the small gasps, murmurs, and yes, even a few claps, as the captain announced the view out both sides of the cabin. I reflected back on other flights, with other incredible sights from the portholes, and quietly congratulated the pilot for his wisdom. I remembered the flights to *Abu Simbel* in the far south, the incredible mortuary complex of *Ramses II* and his wife, *Nerfertari*. Long considered to be the Pharaoh of the Oppression of the biblical narrative, his temple complex was the most publicized action taken by UNESCO in the 1960s, during the building of the Aswan High Dam. Sixteen ancient Nubian archaeological sites had been threatened, with only a half dozen actually being rescued from what would become known as Lake Nasser.

Anyway, with the dismantling of ABS, as we affectionately refer to it (in part due to the airline code!) and the subsequent reconstruction of the saddle-shaped mountain that it was hewn from, millions of tourists have visited the site. Up until the late 1990s, the vast majority took bus caravans from Aswan, 300 km or so north. However, today, the majority of visitors approach via EgyptAir, a thirty minute flight. ALL of the flights approach ABS from north/northeast and, as a result of the flight path, begin the descent to the north of the site.

When the pilot announces, 'Ladies and gentlemen, *Abu Simbel* can be seen if look out the windows on the left side of the plane . . . . ', there is a mad rush, especially by the Asian tourists, to catch a glimpse of this spectacular architectural statement of love and affection that rivals even the *Agra's Taj Mahal.* Every time I take that flight with groups of my own, I imagine the headlines in the next day's *Egyptian Gazette* – 'Ground eyewitnesses verify EgyptAir 737 canted sharply over its left wing prior to crash'. I imagine what the weight transfer of fifty passengers instantly to one side of a plane can do to the trim of the flight . . . or I *don't* want to imagine . . .

* * *

Since I only had a small carry-on, I walked straight ahead, through Passport Control, and practically into the waiting arms of my dear friend and colleague, Sobhy. The last time that we had been together, there was the small matter of an earthquake centered near Cairo, the burning of the famed Egyptian Museum; and, oh yes, the small matter of an artifact of mind-blowing and world changing significance – that we decided to place on the back-burner for the time being given the state of the world.

"*Ahlen, ahlen, ahlen ya habibi! Kif halek ya hamar*?" The love and affection, along with the inevitable barbs, was like I had never left. "How's by you, pah-dih-nair?" Sobhy loved to imitate an aspect of American culture that he felt the he should have been born into.

I kissed him on both cheeks, but that had been preceded by an 'Omar-esque' embrace. He looked well, in spite of the underlying strain that was all too apparent. The Arab Spring, which had started out with such enthusiasm and optimism, had descended into the depths of a 'national identity hell' and had yet to emerge. Every sector of this ancient land had suffered as a result of the turmoil, the chaos, of the last couple of years. But one of the largest segments of the economy, and the hardest hit, was that of the tourism industry. As an Egyptologist, archaeologist and, more often than not, licensed tour guide, Sobhy saw firsthand the terrible tragedy that had befallen his beloved land. The only saving grace for him, if there was one, was that, as Chief Inspector of Antiquities of Sinai, his contact with the tourism industry was as limited as he wanted it to be. In addition, now that his 'royal holiness', Zahi Hawass, was no longer the head of the Supreme Council of Antiquities, the much less politicized position dropped the discipline from the radar of the public eye and, although on smaller scales, excavations could proceed on a limited basis with little or no fanfare, or interference.

We had a lot to catch up on. Our Sinai adventure we had put on hold due to the situation, and it turned out to be good that we did. And anyway, it opened the door to this Moroccan inquiry that was turning out to be even more exciting, if that could possibly be. We went out to his vehicle in the car park, made our way to the exit booth, and hit the road toward the chaos of Cairo, opting for the elevated roadway that bypassed much of the eastern suburbs on our way to Garden City and the cornice along the Nile.

We then took the *Kasr el Nil* Bridge, formerly the *Khedive Ismail* Bridge, on our way to my upgraded set of 'digs' as it were. The *Shepheard's* was now owned by the Helnan Consortium, and was undergoing a perpetual state of renovation. As a result, we headed across the Nile to *Gezira* Island and the *Gezira* Sofitel.

"So, here we are again, but this time headed for the Sofitel. But let me get this straight. We're going to "island, island", right?" I asked my dear friend and colleague for a couple of decades now.

"No, *habibi*, we're going to *Gezira* Island", he replied, with a wink.

"But *Gezira* means 'island', right?" I shot back.

"*Na'am*? What did you say?" he was concentrating on maneuvering his way on the two-lane wide round-a-bout that had four-cars-worth of lanes circling it. There's nothing like Cairo traffic as I always have said.

I repeated myself. He answered "*Aywa*, yes, of course you're right. But we're still going to *Gezira* Island."

What can I say? Sometimes logic has absolutely no place in certain areas of the universe. Apparently Cairo is one of them. We then pulled up to the gated approach and guard booth. After examining our credentials and my reservation, the steel-posted barrier was raised and we entered the upper car park that led to the reception. Once, checked in, we walked down the spiral staircase into the 'real' circular lobby, soaring several stories above our heads. The lounge area was a cacophony of sound – people conversing in twos and threes, a singer and harpist playing together in the far corner, waiters scurrying in and out of the 'Buddha Bar" that was adjacent. I ordered a *Stella*, and Sobhy followed suit. I pretended to tear my shirt and look up inquiringly at an invisible balcony with Blanche DuBois hanging from it. My friend looked at me blankly. So much for my Brando imitation. The waiter brought a dish of olives and pretzels and I proceeded to tell him of this new Moroccan line of inquiry.

Given the vast amount of *proteksia* now that he was re-instated with honor in the SCA and could come and go as he pleased in any of the museums under their authority, I told him about the tombstones at *Volubilis*, and the earliest dates for the one recently re-discovered.

To me, the clues might be found in the corpus of the Elephantine Papyri. These documents shed an unbelievable amount of light on the Persian Era in

Egypt, and, more importantly, the status of the Jewish community at that time. It seems that the community living on Elephantine Island had a major number of Jews living there during the late 6th – late 5th centuries BCE. Apparently this contingent consisted of mercenary troops in the employ of the Egyptians at that time. They were well established, considered to be tremendously loyal, and were allowed to practice their faith unimpeded. In fact, they even went to the extent of building a house dedicated to their God as well.

"I'm familiar with Elephantine", *Sobhy* said. "I am also aware of the vast library of sorts that was discovered there. The Jews of Elephantine kept papyrus rolls in jars under the floorboards of their homes. The legal system of the day, which was really quite sophisticated for twenty five centuries ago, required 'paperwork', and this supported the idea that people should save their papyrus documents. In addition, the official paperwork of the settlement was also saved. Some literature and personal letters were also kept. Nearly all that is known about the Elephantine community at this time comes from archaeological research at the site and from the study of the papyrus fragments. However, I'm *not* all that familiar with the documents themselves. One of the reasons is . . ."

"I know, I think." I interrupted. "They're written in a Hebrew derivative, Aramaic, right? So your familiarity ends because it's not one of the *gazillion* languages or dialects that you know." I winked at him. It was a complement that he acknowledged with a smile and tilt of the head. "That's why you have to put up with me sometimes", I finished. Once again, he smiled and took another sip of *Stella.*

I continued on. "For some reason unknown to us at this point, even nearly a century after discovery and translation, the Elephantine Jews kept lists of their names. Maybe they were tax rosters, maybe they were lists of people who had suffered for their religion. Other Jewish communities kept such lists, or just maybe they were lists of men belonging to military units. After all, the community was clearly mercenary in nature. Don't worry, I'm not a genius, I picked up a copy of Cowley's *Aramaic Papyri* when I discovered the direction that I was headed." I laughed and so did he. But did I catch a look of relief pass over his face ever so briefly? We headed to the restaurant to take advantage of the exceptional buffet and then promised to meet the next morning and head to the museum several blocks, and a Nile crossing, away.

* * *

We stepped out onto the terrace the following morning. It was promising to be another beautiful day in Cairo, once the early mist rising from the Nile dissipated. Located on the southern end of the island, the Sofitel looked toward the enormous 'fountain' that occasionally burbled in the center of the river. Off to the left, just upstream from the *Shepheard's*, the Egyptian naval station's contingent of sailors were doing their morning calisthenics. Even from a couple of hundred meters away, we could see that their hearts weren't in it. Jumping Jacks were lackadaisical at best, and some of them lay face down on the ground – 'doing' push-ups. Or should I say, lying there dreaming about doing push-ups. Others were busy preparing the navy Zodiacs that would later patrol the river in this part of the city. The pool and terrace of the hotel were right at water level – made possible today by the Aswan Dam and its regulation of the river.

We walked around the perimeter and headed up the private drive to the roadway and the *Kasr el Nil* Bridge. As we approached it, I was reminded of one of the more optimistic scenes broadcast around the world immediately following the resignation of Hosni Mubarak, former 'President for Life'. According to the photo, the elegantly carved stone lions that dated to the construction of the bridge between 1931-1933 hadn't been cleaned since the revolution, the 1952 Free Officers Revolution, led by Naguib and Nasser. But during the initial couple of months of the Arab Spring Revolution people had spray-painted democracy slogans on the four figureheads that buttressed the bridge on each end. Common people took it upon themselves to scrub clean the lions as a symbol of a new beginning. They almost glowed in the early morning light of the Nile Valley.

We crossed the bridge and I told Sobhy that I wanted a short detour to walk past both the US and British Embassies along the Corniche, and then swing around *Ahmed Ragheb* Street and head back to the Museum. It was a purely personal, family matter for me. A couple of minutes later we were at my planned destination. I looked up at the new hotel sign that was now in front of us – The Kempinski Nile Hotel. It was now a five star luxury hotel, but by far the most reasonably priced in this part of Garden City. But the hotel that I knew, that my father knew a lifetime ago, was a far cry from this opulence. I told Sobhy that I wanted to have a coffee and tell him a story. We entered and went to the small coffee shop and took a table overlooking the Nile. I began to relate the story of my father in Cairo.

IX

Cairo, 1942 . . .

AS THE DC-3 began its descent as far away as Alexandria along the Mediterranean coast, the ground became dotted with knots of dun-colored, camouflaged vehicles of all shapes and sizes. This was the beginning of the Allied equipment build-up for the final push in North Africa and the opening of the door to the southern belly of Europe.

The Skytrooper banked and made a wide circle around the nearly comatose terminal and runways of the city's *Almaza* Airport. This was the civilian airport that had served Cairo for many years. However, Allied command sought to build a facility that would be modern and suit the needs of the vast influx of men and *materiel* as part of the wartime effort. The result would be Payne Airfield, five kms away; that would eventually be a central hub for the Air Transport Command. Following the war, it was scheduled to be turned over to the Egyptian Civil Aviation Authority and used for international arrivals and departures.

The dust cloud threatened to choke everyone on board the converted cargo plane. After all, it didn't have a pressured cabin as it flew well below 10,000 ft, and got as much light inside the cabin from unpatched bullet holes, popped rivet holes, and improperly patched panel seams as it did from the few portholes that lined each side. After the plane taxied to a stop, the flight deck officer unbolted the hatch and the attached stairs fell to earth from their hinges on the fuselage. The dust-caked GIs tumbled down to the tarmac, spitting and coughing up the fine Sahara sand that had permeated the fuselage.

My father pulled out a handkerchief and began to remove the dust and sweat that had mixed together. The flight crew began throwing the duffels from the rear of the plane down onto the tarmac, and the soldiers sorted out their belongings and stumbled to the shack that served as operations HQ. The non-com had a roster of the flight, and began to read off destination names for each of the passengers and give them a small chit. When he got to my father, the piece of paper with 'orders' on it told him to make his way to the center of town, and a hotel called *El Nil.* No directions accompanied the sheet, no contact phone numbers, no officer in charge . . . in short, nothing to help out. Apparently military personnel were thrown into the melee with no life support system. But you know what, this played directly into my father's hands as he could meander and wander his way, slowly and with a sense of exploration, to his new 'residence'.

Dozens of lorries were moving in and out of the airfield complex, with cardboard placards thrust under the windshield wiper blade arms, hand-scribbled with destinations in the Cairo area. In fact, one of them even said "Downtown Cairo billets". Just the ticket. He threw his duffel in back and joined half a dozen other GIs. Smokes were passed around, small talk made like "Where y'all from, how long you been in, etc" until these 'deep' lines of communication were exhausted. There was an unwritten rule between on-the-move soldiers in a wartime situation. Unless the fellow next to you was there to protect your backside, and vice-versa, you didn't get too close and discover too much. The effects, the tragedies of war were too numerous as it was – no need to compound it by knowing more than the basics. The docs would call it 'shell shock'. Decades later, the shrinks would call it PTSD, 'post traumatic stress syndrome'.

So after a few minutes, they all sat in silence as the street of Cairo flashed by, rolling past them out the open rear deck of the two-ton transport. For some who had just disembarked from the troop ships that anchored off the Alexandrian or Port Said coasts of the Med, the chaotic scenes that they glimpsed boggled their mid-western, healthy, corn-fed minds. To nearly all, the crowded, noisy and frenetic pace that they observed on the street was a universe away from small-town America. Some showed signs of fear as they got closer to being 'thrown into it', others a stoic acceptance, while my father was fascinated, itching to alight from the truck and get into the mix. He had grown up with diversity in South Philly, near the shipyards. He had experienced a dozen cultures, just in the block that he grew up in, and relished the notion of the mixed salad that would be the human experience.

It would take the better part of two hours, at some times moving slower than the donkey carts that wove in and out of the 'faster' motorized traffic. He discovered that Cairo had been designed in a slower, more evenly paced world. Streets were narrow, suited more for the early 19th rather than 20th centuries. Although Mohamed Ali Pasha would raze tens of thousands of houses in order to create the broad boulevards that were patterned after the streets of Paris, or

London, in the 1840s, they still could not accommodate the gas-guzzling, carbon monoxide-belching, diesels of the USAFIME – The United States Armed Forces in the Mid East, part of the North Africa Campaign. Whenever, the vehicle came to a halt, which was more often than not, the back of the truck would start to fill with noxious fumes. The soldiers eventually were forced to roll up the canvas sides as well, in order to get some air flow. They joked about getting a Purple Heart from the ride into town. 'WOW' is how they kidded about it – 'wounded on the way' from CO poisoning.

Once they finally arrived at the *el Nil* the half-dozen or so soldiers with my father were dazzled by the view. Only one hundred fifty meters away was the Corniche and the Nile itself, shimmering in the haze of the late afternoon sun as it slowly sank into the "Goodly West" as the Egyptians themselves called it. Before checking in, the GIs crossed the street, no mean feat in Egyptian traffic, and straddled the low retaining wall to watch the sunset before reporting to the desk sergeant in charge at the hotel.

There's a funny thing about the sun in Egypt. It can seem to be suspended in the sky for hours, not appearing to move a bit down the sky. However, when the orb kisses the thin line of the horizon, where earth meets the heavens, it seems to suddenly be locked onto a magnetic beam; and, before you know it, has plunged the world into the twilight that leads to darkness. The disappearance of the sun in this way is stunning to see – the way it seems so instantaneous. Perhaps that's one of the reasons that the ancient Egyptians were so taken with the world of the west, their Underworld, their Land of the Dead.

With the show so quickly over, everyone re-crossed *Ahmed Ragheb* Street and up the five steps to the very small lobby. As was the case in nearly every hotel on every continent (with the exception of the US), the ground floor lobby was more often than not an area for the reception counter, maybe one or two chairs, a newsstand, and then the flight of stairs and elevator. There was nothing ostentatious, no expanse of leather sittings areas with floor-standing brass cigarette ash receptacles, no restaurant. Instead, it was a small functional space designed to get you registered in and to the important areas of any hotel – the rooms and restaurant on the upper floor. Right in the center of the building's footprint was a single elevator shaft that was surrounded by a spiraling upward stairwell. Okay, it wasn't 'spiraling', but it did wind its way around the square elevator shaft to the upper floors. It was the old-fashioned (even for the 1940s) style of elevator with a metal grate interior door and a robed and 'fezzed' elevator operator. The upper floors then were laid out in a figure-eight pattern emanating from this central service well in the midst of the figure-eight. However, the room numbers were confusing. One would think that they would be consecutively numbered; but remember now, this is Egypt, where all common sense seems to fall by the wayside more often than not. The odd-numbered rooms were on one loop, with the even-numbered on the other. So the soldiers who were being billeted there were constantly in a confused state when getting off the lift.

The top, or ninth floor, was reserved for the lounge and restaurant. It was so constructed as to give mind-blowing views of the Nile, with all the windows facing to the west. The eastern side was reserved for the kitchen and pantry, restrooms and cloakroom. The end result, there wasn't a bad seat in the house.

There was something else about the *el Nil*. It had to do with the 'banking' industry. Since Egypt was considered to be within the sphere of British influence, the Egyptian Pound was tied to the Pound Sterling of the UK. That meant that any other Allied currency, like the dollar, was also linked via the pound to the local exchange. There was an 'official' exchange rate, and then there was 'the exchange rate', if you catch my drift. The black market was alive and well and thriving on the streets of Cairo, and through money-changers. These could be legitimate store-front businesses, or behind-the-scenes shadier transactions. The US soldiers learned quickly. The joke that was currently running among the foreign 'guests' at the hotel was that the hotel had the tallest, and smallest, bank exchange anywhere in North Africa. Because once you stepped in the elevator, and rode to the top where the restaurant was located, you had changed money at a very lucrative rate, slightly better than Bank *Misr*. Whereas the bank rate, fixed, was at $2.15 per Egyptian Pound (Again, related to the British Pound). You could get the 'skyrocketing elevator rate' at upwards to $2.47. This was an extraordinary deal for the boys in khaki, but would eventually be even sweeter for the elevator operator; provided that he held onto the greenbacks for a while, waiting for inflation to catch up. This was all but guaranteed in the near future, as long as the war dragged on.

This temporary living arrangement would last the entire three months that my father's tour of duty in Egypt lasted. And scattered in between the work of the army Corps of Engineers, he was able to visit the sites in and around Cairo. To top it all off, weekend passes to Palestine were all the rage as well. It was a safe and secure locale during the war, and afforded the most soul satisfying excursions that anyone, especially Jewish American soldiers, could ask for.

X

Cairo, the present . . . .

SOBHY WAS ENTHRALLED with the narrative that my father had passed down to me. He found it fascinating that I had ended up in a career that seemed to have been genetically implanted in me by my father's North African/Middle Eastern experience. I hadn't thought of it in those terms, but saw the logic.

"You know, I also have my own *el Nil* adventure," I went on.

"*Stana schwayeh habibi*, just wait a minute". My friend held up his hand and signaled. "*Lohsma*, waiter, a couple of more *ahwa masboot*." He felt that you could never have enough of a good story, and a good, strong, thick, sweet cup of Turkish coffee to wash it down. I couldn't agree more – but with a twist.

As the waiter came over, I put a hand on his forearm and furtively whispered to him, "Do you have any *Groppi* connections?" Once again, the rum balls would haunt me as long as I was in Cairo.

"I'm sorry *rais*, sir, but *Groppi* has been closed since the start of the Egyptian Spring I'm afraid. Because it is only a few blocks from *Tahrir*, during the few days of rage when Mubarak's supporters tried to drive a wedge in the demonstrators with their violent behavior, some vandals and hooligans, mere street thugs, broke into many shops in the surrounding district and looted them. Some were firebombed, and *Groppi* has yet to recover and re-open. But the word on the street is that, for a fee, the baker could send out some of his finest . . . ."

He needn't say more. I slipped him five pounds and waited for a surreptitious delivery in a short while. I sighed with content, life was good.

Meanwhile, I told him of my experience. "We used to stay here in the old days, when finances were tight, and the student groups on a shoestring budget. The location was great, as you well can see, and we were within walking distance of the Egyptian Museum, and the Nile Hilton which faced *Tahrir* at that time. In those days, there was even an elevated pedestrian walkway around the grand circle. Nowadays you cross either on the surface, dodging traffic, or 'go underground' through the Metro Station beneath *Tahrir*."

"*Ya Allah*! Your tale stretches out like the Nile Valley!" Sobhy exclaimed, frustrated by my interjections about the old days. "Get to it before I die".

"Well, as I was saying, I mentioned the Nile Hilton because its small café on the ground floor made the best Tuscan-style pizza at a very reasonable cost." I saw THE look. "Sorry, got carried away with the pizza. Anyway, the second year that we opted to stay at the hotel, we discovered that it had just been purchased by Swissotel the previous week. Now, there's nothing wrong with the hotel being taken over by the Swiss consortium. In fact, it could have even led to great renovation and rehabilitation of what had been a splendid facility prior to World War Two. Many Egyptians still feel today that the allies did some serious damage to Cairene infrastructure – not intentional mind you – but nevertheless damaging the way that a wartime footing can be when civilian facilities are seconded to the military." I saw another look.

"*Qwayes, habibi,* ok, I get it. The hotel was in a state of flux and the early stages of the Swiss takeover. It wasn't like clockwork. The first thing that the consortium management did was to try to set a semblance of sanity to the room situation, and begin to number the rooms in a numeric order that would make perfect sense to any travelers staying in the hotel. The problem was that they had failed to remove the old room numbers from the doors after putting up the new sequence. So the weary traveler was faced with two sets of numbers per room, and of course your guess was as good as any as to which room you really were in. This in turn led to dozens of late key insertions into wrong room door locks, the waking of patrons fast asleep, the frantic calling to reception that someone was trying to break into their room, etc, etc, etc. At first it was hilarious, then as the novelty wore off, quickly became a royal pain and, to some, offensive in nature."

"I couldn't agree more," Sobhy was laughing so hard that he was having trouble breathing, snorting and snuffling. He pulled his handkerchief, wiped the tears from his eyes and blew his nose. I offered him his bottle of water and he gratefully took it. "Ah, that's better," after about five minutes of this. "You do have some stories, don't you" he exclaimed.

"Well, this is the place to get the material isn't it?" After over 40 visits, there really was a wealth of archived anecdotes that could fill volumes. "And of course, finally, the "Bank du Elevator" was still in operation even decades later".

The swinging door from the kitchen opened, our waiter headed toward us with a tray dramatically flourished above his head. He beamed at me with a radiance that rivaled the Egyptian sun.

"*minfadlak, rais*! I am pleased, sir, to return with 'the goods' as you *Amriki* say!" It was evident that he was as proud of his little coup as I was at his ingenuity. It clearly would not go unrewarded.

I bit into the small morsel. I sighed. Life indeed was good. Sobhy reached over and I playfully slapped at his wrist, feigned anger, and proceeded to let him into my little corner of heaven. There's nothing else in this world like *Groppi's* rum balls . . . .

* * *

By that time, the museum was open to the trickle of tourists that braved a country in the midst of change. We paid the bill, I offered the waiter more *bakshish* for his efforts, and we exited to the street. We walked down *Qasr ad Dobarah* past the front of the US Consulate in Cairo. Ever since 9/11 it had begun to look more and more like a fortress amid a sea of greenery. The concrete blocks lining the sidewalk, the pop-up barricades just off the street that protected the driveway, the razor-wired stucco enclosure wall – all made it feel like this outpost of the United States was a wild-west fort under siege. This was only reinforced by seeing the US marines on the rooftop. In the 'good old days', more often than not, they were in their dress uniforms as symbolic guards. Today, desert fatigue battle dress was *de rigueur*, with magnifying scopes for their sharp-shooting weapons; scanning the streets and other rooftops constantly.

On one hand, it was comforting to see a state of preparedness that was a far cry from an earlier time, when embassy protection detail was seen as a cushy job for soldiers; a day when embassies could more easily be stormed and occupied. But on the other hand, it was a sad state of affairs when an ally once considered being a stable partner in peace collapsed into a state of chaos and uncertainty. Yes, of course, Mubarak was a strong man and had dictatorial proclivities; but sometimes there is something to be said for a personality that can maintain a status quo, keep a lid on things, and work in an international framework for the ultimate good of a region. And yet on the other hand . . . talk about a circular argument!

We approached *Tahrir* from the south, and I was stunned. The normal, orderly chaos of that wonderful public space was turned into a temporary land fill. Garbage was everywhere, ramshackle huts of cardboard and tin sheeting sat side by side with tented sheets and other impermanent shelters. Sporadically placed oil drum fires warded off late night chill.

In spite of all that, the energized aura that the place emitted was awesome to feel. In spite of the recent weeks of inactivity by the military council that had taken over in the vacuum that existed after Mubarak's resignation, the sweeping changes that took place over the last few months still inspired thousands to remain in the square to demonstrate daily for the final steps in the evolving political process that would lead to democracy.

We picked our way around the debris, Sobhy shook hands with a few people that he recognized, and made our way to the northern perimeter that fronted the grounds of the museum. We passed several small 'monuments' that had been hastily erected as memories of keynote events in the ongoing 'battle' for Egypt's soul. Here was the location where Mubarak's camel jockeys entered and, with their crops, beat down several peaceful demonstrators before the police belatedly drove them off. A bunch of wilted flowers marked the spot where Copt and Muslim alike stood side by side on a makeshift podium and proclaimed a unity of faith in the face of the toppled thirty year old regime. And just before leaving the vicinity, we saw a battered chair standing, slightly askew, with a photograph of US Secretary of State Hilary Clinton on it. According to a handwritten placard attached to the seat of the chair beneath the picture, it was here in March of 2011 that 'the Egyptian people noted with pride the support of our dear friends, America' as indicated by her visit. All were signs of a proud population that appeared secure in its desire to install true democracy in Egypt and restore her image in the world.

The wrought iron fence and gate stood tall and secure, in spite of the beating that it had taken in the early days of the revolution. It was here that thousands of everyday Egyptians, men and women alike, had stood firm in their commitment to protect their national heritage. Many of them had never even set foot in the museum; yet they linked arms defiantly to try to prevent any looting and vandalism by opportunists taking advantage of the political anarchy in order to steal, and then sell, national archaeological treasures. It would be another couple of days before the riot police were able to establish a perimeter.

Sadly, though, it wouldn't be soon enough. In the dead of night a handful of thieves would enter an unlocked rear gate and scale the exterior fire escape ladder. They made their way across the rooftop of the museum to one of the grimy, nearly opaque skylights that dotted the expanse, designed in the late 19th century to allow the glorious natural Cairene light to filter into the galleries below. It was a brilliant piece of engineering, provided the glass panes were annually cleaned! But over the years, maintenance was reduced to perhaps once-a-decade, if that, casting the interior space in perpetual dullness.

The robbers broke one small skylight that was immediately above the papyrus gallery, and used ropes to lower themselves down the few meters to the floor. From there, a couple of them descended to the main floor, while the other swept through the New Kingdom Gallery on the way to the Mummy Rooms. All told, thirteen cases were smashed. *Shuabti* statuettes, Amarna age limestone statues, scarabs and amulets, all went missing.

On the ground floor, several glass vitrines in the Old Kingdom wing were broken. Priceless objects (okay, they're *all* priceless in the Cairo Museum!) would later be found strewn about, taken out and then dropped and smashed. One tragic example was that of a cedar wood carved boat model, 4400 years old. An 'army' of cedar wood soldiers in a case was opened and several 'men' were tossed to the ground. It seemed that the vandals, in this instance, were more intent on irrational, rage-fueled destruction rather than thievery for profit.

Upstairs, the robbers were more intent on smash-and-grab to escape with as much as they could carry. Cases filled with scarabs, jewelry with semi-precious stones were broken and pieces clearly removed. They methodically moved to the *Tutankhamun* Wing. The precious metals room, with its splendid gold items, was so securely locked that no one could break in. However, a few cabinets with wood-overlaid-with-gold statues and walking sticks were broken into. A lovely statue of Tut on the shoulders a goddess was taken. Another, with Tut fishing on a papyrus boat, was later discovered broken in half.

The final insult was in the second floor wing that held the three mummy rooms. In the hallway outside the entry to the gallery, one case was discovered broken – lying on the floor was a bronze metal frame that helped to secure the mummy wrappings from fraying. Apparently it was too cumbersome and heavy to take away. Adjacent, two mummified skulls were found at the doorway, lying there with no body in sight. However, if there was any good news here, was the fact that these skulls *were not* from the Royal Mummy Room. Its locked door was intact. Rather, these were two lesser mummy heads that were from a work room where they had been undergoing analysis and preservation.

All in all, over sixty-four items were stolen from the museum. *Al Ahram* Daily Newspaper called it a true national tragedy in the midst of so many other tragedies. Zahi Hawass, the director of the Supreme Council of Antiquities, was forced to resign.

But over the ensuing weeks, the end of the tunnel became well-lit. Seventeen of the initial items were quickly recovered, one found in a garbage bag on the grounds of the museum itself. Others that had been damaged were rapidly restored, and the grand dame of international museums began to heal.

* * *

Now, security was tighter than ever, actually a blessing given the irreplaceable contents of that pink-stucco building. Brand new x-ray machines stood just inside the gated entry to the garden. And guess what, THEY ACTUALLY WERE BEING USED! All too often in Egypt, the guards at archaeological and religious sites would simply wave tourists through with not even a cursory look at the X-ray monitor. And more often than not, if a savvy traveler put his or her camera bag on the table adjacent to the machine for fear of radiation damage, the lazy, uniformed policemen would just slide the bag along the table, go back to their coffee and smokes, and wait for the tourist to pick them up after the guests went through the scanner. It really was a new world now.

Once through the security net, we entered the garden area that remained untouched by all the turmoil outside the gate. The lotus pads still floated serenely on the surface of the central pond. The lawn was still immaculately manicured, the statuary clean and pristine. The difference? The throngs of tourists were missing. Gone was the bedlam of trying to listen to a dozen languages, all trying to outshout each other as guides prepared the groups for the hectic tour to come. Gone was the pushing and shoving of visitors hoping to catch a quiet glimpse of some of the world's most incredible relics of the past. Gone was the conspiratorial wink as Tourist Police tried to earn more than their meager salaries via the promise of offering 'private viewings' of items in store-rooms.

And you know what? Sobhy and I both missed it dearly. We saw it in each other's faces as we walked slowly through the main entry and faced the enormous two-storey hall that contained the great limestone statues of *Amenhotep III and Queen Tiye* at the far end. There were perhaps ten other people wandering around in that area. I was truly shocked. Gone was the need for the 'Whispers", the wireless earpieces that allowed guides to speak in normal tones of voice and eliminated the tourist need to crowd around the leader just to catch a word or two in the tumult. It was deathly silent in the museum space. We both shook our heads and proceeded towards the rear of the museum and the offices and extra storage facilities. Our goal was the catalog of the Elephantine Papyri still in the museum. We needed to see if there were any obscure references to Jewish migration and return in the 5th and 4th Centuries BCE.

Although Sobhy had been totally re-instated with good graces following our last 'adventure' in the museum, the governmental 'anarchy' affected all institutions, including the SCA and museums. He wished to swing wide of the director's office for that reason. I concurred; after all, according to all the 'rumors' spreading across North Africa, I personally burned the Cairo Museum! I told Sobhy this, and his response was to fake a call to the Tourist Police, laughing all the while.

"We'll have to put your picture up in various postal service facilities so that good citizens could do their duty after spotting you on the street", he joked. I didn't find it all amusing.

"But does anyone still write letters?" was my response.

"*Ya Allah.* This is Egypt. Although nobody writes letters, *everyone* uses the post office because that's where the majority of Egyptians pay utility bills, taxes, mortgages, etc. It's an entirely different system here than in the States. Actually, I have no idea why it's still called the Postal Service. Should be 'Governmental Banking, Ltd". We both smiled and the tension dissipated as we swung a left to the office of records at the end of the back hall.

There was an upside to the earthquake and subsequent fire damage in the museum. The tens of thousands of documents that had been saved were scanned and transferred to a newly installed computer system. Unfortunately, remote online access via secure password had not yet been set up – things work very slowly in the MidEast. As they say, the standard time is one hour and five centuries behind the rest of the world! So we had to access all data from a terminal in the museum proper.

As we started to scroll through menus, we saw hundreds of references to "file inaccessible due to loss". We mourned the fact that so many records were now gone due to the natural tragedy. The work of hundreds of scholars over the past two centuries would probably be lost forever. The task at hand for the museum staff was to try to re-create as much as possible from other sources – a gargantuan task that would be never ending.

However, as luck would have it, the computerized 'folders' for the Elephantine Papyri were intact; saved from the fire and subsequent sprinkler system flooding. The first place that I went to was the catalogue as published by Arthur Cowley in the 1920s. His seminal work on the scrolls and fragments discovered following World War I are still considered to be the most outstanding analysis of these 2500 year old documents that detailed the life of the Jewish community on the island. His seemingly endless list benefited from the computer age, though. When the data was entered, someone had also cross-listed subject matter and storage location along with catalog number. The end result was a nearly perfect means of referencing the material in a vast number of categories.

Many of the more obscure papyri got the same attention as the more complete ones, and this would be of great aid. One of the problems faced was that many documents had the connotation "N/A", "Not Available", or "Unknown" appended to their entry. Although it was exasperating, I did have one more idea.

"Let's see if there is a separate catalog file that's more recent. The Israeli scholar, Bezalel Porten, researched and published new material on the papyri in the 1960s." Sure enough, a few keystrokes revealed another catalog that seemed more complete, more up to date. "And this one has more subject matter categories than the Cowley file." We now could enter in more precise parameters and get even better results.

We spent the better part of two hours searching the database and came with a couple promising entries. But we discovered a real flaw in the system. As yet, there were no transliterations or translations of the texts proper. We needed to actually dig them up in either the archive store-rooms or see them if they were on display in the gallery. I told this to my friend and he groaned.

"You didn't really say that did you?" The grimace on his face said it all.

"Say what?" I hadn't a clue.

"That 'we needed to 'dig' up the scrolls in the archive room.' Really . . . . *Ya hamar*! *Enta mush qwayes*!" He muttered under his breath, "You're really quite the idiot." (I paraphrase)

It dawned on me. "*Ma'alesh*, what can I do?" I smiled back ruefully. I'd need to watch my phrases more carefully or I'd continue to get an earful of colorful language from him.

But by now it was time for lunch. I suggested the *Felfela*, a few blocks away on *Ta'alat Harb* Street. It was reasonably priced, with excellent *schwarma*, outstanding *babaganoush*, and *humus* that melted all over your taste buds. As we walked out the entry of the museum, Sobhy's final words to me hit me in my wallet – " . . . and you're buying . . ."

XI

Syene, 419 BCE . . .

FINALLY, AFTER SO many months of inundation, there was evidence of the Nile's return to its normal depth. The season of 'Akhet' was coming to a close. The life-giving silt had been deposited, the waters were receding, and the peasants were preparing once again for the fall planting to begin. That season, 'Peret', would then last until the equivalent of late Spring, when the harvesting would begin. 'Shemu' would then last until the floodwaters began to return in late Summer. This was so predictable that the calendar used by the Egyptians for centuries was based on this timetable. In the midst of an uncertain world, with the Persians knocking on the eastern doorstep, such regularity was a welcome respite in these chaotic times.

The Vizier looked out of the second-floor window of his estate, high on a ridge along the eastern flank of the island, and thought that all was right in the world. His family had been here for nearly 4 generations, and the men had quickly risen to positions of authority within the leadership of the first nome, or province, of Upper Egypt: 'ta-Seti', 'the province of the frontier'. The house was built in a somewhat unusual fashion for Egypt,; but apparently the style was catching on with the Jewish community here. It was a four-unit house, with three long rooms and a broad room across the front. The flat roof was accessed via a stone and wood staircase; for here, much of the year, family members would sleep because of the extremely moderate evenings in the Nile Valley. The central long room was actually an open-air courtyard that let light and air into the adjacent rooms. It was also the location of the oven, allowing smoke to gently rise into the sky and not fill the interior with a sooty residue and even smokier smell. According to his ancestors, this was the same style of house that the Israelites used over a thousand years earlier.

As their political and economic acumen caught the attention of the Achaemenid Kings from Persia who ruled Egypt from one generation to the next, the current satrap, or Persian governor, felt the need for a strong representative to deal with the Kingdom of Meroe to the south, and its king, Amanineteyerike, meaning 'Begotten of Thebes'. For many years now, the Nubians had coveted the southern extremity of Misr, and constantly sent forays to probe what they thought was the soft underbelly. They even adopted aspects Egyptian religion, culture and language in a blatant attempt to woo the peasantry to their side.

The Jewish community of Egypt was not just tolerated, but embraced and granted full rights. However, the Vizier, being the pragmatic man that he was, preferred to downplay his Berber and Jewish roots, and simply refer to his family as Saharan in origin – fully embracing their adopted nationality. Additionally, though, in the privacy of the tight-knit Jewish community on the island, his pride in his ancestry forged a solid relationship that, when the military threat from Nubia became increasingly apparent, enlisted the mercenary aid of all capable men in defense of this land. This played well in Syene, and served to support his role as presented by the Satrap.

Even his family, although vaguely aware of their background, was unfamiliar with the details of their ancestry. It was a secret that was held close to the hearts of all the heads of the family for generations. It was better this way, and what they didn't know couldn't come back to cause damage should the situation ever arise. After all, in the minds of many, once a foreigner, always a foreigner. To be a stranger in a strange land meant that, according to human nature all over the world, you were at risk as the scapegoat for all the ills that might befall a people – even if it had nothing to do with you.

As the evening approached, and he gathered the family on the rooftop terrace for the last meal of the day, a dusty traveler approached the enclosure from the eastern boat ramp not far from the Nilemeter. From the rooftop, he could see the man stop adjacent to the papyrus bundle fence and consult a scroll. Since the Vizier held a position of prominence, people needed to know where he lived, so a small placard gave his name and position only; no one had 'addresses' on Syene because everyone knew everyone else. This shingle was designed for outsiders. He knew that this person was an outsider for a couple of reasons. First, he was wearing different robes than those in the Nile Valley. The 'djellaba' that he wore was hooded, and of a coarse wool. No one in Egypt had need for a hooded gown, the Hamsin winds that blew here had lost their ferocity by the time they had crossed the Great Desert. And second, the approaching man was clearly of North African, Berber origin. His facial features gave this away. The Vizier was intrigued, but made no move to descend to greet the visitor. The servant at the door would handle that and, if necessary, summon the master of the house.

A few moments later, one of the house attendants bounded up the stairs and relayed that a messenger from far off in the Great Western Desert was waiting with a document that the Vizier needed to see immediately. He set down his ceramic cup of date wine, gathered his thoughts, and went downstairs to greet his guest. After all he was the Vizier of the province . . .

* * *

The traveler sat in the shade of one of the sycamores that graced the property. He gazed in awe at the great river that flowed just a few dozen meters away. He hadn't seen anything like that at all, not even in his native Berber land far to the west. Yes, there were streams and mountains that bordered the desert, but nothing as majestic, wide, and apparently deep like the Nile. After the weeks of travel eastward across the Sahara, the water was intoxicating to say the least. He picked up the earthenware mug and took another draught of the mild beer that the attendant had given him. He wracked his brain for the proper prayer to say before drinking, and he could only come up with 'Boreh pree ha-gafen', for the fruit of the vine in biblical Hebrew. Okay, so it was the fruit of the barley in this instance, but he was sure that YHWH would accept his 'blessing on the fly'. As he silently finished, the master of the house approached, resplendent in finery fit for a king; or in this instance, a vizier.

"Greetings to you, you are a guest in my home. To whom do I owe this honor?" The Vizier was cordial yet a bit wary. There were constant impositions on his private time, and he did cherish his privacy with his family. His ancestral tradition respected this need; no, demanded this need – as one's personal life was seen as more essential to one's well-being than one's public persona. It was the rare occasion that his trusted attendant allowed for the imposition to occur.

"I come to you with word from your ancestral homeland." The messenger looked around at the wealth of the Vizier; muted, quietly elegant, yet indicative of vast power and authority. "It is true what they have said of you back home in Tingis – that you had risen to great prominence and respect in Egypt, in spite of your, hmm, shall I say, family ties. We have watched from afar, and have noted with tremendous pride, your successes, 'Baruch HaShem'.

The Vizier was slightly taken aback. He certainly had not expected this. No one knew of his 'ancient past', his family lineage, or the faith of his father and his father's father. He had been very circumspect with his image, but had always found ways to avoid religious activity in the public forum. No one had apparently noticed or paid much attention to it, and his secret had remained safe. Yet now this individual was in his salon, enjoying the hospitality that was not just a given from people of a desert society, but a hallmark of his own people, often referred to as People of the Book. After all, the spiritual imperative went as far back as Avram Avinu, 'Our father Abraham', and his wife, Sarai. They opened their tents to anyone who strayed from the path, gave them food and drink; provided shelter. It was just one aspect of taking pride in and observing the 'blessings', the 'mitzvot', found in the biblical narrative. Take pride in observing God's precepts, don't see them as something cumbersome and weighing you down; and you will delight in this world and be successful – preparing for the world to come.

"Baruch HaBa, you are welcome in my home as well. And to what do I owe this audience from one who has journeyed so far and at such a risk?" The ancient language rolled easily over his tongue. Some things never were forgotten in spite of the lack of use.

The traveler walked over to the window and ensured that there was no one within either earshot or viewing distance. But as a precaution, he pulled the fine linen drapery a bit tighter across the frame. He then reached deep into the folds of his Djellaba. The attendant was standing discretely off to the side, far enough away not to hear the muted conversation but close enough to defend his lord. He stiffened and took one step toward the pair and put his hand on the hilt of his dagger. It wasn't necessary, for all the stranger did was to pull a small, tattered scroll from within. He silently handed it to the Vizier, who took it gracefully, uttering his thanks.

As he read the document, a million scenarios crossed his mind. But foremost in his thoughts was the opportunity of a lifetime.

XII

Cairo . . . .

AFTER OUR RETURN to the museum, we spent several more fruitless hours pulling the papyrus fragments, with Sobhy doing much of the translating. This was his bailiwick, certainly not mine. He relished the work, although it was very tedious. I left him from time to time to get glasses of tea to refresh us.

As the angle of the sun dipped lower and lower in late afternoon, he became more frustrated. The documents that we had isolated as 'possibles' from the computerized database proved to be dead-ends. Although fascinating in their own right, they shed no light on our quest. I was disappointed, but clearly not as 'bummed' as my dear friend. He sat back, and I could see that the empty search had drained him. Whatever advice I proffered would not be accepted graciously at this point, so I kept my mouth shut and waited him out.

As he absently gazed out the window and the ever-increasing dusk, I surreptitiously grabbed by pack and removed a couple of tissue-wrapped items. After a few sips of tea, while he still was pondering the lack of progress, I slipped the rum balls from *Groppi* onto the plate between us. Apparently his sense of smell hadn't abandoned him in his reverie. He turned, and it was if someone turned the lights on in the room. He was positively beaming now.

"*Groppi*!" he exclaimed with delight and swept up one of the delicacies with a blinding speed that really caught me off guard. He then wolfed it down in two large bites; wiping his chin with a paper napkin; murmuring contentedly. A quick sip of more tea to wash it down; and suddenly he was reaching across the plate for the other treat. Alarmed, I grabbed the plate and swung away from him.

"*Ya Allah*! What are you doing? I brought one for each of us and here you are trying to make a *Hazar* out of yourself! A pig! Of all things!" We both laughed and finished our tea. I *did* get my delicacy after all.

We decided to call it a day, exited the museum and went for a stroll along the *Corniche*.

The Nile was dotted with a handful of *feluccas*, the ubiquitous sailboats that could be found up and down the river. However, here, they needed to dodge the more numerous powerboats that belonged to the Cairene elite. It appeared that at least the wealthier classes of Egyptians were untouched by the political upheaval in the country that persisted long after Mubarak's ouster. Only the lower half of Egyptian society (economically speaking) seemed to suffer due to basic shortages. However, this 'lower half' actually numbered closer to eighty per cent of the population. So it was a huge demographic issue.

On the ground, the reality was that only a couple of districts in Cairo in and around *Tahrir*, and a couple of neighborhoods in Alexandria, were still affected by the demonstrations and a heightened military and police presence. The truth of the matter was that by now, months after the initial euphoria wore off, everyday Egyptians would demonstrate and protest in the heart of downtown, around the square that was named for an earlier revolution, "Liberation Square". But then, even in the midst of the social and political change that was occurring, would go home to their residential districts for dinner and a shower, etc. To ensure that all was well in their suburbs while they were away, wonderfully effective neighborhood watches were created. Any outsiders on the streets were politely asked by patrolling guards what their business was. If they were deemed legitimate, they were allowed to pass. If they were intent on disruption, they would be prevented from entering the area and detained for a while as police were called. Unfortunately, the majority of the time, the police, stretched so thin, failed to respond. The result was that the intruders would eventually be let go with a fairly stern warning that this neighborhood was off limits. Usually the warning worked.

Sobhy and I headed a bit north, then turned east on the road from the 6 October Bridge. We meandered through a few small side streets and then returned south down *Meret Basha* Street, skirting to the east of *Tahrir* Square. We passed by the shuttered KFC franchise, closed due to the fact that early on vandals had broken out the front windows; yet to be replaced, and as we continued left the entrance to the Sadat Station Metro stop behind. We opted to keep walking a bit to build our appetites, dulled just a touch by our mid-afternoon tea. As I have always said, "blame it on the British". We passed a small passage, actually nothing more than a wide alley, called Champollion Street. Sobhy remarked about the name and the re-discoverer of the key to breaking the hieroglyphic code. However, in light of the recent revolution and turmoil, the street had a new meaning as well.

"Isn't this the street of the residence and gallery of that avant-garde artist, Huda Lutfi?" I asked my friend. He replied that he thought so, but didn't know exactly where. She was one of the voices of the modern-day revolution as a cultural historian and artist. Having lived for thirteen years in the shadow of *Tahrir*, she has been intimately familiar with life on the streets in and around the square. Her exhibitions were described by art critics as 'archaeological research on the streets of modern Cairo'.

"One thing that I do know" Sobhy said. "Her work about social change and the last couple of years of Mubarak's regime was strongly supported by the middle class of Egyptian society. Because of that, many in the government felt that she was untouchable – that her arrest would cause an even greater uproar. So her work continued unabated. But I'm not quite sure that I like her style. Her message is one thing that I can support; but military police wearing lipstick? Not for me."

I somewhat agreed, but did find some of her collage work compelling. I let Sobhy take the lead, for he knew now which restaurant we should visit. He led me through a couple of smaller side streets and we then came to the *Koshary el Tahrir*. It was one of his favorites that served his favorite – *koshary*. No, it had nothing to do with Jewish cuisine. Rather, it consists of rice, lentils, chickpeas and macaroni. Toppings include tomato sauce, garlic sauce and fried onion. Many believe its mixture to be uniquely Egyptian. As a vegetarian dish that is relatively light, it has formed a staple of Egyptian society. Served in steaming hot bowls, along with a bottle of water, one doesn't even need *pita* bread with it.

By the time we finished, it was approaching eleven or so. The streets were still crowded with people, and a bit farther away the die-hards in the square were still chanting slogans and preparing their tent camps for the evening. We parted company and agreed to meet at the museum the following morning at nine-thirty to complete our survey of material at hand. Perhaps that be the day that we got some of the answers we were looking for.

* * *

The *muezzin* had no effect on me the next morning. I slept solidly through the call to prayer at sunrise, surprisingly. It must have been the later-than-usual *koshary* meal that lulled me into a deep, dreamless sleep. I welcomed it after all the travel that had taken place over the last couple of weeks. But of course 'late' for me is six thirty or so. I got cleaned up (yes, some people think that I 'clean up' nicely, thank you) and went down to the buffet breakfast. Who needs lunch after the kind of spread that is offered by the Sofitel *Gezira*? One of the greatest surprises that I have rarely found in the States is beef bacon! Along with Egyptian-style French toast and a couple of cups of rich coffee, and I can do nearly anything. I sat there, drinking, pondering the fresh fruit table, reading the *Egyptian Gazette.*

I felt the paper rustle a bit from a stray wind current in the dining room and heard the chair on the other side of the table scrape across the marble floor. I pulled the paper down and saw another old friend start to pour himself a cup of coffee across from me. It was someone that I considered a brother, a friend, for nearly 25 years. *Haytham* had been in the travel industry for all of his adult life, primarily in the English and Chinese sections of the agency that he worked for. "*Wing-ess"* Tours and Nile Cruises was one of the foremost agencies in all of Egypt. (Yes, it's not pronounced *Wings* as we English speakers would expect, but the two-syllable Egyptian approach to English words: *wing-ess*).

"So you were going to tell me that you were here in Cairo . . . when exactly?" He looked kind of hurt. But, you know, *this* time I had it covered from the get-go; for I had left him a text message and voicemail before I got on the plane in *Casa.*

"*Ahlen habib, kif enta*? And it's nice to see you too." I smiled, got up, and kissed him the prerequisite number of times on his cheeks. It really is way cool to know that he doesn't know that I know that I have the upper hand on this one. "I'm very well, thank you for asking", rubbing it in a touch. "When was the last time that you checked your phone?" I asked innocently. The look on his face told it all. Boy was I happy – but tried not to show it.

"Well, er . . ." there was dead silence now for about half a minute. "Well, you see, my battery died, first on my car, then on my phone." I was totally lost. "Okay, here's how it was. I was driving from home in *Heliopolis* to the Wing-ess office on *Salah Selim* Road. Got there, went into the office for some vouchers for a Chinese group, came back to the car. That's when I discovered that the battery was dead."

"The phone battery?" I played dumb.

"No, the car battery. So I went back into the office and borrowed *Adly's* car. You remember him. So I drove to the Sheraton Casino and Towers where you used to stay to meet with *Mohamed Helal* and introduce him to the Chinese group."

I had no idea where this was all going, but I was having a good time.

"So then, I stayed for dinner with the Chinese, and then went home. I forgot that I had *Adly's* car . . . I told you that, right?"

"No, you didn't tell me that you forgot. But go on." I was really enjoying myself now.

"*Tayib*, okay. So I went home and went to bed. The next morning I got *Kareem* up. You know how slow the kid can be, especially when getting ready for school." I did know his son, and knew that he took after his father when it came to anything before ten in the morning – both of them thought that earlier hours shouldn't exist.

"Continue . . ."

"So by the time I got *Kareem* to school and returned to the Wing-ess office it was already time for lunch. So *Adly* and I went to lunch in the *Ahlen* Restaurant in the Marriott a few blocks from the office, you know it, and by the time we got back to the office it was late."

The stage was set now for the 'mother of all excuses'. I was waiting with baited breath – maybe Nile Perch. It kept on getting better.

"So *Adly* dropped me off at home, where *Kareen* was waiting after school. We did homework together, then I made his favorite *couscous* and after an hour of video games he went to bed. I was tired so I did too. The next morning, I woke up and got *Kareem* off to school and walked out to my car. But there wasn't a car to walk out to. I panicked for a moment, and then remembered that the car battery had died."

I was rolling in the aisle now. The way that *Haythem* tells a story, well, as the Mastercard commercial goes, '. . . it's priceless!'

"I was all set to punch in '122', the police emergency number, when I realized that I didn't have my mobile. I had left it in my car, which was outside the Wing-ess office. So obviously I didn't call the police – they would have thought me an idiot."

Tears of laughter were now streaming down my cheeks. "It's a good thing that you didn't call with your non-existent phone!" I was merciless.

"So I caught a taxi to the office . . ."

"The Wing-ess office." I laid it on now with my thickest accent.

"Well, right. I found my car just where I left it. From the office phone I called the Middle East Egyptian Auto Club on *El Nozha* Street to bring me a new battery."

"For your phone." Fun, fun, fun – for me.

"*Cus emak enti,* no, you idiot, for my car!" He suddenly knew that he'd been 'had'. "When I met them down at the street, I found my mobile. It was in its holder, but by now its battery was dead as well."

It was an 'ah-ha' moment for me, and for *Haythem.* "So what happened then?"

"Well, I paid well over seven hundred Egyptian pounds to have it installed. So finally I got the battery repaired . . ."

"The mobile phone battery?" It was the time of my life.

"No, you idiot, the car battery. The car's running fine, the mobile is dead. I got home and plugged the phone into the charger and because the battery was entirely drained it took all night until the following morning. But then I had to go to *Sharm* in Sinai to meet a group returning from *Jebel Musa.* So I borrowed *Adly's* phone. Then when I returned from . . ."

"You just seem to take anything of *Adly's,* don't you?"

He glared at me, obviously uncomfortable because I had the upper hand.

"Then when I returned home I found that my mobile was fully charged."

"And this was?"

"Late last night, two days later. I looked on my email account and saw a message from Sobhy that you were here at the Sofitel, so here I am."

"Have you checked your phone yet?"

"No, but the way that you are looking and laughing right now, I assume that there is considerable evidence that you contacted me, right?" Now he was laughing as well. He does tell a good story, I'll admit.

* * *

We finished breakfast and walked up one flight to the exit by the reception and entered the car park. I was a bit nervous getting in the car with him. Who knew what else could fall apart at that moment. But he turned the key and the engine roared into life. I mean it, it really roared. Apparently the next thing to go would be the muffler.

Ten minutes later, after maneuvering around the traffic circle, we pulled into the small carpark to the rear of the museum. Sobhy had left word with the guard to allow us a space for the morning. However, he forgot to also tell the guard to let us in the service entrance adjacent. We walked the perimeter of the museum grounds and gave our names to the tourist policeman operating the turnstiles at the front entry. He radioed in and we were allowed to pass. Just as we reached the top step, Sobhy emerged from the shadows just inside the massive doors to usher us in. He escorted us back to the offices first; there was always the prerequisite coffee before business. I quickly excused myself for a moment and bounded halfway up the flight of stairs to the men's room. As I made room for more coffee, I was reminded that this very place was where the first adventure started for us in what seemed like a century ago. There was the statue fragment, the mysterious circumstances of its discovery in the middle of the 20th century, the bewildering inscription that would set Egyptology and the history of the Middle East on its ear if it ever came to light . . . and of course the mutual decision to let sleeping dogs lie for the time being.

I shook all that off and headed back down and to the rear offices. Soon enough we would try to decipher what the database had to offer.

"It's all *majnoon*, craziness." Sobhy muttered under his breath for the third or fourth time since we had entered the office. We were having a hell of a time finding out anything substantial in the archives that would shed further light on the historical nature of the Jewish community on the island. The actual files, not the computerized database, were sketchy due to the fire. We already knew that coming in – but the incomplete nature was appalling. I thought of something else. We fixed some tea and sat back.

"You know, many scores of papyri were shipped around the world for study in the late 1920s after Cowley's discovery. He wanted as many scholars as possible to work their way through the documents and give the world their individual 'takes' on the content."

Sobhy sipped thoughtfully. "*Habibi*, you may be on to something here. If I recall correctly, there should be both hardcopy files and computer entries that were designed to track that information. Let's see what we can come up with. You do the computer, you're much better at that. Anyway, the database is in English. I'll look through the folders in the file cabinets. Between us, there should be an answer. *Yallah*! Get to work you Upper Egyptian!"

I knew that he was happy and back on 'the trail' again. The tip-off was that he called me an 'Upper Egyptian'. It was an inside joke and term of endearment.

Cairenes have a certain disdain for anyone not from the city. It is an arrogant attitude that is certainly not deserved. In fact, as the cliché goes, "some of my best friends are Upper Egyptians". But there is truly a pattern of living 'up there' (okay, it's really 'down there' to the south, but remember how the Nile flows). It is a slower pace, a more laid-back approach to the world that is timeless, dating back thousands of years. After the 'nightmarish' city life of Cairo, the slow-down and relaxed 'fit' of the gentle people to the south is refreshing and invigorating.

The vast majority of people there, between Luxor and Aswan, are Nubian Egyptians. Their sense of hospitality and friendship endures through everything one can imagine. One of my dear friends in the south is the 'boatman-turned-High Dam employee' Mohamed Ibrihim Hassan. I met him well over 30 years ago as a *felucca* sailor, shepherding tourists from one bank to the other, in and around the islands and down to the First Cataract. We became close because of the groups that I brought from university every year, and sometimes twice.

Eventually, we would add to our sail a stop in his village on the western side of the river; meet his family and be offered the hospitality of sweet tea or *karkade*, an hibiscus tea drink that could be served either hot or cold. Female family members would offer to 'henna tattoo' women in the group (for a fee), and my unique journeys to Egypt became even more 'unique' as we would always include this as well. Over the years, I would see his family grow, his daughter get married, and grandchildren toddle around.

But city dwellers in Egypt seem to disdain this lifestyle, this human closeness. And here's the case in point via a really 'bad' story. An Upper Egyptian wanted to earn a better living and have his family enjoy a nicer lifestyle. So he went to Cairo to get better employment, because in the big city wages were more substantial. He arrived at a construction site and asked for a job as a carpenter. 'What kind of skills do you have?' asked the foreman. The man replied that he didn't need any tools to hammer things because his head was so hard. The foreman was dubious but asked him to demonstrate. He did, and 'tuk, tuk, tuk' – he drove a nail into a board with his head and didn't feel a thing. The foreman, impressed gave him a task – to build a fence along the perimeter. The Upper Egyptian went about his job happily. 'Tuk, tuk, tuk' went the nails into the boards. Until he got to one board and had a problem. He drove a nail part-way into the wood and it stopped, and bent over. 'Hmm,' he thought, 'must be a knot.' So he repositioned the nail and 'tuk, tuk, tuk' it went into the board halfway and stopped and bent over on itself. Now, the Upper Egyptian was getting upset. 'What gives?' he thought. Well, he decided to check things out and walked around to the other side of the fence. You'd never believe what he found there. *Another Upper Egyptian sitting along the fence with his head resting against the board that the man was trying to nail!*

This is the 'big city attitude' toward a wonderful part of their Egyptian society that's just different. It's an attitude that reflects a peasant-style 'hard-headed dullness' that the urban dwellers choose to mock.

But in Sobhy's case, it was a term of joking affection.

* * *

We were close to calling it a day. It had been a fruitless search until now. The paper files were in shambles, as we had already assumed. I had had some luck in reviewing the computerized files, but nothing that appeared promising. I told my friend that I would go through another couple of locations that had been put on a table of contents of sorts, and then we would need to re-assess. It was that frustrating.

My last stop was, in all places, Berlin. Apparently, between the wars, there was a solid conduit of scholarship between Egypt and Germany. This was due to the fact that so much of Egypt's glorious history had been purloined by German 'scholars'. I know, I shouldn't be so hard on them, or *any* international scholars of the day; simply because they 'stole' stuff. The regrettable truth is that it was a common, everyday, sanctioned process in the archaeological world at the time. For example, the British Museum has over 60,000 objects of Egyptian art in its collection, while the famed Cairo Museum has only 120,000. Europeans, in their ignorant arrogance, *actually* felt that it was their civilized duty to save art from the 'uncivilized' native population of the Middle East and North Africa. In fact, the Brits came up with an acronym for it so that it wouldn't sound quite so insulting. They would call all natives that they lorded over, *WOGs*. It stood for 'Wiley Oriental Gentlemen" – not quite a name that I would accept graciously either.

This horrendous practice came to an end following World War II, when so many of these 'provinces of the realm' gained their independence and the sun finally began to set on the British Empire; not to mention the defeated Axis powers of Germany and Italy. With this nationalist fervor sweeping the lands, the new governments began to request, no, *demand*, that their own ancient histories be returned to them. It was now a matter of pride and honesty.

But this certainly wouldn't sit well in France, or England, Italy or Germany. So now, for decades, artifacts have remained in the various venues scattered about the continent (the *wrong* continent) in spite of threatened legal action. Perhaps the most infamous case regarding Egypt and Germany began in 1913. At *Tel el Amarna*, Ludwig Borchardt would unearth the most photographed (outside Liz Taylor) bust ever discovered – the painted limestone image of Queen Nefertiti. In late 1913, it was smuggled out of Egypt – tightly wrapped up and placed deep in a box to fool the chief antiquities inspector. A photograph of the bust was deliberately unflattering. The specifications stated that the bust was made of gypsum, which is almost worthless, although the features were painted on limestone. Every year since 1952, the year of Egyptian independence, the Supreme Council of Antiquities has written an extraordinarily polite letter to the German government, requesting that the statue be repatriated to Egypt. Of course, we all know the answer . . . "*NEIN*". She still resides in the *Neues Museum*, the Egyptian Museum and Papyrus Collection in Berlin; in a room all to herself.

In a bizarre twist, I thanked God for a variety of German efficiency. The computer folders were well organized, precise, and clear. In fact, they even were with bi-lingual headings. This made finding avenues to explore painless and quick. But I would discover one fatal flaw – the Germans were loathe to give up any secrets. There would be detailed lists of items, subjects in the database that they supplied to the SCA, but there the detail ended. There were no digital images, there were no translations, there were no real descriptions. A 'tag line' made vague references to subject matter but that was it. I went to the section on Elephantine Papyri.

I sighed and got down to it; scrolling at a fairly good clip as I had learned to skim the material easily once I knew what was and what was not recorded. It was kind of like using *microfiche* spools back in the last millennium. But instead of cranking I was clicking.

The tea finally caught up with me. I took a break and hit the head as they say. I wondered if any answers would ever be discovered. But being the eternal optimist, I returned with a renewed enthusiasm, determined to learn something one way or another. As I settled back in front of the LCD monitor, I looked over at Sobhy and saw that he looked as dejected as I had felt a little earlier. Apparently there was nothing on his end – although he had been prepared for it all along. We both realized that the earthquake and subsequent fire and water damage in the offices turned the vast majority of material into so much soggy, charred pulp. But we needed to give it a shot. He felt my gaze and looked up. A rueful smile said it all, and at that point I was determined to find something, anything, to hearten my friend.

The Elephantine Section of the computer files had the subtopic of "Papyri" listed. There was a submenu that indicated that the scrolls and fragments were catalogued in thousand-number increments. But that didn't mean that there were 999 items per folder. As is the case in all archaeological research, it is always safer to have large blocks of stuff set aside rather than have to re-create files and add new categories because you didn't leave enough room. In the case of pottery baskets of material found in each area of excavation, it was simple to assign before the dig season starts something like this: Area A, baskets 1-999; Area B, 1000-1999. If you don't use all the numbers up, it's no problem. Dozens of scroll and scroll fragment catalog number flashed by on the screen.

I had reviewed a dozen such folders, and although I had slowed down to look at maybe thirteen or fourteen catalog numbers with interesting sounding reference lines, none seemed to really grab me. That is, until I hit the thirteenth folder: nos. 13,000-13,999.

In the midst of it all, a reference called 'P.Berlin 13737' caught my eye in a big way. Its reference information stated that it was the fragment of a letter written around 419 BCE. The language was Aramaic and it was preserved with six lines of text. However, what caught my eye was the fact that it was not a papyrus document, but rather it was parchment. Parchment is a specially treated form of leather that is soft and durable, making it an excellent writing material. But its use in Egypt at the time was limited. Compared to the cost of producing the more abundant papyrus, it was worth a small fortune.

I called Sobhy over, and he could hear the excitement in my voice. As I told him about this particular text, he interrupted me.

"I think that it is apparent, at least to me, that this document may have had origins in somewhere other than Elephantine. The value is not in the material itself, but instead the fact that it *is not* written on papyrus is its value."

Of course, he was 'spot-on' as the British would say. Parchment was not seen as more valuable in other parts of the world, if there was nothing cheaper to compare it to. Taken from that perspective, the import of this document for our needs became even clearer. As the description stated, it was written in Aramaic.

"No one used Aramaic in the 5th century BCE other than members of a Jewish community. It wouldn't become the *lingua franca* of the eastern Mediterranean until the 1st century BCE." I said. "So if this was written by a member of a Jewish community, where did it come from? How did it arrive in Egypt? Who was the recipient?" The questions kept piling up.

"Let's email them", Sobhy simply stated. I hoped that it would be that simple. He logged on to the terminal, and brought up IE 8, connecting online. He then opened his email account. "It will look much better this way if it came from the SCA domain. When the Germans see 'SCA-egypt.org' they'll be more likely to open it up and take it seriously." If course he was right. Remember what I said about *proteksia* before?

He finished composing the email, had me proof read it, and fired it off over cyberspace. Although Germany was an hour earlier than Egypt, it was still just past quitting time. Neither of us expected an answer until the next day at the earliest. Congratulating ourselves on a potential breakthrough, we packed up our things, left the museum, and went out to celebrate.

"You know, I know just how we should relax" I said. "Let's drop our things at the hotel, and get a taxi over to the west and take the *Nile Pharaoh.* The food is decent and plentiful, and it's a great night out – and cruising for a couple of hours on the river, going out on the upper deck and feeling the breeze – just what we need to unwind." He agreed, and off we went.

* * *

As usual, the day dawned misty but clear. The sun peeked over the *Mokattam* Hills and started it march to the Goodly West. I opened the drapery and stepped out onto the small balcony. The one stunning thing about the *Sofitel* Gezira was its shape. The hotel was circular, built around the central column of fire escape stairs and elevator banks. This meant that all the rooms faced outward, with absolutely breathtaking views. To the east and south was the river, north faced the rest of *Gezira* Island with the relatively new opera house, *Dār el-Opera el-Masreyya,* immediately below. It was inaugurated in 1988. The original, dating back to 1869 was built by *Khedive Ismail* to honor the opening of the Suez Canal. It suffered a tragedy in 1971, burning to the ground. To the west, the view faced *Giza*; and, if you were lucky, and higher than the fourteenth floor, you could faintly make out the Pyramids on the horizon. My room this time faced east, and being on high floor, could see above the rapidly clearing mist. The Citadel of Mohamed Ali Pasha dominated the horizon. I looked in vain for the great creator god *Khepher,* the dung beetle. After all, according to Egyptian myth, a great dung beetle pushed the sun across the sky til it was swallowed by the sky goddess, *Nut.* As the canopy of the earth, she faced west. She then passed it through her body, giving birth to the sun once again in the morning – the lower portion of her body to the east.

I called Sobhy on my mobile; he was still shaking the cobwebs out even though it was approaching eight-thirty. Apparently he had a somewhat restless night thinking about what the Berlin papyrus might hold in store. I told his that I had suffered the same fate, but that when sunrise approached couldn't fall back asleep. We agreed to meet in the museum garden because he had to take his son, Moustafa, to school – and really needed to rush out the door. He said that for sure he'd be there by museum opening at nine-thirty.

I went down to the buffet in the lower lobby restaurant, read the *Egyptian Gazette,* and strolled over the bridge to the museum. Since I still had a bit of time to kill, I walked over to the old museum shop, now just a tiny hole in the wall. A major remodeling of the entry/exit network of the museum had allowed for the creation of a 'mega mall' along the western side. Now, one exited the museum from a side door and was forced to 'walk a gauntlet' past over a dozen 'legitimately licensed vendors' as their permits clearly stated. In essence, any shopkeeper who paid enough *proteksia* to the proper authorities could gain a stall.

From there, you proceeded to the front garden and then out onto the parking plaza facing *Tahrir*.

The 'old shop', adjacent to the main front entry, but located to the east, was run by an ancient Armenian who must have been as old as many of the artifacts inside. He was 'old' when I first met him in the 1980s, and now was even 'older'. *Onig Alexanian* was a scholar of antiquity in his own right, and a shrewd, savvy businessman. His family had originally made a living off selling antiquities of dubious provenance in the midst of the 20th century. But as governments began to crack down on the illicit artifact trade, he turned to the selling of high-end replicas. Made of the finest gold, silver or precious stone in the image of the originals, wealthy tourists flocked to his small store. The location was ideal, and, although the *bakshish* price was high, was worth its weight in gold – literally. The new mall was a mixed blessing to him. On one hand, it culled the low-end, low budget tourists from blocking access to his shop; allowing those who would buy more space to view the luxurious items. Yet on the other, very few tour guides had the clientele these days who were potential customers, so they send their flocks to the western side.

However, by now, *Onig* had amassed enough funds for a well-deserved retirement should he ever wish it. The few sales that did occur were of such a level that they more than kept the shop afloat and the family in a well-to-do lifestyle.

"*Ahlen habib, kif halek*?" I walked in the door and greeted him. He looked up and his eyes widened with recognition.

"*Allah* be praised, the wandering *Amriki* has returned", and then there was the prerequisite kiss on each cheek. Although he was an Armenian Christian, he, as all others, would oftentimes evoke the name of the God of Moslems in everyday language. I laughed at this and returned the greeting.

"Blessings on your family, *Onig*, and all your friends". We passed a few moments' time catching up, over the ubiquitous demitasse of *ahwa masboot*, until I was forced to bid him goodbye. I had purposely omitted any reference to what the latest quest was all about, for *Onig* had been offended that I hadn't come to him for help, and perhaps offering a bit of a financial reward, for information about the New Kingdom statue fragment that had caused such an incredible stir the last time I was in Egypt. I knew that if a fairly well-healed wound were re-opened, there may have been consequences. He still was *very* connected in circles that were considered 'out-of-bounds' in some ways. I promised to try to stop back later, when things were considerably less hectic.

By this time, the Regional Director of Antiquities for Sinai had arrived at the museum grounds. Sobhy saw me leaving the shop, and playfully tapped his wrist.

"You call me in the middle of the night, order me to rush down here, and then keep me waiting?" he joked. First, he held wrist watches in disdain and never wore one; except for the 'permanent' watch-face scar on his forearm near the wrist – a souvenir of the 1973 war in Sinai. But second, he felt that he was a 21st century man on the cutting edge of technology, so his mobile smart phone told him what time it was anywhere in the world should he require that information. He knew I was within a minute of our scheduled meeting time.

We headed in and back to the office with the computer terminal. He logged on and waiting patiently for the system to boot up. Following that, he went to his email account and started searching through the new ones. There it was, what we had been waiting for since identifying a possible papyrus link. Apparently the staff all used the same email address, as no name was indicated. It read, 'aemp@smb.spk-berlin.de'. The news wasn't all that heartening. It read:

FROM: Volkmar@ aemp@smb.spk-berlin.de
TO: Sobhy@ SCA-egypt.org
SUBJECT: Papyrus P. Berlin 13737

Dear Sobhy,

Thank you for your kind email. We will do whatever we can to assist you in your search. However, due to the age and nature of the collection, no one has had the opportunity yet to digitize any images of the corpus of papyri. The one in particular that you wish has only the following information. Its language is Aramaic. Six lines are preserved that are parallel to the grain on parchment that seems to have come from Northwest Africa. It is measured 8 cm wide x 14 cm high. There is no record of translation here, perhaps due to the vast number that we have.

I wish that I could be of more assistance,
Best regards,
Conrad Volkmar
Curator, Neues Museum, Berlin

As Sobhy read it, I told him that I thought that it was a dead end in the least. "At least we know that the obscure papyrus still exists."

But he reminded me, "That's what the curator said, from his files. I wonder if anyone has seen it in the last forty years? I suppose that I could email and ask him to try to locate it. But again, even if he did, who would translate it, and who else would be involved, etc?"

"It seems as if there's only one answer. Go to Berlin to see it for ourselves." I certainly didn't want to do this on my own. Sobhy looked at me.

"You want to go to Germany, you want me to go with you. The last time we did something like this you dragged me to Israel. OK, so that was a bit closer and it really was the time of my life. It opened my eyes to 'the other side' as you put it. I appreciated it and grew from it. But I can't chase a windmill on a whim."

I understood his concern. But then an idea flashed through my brain. I did have them on occasion.

"Perhaps there is a way to link this to the Supreme Council of Antiquities and its quest to have Egyptian artifacts returned to their rightful place, in Egypt. If we could only get the new Secretary-General of the SCA to put in another request, in this instance, 'low-profile', minor antiquities like a couple of papyri, it could thaw the icy relations that had been ongoing; in part due to the grandstanding of the former 'TV star' secretary general."

Sobhy thought a moment, and liked the idea. He said that he would run it past his new boss, pushing it hard. And in that way, if all worked out, he could go to Germany on the Egyptian government's 'dime' to bring back the artifacts that were agreed upon, including P. Berlin 13737. He hurriedly made a couple of phone calls to get an audience with the secretary general's secretary. Meanwhile, I went online to check flight schedules.

XIII

Volubilis (Walili), 1348 CE (748 AH) . . .

AFTER A HANDFUL of years, the Berber explorer Ibn Battuta was returning home. Considered to be one of the great travelers of his age, he had just completed his second journey throughout the Islamic world. He was looking forward to resting for a while in Walili and completing his second volume of the 'Rihla', the 'Journey'.

The city had been prospering for centuries under Amazigh, or Berber, rule. For longer than anyone could remember, the dynastic leaders, who traced their obscure roots back to Egypt over a thousand years earlier had seen the Carthaginians and Romans come and go. And yet this family continued to work to benefit all in the revived Berber town. Peace, prosperity, and security were the motto of these leaders – and their people loved them for it. No matter that their origins were somewhat mysterious. However now their rulers, known as the 'Agella', the king, were referred to in the Arabic, called Caliph. It was seen as a continuation of the millennium-old leadership of the Islamic World initiated immediately after the death of the Prophet Mohamed. 'Calipha' in Arabic meant 'successor'. Abu Bakr, Mohamed's closest friend, confidant and ally, was the first caliph. The family leaders quickly adapted to the ways of the foreigners, and even adopted the title.

This was precisely the environment that Ibn Battuta needed to get his memoirs written. After the Moslem conquest by Oqba Ibn Nafi, the 'marriage' of Berber and Arab tribes allowed the city of Walili to thrive in a way that had not been seen since the days of Rome. Its wealth and prestige actually came about due to the rise of the dynasty of Ibn Yusuf.

No one knew for certain when the family first arrived in the region, or how exactly they came to power. No one cared for that matter. All that mattered was the success that the city now enjoyed. According to rumor, they had both Egyptian and Berber blood in their veins; and this served as the model of unity for all in the Maghreb, or North Africa.

Ibn Battuta had requested an audience with the caliph, and his request had been granted with such speed that he barely had time to rest from his travels. But he appreciated the fact that the caliph was open and welcoming to all. That was the trademark of this remarkable Ibn Yusuf family; respect for diversity which led to internal harmony and a camaraderie that was somewhat rare in a world of so many great cultural and spiritual differences. He wondered about this from time to time; and wondered about the background of this caliph that would give him such insight.

After a few days of rest, a messenger came to the Riad, or small courtyard palace, of Ibn Battuta. The Caliph of Walili would be honored to host the famous 'son' of the city with a small dinner party the next night. He should rest assured, though, that it would be a private, intimate affair with only a handful of guests. (He wondered what 'a handful' meant to the provincial leader, and certainly hoped that it could be taken literally). Should he wish to bring a guest, he was more than welcome. Since the explorer had been away for so many years, he really didn't know who to approach, so he decided to go alone.

The evening was not as expected. True to his word, the Caliph had indeed meant 'a handful' – even though it was just under 'two handfuls'. The Caliph, his wife and sons, his two principal advisors and their wives were all that awaited Ibn Battuta. It was clear to him that this was indeed a new age, with women being included in all matters, not just as ornamentation in public events. Was this a subtle clue into the background of the ruler's family – he hoped to find out?

The meal was sumptuous, the mulled wine just the right tartness for his taste, and the conversation was stimulating. Ibn Battuta hadn't enjoyed himself so much in a couple of years; at least not since his stay in Al Kuds, Jerusalem in Arabic – 'The Holy'. As the evening wore on, it seemed that everyone had a brief respite from conversation and entertainment – resting a bit before resuming the festive occasion. He reflected on his visit with certain warmth.

According to a Christian journal that he had read in Latin, the "Gesta Francorum', 'The Deeds of the Franks', purportedly written around 1101, the city had returned to a state of civility because of the Moslem conquest. In 637 the Caliph Omar successfully concluded what most scholars considered a true miracle – a bloodless conquest after only four months of siege. The Jewish residents enjoyed a renaissance of culture and respect, not to mention legal spirituality – something certainly not seen during the Byzantine Christian rule of the city.

For the first time in over five hundred years they were allowed to return and live within the city walls. As a major city of 'Palestina Prima', the province within the Byzantine Empire, Jerusalem had suffered only a generation earlier at the hands of the Persians. Sharhrbaraz, the leader of the Sassanian Army, captured and looted the city. According to the stories, over 90,000 Christians were massacred and the 'True Cross' captured and taken to the imperial city of Ctesiphon. It would only be returned after Heraclius re-captured Jerusalem and won a decisive battle against the Persians in

628. Within a half century of this victory, The Caliph Omar would begin to build the magnificent Haram esh Sherif, the 'Noble Sanctuary' – commemorating the triumphal nocturnal journey of the Prophet Mohamed to meet with Allah in Heaven. This would solidify Jerusalem's place as the third holiest shrine in Islam, behind Mecca and Medina.

However, the Holy City would once again suffer at the hands of religious fervor. Pope Urban II called on all Christians of good conscience to mount a 'crusade' to liberate the Holy Land from the Moslem infidels; all done in the name of Christ. He made it all too clear that anyone undertaking this quest would be absolved from sin. As they sharpened their blades on the mentally and physically deficient, Gypsies and Jews as the hoard marched south and east through Europe, it also became clear that the Papacy hoped to rid the continent of those considered to be 'outside the realm' of Catholic Europe as well.

The siege began June 7 and lasted until July 15, 1099. Fatimid Egyptian rule over Palestine and Jerusalem would end that day. Although Crusader numbers had been sorely depleted during their journey that so far had lasted nearly three years, they rallied around the claims of a vision by the Priest Peter Desiderius on July 5. He stated that if the Crusaders were to fast for three days, then to march barefoot around the fortified walls of Jerusalem, following the example of Joshua at Jericho, the city would fall to them in nine days.

On the night of July 14 the massive siege machines that had been constructed were guided up to the walls. The next day, following a very heavy battle when a number of attacks were repulsed by the defenders, Flemish knights first stormed into the city. They were quickly followed by those under command of Godfrey, Tancred and Raymond. Soon after, the city fell.

Many Muslims sought shelter in the Al-Aqsa Mosque and the Dome of the Rock, on the Temple Mount. The author of the Gesta Francorum, written in 1101, stated that a terrible massacre of Moslems occurred at the hands of these 'Crusaders of God'; ' . . . where the slaughter was so great that our men waded in blood up to their ankles . . ." Baldwin of Edessa would write, "In this temple 10,000 were killed. Indeed, if you had been there you would have seen our feet colored to our ankles with the blood of the slain. But what more shall I relate? None of them were left alive; neither women nor children were spared".

The Jewish community of the city wasn't spared either. According to the Moslem chronicle of Ibn al-Qalanisi, the Jewish defenders sought refuge in their synagogue, but the "Franks burned it over their heads", killing everyone inside; singing "Christ, We Adore Thee! Thee are our light, our direction, our love". But apparently there were survivors as well. Contemporary letters from the Cairo Geniza sought aid for Jews who escaped Jerusalem at the time of the Crusader siege.

The city would be restored to Islamic rule within a century. On September 17, 1187 the Muslim troops arrived at the walls of Jerusalem. By Oct 2, Balian of Ibelin surrendered Jerusalem to Saladin, who allowed citizens to leave if they wanted by paying a ransom. Those who could not pay their ransom could be sold into slavery. With the defeat of Jerusalem it signaled the end of the first Kingdom of Jerusalem. Many holy sites, including the Haram and the Al-Aqsa Mosque, were ritually purified with rose water. Religious freedom of worship was also re-instated at this time, and the Church of the Holy Sepulchre remained administered to by Christian clergy. The Jewish community also enjoyed limited freedoms as well.

And this was the city that Ibn Battuta remembered with fondness as he sat back on the luxurious silk pillows that rested along the walls of the central courtyard in his host's riad. But now, back to matters at hand. It seemed that his gracious host was now of a mind to talk. It was clear that the Caliph wished to know of events on the other side of the continent, especially in Misr and its capital city. One thing stuck in his mind, though. The Caliph kept referring to the city with its archaic name, Fustat – as if it was the city that he remembered. In fact, it was not only that city that he inquired about, but also the Island of Syene, near the First Cataract. What was it about these two places, and their own antiquity, that stirred the imagination of this great ruler in Walili?

'I suppose that I should begin by answering some of his questions,' thought the world traveler. 'Perhaps then I can get some insight as well in his response'. And so it began.

XIV

Cairo and beyond, the present . . .

"DO YOU HAVE any idea how frustrating it is to try to 'talk online' to an airlines website?" I was stressed to the max. I hadn't gotten very far in my quest to find a relatively inexpensive way to get to Berlin from Cairo. It seemed that Berlin, although the capital of the united Germany, was a 'backwater town' when it came to air travel. In spite of the fact that Lufthansa is considered *the* airline of Germany, it has hubs in Frankfurt, Dresden and Munich – not Berlin. As a result, I couldn't find a non-stop flight there from Cairo if my life depended on it. In fact, I couldn't even find a Lufthansa flight that could accommodate me in a timely fashion. I even considered flying somewhere like Frankfurt and then taking a Eurail journey on to Berlin. I told this to Sobhy.

"The options are so limited that you'd think that Germany was a third world country." My stress level was peaking. "So here's one option. Take an EgyptAir flight nonstop to Frankfurt. That's about 4.15 hours. Then, I can take the express train to Berlin, but that's still another 4 hour ride. The connection timing sucks as well."

Sobhy looked over at me and commiserated. "At least it's not the 13-hour overnight sleeper from Cairo to Aswan." He laughed as he remembered one such ride. Do you remember the time that we . . . ."

I cut him off. "Do we really have time for that?" I smiled as I too thought back. So now I was reminiscing as well. Although recently remodeled, the express sleeper was in many ways just an updated version of carriage 'cast-offs' from the Orient Express. I always welcomed the ride, for I found that I could easily sleep in the berths, lulled to bed by the monotonous clacking of the wheels on the rails. Others stayed up a lot of the night simply to share in the excitement of yet another mode of once-exotic travel. In the past, there had been a dining car attached to the train. It was an experience not to be missed. With the car swaying in time to the train's rhythm, it was tough to eat, let alone drink. But the waiters had it down pat. In fact, they could pour coffee from a carafe from a foot apart and not miss a drop; swaying in time with the lurching dining car. But today, it's more like an airline. Each car steward brought you airline-style meals on trays that you ate in your compartment. So, you may ask, is the camaraderie of a train ride gone? Not at all. There is a club car located somewhere in the train. Many of the younger people go there for the fun of it. However, you can't hear yourself think due to the loud volume of disco (yes, I did say disco) music being played. You can't see things higher than three feet off the ground due to the bluish smoke hanging in the air. (Don't forget, Egypt is not a non-smoking entity). And the drinks are so watered down that you couldn't get a buzz on if your life depended on it. But it still was a shock to the system to awaken ten hours later and find yourself in an entirely different world, nearly six hundred miles and a lifetime away from Cairo.

"I shouldn't have cut you off like that . . . ." And we reminisced a bit before I continued the travel exploration. On an adjacent terminal, Sobhy opened his email and was delightfully surprised. He was as bright as the Nile Valley sun as he told me the good news.

"The Secretary-General has decided to open a line of communication with a number of governments, their national museums, *and* many of the well-known private museums with Egyptian treasures in their collections. Because of the way that I worded my request to him, he is in the process of securing audiences with a number of his counterparts throughout Europe. And because of the interest in the papyri, he said that he would start with the *Neues* Museum! He is expecting confirmation from them to accept 'a visit', as he put it, at any moment. See, he can get things accomplished if it makes him look good. And how good does he look in Egyptians' eyes if he starts to have objects, no matter how insignificant, returned to the homeland! Now start looking for *two* tickets to Berlin . . . . *schnell*!

Thank God for Kayak! I was able to find decent transportation on Air Austria. Finally, I settled on that airline and two segments. #864 would get me, rather, *us*, to Vienna, and, with a nominal layover, #273 would get in to Berlin at a reasonable hour. The total travel time was six hours – much shorter than the plane/train combo. Now we only had to await confirmation from 'the head office' in order to book the flights and be off to Europe. I was excited, Sobhy was ecstatic. But he also was glad to get away from Cairo for a while for another reason.

The chaos that was Egyptian politics was coming to a head in a few days. Months of sparring with the Supreme Council of Armed Forces that currently was ruling the country, and months of civil unrest and, at times, great violence, was taking its toll on all Egyptians. For the first time in almost 60 years, the Egyptians would be going to the polls to vote for a president *NOT KNOWING* the outcome in advance. To all of us from the western world, we couldn't fathom that fact. But for Egypt, whether it was *Gamal Abdul Nasser, Anwar Sadat, or Hosni Mubarak,* every Egyptian citizen knew in advance who would win – the elections were that . . . orchestrated. In the last election that took place in 2005, it was announced that *Mubarak* had won the presidency for another six year term, with 88.6% of the vote.

With the increasingly violent demonstrations in the street, after the first open and public debates between candidates had taken place, my friend would rather vote with an absentee ballot and be away from it all when the actual polling was scheduled. He fervently hoped that the Secretary-General's overture was accepted as soon as possible.

It only took another 24 hours for German efficiency to kick in. An audience had been granted with the chief curator of the Egyptian Collection of the museum in 3 days time. It couldn't be more perfect.

* * *

We arrived early at *Heliopolis* Airport. Even though the new terminal was a grand, spacious, technological wonder, it was still an overcrowded nightmare. Why there weren't more airline employees remained a mystery that only the pharaohs could comprehend. Nearly a dozen ticket counter positions were empty of personnel. The Air Austria flight aisle had only four coach-cabin counter-spaces working a flight scheduled with a Boeing 777. That meant nearly 250 passengers had to pass through one of these four. Talk about delays, and insanity that could have been avoided – and Sobhy was ready to turn around and walk out to leave me to fend for myself.

Suddenly I heard someone shouting our names from across the spacious hall. We both turned in unison and saw our pal *Haythem* waving us over. I was more than reluctant to lose our place in the ever-growing line, and pantomimed this to him from afar. He shrugged his shoulders in the 'not to worry' way that he always did. Sobhy felt that we should take the gamble; after all, we'd simply get pushed back in line, oh, a half – hour!

So we wheeled the roller bags around and weaved our way past a number of grumbling fellow passengers-to-be and greeted him.

"How'd you know that we were here? What are you doing here? This better be good, *Haythem.* We've already waited a long time in line and . . ."

He cut Sobhy short. "I didn't know that you would be here *habibi.* I just brought a group of *Anglisi* to the airport to get rid of . . . er . . . escort them out of the country after their tour was over. Thanks God I don't have another group of them for two weeks. I just happened to see you two standing in line like Nile Valley sheep. Believe it or not, I saw you two there for 10 minutes. At first, I laughed to myself at your helplessness. Then, out of the enormous sympathy that I have for lost souls, well . . . I don't have *proteksia* in this place for nothing you know." Flashing his Ministry of Tourism ID card, he led the way around the far side of the lines and ushered us to the Business/First Counter that was vacant. He had a word with the agent. She had a smile that required sunglasses if you stared at her directly. Sobhy did, and I swear he was blinded for a moment or two. He stuttered and stumbled when asked for his ticket and passport. She took it and proceeded to tear it up, waiting for the machine to spit out a new boarding pass – 9G, up front. She then handed him an entry card to the EgyptAir Business/ First Lounge. Once done, she turned to me.

"Sorry, but you're still in coach" she said with all seriousness. Then she broke out laughing and winked at *Haythem.* Apparently he had put her up to this as well. Now he got the best of me. A 9H pass later and the 3 of us paused before passport control. The newest rules and regulations for air travel now forbade any agents or reps from escorting their clientele to the gate area as in the old days.

"Have a safe flight and productive search in Berlin", he said. How he knew was beyond me, but I didn't say anything. With warmth and hugs, Sobhy and I proceeded to the control booths as our friend waved goodbye and turned to head out of the terminal.

The next phase of our quest was just beginning.

XV

Berlin, the present . . .

THE FLIGHTS WERE uneventful, except for a brief moment of turbulence over the Alps that scared Sobhy witless. The 777 had hit an air pocket and then plummeted a couple of hundred feet before arriving at calmer air. The closest that he'd come to dropping precipitously in a matter of seconds had been on the *Ringespiel,* or merry-go-round kiddie ride at Cairo Land with his son *Moustafa.* He was thoroughly thrilled with the amusement park ride; his father not so much. Cairo Land is the Egyptian version of the Midway at any state or county fair, but permanent. It was located just southeast of the *Mokattam* Hills and the Citadel. Nearly every Cairene kid had been there at least once. To Sobhy, contrary to James Bond, once was enough.

As we taxied to the gate, I noticed how clean and precision-oriented *Flughafen Tegel-Berlin* was. It was a far cry from the controlled chaos that we had left in Egypt just a few short hours ago. However, the interior of the terminal had nothing over the new Terminal Five at *Heliopolis,* and I could see that Sobhy noted the fact with pride. Passport Control was equally efficient and, with only roller-bags, we were able exit quickly.

Rather than mess around with the bus and train system, although efficient and reasonably priced, we opted to take a public taxi from the airport, northwest of the city center, to the Rocco Forte Hotel de Rome, near to the museum. It would cost about twenty-five Euros. I had heard very good things about this hotel, and had gone online to book a junior suite. I was sorely tempted at booking one of the historic suites, created from the former offices of the bank directors.

But as it was being graciously paid for by the Supreme Council of Antiquities, I didn't push our luck.

At Behrenstraße 37 on *Museuminsel*, Museum Island, it was named after the British hotel magnate, Rocco Forte. The building originally was constructed in 1889 and housed the Dresdner Bank until the end of World War II. Renowned for its personal service, Anne Raber, the head of concierge services, had left a note of welcome for us. We both thought it unusual, until we learned that an email from the Secretary-General of the SCA arrived ahead of us. A box of chocolates in the room would greet every traveler who stayed there. I know, they're not rum balls, but they'll do in a pinch. I thought that Sobhy would be delighted. I was.

After settling in, we headed to the rooftop bar and had dinner, enjoying the glittering lights of Berlin from several stories up. We could almost see the complex of museums on the island in the midst of the *Spree* River. Our plan was formulated there, and we decided that a mid-morning start would be sufficient since it had been a long day of travel.

* * *

The next morning still dawned early for me. My body clock just wouldn't let things slide into a mid-morning mode. Sobhy, on the other hand, slept like the pharaohs. I had filled out the continental breakfast card and hung it on the door before turning in. Along with a copy of the *International Herald*, I sat there, munching and enjoying the solitude until around 8:45. The door to the other bedroom opened and Sobhy staggered into the central sitting room. Rubbing his eyes, he wondered at the time.

"It's already late afternoon," I teased. He had no idea which way the room faced, and judging from the angle of the sun it easily could have been the opposite of morning.

"*Ya Allah*! Why did you let me sleep so long? We're not here on holiday you know!" He began to quickly pour a cup of coffee and turned to run toward his shower. I grabbed his arm, laughing.

"Relax" I said, laughing all the while. "The room's facing east, not west. It's only around nine or so. We're in plenty of time for the midday meeting at the museum."

He spun back to me, pantomimed the back-handed cheek slaps to my face, and plopped down on the chair, one leg sprawled over the arm. He plucked a few pieces of fresh fruit from the plate, grabbed a napkin, and let the tension ease from his body. I had no idea how wound up and frantic he got over the 'misunderstanding' of time.

As he sipped the coffee, he explained. "This is the first real test of the Secretary-General, and the first overture under his tenure to make inroads with the international antiquities community. It is tremendously important for the new

Egyptian government to be taken seriously. And for a matter of importance like the return of our antiquities, it would be an incredible coup. In addition, my new boss can really 'stick it' to our past 'pharaoh', Zahi Hawass, if he can secure even a couple of insignificant papyri and get them back to the Cairo Museum. After all, even with all the grandstanding, blustering, and TV appearances internationally, Hawass was viewed as Egypt's 'class clown' and was never taken seriously. His pompous arrogance couldn't hide all his flaws, and museum directors around the world knew this."

"Wow, I had no idea it was that heavy of an issue. We always saw 'King Zahi' in that light – but never thought that behind his back the other professionals in Europe really laughed at him. I remember the German robot that was specially designed to enter the air shafts in the Great Pyramid of Cheops. That was, when . . . . mid 1990s or so. Hawass timed it in such a way that the long, slow crawl would take place around five in the morning. That made it Prime Time back in the States and on live TV – it was all set to blow the socks off the viewing public."

"*Na'am*, what do you mean by 'blow the socks off'?" He was confused; my use of English idioms sometimes really put his off his game.

"Never mind," I replied. "Suffice it to say he planned to secure his place of greatness in live, reality TV all over the world by making an incredible discovery. I simply remember his hectic pacing while trying to take control of every aspect of the robotic action. Even though he was inside the Great Pyramid, he had his signature cowboy hat firmly placed on his head. His blue denim workshirt, another Hawass trademark, was stained with deep blue rings of sweat around his neck and under his arms. He was *schvitzing* like a stuck pig!"

"On no, here we go again. What is this '*schvitzing*' you're talking about? Another Hebrew expression?"

"No, this time it's Yiddish. 'Sweating'." I could see the confusion and the resignation that sometimes I don't speak coherently. He may have been right.

* * *

A clear day, and we decided to 'stroll' to Museum Island to meet with the curator that Sobhy had been in touch with, Volkmar Conrad. We walked down *John Foster Dulles Allee*, across the *Platz der Republik* in order to cross the *Unter den Linden* Bridge. We estimated that it would take about half an hour. As we approached the *Spree* River, the lushness and greenery was really nothing like the banks of the Nile. Here, deciduous trees vied for places of honor along the cornice. Their leafy canopies gave a great deal of shade, unlike the more scraggily-fronded palms of Egypt – even if they were called 'Royal'. The added shade then afforded a greater trapping of moisture in the air, so the level of humidity, although not oppressive, was still noticeable to an Egyptian.

As we crossed the channel of the river to the island, I noted that the avenue changed names as well. Now it was *Schlossplatz.* Arriving at the grounds of the museum complex, we still had ample time before the meeting, so we opted to visit the Café Allegretto located within the ground floor of the museum itself. The coffee was rich, thick and aromatic. Sobhy noted that it rivaled even the finest that Cairo coffee houses had to offer. But he missed the noise and hectic atmosphere found there. In Cairo, as in all Mideast cities, the coffee house was *the* center of activity. Here was the location of 'male' gossip, discussion of politics and economics, viewing of eastern hemisphere 'football' on the TV, and people-watching. Although the volume of conversation in general was somewhat high, the thing that Sobhy missed most was the clacking of either domino-tiles or *shesh-besh,* backgammon, pieces following rolls of the dice.

"Do you remember that one night outside of Giza, while your group was watching the *Son et Lumiere*?" he asked, with a gleam in his eye. *('Oh no', I thought, 'here we go again.')*

"Ah, no, why don't *you* remind me!" I took a sip and waited for the inevitable.

"Your group of students had just entered the show, and we had about an hour fifteen until it was over. Since you had seen the show, oh, a million times before, we crossed the street to wait at *Coffee Shop el Sokarya.*" He was starting to warm up. "You had your usual *ahwa masboot,* with plenty of sugar. I opted for *Nescafe."* There's no one who can draw out a story and inflict pain better than my friend.

"Okay, okay-I get it." I wanted the agony to go away fast.

"*Tayib,* fine, as I was saying, the boy brought over the drinks, I got a 'hubbly-bubbly', and then he brought the *shesh-besh* board."

I interrupted, trying at least to get one shot in. "I know what's coming, and I think that it was only a matter of fact that the molasses and tobacco went to your head and you had no idea of how you were playing . . ." The 'hubbly-bubbly' that he was referring to was a water-pipe. Contrary to the popular perception, or misperception, that people all over the west have, the water-pipes seen in coffee houses all over the Mideast and North Africa are not paraphernalia for rampant narcotic abuse by locals. Rather, they are simply a smoking venue of choice for millions in that part of the world. Not all could afford to purchase a pipe, because many are really works of art, but instead see it as a social, public interaction. These locales are not dens of iniquity, but simple gathering spots. The pipes are filled with tobacco and spices, like molasses, to temper the harshness of the smoke. Sitting in a shop you are surrounded by an exotic mix of aromas that creates a very pleasant olfactory sensation – to a degree. I went on.

"So now that we know that you knew that you were playing out of your league . . ." Now I was cut off.

"As I remember it, I took every single game from you, doubling down at least twice . . . for a total of, hmm, let's see, seven games was it?" He was grinning like the *Sphinx.*

"Actually, it was eight". At least I could take comfort in my honesty.
Fortunately, it was time to head up to the offices, my nightmare was over.

* * *

It's a good thing that we arrived at the secretary's station exactly on time. Even though the Swiss are the ones who are noted at being punctual, it actually seems to be a Nordic thing in general. We presented ourselves at the precise moment when the large clock on the wall saw the minute hand give a slight clunk at it rolled over the '12' spot. The woman at the desk noted us, and the clock, and smiled a smile that only could signify the 'you passed the test' smile that must be a genetic thing with secretaries who are of a higher breed. Nevertheless, it was *de rigueur* to have us wait just the briefest of moments as protocol insisted. Sobhy gazed around at the deep, rich wood paneling and a couple of lesser-known 'masters' hanging on the walls. To him, the opulence was on the verge of being offensive. Actually, to me as well. But we both bit our tongues.

At exactly one minute past the scheduled meeting time, a middle-aged, 'middle-management' gentleman exited an inner office and strode towards us with a keen sense of purpose, and a quiet, but not overly arrogant, attitude of competence. I immediately liked what I saw, and felt that Conrad Volkmar would do anything in his power to help us. We were off to a good start right at the get-go.

We made our introductions, and Sobhy pulled a small cardboard 'barrel' about twenty cm. long from his small satchel. As is the custom in the Mideast, one always brings a small gift to a host, a sign of friendship, trust, and respect. In this case, Sobhy brought with him a small papyrus piece with a cartouche and the initials 'V.C' painted within. One of the most enjoyable gifts that anyone can get is an art item of this nature. It is uniquely Egyptian and personalized so that the recipient knows that it was created just for him or her.

There is a corner of the souvenir industry in Egypt that is a thriving business – the art of papyrus painting. It also helps the arts, and art students. There are scores of papyrus 'institutes' located up and down the Nile Valley. Tourists can purchase exquisitely created works of art for upwards to a thousand dollars or as inexpensively as just a few. They can stunningly beautiful replicas of tomb paintings, or *kitschy* scenes that remind one of Velvet Elvises draping a rusty mini-van outside the entrance to a county fair. But by far, the most personal is the *cartouche*. Seen as the royal thread of eternity, the *cartouche* would surround the royal name of a pharaoh. As a matter of fact, it would be this style of name identification that would allow Jean Francois Champollion to break the hieroglyphic code found on the Rosetta Stone, discovered back in 1798.

Today, art students from Egyptian universities are able to intern or get paying part-time jobs creating these modern masterpieces. When tour groups come to these locations, like my personal favorite, *Mondy*, locating on Pyramids Road in Giza, they simply wait a few minutes while the hieroglyphic letters are painted onto pre-painted gilded *cartouche* ovals already on small sheets of papyrus. The reason that I mention this one shop is due to fraud that is rampant in the tourist industry in Egypt. Okay, it's rampant throughout the world. However, with regard to the papyrus industry, there are street vendors out there who sell incredibly cheap 'papyrus' scrolls to the unwitting public. But in these cases, the material is actually dried banana leaves, which break down and disintegrate within a couple of years. The real deal, as evidence in museums around the world, lasts for thousands.

"*Ach*, this is a most incredible and gracious gift that you have brought me!" Volkmar was delighted beyond words. "I will have it framed and placed in my office as soon as possible. So now, would you care for a cup of coffee and a *strudel*, and fill me in on how I can help?"

More rich, unhealthy stuff – just what the doc didn't order. But I saw Sobhy watering at the mouth . . . that man can eat, and eat, and . . .

"I'll just have the coffee, but I'm sure that my friend will share your pastry!" We continued with a bit of small talk for the few moments that it took for the refreshments to arrive. I decided to let Sobhy take the lead, since he was the governmental representative here. We had to continue the pretense if we had any hope in getting a look at the Elephantine document and just maybe getting it back to Egypt.

"As you know, Mr. Director . . ." Sobhy began, but was immediately cut short.

"My dear Sobhy, you flatter me." Volkmar broke in. "But I am merely a curator here in the museum. Perhaps someday . . . ." His voice trailed off, as if recalling a dream.

"My apologies, but I'm sure that one day this will 'all be yours' as they say." The Egyptian continued. "In this new age for Egypt, an age of democracy and a re-assertion of Egypt's role in the world as a cultural leader of both the past and present, *(I thought that he was really laying it on thick but kept quiet)* we would quietly like to renew our requests for a return of some of the objects that Germany had assisted in 'discovering' in the early twentieth century" *(Now, in spite of myself, I was impressed with his diplomatic tact!)*

"I personally couldn't agree with you more, *mein herr*, but as you are all too aware, protocol and channels need be followed. However, there has been a subtle mood shift in the *Bundestag* in terms of international relations. What better way to start mending fences as it were than to begin on a small, yet significant scale." The German intellectual had actually hinted at even greater things to come regarding the possession of antiquities and their repatriation. He went on, "Perhaps this Aramaic papyrus is just the place to begin. Now, which one exactly are you referring to?"

Sobhy pulled out the stat sheet on the target of our quest. He also submitted the official letters from the Secretary-General of the Supreme Council of Antiquities that outlined both the legitimacy and *bona fides* of the archaeologist and my role as advisor. Volkmar perused them ever so briefly, for to do so with great detail would be an affront to us, a questioning of our validity. But we also knew that he had had us thoroughly 'vetted' before ever agreeing to see us anyway.

"Here's what our antiquities division would like to start with in terms of artifact return. As a sign of good faith, I have been authorized to extend the offer of identifying a handful of items in your museums that could be re-classified as part of a permanent 'teaching and display collection', those are the precise words from my boss, to remain in Germany in perpetuity as long as they are on public display. If all proceeds as planned, you and I can work together on a list that can be submitted to both our governmental reps and then approved. Here is all that I could glean from our files." Sobhy showed him the scant catalog information:

Elephantine Papyrus P. Berlin 12737
Language: Aramaic
Date: approx 419 BCE
Material: parchment
Size" 8 x 14 cm
Provenance: Egyptian Museum, Berlin
Acquisition Date: unknown, approx 1920s

"That's all that we have I'm afraid."

Conrad Volkmar was smiling the entire time that he read the entry. "I have no doubt that we will be able to accommodate you and even come up with an equitable letter of intent for the future. That will take passage by a subcommittee of the government once the museum director has approved. Between you and me, he has already indicated his pleasure of cooperation based on the intent of the emails. *(Sobhy thought, 'Of course, it gets them off the hook for thievery', but he smiled that infectious grin of his and said nothing).*

"As you no doubt are aware, A.E.Cowley, the epigrapher, first 'brought together' all the documents in England, Egypt, Germany and the United States to publish them in one document. Of course, I don't mean literally. They are still physically scattered among the nations. But his comprehensive work allowed all of them to be seen side by side in photographic plates, and written analysis. Of course, to many of us, the finest examples reside right here in the *Neues* Museum. Built between 1843 and 1855, it was designed by the architectural giant Friedrich August Stuler." He smiled at us in a somewhat condescending manner. I looked at my Egyptian friend. He caught it too, and was none too pleased to say the least.

"Allow me a few moments to see if this papyrus fragment is sufficiently documented in the database to come up with it quickly." He went to the outer office and left the two of us sitting there, wondering.

* * *

Within a few moments, my stereotypical imagery of German efficiency walked through the door to the inner office we were in – but in the guise of the prim, almost prissy secretary for Herr Volkmar. She bore a silver tray with a complete coffee service. To my untrained 'modern art' eye, it looked to be every bit an early 19th century. Sobhy and I glanced at each other again, and he rolled his eyes.

"*Fraulein . . .*" (her name escaped Sobhy) "this is an extraordinary reproduction of 19th century silverworking. Is the original available to see in one of the galleries?" Sobhy innocently asked.

She huffed and puffed, a strange blend of indignation, arrogance, and pride. I couldn't help but stereotype again. Just the impression of Teutonic culture that had plagued Germany for centuries in the world's eyes.

"*Mein Herren*!" Her eyes blazed with anger. "This set was created by the great silversmith David Peter Hermann Baumann for the municipality of Hamburg somewhere between 1825 and 1830! It *is* the original!" She practically spat the words at us as she banged down the platter on the table, turned and stomped from the office, head held high with jutting chin. Once more, the opulent arrogance of the German mindset came to mind. Where else in the world would museum pieces be used on a day-to-day basis, I wondered.

As her footsteps were drowned out by the not-so-subtle slamming of the heavy oaken door, my Egyptian friend poured the coffee and then grinned and remarked, "At least the coffee's 21st century vintage". We both savored the rich brew and resumed our wait for the associate director.

A 'few moments' turned out to be nearly half an hour, and when Conrad Volkmar returned he was wearing a perplexed look on his face. Yet underneath it, I sensed a growing rage that was barely in check.

"Gentlemen, my apologies. I'm afraid I have terrible, and confusing, news." It seemed that when *Herr* Volkmar became upset his accent thickened measurably. 'Have' had come out as '*haf*'. We sat back and listened.

"I began to search the database, as I indicated, *und* I *vas* (there it went again) able to download and print out the information about the papyrus that you are inquiring about. Here's *vat* I found. The esteemed German archaeologist Otto Rubensohn, *af der* Berlin Museum excavated under a license granted by the Egyptians between 1906 and 1908. His daily journals were meticulously written, but his scientific data entry was haphazard and spotty at best. The journals described the discovery of several papyri, including your 13737. However, when it came to the recording and documenting the loci, depth measurements, even the properly identified trench, the information is severely lacking. All of this came to light when Eduard Sachau eventually published the material in 1911."

Volkmar went on, now clearly agitated and building an intense head of 'angry steam' that threatened to blow his lid. He consulted his notes. "According to Sachau, and I quote, '*Die Schriftrollen wurden entführt weg* . . . the scrolls were whisked away', with great alacrity before Egyptian officials caught wind of it".

Sobhy jumped up and jabbed his finger into Volkmar's chest. I too rose from my chair, preparing to separate the two archaeological gladiators should it become a necessity.

"There you guys go again. You Allemani, you Germans, have been all alike for over a hundred years! Just like Borchardt in 1913!"

He was spluttering and waving his arms and pacing back and forth like a man obsessed – which he clearly was. Egypt had been suffering from art and archaeological thievery ever since Napoleon deemed it necessary to 'save ancient antiquities' from potential destruction at the hands of the native population. The result would be an ongoing European attitude that it was their God-given duty to rescue antiquities from whatever country they occupied; transporting them back to their respective national and private museums for local consumption.

Whatever wasn't 'bolted down' was carted away with impunity until the post-World War II era, when emerging nation-states took matters into their own hands with the aid of the fledgling United Nations. The particular episode that Sobhy was refering to had to do with the world famous bust of the most beautiful woman in the world (before Elizabeth Taylor of course), the exquisite Nefertiti, wife of Akhnaton. At Amarna in 1913, Ludwig Borchardt would unearth the most photographed bust ever discovered – the painted limestone image of Queen Nefertiti. In late 1913, it was smuggled out of Egypt – tightly wrapped up and placed deep in a box to fool the chief antiquities inspector. A photograph of the bust was deliberately unflattering. The specifications state that the bust was made of gypsum, which is almost worthless, although the features were painted on limestone. For years, Zahi Hawass had been trying to recover this priceless artifact – always to get the same answer, 'nein!' (they didn't rate a 'ten')

I tried in vain to placate my friend, but he would have none of it.

"If the Anglisi can see fit to return the Elgin Marbles to Greece, what's holding back you Germans?" He was seething. I was afraid that either he would so insult the German director that everything would be called off, or he would blow a blood vessel and stroke out. Neither were events that I wanted to witness.

Conrad was contrite almost to the point of groveling. I was confused. I thought that he had the upper hand here. He commiserated with Sobhy and me, wholeheartedly agreeing all the while that his governmental policies were flawed; but what could he do as a mere associate director/curator in the convoluted museum bureaucratic system, etc, etc, etc. It sounded sincere, but I was still leery of his stance.

He further attempted to forge a truce, linking us as comrades in arms against a common enemy, by reaching into an ornate Empire Period sideboard (no doubt real as well) and withdrew a bottle of schnapps and three crystal glasses.

"If we can call a truce for a moment, the news that I was trying to get at may alter things considerably. But first, I think that we need this to fortify ourselves for the shock to come."

I eyed him questioning his choice of words. Sobhy landed heavily in his chair and sighed resignedly. The amber liquid poured, we all raised our glasses and downed the shots in one gulp. Volkmar then proceeded and what we heard had both of us reaching quickly for the decanter simultaneously.

XVI

Berlin, September 1932
The handwriting on the wall

IT WAS JUST after the close of the *Maariv* service, the evening prayers. Several of the old men hurriedly left the *Rykestrasse* Synagogue in the borough of *Pankow* to get home to the meal that their wives were preparing for them. The darkened streets afforded a sense of security in spite of all the talk coming out of the Germans who were so enthusiastically embracing the doctrine of the National Socialist Party.

Yet a handful of young men, student-scholars, remained in the pews of the small side chapel that was used for daily prayer. As opposed to their older counterparts, these young men didn't dismiss the statements made by the Nazis pertaining to Jewish involvement in the economic, social and political demise of the German Republic. The old men clung to their memories of the glory of Germany in the days of World War I, and serving the Fatherland. In fact, one of them insisted on wearing the Iron Cross that he received for gallantry in action in the Ardennes Forest. Little did he know that it wasn't the magic bullet-proofed talisman that he envisioned it to be.

As street thugs became bolder and bolder with every new law and edict passed by the rising government, the situation became more and more tenuous for the Jewish community. Generations of mistrust fueled the growing anti-semitism that now was officially sanctioned. The young men, modern Germans in every sense of the word, were still on the outside because of their faith. They had already discussed a broad range of things that they felt they must do to preserve Judaism. One of them was a photographer in the *Neues* Museum. He was going to be assigned the task of photographing the papyrus collection of the museum, material from Egypt. As he made early preparations for the shooting to be scheduled soon, his eyes fell on the scripts found on these ancient scrolls, and he did a double-take. Some were written in Aramaic, the ancient language of the Jews during the reign of Herod the Great.

As he mentioned these documents to his friends, the general consensus was that they needed to be protected for future generations – who knew exactly what the Nazis were planning. The only thing that these young men were certain of was that their Jewish world was in dire jeopardy. Little did they realize how close to extinction it really was.

One of them remarked that the *Haftorah* portion of the coming Shabbat's readings involved the Book of Daniel. What an omen! Chapter five discussed the story of Belshazzar, the ancient king who had profaned the sacred ritual vessels that had been pillaged from Solomon's Temple in Jerusalem. During a banquet that ended as an intoxicated, rabble-rousing affair in his palace, a disembodied hand appeared, floating in the air. It traced mysterious words onto the palace wall – **מנא מנא תקל ופרסין** Mene, Mene, Tekel, Parsin.

As the story went, the Babylonian king summoned Daniel the Prophet to interpret the message because the words themselves, dealing with numbers and counting, were meaningless in translation. Daniel interpreted the words to mean that the days of the Babylonian king and kingdom were numbered. That same night, Belshazzar was killed and the Persians sacked the capital city.

Although they were singularly secular German Jews, these fellows were stunned at this coincidence and vowed to take some action immediately. As one put it, "*HaShem* has seen fit to inspire us and use us as vessels to preserve and protect German Jewry in the dark hours ahead". With a collective 'Amen to that', they began to formulate a plan to steal away the papyrus scrolls and hide them for however long it took to restore the former Germany that they all knew and accepted.

The photographer, a young man named Kurt Loewe, who was assigned to do the documentation at the museum, would find a way to secrete the papyri in his camera equipment box and bring them back to the synagogue during the night. The group would then formulate a plan to hide them 'in plain sight'.

* * *

A couple of weeks passed, and the audacity of the common Berliners who had already harbored a dislike for their Jewish neighbors grew by leaps and bounds. Emboldened by the Nazi regime's edicts that were aimed at limiting the rights of her Jewish citizens, vandals and thugs harassed residents and randomly destroyed property; even if there was the only the merest hint at Jewish ownership. The synagogue leaders hired additional guards and the time of Shabbat services would be modified slightly from week to week in an attempt to throw off potential stone throwers who would gather just before services would begin. The rabbi told the congregants that God would not upset if Shabbat prayers began well after sundown, as long as the prayers would eventually be said. Other precautions were taken as well. Valuable ritual objects were removed from the building and taken to various members' homes, to be hidden far from the temple.

Meanwhile, the Nazi regime began to take on a heightened interest in the art objects that were part of the national museum network. It was becoming a well-known fact that *Der Fuhrer* had a fascination with art, and considered himself to be an artist of considerable talent. (this in spite of the fact that he was expelled from art school in Vienna). To promote "proper" art Hitler had the *Haus der Deutschen Kunst* (House of German Art) built in Munich, to be the scene of special yearly exhibits. In addition, he ordered all the collections in Germany be photographed and accurately cataloged for future reference. Many took this to mean that whatever Hitler and his cohorts deemed to be improper would be removed from exhibitions, thrown in store-rooms or, even worse, destroyed.

Finally the opportunity that the young Jew was looking for had been scheduled and he prepared his equipment. At that time, there were no work restrictions yet placed on Jews and other 'undesirables' in Nazi Germany, so the man easily went in and out of the museum at will. Also, because of his work photographing the various collections at the behest of the government, his museum identification badge gave his access to all areas of the building and at all times. Often it was inconvenient to photograph during the open hours of the galleries with all the people milling around; so he could come and go at all hours in order to work unimpeded.

With his pass in hand, Loewe made it a point to come into the building many evenings to shoot innocuous pieces of the collection. The guards became accustomed to his presence, his comings and goings. After several days of this, and with the bringing of cardboard boxes of strudel that he shared with the security men over coffee, they began to consider him to be 'one of the gang', trustworthy. Eventually, when the photographer would leave, the guards stopped asking him to open his camera cases for inspection.

As his preparations advanced, the status of the *Rykestrasse* Synagogue became clearer. After the new Nazi government had widely banned Jewish performers, artists and scientists from public stages and lecterns, the synagogue became designated as a forum for their concerts and lectures organised by *Kulturbund Deutscher Juden.* Because of this, the building was exempt from traditional heavy taxation, and would ultimately be spared from destruction in November, 1938 during the infamous *Kristallnact,* the Night of the Broken Glass. The Nazis ordered a 'mere vandalization' of the synagogue, since its location was in the heart of a block of residential buildings housing Jew and non-Jew alike. Instead it was reported that furnitures were stored in the prayer hall. The furnishings (chandeliers, *lustres, menorot, ner tamid,* and copper coverings of doors) of the synagogue made from non-ferrous metal, which was scarce and much needed for war production, were not dismantled. This categorization would allow the men's plan the possibility of success.

His best opportunity would come in a few nights. An art opening was scheduled take place in the museum on September 11. The small reception that would follow was scheduled to end around ten in the evening. This opened the door for Loewe to come into the museum after the doors were closed to the public to 'shoot in peace' as he hinted to the guards time and time again.

Like Teutonic clockwork, the art opening reception ended on the stroke of ten. There was something to be said about German efficiency. At precisely 10:15, Kurt Loewe waved his credentials at the two overweight security guards flanking the loading dock entry to the museum building. He turned on a two hundred-watt smile as he flashed his ID and set the box of strudel on the table. The most senior of the two muttered his thanks, the air redolent with the smell of garlic, braunschwiger and kraut. Apparently the sugary desert was just in time for these two defenders of public art. He barely broke his stride as he headed off to the photography lab. Receding in the distance, he heard what could be mistaken for the sound of a wild animal tearing its prey into small pieces with a tremendous ferocity.

In spite of his mission on behalf of the Jewish community, Loewe still felt obliged to carry out his duty to the museum as well. After all, in spite of the Nazis, art was art – and needed to be carefully recorded and documented for posterity. What if his mission failed, then some sort of record needed to be maintained, if only in the form of photos and documentation. The post Nazi world would return to appreciating art regardless of its origin.

It would take a few hours to adequately bracket and shoot the several papyrus scrolls in Aramaic that he had identified. In order not to draw undue attention to himself, he would return for a number of nights to finish the work on the other documents, return them to their storage areas, and develop the pictures. Then his work would involve the various forms and paperwork that would be filed away in the office of records and documentation.

Loewe spread out the black faux-velvet drapery on the table, and draped it over the easel just behind it. This gave a seamless black background and tabletop upon which to lay out the beige/tan scrolls. As he peered through his lens, he saw that it made a very good contrast. Carefully, he unrolled document after document; photographing each with bracketed F-Stop settings so that he would have three different exposures to choose from. With each, he meticulously wrote down the information that was appended to each scroll in its hard case.

When he finished photographing the Aramaic scrolls, he set them aside. After a few hours of work, well into early morning, he began to pack up. He carefully laid out the black background cloth. Gently, he placed the scrolls side by side on the material. Once he did that, he cautiously rolled it up and inserted it in the tube that it had been packed in. He popped the cap into place, slung it over his shoulder with the carrying strap, picked up his camera bag and headed to the rear door. On his way out, he placed the registration cards of the objects into the 'in' basket of the recording secretary. By late morning the next day, he hoped, the files would be in their proper place, once again gathering dust. He muttered a silent prayer that no one would come looking for the files, or the papyri, in the near future. They would be in for a shock.

He quietly, nonchalantly, came down the stairs in full view of the guards – full view, that is, if they had been awake! As had been the case more often than not, the dullness of routine, the intense quiet, and full stomachs of the part-time guards ensured that they would be sound asleep. As they say, 'the darkest hour is just before the dawn', but the gendarmes would never know it.

Loewe walked past the gently snoring duo and silently exited the museum with ancient documents of a Jewish past from centuries ago and a continent apart.

* * *

Kurt made it to the *Rykestrasse* Synagogue just a little after dawn, in time for the *Shaharit* morning prayers. His colleagues had agreed to meet him that morning before they all headed to work. It was not unusual for the young men to be seen alongside their elders, because they had often come to the relatively short service – in part due to the bialys, lox, cream cheese and herring that was served afterward as an incentive to get younger members of the temple to attend daily prayer. For them, a few moments of prayer were worth the price in order to get a free breakfast. Inflation was eating away at their salaries at an alarming rate.

Over coffee and platefuls of food, his friends whispered excitedly among themselves. Loewe was afraid that they'd blab their secret all over the social hall, and he constantly had to tell them to keep their voices down when discussing the acquisition, yet speak normally about mundane things.

One of his more cynical companions quipped that they could speak as loud as they wished, for the *altekockers*, the 'oldsters', couldn't hear the roar of a cannon from the Krupp Foundry if it went off right next to them. Loewe shot him a look that was withering in its intensity. After all, no matter their age, they were the Jewish community that these men were trying to preserve for the future.

Now the only question was where to hide the scrolls.

The men silently pondered their predicament for a while. A couple of Loewe's companions wanted to remove the scrolls from the building and hide them in private homes. Others felt that the risk was too great because of the growing danger to the Jewish community in general. They were at an impasse.

The photographer sat apart, sipping his coffee, thoughtfully watching and listening. After a short while, he got up to relieve himself of what seemed like litres of coffee that he had drunk overnight while in the museum and then at the synagogue. He walked down a short hall to the w.c. that he knew was adjacent to the social hall. However, when he got there, two banners were taped across the door with a sign that said, *Eintritt verboten. Arbeiten im gange.* 'Entry forbidden. Work in progress'.

He was irritated at first; now he'd need to either go around and through the sanctuary to the restrooms at the main entry, or go upstairs into the school and library. He opted for the front of the building. As he began to walk back to the reception hall, he once again passed the closed lavatory. He decided to see where his Deutschmarks were going with regard to the renovation. He gently pulled one banner down and entered the facility. The entire restroom was torn apart. The plumbing was in the process of being replaced. Apparently, one of the vent stacks was entirely perforated. It had been cut and capped off. A new one rose through the ceiling to the roof immediately adjacent to the old one – so the plumbers would not have to cut another hole through ceiling joists, floorboards and roof. It was a smart move, thought Loewe.

Curiosity satisfied, he turned to leave and put the tape up when it hit him – the perfect spot to hide the documents until all was safe once again. He hurried back to his friends, told them, and they all returned to the construction area. Their excitement grew, until one of them remarked about the possibility of discovery. Loewe assuaged their fears. He noticed the building inspector's tag stuck on the wall – signifying a passing mark for the roughed in plumbing work. To his knowledge, this meant that the replacement tiling could go up immediately and cover the hole. Finish work and installation of the floor and fixtures was imminent. He assured his friends that within a day or so no one would have a clue. Plus, as an added bonus, the plumbing would work splendidly since the old stack was rendered obsolete.

They all breathed a sigh of relief as the photographer uncapped the cast iron stack, gently inserted the tube with the black cloth and the Aramaic scrolls, and replaced the cap. He then smeared a bit of plumber's putty around the base of the cap, imbued with a bit of dust and construction debris to make it look untouched, and stood back. No one, including the plumbers and wall board installers, would know that anything was amiss.

The men then left the remodeling project, Kurt Loewe replaced the tape, and they all headed off to work – knowing that they had done their part in trying to save a portion of their Jewish heritage from the Nazi world.

XVII

Berlin, the present

WE SAT IN stunned silence as Conrad Volkmar told us his unbelievable news – not only was the Aramaic document P. Berlin 13737 missing, but so were all of the Aramaic Elephantine Papyri! The only thing left were the intact file folders with the information that had been recorded decades ago. Much more than alcohol was needed to ease the shock and pain that all three of us felt.

"I have no idea as to how, or for that matter, when, this breach of security occurred. In fact, I have to say, we don't even know if it is a breakdown in security – the scrolls may in fact simply be misplaced somewhere in the museum." Volkmar went on to explain in depth this possible assumption of what might have happened.

The *Neues* Museum suffered severe damage during World War II in a series of massive aerial bomb blasts. However, the collection was for the most part saved because museum officials were able to store the priceless collection in underground vaults when the museum was closed in 1939 due to the coming war. In an allied aerial bombardment in November 1943, the central stairway and its frescos were burned, along with other great pieces of architectural sculpture. In February 1945, another Allied bombing destroyed the northwest wing as well as the connection to the *Altes* Museum and damaged the southwest wing as well as the south-east facade However, the ruins of the building were left exposed to the elements, and the weather wreaked havoc on the structure for decades. It would only be in the 1986 that emergency measures would be taken by the then East German government to begin the arduous task of reconstruction and restoration.

Following the fall of the Berlin Wall and the reunification of Germany in the early 1990s, work on many projects, including the museum, was halted.

It wouldn't be until 1997 that the English architect, David Chipperfield, would drag out the old reconstruction plans and begin anew to finish the *Neues* Museum project. He would discover that many of the architectural elements of the original building, such as the spectacular Egyptian Courtyard, had been either lost or destroyed over the decades. As a result, many of those elements simply were not included in the new master plan.

Finally, by 2003, the government would announce that nearly all the pieces had finally fallen into place in order to complete work on a cultural icon. The icon referred to was the entire *Museuminsel,* or Museum Island, with all of its buildings. This grand undertaking was priced out at 1.5 billion Euros. The Neues Museum itself would cost a whopping 295 million Euros. On October 16, 2009, the museum officially reopened. At the reopening ceremony, the Chancellor of Germany Angela Merkel described Chipperfield's work as "impressive and extraordinary" and the museum as "one of the most important museum buildings in European cultural history".

"The sad part of the entire affair was that, because of timing insisted upon by the government, the re-installation of the stored art was hurried, haphazard and horrific in its oversight. Museum curators were not the primary personnel involved; but rather mid-range government officials who didn't have a clue as to what they were doing or what they were installing. I must say, at least Nazi efficiency brought in art historians, curators and the like when they pillaged the great museums of Europe so they knew precisely what to take and how to store it. I'm very sorry, but I do have to give them credit for that. Even the incredible blimp, Heinrich Goering, took extreme care for the artwork that he privately plundered for his collection." The German sighed heavily and scrubbed his face with his hands, wiping away the tears that were freely flowing.

He excused himself to go to the w.c. to splash some cold water on his face and compose himself. As he left, he slid a single piece of paper across his desk for us to peruse.

The Table of Contents page for the folder of 'our' particular scroll read as follows:

Registration Card
Black and White Photographs
Translation Card
Miscellaneous notes

Conrad looked 100% better now, refreshed and recomposed. If I didn't know better, I'd say that he was obsessive compulsive – having even put on a new shirt with freshly knotted tie.

"So what are our options now gentlemen?" he asked of us, this time pouring us coffee from an urn on the sideboard. The initial shock had worn off, as had the need for the shot of whiskey that had momentarily calmed our nerves. We began to reconstruct the sketchy past.

"Do you really think that these documents disappeared during the war, still waiting to see daylight again once found in some long lost bunker?" I was skeptical at best. Sobhy came up with perhaps the best idea yet.

"We should try to trace the very last moment that the scrolls were seen, studied, or in some what handled. Then maybe we can re-imagine where they might have gone from that point." It was solid thinking, and we both congratulated him on the notion. The question then was exactly when the scrolls were seen.

By now it was early evening, and we all realized that we were famished. The stress of the afternoon had taken a toll on all of us, so we decided to find a place for dinner, then call it a day. Conrad suggested the Corroboree Restaurant. It was located on George St. under the S-Bahn arches, quite convenient to us. The food was ample and very good. Although the service was a bit slow, we certainly were in no hurry after today. The three of us deliberately steered away from any conversation that was related to the scrolls, and simply sat back and listened to the live music. We adjourned with the prospect of making headway the next morning – giving us all a glimmer of hope.

* * *

The following morning, over croissants and coffee, Sobhy and I laid out our plan of attack. It was apparent that we needed to research all documents in the archives that might remotely shed some light on the disposition of the collection of the *Neues* Museum in the few years before the outbreak of war. From there, we could ostensibly trace the movement of some of the pieces that had gone missing. By mid-morning we were on our way back to the museum. Conrad had a full day of meetings already scheduled, but as promised there were two visitor ID passes waiting for us in the lobby. These would give us access to the archives on our own so we didn't need to be delayed by waiting until his meetings were finished.

As we entered the archive storage area in the southern wing of the museum, I was immediately struck with a sense of déjà vu. We approached a glass wall a couple of meters past the reception desk. I stared into the dim room beyond, lit by faint bluish neon lights that gave the area an 'other-worldliness' appearance. I noticed one thing immediately – tables were strewn with materials somewhat haphazardly. It looked as if a few archivists had been hard at work and then simply picked up and went out to lunch; leaving everything in a state of limbo, out in the open. (They even left their sweaters draped over their chairs, I thought).

"What does all this remind you of?" I asked my Egyptian friend. He looked around, shrugged his shoulders, and scratched his head.

"An archive room in a museum?" he smiled innocently.

"EXACTLY!" I proclaimed. "It's in as bad a shape for an archive room as the archives in the Cairo Museum! Perhaps even worse!" I shook my head in disbelief. Whatever happened to that renowned German efficiency that was always being lauded by the press. "I think that we'll really have a tough time of it here – like . . ." I was cut off.

"*Ya Allah!* I know! A nail in a hay bin!" Sobhy grinned at me triumphantly.

"Do you mean a 'needle in a haystack'?"

"*Min fadluk*, please, that's exactly what I said." He looked crossly at me. I was too frustrated at the situation to even bother correcting his idiom. (Or did I mean 'idiot')

"Anyway, yes, we're in dire need of some assistance." I returned to the archive desk and asked the intern stationed there to give a hand.

He was able to maneuver the German language mine-field of colloquialisms and actually find the online page that referred to the individual folders that were designated for each artifact. He quickly brought up the folder for P. Berlin 13737. He then scrolled the table of contents and asked us exactly what we'd like to see. I told him that we'd like to scan through all the pertinent material for that particular scroll, and he readily obliged us.

Sadly enough, the digital age had not yet caught up with this portion of the archive. Yes, the online page listed the items in the original folder; but no, the separate materials within the various folders had not yet been digitized. As a result, I asked if we could see the actual folder and its contents. Although the intern said that protocol in essence forbade the handling of the real files due to their fragility, the fact that Conrad Volkmar had vouched for us spoke volumes. He acquiesced, as long as we told no one other than Herr Volkmar.

He then proceeded to lead us to the door, the likes of which I had never seen before. Maybe there was truth to the notion of German ingenuity and efficiency after all. It looked faintly like an air-lock on a modern U-Boat, or the International Space Station. In actuality there were two sets of doors with heavy gaskets that made them airtight. Before entering, he pulled on a heavy cardigan sweater, looked at us in our short sleeves, and simply shrugged. Keying in a passcode, he then pulled open the heavy door. A whoosh of slightly chilled air greeted us as a preparation for things to come. Sobhy and I glanced at each other more nervous than curious. Volkmar handed us UV goggles.

As we stood inside the airlock, the massive door hissed shut behind us. As we somewhat impatiently waited for the computer to assess the seal, and thus feel free to eventually open the inner door that led directly into the archive vault, I felt for my Egyptian friend. Although a superb archaeologist, Sobhy had an inordinate fear of enclosed places. He could never be a tomb robber! I smiled at that thought. But, in addition, he could never bring himself to voluntarily enter a small space on any excavation, without a number of people around him 'just in case' as he would put it. 'Just in case' his claustrophobia would kick in and he would have a mild panic attack. I whispered for him to close his eyes, count to ten, and by then (I hoped) the inner airlock door would unseal and we could proceed. During the count, we were bathed by UV light, designed to kill any airborne pathogens floating around or clinging to our clothing.

I silently counted as well, and I hadn't reached nine yet when the green light above the second door came on and another whoosh gave us access. The German curatorial intern handed us paper masks and booties as an added precaution. As we stepped in, the first things that I noted had to do with the climate. The air was noticeably cooler . . . did I say 'cooler'? I meant colder! The ambient temperature must have been at least fifteen degrees Fahrenheit lower than the reception area. (Hence, the German's cardigan sweater) In addition, I noticed a distinctively higher air pressure. This would further ensure that all air flowed out into the airlock and exterior space, rather than into the chambers within. I also recognized a humidistat on the side wall. The humidity was strictly regulated as well. The stored documents were in as climatically-controlled an environment as could possibly be created.

The young man headed over to an IPad mounted to the wall. He 'touched in" a series of commands, and a floor plan of the archive popped up onscreen. He consulted another menu, and then touched a room on the map. This expanded into a catalog, and, voila, he was able to unerringly lead us directly to the shelf that contained the acid-free cardboard box that held the folders for the Elephantine scrolls in possession (supposedly) of the Neues Museum. He then handed us latex gloves. There's nothing like the oil on skin when it comes to degrading ancient paper.

As he had mentioned, the folder indeed was thin – a few sheets of rather basic information, including registration card. However, an added sheet contained a translation in English of the fragment, carried out by Cowley in the 1920s. It said:

> *". . . . thus if it is pleasing to the priesthood, we currently*
> *. . . [re]quest that Yohanon ben Yaakob of the priestly family*
> *. . . [of] Yusuf be allowed to return to us to serve-from the*
> *. . . [tri]bal home of many generations, in the venerated land*
> *. . . [of T]ingis on the far side of the western desert, beyond Libue.*
> *Written in the year 17 . . . .*

We read it and were taken aback. We had known that it most likely had come from a land other than Egypt, due to the material being parchment – a material that was used rarely if at all along the banks of the Nile. But now, we had the name *Tingis* as an added measure. We were surprisingly delighted at this turn. Now we knew for certain the provenance of the document; the Roman city that was the foundation of modern Tangier today. I was giddy.

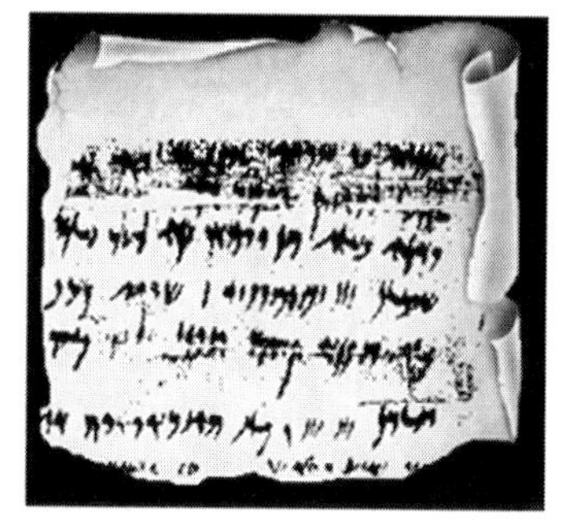

As we smiled at each other, Sobhy turned the page to see the next document. It was a grainy black and white photo of the piece, P.Berlin 13737. We knew for certain that the link with Morocco and its Jewish community at least extended into the 5th Century BCE and not just the Roman Era.

I held the 70+ year old photo in my hands, trembling ever so slightly.

We both looked at it in awe, at the same time with an incredible sense of loss. Perhaps this was the only remaining evidence of this scroll fragment; the original lost during the war. But in the greater scope of things, if all of the other scrolls were lost as well, and only their documentation still existed, then the tragedy of war would be greatly compounded.

Too stunned to speak, we simply gazed at the picture for a few more moments.

After a couple of deep breaths, I put the photo aside and sorted through the other bits of paper. One thing immediately struck me. The basic registration card was there. But something that we didn't know gave me a glimmer of hope. On the registration card was a box that was entitled 'photographic record', or some similar translation. Typed into the space was the name of the photographer, someone named Kurt Loewe, and the date of photo session, September 12, 1932. We now had a thread to follow.

* * *

We were able to obtain copies of all the pages in the P. Berlin 13737 folder, and returned to Volkmar's office. By now, both of us had warmed up to the ambient room temperature, accelerated by the steaming cups of coffee in the curator's office. He was still at a loss for words. The missing scrolls were clearly an embarrassment to the museum and a direct affront to the curator. He vowed to do everything in his power to begin to trace when and where the scrolls seemed to vanish into thin air.

When we mentioned the provenance registration card and the information about the photographic record, he brightened perceptibly. In fact, he was downright excited that we actually had some sort of lead to follow in this mystery.

Perhaps, just perhaps, employment records might still be available somewhere in the dusty confines of the museum sub-basement. After all, the museum was shuttered well before the war began, and the lowest levels had been safe and secure throughout the war years, in spite of what transpired above ground.

He dispatched one of his aides to see what could be gleaned from a search of the administrative archives. This task was not looked upon with relish by the young fellow, he had been dispatched down 'to the dungeon' once before, several months back. The thought of the cobwebs hanging low off bare, low-wattage light bulbs, the musty, moldy air, and the pitter-patter of little feet (certainly not of a children's tour group) still sent shivers up his spine. However, it was his job. Any hope of moving up in the museum hierarchy meant following orders. He also hated that notion in light of his heritage. He took one of the air-filtering masks from the archive reception area and headed to the basement.

Once there, the intern headed directly for the file room that housed the administrative documents of the museum. A beaten up, olive drab file cabinet tinged with rust and mildew bore the faint label, *Personalakten,* 'Personnel Files'. Each drawer contained a decade's worth of information, so it was very easy to find the 1930s. Based on the information that the curator and his curious foreign friends had uncovered, he sought out the folder for 1932. As he pulled it out, he started to cough uncontrollably. The file itself was covered in brownish mold spots – and given the young man's allergies, the spores that now filled the air caused a reaction in spite of the mask that he wore. He grabbed his inhaler and took a shot. Immediately, relief flooded his lungs and the coughing spell cease. But he knew that he needed to take down the information and get out as quickly as possible.

The first thing that he did was look at the employment roster for the year. He scanned it quickly and noted that there was no Kurt Loewe on the list. He huffed irritably. All the way down here, with the health threats it presented, all for nothing, he thought. He then noticed another sheet that was labeled *Aushilfen,* 'temporary personnel'. Suddenly his luck changed. There, as clear as the faded type could indicate, was the name that he was looking for. Apparently Loewe was one of a couple of freelance photographers added to the roster as the museum pushed for documentation in preparation for the closure of the facility and the subsequent storage of its collection. He pulled out his mobile phone and quickly snapped a couple of photos, re-inserted the page, snapped the folder shut in a cloud of dust and mold spores, and slammed the file drawer closed. The intern practically sprinted back down the corridor to the stairwell and the promise of clean air.

As Volkmar, Sobhy and I wrapped up our divided duties as the next phase, the intern wrapped sharply on the door and threw it open even before the curator could get out 'come in'. It was as if a small dust devil flew into the room; motes reflected off the sunbeams that filtered into the room from the tall windows. However, this particular whirlwind was smiling behind the air mask.

"I be god did!", is what the statement sounded like.

"Pull of the damn mask, calm down and speak to us!" Conrad said.

"I've got it", came the clearer, mask-less reply. "I found the files but had a hard time due to the air and mold, you know about my allergies . . . ."

"Yes, yes go on . . ." was the impatient retort.

"Well, at first I saw nothing regarding this Loewe person. But then there was a sheet of temporary hires and he was named there. Here, look at this." The intern took out his phone and scrolled through the pictures in the memory. "Oops, sorry, no clearly not that one!" His girlfriend in a fetching bathing suit on the deck of a Rhine River barge caught all of our eyes. "Here it is." And we saw the names of three photographers listed as adjunct technicians – with the second one being Kurt Loewe.

I was delighted. "Now, we need to trace this man, find out if he survived the war, might still be alive today, and ask if he knew what might have happened to the scrolls that he photographed." Seven decades later it seemed a gargantuan task. But our leads were few and far between.

Because of the sensitivity of the matter, the intern hadn't been apprised of the exact situation. As a result, Curator Volkmar decided that he himself would continue to trace the photographer Loewe and his status in the 21st century. His obvious first step was the Greater Berlin Area phone book. We all would be surprised at the usefulness of this basic tool in spite of the digital age of this century. But nothing would come of it. Neither did a Google search. I suggested that he return to the immediate post-war era, see if any documentation existed on this man just after the war.

The Allied Command in Europe, before re-inventing itself in the post war era, enabled the Germans to conduct a haphazard census in October of 1946. It attempted to identify and record civilians and their movement in the first year following the cessation of hostilities. One of the more spotty groups of records came in Berlin, as it was divided into military zones by the western Allied forces and the Soviet Union. This is where the bulk of the search was conducted.

Fortunately, academic interest in this material was so high that the university system in Germany allocated many of its resources to having the old documents scanned and entered into a database that was part of the public record. So whatever information that could be gleaned was immediately accessible from his museum office computer terminal. Conrad breathed a sigh of relief. No traipsing about in various administrative buildings in order to track down the photographer. He could simply sit back, sip coffee, and browse the websites as indicated. It could boil down to only a few moments online if he was lucky.

Luck is in the eyes of the beholder, and some luck fell his way in this instance. On a hunch, he had keyed in 'photographers/photographers' guilds/museum employees' as part of his Google search. The first search came up empty-handed, the database was scant. However, the second two subjects cranked out fairly long lists within a few moments.

"Now we're getting somewhere!" Volkmar thought. But he was disappointed with the first list. Nowhere was the name 'Loewe' to be seen. He hoped that the museum employee list would have better results. As he glanced over the list, at first he couldn't believe his eyes. He rubbed them, allowed them to re-focus; yet there it still was. The name 'Loewe, Kurt.' Volkmar pumped his fist in the air triumphantly. But, once again, the joy was short-lived. The entry that was handwritten so many decades ago identified a wraith, a wisp of smoke that seemed to vanish into the netherworld, with very little substance to it.

Loewe, Kurt, contract photographer, address unknown – contact 'Emigdirect'.

Now he was really confused. Emigdirect? What the hell was that? After bookmarking the previous search so that he could easily return to it, he 'Googled' the word and several hits appeared. He surfed through several of them, but they all yielded the same stock information. "We've got some of the information, and it's a start. But I'll tell you, it's tenuous at best." The look on his face was a mixed review. The entry shed a bit of light on the generalities of what the word meant. We were out to sea. Then a key passage gave me an idea. I felt certain that I had a clue.

"You just mentioned that *Emigdirect* was part of a greater agency. Could it have been *HICEM*?" Sobhy looked at me as if I'd lost my mind. "Why are you talking about *Haythem* at a time like this?" He was really confused now. We had an Egyptian colleague in the tourism industry name '*Haythem*', but it was pronounced as '*Hysem*". I saw the bewildered look on his face and laughed. "No, no," I was laughing hard now. It got contagious and we all started. Boy did we need this comic relief break. I took a deep breath. "The acronym of HICEM was a combination of the names of three major Jewish relief agencies that operated in Europe immediately following the war – designed to aid the surviving remnant of Europe's devastated Jewish community. They were the New York based Hebrew Immigrant Aid Society (HIAS), the Paris located Jewish Colonization Association (ICA) and Emigdirect, a migration organization that had its headquarters right here in Berlin. So the combination of the three with their initials would eventually yield HI-C-EM; the agency, not the Egyptian". I smiled. Sobhy smiled. Volkmar just looked confused. "Where do we find any records, data, that might get us further down the road here." He warmed up to the idea that all was not at a dead end. "I think that the combined agencies helped well over 300,000 displaced Jews, and over 15% ended up in Israel by the early 1950s. Yad Vashem, Israel's national memorial and research facility dedicated to the Holocaust contained all the records.

XVIII

Egypt, Israel . . . the present

WE NOW KNEW that a division of labor was essential. Volkmar would continue to try to track down the missing scrolls. Sobhy needed to return to Egypt for a few reasons. I, on the other hand, needed to get back to Morocco, but via Israel. The HICEM connection for the photographer Loewe was the potential breakthrough that could lead to the rediscovery of the missing museum collection. Good-byes, handshakes, promises to rendezvous as soon as possible when answers were found, were short but heartfelt.

The following morning, Sobhy and I headed to Berlin-Tegel. He had worked out a deal with the curator to take back three other Elephantine Papyri and have them installed in the Cairo Museum. Fawzi Abu Hassan, the new director for the Supreme Council of Antiquities, would be thrilled. The new Egyptian government badly needed some sort of exciting *coup* to instill faith in the electorate. For weeks, the people had grown restless after the presidential elections. The initial euphoria, which was similar to that of over a year and a half earlier, when Hosni Mubarak had stepped down peacefully, was waning. The outpouring of support for Mohamed Morsi was starting to turn sour.

Abu Hassan, via the persistence of his director for Sinai excavations, Sobhy, would achieve something that the extremely visible face of Egyptian antiquities for the world, Zahi Hawass, had *never* been able to do. He actually got items of Egypt's glorious past returned to the homeland from foreign governments. To many educated Egyptians, this was a real slap in the face to Zahi Hawass, and in extension, the old regime. It marked a turning part for the world as well – indicating a sense of legitimacy in the eyes of other governments. This, more than anything else, buoyed the flagging heart of the revolution.

Sobhy, for his part, would not mention the missing Elephantine documents for the time being. He knew as much of the story as we all did. He also understood that the missing collection had nothing to do with the current German government or its national museum system; but rather it dated back to a seven decade old time of Nazi domination and its greedy obsessions. Abu Hassan would be delighted in whatever Sobhy returned for the time being. He then could return to Sinai to conclude a couple of seasons of work at the site of *Serabit el Khadem*; which had been briefly put on hold due to this new adventure. As soon as he wrapped things up there, and had given me and Volkmar some breathing room to continue our inquiries, he could return to the matter of the missing scrolls.

We each made our way to the proper ticket counters – both at the Lufthansa desk. Even though Berlin is the most vibrant capital in Europe today, it still plays a secondary role in international air travel. Frankfurt maintains its position as the hub for Lufthansa. After completing our booking and checking in, we met up and went through Passport Control together. However, I needed to wait for my Egyptian friend on the other side, since he had considerably more to sort out. Remember, he had with him Kevlar-lined tubes that held the precious Elephantine papyri being returned home after nearly a century. After several 'dog-sniffs', re-run x-rays, and eventually the opening of the tubes to inspect the contents and correlate them with the documentation, he finally joined me in the 'international' zone.

Although the thoroughness was impressive and essential, the Egyptologist was exhausted from the ordeal. He looked forward to trying to get four hours of sleep on his second flight to Cairo. I, on the other hand, was amped up for the task that I was given – to try to locate the missing photographer in Israel, *if* he was in Israel; or still alive at this point. Since all indications pointed to him being the last to see the scrolls, the pieces might now fall into place and all questions could be resolved. 'If' was the operative word.

Our flight was the same to Frankfurt, so we headed to our gate. Once in Frankfurt, after only an hour and fifteen minutes, we found that we needed to run to our other gates for our connections. As usual, connecting times look wonderful and minimally efficient on paper; but not everyone can 'pull an OJ' and fly through a terminal at groundspeeds approaching Olympian times. Virtual reality from a computer-booked connection and 'real' reality are as far apart as one can possibly imagine. We promised to be in touch the following day, after settling in at our respective destinations, and then both turned and dashed in opposite directions.

* * *

The Cairo flight for the Egyptian seemed as if it didn't exist. As soon as he buckled in, he was asleep. He needed the rest. The first thing that he remembered was the command in English and Arabic to 'return seats and tray tables to their upright and locked positions'; and the admonishment by the lead flight attendant to turn off all computers. As soon as the wheels hit the tarmac, the pinging of powered up mobile phones filled the cabin. Dozens of languages and dialects started yammering about baggage claim carousels and car-park locations. The serenity was gone. In addition, as the Airbus 320 approached the jetway, dozens of passengers got up and began opening overhead bins. (*Remember – take caution as bags may have shifted in-flight!*) All the while, the flight attendants tried in vain to get passengers to remain firmly buckled in their seats until the plane would come to a complete stop and the seat belt signs were no longer illuminated. *Good luck with that one,* Sobhy thought. *Welcome at Egypt!* Although tired, he simply didn't want to fight the crowd. He stayed in his seat, and as people filed past they looked at him as if he was crazy, or at the very least someone mentally impaired who needed a flight attendant to escort him off the plane.

Once out of the new, air-conditioned, clean terminal, Heliopolis was as dusty, polluted, noisy, hectic and crowded as always. Gone was the relative serenity of German order. But Sobhy drew it all in as a breath of fresh air. In spite of its flaws, he missed the Egyptian way of doing things. A slower, gentler, more laid back attitude was a part of his nature as well.

In the hazy air, Sobhy made out the dun-colored Land Rover vehicle emblazoned with the Supreme Council of Antiquities logo on the doors, waved to one of his colleagues in the driver's seat, and threw his roller-bag in the boot area. However, he cradled the tubes with his precious cargo in his arms like he had done with his infant son, *Kareem,* many years earlier. They wouldn't leave his sight until they were safely ensconced in the museum labs for inspecting and cataloging. He sighed happily. All was right along the Nile . . . .

As the driver paid the airport exit fee, Sobhy asked that they swing by his flat in Heliopolis to drop his bag and check the mail. It was only a few minutes out of the way, but allowed him time to go over the events of the past few days, and decide what and how he should tell his boss, Abu Hassan. He concluded that there was nothing earth shattering to tell – as yet. Yes, the Aramaic Elephantine documents were 'misplaced', for lack of a better word. But until, and yes, if, his American colleague and the Israelis were able to sort out things, the 'need to know' by the Director of the SCA was not necessary. He had faith that some resolution could be in the offing. He also had learned from his past encounter with the granite statue, referred to as 'Israel's Pharaoh', that his friend and the Israelis were very innovative and would doggedly pursue evidence until answers came to light.

He grabbed the *Baraka* bottle of water offered by the driver and drank deeply. He then sat back and thoroughly enjoyed the ride toward *Tahrir* Square. As usual, in order to bypass a considerable portion of the city's vehicular traffic, they took the flyover, the 6 October Bridge, that soared fifteen m. or so above the older roadways. This limited express gave Sobhy a wonderful overview of the city that he so dearly loved. From there, as they passed the famous *Khan el-Kalili* Bazaar, and just before the bridge proper that spanned the Nile, they exited at *Meret Pasha* Street and approached the museum from the north. This then allowed them to put the museum between them and *Tahrir.*

Even though the elections were over (for the time), thousands of Cairenes still inevitably made their way to the 'square seen around the world' as the focus of the Egyptian Spring of 2011. In spite of everyone's best efforts, it was still laden with the detritus of a revolution; torn and crumpled banners and pennants, improvised make-shift shelters, and garbage – lots of garbage. City municipal services tried to keep up in vain, and the noble attempts by the local population to keep the area clean fell far short of success. In addition, nightly rallies still persisted – although no one was quite sure from time to time what the rallies were aimed at. The sharply focused crowds of 2011 lost their edge except on rare occasions. Now, it seemed that pickpockets outnumbered protesters during daylight hours.

The newly installed security system protecting the service area by the north gate was also manned by members of the Tourist Police. Their image had taken a beating in the early days of the revolution, and now this division of the Supreme Council of Armed Forces was looking to redeem itself. Even though it was an SCA vehicle, the passengers' IDs were scrutinized, a bomb-sniffing dog walked around a couple of times, and one of the officers waved a mirrored scope beneath the undercarriage of the SUV. All in all, Sobhy was impressed and profusely thanked the officers for their diligence. The driver rolled his eyes a bit as he headed through the gate to the loading dock. Sobhy saw this and reprimanded him.

"*Yom asal, yom basal*" he said. "'One day its honey, the next day onions!' You get much more out of people and situations with honey. Remember that the next time that you deal with people and perhaps need a favor down the road." His glare burned a hole in his museum colleague. Chagrined, he parked and deferentially opened Sobhy's door as a chauffeur would. (*Maybe the young man learned a lesson here,* he thought). They then walked into the museum with the priceless papyrus scrolls.

Museum Director Abu Hassan was waiting patiently for them in his inner office. He ushered Sobhy in and perfunctorily dismissed the other man. Some things bureaucratically never changed – a pecking order was still a pecking order, whether under Zahi Hawass or Fawzi Abu Hassan. The new director walked over to the sideboard and poured demitasses of thick, sweet Turkish coffee and brought them over to a small table flanked by armchairs. Sobhy sat down and placed the tubes on the floor next to his seat. After all that had occurred, in spite of the director's 'champing at the bit' to see 'Egypt's coup' regarding taken antiquities, he still had the presence of mind to observe protocol.

"I trust that your journey was not too taxing, *habibi,* and that it wasn't too much of an imposition on our friendship to send you to the Germans," he said as he took his cup.

Sobhy saw the gleam in his eye, a hungry look that was barely reined in. He actually enjoyed having the director over a barrel, as his American friend might have said. So he milked it for all it was worth.

"It was a bit tiring, somewhat stressful. You know how the Europeans, especially the Germans, think. But, *al Hamdu illah,* everything progressed at a reasonable pace and we were able to come to terms directly. Praise God, I have with me the beginning of the end of foreign ownership of artifacts from our beloved ancient past, *inshallah.*"

"*Qwayes! Qwayes Ow-ih!* Wonderful, wonderful news. I am delighted that the line of communication has now opened and we can negotiate from a position of great strength. A precedent has been set. All thanks to you, Sobhy. Now, show me what you have gotten returned to us before I die . . . of anticipation!"

The coffee cups were moved to the sideboard, out of the way of causing any potentially tragic spills, and the tubes placed on the oval table. Sobhy removed the caps and gently, reverently, removed the felt rolls stored within. He then proceeded to unroll the material. Slowly, slowly, the papyrus fragments from Elephantine Island came into view – resting on soft material. After nearly one hundred years 'in exile', the twenty-four century old documents had come home to the Nile Valley. Abu Hassan unapologetically let the tears flow, and suddenly the impact hit Sobhy as well, as he grabbed his handkerchief to prevent any 'salty spillage'.

The black cloth background allowed the scrolls to stand out sharply, clearly – their hieroglyphic symbols in black ink stood out in contrast to the tan colored papyrus sheets. The carbon and beeswax mixture favored by the ancient Egyptians in the 5th Century BCE didn't deteriorate as quickly as did other formulae; so the ease with which Director Abu Hassan was able to translate was apparent.

"*Ya Allah!* Look at this one Sobhy!" proclaimed the Director. "See here, this document was even 'signed' as if it were by the scribe *Amenhotep*!" He clapped his hands with delight, as if he were a ten year old school boy again, cheering on his favorite football team, *Aly,* as it won victory after victory on the way to winning last year's Africa Cup. "Look how clear the palette and bag of pigment are, serving as the identifiers for the royal scribe." His unbridled enthusiasm was quite contagious.

"*Aywa,* I can see it too. It's quite stunning you know." The younger Egyptologist tried his best at restraint but it didn't quite work. He too was thrilled at his success in bringing back a portion of Egypt's past. Although the documents were simply common secular texts, they were important in the quest to fill in the blanks of ancient history.

One of Egypt's greatest challenges had been its embarrassment of archaeological riches. The SCA was now trying to shed the elitist image that it had been saddled with for decades. On one hand, it was entirely understandable. After all, when you are blessed with a wealth of major, phenomenally preserved treasures such as temples, tombs, and pyramids, as a nation you run the risk of becoming jaded. This was exactly the attitude of archaeologists of the late 19th and early 20th centuries. Why bother with the everyday when you had ample 'royal' material to work with. Taking it even one step farther, many of the early 'archaeologists' working in Egypt and the Near East felt that 'if it was broke . . . . Don't bother with it!'

Sobhy recalled hearing one such story about the venerable Auguste Mariette. Mariette was often called the Father of Egyptology, because of the great scientific strides that he made in the midst of the 19th century. His work would begin in 1843 as a cataloger of Egyptian manuscripts in the Boulogne Museum. His excavation career would begin in Sakkara, in 1850 with the blessings of Said Pasha, the ruler of Egypt on behalf of the Ottoman Turks. He discovered an Avenue of sphinxes that led to the long-lost *Serapeum*; an underground burial network that held mummified bulls, the God Serapis. These chambers were carved out of the Red Nubian Sandstone of the Western Desert, adjacent to the pyramid complexes of the IIIrd and VIth Dynasties. In addition, Mariette worked on the IIIrd Dynasty Stepped Pyramid of Zoser. Another spectacular find of his was a Persian Era pit (4th Century BCE) where scores of more ancient mummies had been "dropped" after their tombs were robbed. In 1854, Said Pasha ordered an Egyptian Museum to be built. He chose Mariette to carry out his plans. The original building was completed in 1858, called the *Boulaq* Museum.

But in spite of his brilliant excavation techniques, and intuitive perspective on ancient Egyptian archaeology, he had a fatal flaw. According to many, he either ignored or failed to appreciate the thousands of broken potsherds that littered the archaeological landscape on dozens of sites. There is an unwritten rule in archaeology – 'everything ancient works its way to the surface, and everything modern finds its way below ground.' He paid little attention to these broken bits of ancient civilization, preferring to 'go for the gold', the intact evidence. In one such case, Sobhy remembered, when dozens of fragments of beautiful bi-chrome pottery were brought to him, he turned his nose up and walked off, yelling over his shoulder in broken Arabic, 'Trow eet all avay!'. Today, as everyone working in the field knew, a large percentage of these broken sherds had the potential of being restored into lovely, fairly complete vessels that would add enormously to the knowledge that we have to life in the ancient past. It had only been in the 1990s that Egyptologists had begun to really pay attention to everyday life, as they zeroed in on excavations of ancient villages, rather than strictly focus on major monuments and tombs.

"I think that we should create a separate exhibition space in the Papyrus Gallery on the second floor. We should also make it very clear that we welcome the new cooperation between our government and the Germans as we make strides in working to bring artifacts from around the world back to their native lands; whether it be *Misr* or any other country. Perhaps now we can be seen as leaders in the recovery of the ancient past. This will be a glorious achievement for us in the SCA, *and* the leaders of our country in the SCAF. Maybe, just maybe, everyday Egyptians will see it as a sign that stability is right around the corner for all of us. It's been such a trying time." The Director certainly was one of the more optimistic people in Cairo at this point in time.

"If you like, Director, I can begin to sketch out the options for you . . ." Sobhy began.

The Director waved him off. "*Yallah habibi!* Get to it immediately! But once you've planned the layout, I want you back in Sinai to finish your salvage work at *Serabit.* The Israelis have offered support in a combined effort. Their initial work decades ago while they occupied Egyptian land will be invaluable to us, along with their incredible technical expertise. And the joint effort will once again be of value to SCAF as well." Abu Hassan always had politically advantageous opportunities uppermost in his mind. Sobhy couldn't deny him that, but at the same time grudgingly felt that the rediscovery and preservation of Egypt's past could use all the help that it could muster. He already had a considerable amount of admiration for the IDAM, the Israeli Department of Antiquities and Museums. He remembered with pride the day that the Director, Dror Amnon, had issued him a permanent visitor's pass to work with them. This could be a coup for him, personally, as well and he savored the idea. He smiled at Abu Hassan and agreed to get on it immediately.

* * *

Meanwhile, over in Israel, tracking down the elusive 20th century past was proving to be more difficult. The Assistant Curator for IDAM, Kati Ben Yair, was waiting out at the car park at Ben Gurion International Airport. As I exited the terminal and was smacked in the face by the intense Mediterranean sun, she whistled and waved her arms wildly. It had been a while since the 'adventure' surrounding the Egyptian statuary. Although we had celebrated a bit of RnR following the episode, necessity had initiated the return to the States for a few months. It was great to see her. Don't let anyone fool you, Skype really isn't all that it's cracked up to be. Yes, the computer age has made distances shrink, but there's nothing like the real thing, baby – as the old commercial went.

A hug and a brief kiss, and I practically threw myself into the air-conditioned cab of her Fiat Panda. Relief rolled over me. But as they say, 'it's not the heat, but the humidity'. The *Shephelah* in Israel was still home to the coastal humidity that always enveloped *Tel Aviv,* and wouldn't dissipate til the rolling hills of the Jerusalem District were approached, forty km further inland. As she maneuvered the small car around the rotary that eventually led to Highway 1 and Jerusalem, she outlined the appointments that she had made with staff at *Yad V'Shem,* Israel's National Memorial to the *Shoah,* or Hitler's Final Solution. Over the years, it had developed the world's greatest database regarding humankind's most horrendous tragedy to date. And it wasn't simply for the 6 million Jews who perished at the hands of the Nazis, but the five million Gypsies, physically and mentally deficient, gays and lesbians, Catholics who suffered the wrath of the paperhanger from Bavaria.

I started to nod, whether from the last few days and their hectic activity, or the humidity, I had no clue – but I quickly drifted off. The next thing I knew, I was being lightly (or not so lightly) punched in the shoulder by Kati.

"*Boker tov habibi! Yeshanta tov?*"

She welcomed me to the world of the awake as if I were an Israeli child. I hadn't realized that I had slept soundly for 45 minutes. We were approaching the outskirts of the Arab village of *Abu Ghosh.* Home of the world's finest (according to the village elders) and largest platter of *hummus,* that creamy, garlicky, chickpea-ey concoction swiped onto hot *pita* bread, it played a fascinating role in the history of Israeli Jews and Palestinian Arabs in the region.

Abu Ghosh is a bustling Arab village with a colorful history. Much of its importance is due to its location – for centuries the main highway running from Jaffa on the coast to Jerusalem passed by the community. According to Chronicles and 1 Samuel, the Ark of the Covenant rested for two decades in the nearby village of *Kiryat Yearim* before King David transferred it to Jerusalem. (1 Sam. 6:21-7:2; 1 Chron. 13:5-8). Legend has it that in 1099, Richard the Lion heart caught his first glimpse of Jerusalem from *Abu Ghosh.* Here is the Church of the Resurrection, 1132 CE.

The view is still breathtaking today. The name *Abu Ghosh* is in fact the name of the Arab clan which settled in the area in 1520. They were sent from Turkey to the Holy Land by *Sultan Selim I* to restore order in this part of the Ottoman Empire. The nearly 6,000 Muslim residents of the village today are almost all descendents of this clan. Part of the local folklore involves tales of the toll charges extorted from travelers and pilgrims passing through the village on their way to and from Jerusalem; ordained by the Ottoman Sultan. In 1947 and 1948, passage through the hills surrounding Jerusalem was crucial in getting supplies to the besieged city during Israel's War of Independence. Of the thirty-six Arab villages nestled in these hills, *Abu Ghosh* alone remained neutral during the fighting, and in many cases proved friendly and helped to keep the road open.

"From here it was possible to open and close the gates to Jerusalem," said former President *Yitzhak Navon* when discussing the village's regional importance. *Issa Jaber,* director of the local department of education for many years, felt that the personal relationships created with Zionist leaders during the pre-state period set the basis for later cooperation.

"We had a perspective for the future. That was because the people in *Abu Ghosh* have always attached great importance to being hospitable. We welcome anybody, regardless of religion or race. Perhaps because of the history of feuding with the Arabs around us we allied ourselves with the Jews . . . against the British. We did not join the Arabs from the other villages bombarding Jewish vehicles in 1947. The other Arabs never thought that there would be a Jewish government here . . . They accused my father of being a traitor and tortured him for six days."

Abu Ghosh today is governed by a local council, and is part of the Jerusalem District. Since 1997, *Jaaber Hussein,* a Muslim Arab-Israeli hotel food manager from *Abu Ghosh,* has signed an agreement with Israel's Chief Rabbis to purchase all of the state's *chametz,* the leavened products not kosher for the Jewish holiday of Passover. This symbolic deal allows the state to respect religious edicts without wastefully destroying massive quantities of food. The community prides itself on its hospitality with regard to the Israeli community and tourism.

Restaurants are the heart and soul of the village. A giant serving of *hummus* weighing 4,087.5 kilos is seen resting on a 6 m. satellite dish breaking the world record in *Abu Ghosh* on January 8, 2010. Fifty chefs in the village mashed up over four tons of *hummus*; beating the Guinness World Record set in Lebanon just months earlier. The weight is about twice as much as the previous record set in October 2009.

I roused myself just in time.

"*Stana Schwayeh*! Wait a minute!" I yelled. "I'm starved. Pull over into the *Abu Ghosh* Restaurant car park. *Hummus* and pita are on me."

She laughed playfully. "Be careful what you wish for! If you're not behaving, well . . . ." We got out and entered the cooler confines of the cafeteria style eatery.

* * *

Our thirst quenched, our hunger (or at least my hunger) slaked, we got back into Kati's car and headed for the western side of the city. Now we were in the Judean Hill country and the road meandered a bit with wide, sweeping curves as it led up to the city that was sacred to all three great western religious traditions. Considered to be the birthplace for Judaism, Christianity, and, to an extent, Islam, three thousand years of holiness would shape its nature culturally, spiritually and, of course, politically. If one were to rank the nature of Jerusalem for these three faiths, perhaps the following paradigm could be applied.

To the Christian world, there is Jerusalem, Rome, and Constantinople as epicenters of faith. To the Moslems, there is Mecca, Medina, and Jerusalem as key cities. But to the Jewish world, there is Jerusalem, Jerusalem, and Jerusalem. The *Babylonian Talmud,* commentary by early Rabbis on the essence of interpreting the faith, stated that "Ten measures of beauty were delivered to this world. Jerusalem took nine, leaving the rest of us to divide the other share." But in the same breath, "Ten measures of sorrow were given to the world as well." You guessed it, Jerusalem took nine . . ."

No matter how the interpretation is understood, the city's holiness to all is never a question. In fact, in the language of faith, 'ascending' is a metaphor for a high level of religious piety. "Going up to Jerusalem" weighs very heavily on the souls of spiritual pilgrims. But this is not just a metaphor. The physical setting of this extraordinary spot calls for one "to ascend" no matter which direction you approach it from.

The road from the west, from the coast, through the *Shephelah,* the transitional foothills, is known as the *Bab el Wad,* in Arabic called 'the Gate to the Valley', had dominated access to the city from the coast for thousands of years. Prior to the June 1967 war, the road was a narrow, sharp-bended affair that was, in some spots, a maximum one and a half lanes wide. As another vehicle would approach, you would play 'chicken' until the opposing traffic (and you) would finally gently nudge your right wheels off the paved surface a few inches so that each could pass. Sometimes, if you were unlucky, an oncoming *Egged* Bus simply wouldn't give way, so you had to move perilously to the side.

Littering the sides, along the ravine edges, dozens of rusting vehicles dotted the landscape. They were the burned out remains of some of the most violent battles of the 1948 War – those Israeli troops trying to defend the beleaguered city under siege. Today, daubed with black-painted dates of those battles, now fading in the intense Mediterranean sun, they serve all as reminders of those tenuous days even before the State of Israel was declared. Today, Israelis zip past these monuments at rates of over a hundred kph on three broad, smooth lanes for each direction; the sense of a dangerous passage all but a memory.

As we went around the final couple of sweeping curves, we passed the sleek, rocket-launcher like memorial created by Naomi Henrik in 1967. Looking as though it were leaping out of the hillside, it was dedicated to the soldiers who lost their lives trying to save Jerusalem.

And suddenly we were on the outskirts – Jerusalem the Holy, Jerusalem of Gold.

* * *

Having just sent the director an email with the proposed layout of the papyrus exhibit, Sobhy began to throw a few things in a duffel, so that he could begin the several hour journey back to Sinai and the site of *Serabit el Khadem.* He drove his son, *Kareem,* to his mother's apartment, with the promise to bring him back something 'way cool' from the excavation, and for him to remain a good boy until the weekend, when Sobhy would return from the dig.

He drove through the eastern suburb of Nasser City and hit the Cairo/Suez Road. 50 minutes saw him flash past the road marker that announced that he was leaving the Cairo Governate and entering that of Suez. A few km past that, at the *Genaiva* Junction, he made a pit stop at the snack bar there. He grabbed a *falafel* and *Orangina* Soda, and took the chance and called his mother to check on the boy. After ascertaining that all was well, Sobhy continued on into the late afternoon light, as the sun slowly set at his back.

Once he reached Suez City, he entered the engineering marvel known as the *Ahmed Hamdi* Tunnel, that linked Suez City with the Sinai Peninsula. It was named for the Egyptian general who, in 1973, devised the water cannon which allowed for the successful crossing that was the opening volley of the 1973 *Yom Kippur* War with Israel. Built in 1981, it is only a mile long, but saves a several hour drive from Luxor far to the south to the ferry from *Hurghada*. From there, it was a straight shot south, along the west coast of Sinai, following the *Ras Sudr* Road. He suddenly realized something and smiled a great, broad smile. This easy route was only made possible by the Israelis, between 1967 and 1973. He had a whole new perspective on his former enemies since his work with them and his visit to "the other side" to find answers.

After the '67 War, when Israel occupied the entire Sinai Peninsula, they brought the 20th century to the desert region. Regrettably, in Sobhy's eyes, the Egyptians had mistakenly ignored the vast wealth of Sinai, for Egypt's benefit. The mineral and oil wealth was astounding provided you had the means to exploit it. The tourist value, with the natural beauty of the desert side by side with pristine beaches, was immeasurable had it been developed. And of course, the archaeological record could not be denied; including the extraordinarily sacred nature of *Jebel Musa*, Mt. Sinai, birthplace of true western religious monotheism.

Of course the Israelis realized this almost from the beginning of occupation. Following in the footsteps of another conqueror a couple of centuries earlier, Napoleon, they brought two armies with them; the military one and the scientific one. Napoleon felt that if he only understood that which he had conquered, he could 'woo' them to accept his benevolent rule. This was a radical break from the traditional relationship of conquered and conqueror. Now, if you offered a 'better life' (albeit one whose lifestyle was alien to yours) to the vanquished, they would welcome you rather than fight you tooth and nail. So, the 'woo-ers' would win over the 'woo-ees' . . . hopefully. The Israelis would offer 20th century amenities to the Sinai *Bedouin*, such as healthcare, education and economic 'stimulus' packages that included expanded tourism. In exchange, they hoped for relative peace and tranquility until the resolution of the Sinai status. They actually got it, too; quite an achievement. However, Sobhy remembered, it was Egyptian incompetence and the arrogance of Nile culture vs. *Bedouin* lifestyle that allowed the desert denizens to accept what Israel had to offer.

The road that he was now driving south on, the *Ras Sudr* Road, was just one of the fruits of the Israeli labor. Until the Six Day War, at best, there were a mere handful of hard packed roads in the desert. The majority were nothing more than beaten tracks that had been created over the centuries by desert caravans. After Israel's stunning lightning victory, they paved roads and created way-stations that were initially designed for military ease in movement, but eventually were taken over by the booming desert tourism industry. In addition, they radically expanded the *Ras Sudr* oil fields and successfully drew millions of gallons of oil out of the Sinai until 1982, when the Israeli withdrawal from Sinai was completed. Even today, there is a unique clause in the peace treaty that calls for Israel to buy Egyptian Sinai oil at a slightly reduced cost due their development of the facility. Sobhy chuckled when he remembered that . . . 'those Israelis,' he thought,' always thinking!'

As he approached the community that had sprung up there, his eyes began to droop. Weariness overcame the Egyptologist, and he opted to spend the night along the Sinai coast before heading inland the next day to *Serabit*.

Since it was on the government's tab, but since he also wanted to show a wee bit of responsibility without giving up comfort, he opted for the Moonbeach Resort. With his SCA identification card, he got an added 15 percent discount, so his night was only about the equivalent of $40 USD. There was a restaurant on site that was as reasonable as well. He saved the government, and his sanity.

By the time he showered and ate, he was ready to collapse into bed. As he lay there, he recalled the story his American friend told him about 'the good old days', when Sinai was still the wild MidEast. It was in the late 1970s, after the *Yom Kippur* War, and both sides were well on the way to a peace agreement. It was also after Sobhy's wartime adventure when he was mildly wounded in the wrist by the Israelis. Ever since then, he referred to the round, three cm scar as his 'permanent watch face'. A reminder of a time that everyone wanted to forget.

Before the *El Arish* Treaty signing of 1982, the Israelis were still sending hundreds of desert tourists into the region, camping out along the way. However, there was a twist. As Israel and Egypt worked toward the arrangement, the UN sent a special Emergency Force to oversee the disengagement in an orderly fashion. Because of the nature of the *Ras Sudr* road, both Israeli and Egyptian military forces needed to use it for troop movement. So the UN, in its infinite wisdom (that's an oxymoron, to say the least!) would open the road, under their supervision, to the Israelis for three hours, then the Egyptians. If you arrived too late at a checkpoint, just before the road was scheduled for the other side, you were written up as a violation of the UN accords, and forced to stay overnight in the UN camp. (certainly NOT the Moonbeach!).

Sobhy couldn't help smiling now. The story now became way too funny, in spite of the fact that it was seen seriously by the UN at the time. He continued to grin to himself as he recalled the rest of the tale from his friend, *el Majnoon*, the crazy one, as he called him with affection.

One year, while traveling with a group of archaeology students in Sinai, they had been delayed a bit by one of the students who had come down with a bad case of *Shilshul,* as they called it in Hebrew. Of course, 'Mummy tummy or Pharaoh's revenge' works just as well. Off he went, to the far rocks. After a half hour's delay, they were back on the road again in the Mercedes six by four desert truck re-invented by Ora Lifschitz and her driver/engineer, Moshe; from the Hebrew University. As they approached the *Ras Sudr* UN checkpoint, they noted that they were cutting it very close as to timing. The UN staff, were anally precise in all matters of administration, but woefully inadequate as peacekeepers. To show you their priorities, the current detachment here were Swedes. They insisted that the UN ship them a semi-trailer that had been converted to be used as a *sauna,* of all things! A SAUNA! In the midst of the Sinai in the summer when the temperatures approached 52 degrees . . . . CELSIUS! A phrase came back to him; a Yiddishism that he learned while in Israel . . . *Oy Fa Voy*!

Now Sobhy was laughing out loud. The group of students was forced to spend the night at *Ras Sudr,* under the watchful eye of badly sunburned Swedes, until the following morning when the road was reopened to the Israeli side. Meanwhile, the Swedes duly noted in their logbooks the violation of the international UN sponsored cease-fire of 1977 by the Israeli side of the coin. Somewhere in the annals of the UN, the name of an American archaeologist is recorded as a violator of UN peace accords in the Sinai. Sobhy fell asleep with a smile on his face, plotting ways to rib his close friend about his 'international record'.

XIX

To Fustat, 417 BCE

IT HAD BEEN an incredibly long journey for the Vizier and his family. From the outset, the difficulties seemed to keep mounting. First, he had to gently, gently break the news to the family and friends. How indeed do you explain something without explaining anything. How do you get those who love you to trust your judgment, no matter how much it seemed a fanciful dream that flitted tantalizingly in front of your face like a beautiful butterfly. No, they would have to accept his decision and share the dream however it may end.

Then, the really hard part – explaining to his Pharaoh that all that had been given to him and his family for generations was about to be cast into the Nile, carried off in a way that no one could imagine. That was the really hard part, yet he felt compelled, no, obliged to follow what lay in store for him beyond the great desert to the west.

After weeks of preparation, and not so gentle prodding of the family at times, the day for embarkation finally arrived. The Pharaoh, although somewhat put out by the whole scope of the affair, graciously lent his royal barge for the downstream journey to Fustat, far to the north. It would take over a week of sailing, but the ease and comfort afforded by the luxurious vessel allowed for adequate rest for what was presumed to be an arduous trek across the western desert. The family was actually quite supportive in their preparations. There were no major arguments about what to take, and what to abandon in their villa in Syene.

As the rosy fingered dawn broke over the eastern desert hills, and Syene roused itself into wakefulness, dozens of friends, relatives, and even government officials lined the quay and waved as the boat silently glided into the middle of the great river, caught the current, and began its northern journey to Fustat. Nearly 5 thousand stadia (about 1000 km) were ahead of them and the family reclined on cushions under the linen canopy to watch Upper Egypt recede to the south. They all spoke in an animated fashion about the adventure ahead. Standing by the prow of the vessel, the Vizier pondered his move – too late to turn back now.

The Vizier guessed that all would be waiting in far off Tingis to make life instantaneously comfortable for them. At least that was the scenario that he fervently wished for. However, he did make sure of one thing. It didn't matter how far, or how foreign, the destination was. As long as there were some basic elements to the new life that were familiar, that served as a foundation stone upon which to build a new life, then all would be alright. Yes, there was their faith and their cultural identity that was easily carried in the backpacks in their minds. But something physical also needed to be clung to as well. In this case, it was the unique architecture of their culture. Rolled tightly in a wooden tube were a couple of papyrus scrolls with building plans. These were the floorplans of the four-unit houses that were the trademark abodes of ancient Israel since time immemorial – or so it was presented to the Vizier from his father, and his father's father. It was said that this style of home originated with the ancestors who were enslaved to the Egyptian pharaohs as early as the days of Yosef Avinu, the blessed Joseph ben Yaacov ben Itzhak ben Avraham Avinu. The plans were brought from the land of Canaan, according to tradition, in the memory of Joseph, who was sold into slavery by his brothers; all due to sibling rivalry and jealousy over some sort of amazingly colored dreamcoat. It was indeed quite a tale. But he wondered idly as he watched the Nile flow beneath the prow of the boat, if it was a tale told by an idiot, full of sound and sometimes fury – actually signifying nothing of substance. Regardless, he planned to build an identical villa for his family once this incredible journey reached its terminus in Tingis.

In addition to the floor plans, another wooden tube carried an even more precious cargo – a series of scrolls with the sacred texts of the Taanach, the Hebrew Bible. Viewed as a 'people-making instrument', it served as an outline for all life; a primer on how to live as Godly a life as humanly possible, a letter written by our parent in heaven to each and every one of us. This scroll would preserve their way of life wherever it was on earth, and the Vizier took heart in this knowledge.

*　*　*

After a few days on the river, the novelty of the journey, the excitement of the adventure, began to wear thin. Family members on board became restless, bouncing around the deck with pent-up energy that was no longer dissipated by the activities associated with life on the river – fishing, swimming, sunning, and even simply contemplating the changing shoreline as it glided by. Yes, one night they had tied up along the riverbank at the sacred city of Abydos, but because of the wild beasts that came out of the desert hills in the evening after the sun set, no one was allowed to lay a foot on land – lest they become a desert buffet for the animal kingdom.

The Vizier saw this, anticipated this. So when the boat approached the community of Minya a couple of days later, he made an executive decision. They would dock for two days, re-provision the ship, perhaps explore a bit during the daylight hours and regain their land legs, and then complete the journey.

It was toward sunset that the crew began to maneuver the ship toward the quay on the east side of the river just around a stadion from the town. The western hills on the opposite had been turned a fiery color with the sinking sun. The red Nubian sandstone cliffs caught the dying light in an extraordinary way. Everyone turned to marvel at the light show. And suddenly it was gone. One thing that never ceases to amaze is the timing involved in a sunset across the broad expanse of desert. The sun seems to cling to the sky, refusing the pull of gravity, seeming to fight for its life. It hangs there, suspended, for an eternity. Then suddenly, as if it had given up the fight on impulse, reluctantly, rapidly sinks into the horizon; immersing the Goodly West in a cloak of darkness, making its journey through the body of the Sky Goddess, Nut. It would be reborn in the east, bathing an awakening world in its luminous glory once again the following day.

There was an electric air of excitement that evening, everyone was ready to disembark the next day and shake out the little used leg muscles on the day trip off the boat. The Vizier opened his copy of the Taanach, his spiritual 'letter' written to him from his heavenly parent, to study up on his ancestors' entry into Misr, Egypt, centuries ago. After all, if he was to serve as tour guide the next day, he'd best be prepared to answer any and all questions there might be.

* * *

The next morning, bright and early, with an air of anticipation, the family of the Vizier and several of the crew members who decided to join them walked down the rickety board that served as a gangplank. Their feet sank into the wet sand ashore, and one could see the joy in many of their eyes as they worked their way up the gentle slope of the river bank. Firm, solid land never felt so good – they just weren't used to the idea of living days on end on the water like the sailors of the royal boat. Once up to the grassy bank a few cubits above the present water line, many simply flopped down and soaked in the warming rays of the early sun. The youngest family members frolicked a bit, running north and south along the riverbank, burning off some of that pent-up energy from several days trapped on the Nile cruiser. The Vizier took great pleasure in this, and, somewhat wistfully, questioned for a moment why he opted to pack it all in, leave this magnificent land, and head west into the unknown. But it was just for a moment; he considered the fact that even greater things may lie in the future, and the wonderful memories of life along the Nile would always be with them, no matter the outcome.

He gathered the group together and pointed upslope a couple of hundred meters away.

"See those black spots on the plateau near the crest of the embankment? Those are entries into a series of tombs that the ancients referred to as the Tombs of the Governors of Hebenu, one of our ancient provinces. But in fact that's not what's so fascinating about them. They are brilliantly decorated, and tell a story that is dear to our hearts. Care to see?" He knewthat his last statement revealed a tantalizing tidbit that none could resist.

After half an hour's climb to the plateau above, they all sat in the shadow cast by the rock-cut tomb entries, for the sun was far from its apex at noon. A couple of the ship's crew had carried bladders of water and now dispensed it generously. While everyone caught their breath, the Vizier unrolled one of the papyrus scrolls that he had brought from the ship and began to read. It was the story of a young Israelite's sojourn in Misr, and how, centuries earlier, he had risen to a position of great power and authority, not unlike the Vizier himself. It came from the Book of Bereshit, Genesis; for it was the opening of a great saga . . . "In the beginning . . ."

So, after the short reading, some were curious. Where exactly did these ancestors come from, what did they look like? And the Vizier had some sort of answer here. "Now we enter into the tombs and take a look around. You'll be surprised, because here a possible answer to your question might be found on the walls. Let's go into this one first, the third in the row. According to the cartouche found adjacent to the doorway, it belonged to a man named Khnumhotep, a high-ranking official of this Province of Oryx."

He led the way into the first chamber from a small, columned portico. The ceiling was curved slightly, like a barrel vaulting so typical of Egyptian houses. The curve high above trapped the hot air, and small vents allowed it to escape – cooling the interior. However, in this case, there was no need to cool an interior – the occupants didn't mind the heat! And since it was rock-cut, there could be no escape outside, so only the ceiling was replicated to give the deceased a familiar setting.

But there was one scene that needed no translation for the group. It showed Khnumhotep himself receiving offerings of goods from a group of Asiatic, Semitic looking people. They all oohed and aahed at the detail. The scene showed a group of 37 family members sojourning in Egypt. According to the narrative, the Patriarch Joseph had a family of 70 with him. Of course, in any text, numbers can be suspect, but the indication of a very large extended family was an evident fact. They looked entirely different from the Egyptian community. First, there was the matter of skin tone on the wall paintings. The Egyptians were painted a 'sun-burnt red', due to exposure to the intense Nile Valley sun. The Semitic tribespeople, on the other hand, were painted in an olive-skinned tone. One thing that the Vizier's family had always wondered about was their hirsute nature. The men in the family had more facial and body hair than their Egyptian counterparts. This too was indicated in the artwork. So clearly there were associations ancestrally here that were not shared with the native population.

"Look at the kilts that they are wearing!" shouted one of the children. "It's truly a many-colored dreamcoat, like in the story!" he exclaimed. And yes, it was true. The Semitic men and women wore beautiful, colorfully banded dresses and kilts, and everyone thought back to the story of Avinu Yoseph's selling into slavery by his jealous brothers – over a

piece of clothing. The Egyptian guides who led them, on the other hand, wore elegant, but simple, linen kilts that were totally devoid of color.

The imagery of a semi-nomadic group was quite clear as well. As once glanced over the entire scene, the items that were essential for itinerant journeyers were clearly seen. The traditional pack animals that were used, the donkeys were numerous, laden with personal possessions. Other animals seen would be utilized in every way imaginable – sheep and goats. They were the ultimate bio-degradable, environmentally friendly, beasts. They offered wool for clothing, and milk for drinking. Then, in their next phase of use, offered meat, horn and bone for tool and utensils, and finally bladders for water storage and transportation. Almost every bit of the animal had some practical use.

The final act of this wonderfully depicted story showed the Semites offering precious items to Khnumhotep as royal administrator, in exchange for food. The Vizier knew well the vagaries of nature, and the fact that surrounding lands were constantly in a cycle of plenty and famine, caused by re-occurring droughts. After all, wasn't that how Joseph came to be reunited with his brethren after so many years – because of famine in the Land of Canaan?

But this caused him to reflect on his monumental decision to pack up his family and leave their adopted homeland based on a document that an unfamiliar courier had delivered. 'Egypt was the gift of the Nile' was the mantra that every Egyptian chanted each year that the life-giving flood came, replenishing a land with rich, fertile soil. While everyone around them might be dying of starvation due to a lack of rainfall, Egypt never suffered. So everyone would constantly thank the Nile gods for their bounty.

What lay beyond the western desert, would they be subject to the whims of nature, and be forced to fight for their lives in a harsh environment? Yes, he questioned his decision always, but vowed to persevere, because it was truly a calling that would lead him back to Tingis.

The excursion began to wrap up, as the sun started its downward arc to the Goodly West, and the intense heat built up quickly. The group headed back down to the river, the cooling breezes and shade under the canopies that were erected on deck. The next morning, rejuvenated, they would continue the final leg of the journey to Fustat. From there, the westward trek across the desert along the Great Sea would begin. Who knew how long it might take, but the anticipation made it all well worth it.

There were two days of uneventful sailing. The evening of the second day saw an ever-growing impatience on the part of passengers and crew. They were so close to their destination now. As they passed the canal that led west to the Fayum, the Vizier made an executive decision. He told the boat captain that he wished to arrive by the end of the next day in Fustat. This meant sailing well past dusk that day. For seasoned boatmen who plied these more northern waters quite often, it was not views as a problem. However, the royal barge's captain was somewhat unfamiliar with these waters, these currents and unexpected eddies. He respectfully asked the Pharaoh's advisor to allow him to tie up just after sunset, to play it safe with his precious passengers. After all, his neck would be on the chopping block should anything happen.

The Vizier took it all in, weighed pros and cons thoughtfully. He respected the captain's expertise and knowledge, and certainly understood his caution. But he also saw the toll that the long voyage was taking on his family, in spite of the luxurious surroundings of the Pharaoh's ship. As a result, he politely, yet firmly, denied the request. To assuage the fears of the boatman, he hastily scribbled a note on a papyrus scrap that exonerated the barge captain of all blame should an event occur. He took full responsibility for the decision to sail into the night.

The captain, although relieved, still was worried a bit about night journey – and rightly so. A couple of hours after sunset, when the watch was changing, a sudden, rather dramatic jolt shivered through the hull of the ship. Several people on their pallets were thrown unexpectedly to the deck, rudely awakened. Although no one was hurt, cries of alarm echoed the length of the royal barge. It was more shock than anything else. Apparently, the vagaries of the Nile came back to haunt the vessel. The navigable channel in the Nile was always shifting due to the constant changes in sand bars from one month to the next. That was why captains loathed sailing at night. At least during daylight hours a watch could be posted on the prow and many sharp-eyed crewmembers could shout out a warning in plenty of time. Darkness was the enemy, and many ships that dared to sail past sundown ran the risk.

The ship ground to a stop on one of the many sand bars that lay just beneath the surface. Although the flat-bottomed vessel only drew 3 cubits, about 4.5 feet, it was riding deep enough to become wedged onto the spit of sand that projected into what had been a deep channel just a couple of weeks before.

The captain assessed the situation with calm precision, although his embarrassment was clearly evident. His first mate reported to him that no injuries had been sustained and no damage had been inflicted on the boat. No supplies had been lost overboard as well. In essence, it was nothing more than a slight mishap; although it certainly would be a smear on the record of someone who had gained the trust of the Pharaoh, and was expected to perform perfectly. He knew that, once the episode was over, he would be the brunt of severe ribbing by many who plied the waters of el Nil.

Once everyone had calmed down, they returned to sleep. Actually, several of the family members slept better because the ship was no longer moving on the river. The captain ordered lights hung from the prow and stern of the boat, and in addition sent a couple of small skiffs out with lights attached. They anchored them a couple of dozen cubits from the boat, to warn off any river traffic and prevent another accident from occurring. At that point, he settled down in his chair to wait out the morning and get his vessel off the sand and back on its way downstream.

At sunrise, he roused himself, grabbed a piece of bread and a flagon of date wine, and surveyed the scene before him. It was evident in the morning sun, as the mist fled the river's surface, that a new sand bar had been created over past few weeks, jutting out from the eastern shore into the shipping channel. They were firmly stuck since they had slid well over 40 percent of their length before coming to a stop. As the crew ventured to the rails to look at the situation, the captain ordered the oars out in an attempt to pull themselves free. This quickly proved itself to be folly, as did any attempt at pulling the ship off the sand by crews in the small skiffs. The only recourse was to wait for another vessel and request a tow off the submerged obstacle.

In the meantime, the rest of the crew and passengers were able to enjoy themselves fully, wading in the water and relaxing – savoring the moments of a short 'vacation' from the trip before landing in Fustat. No one complained about the delay; a good time was had by all, except the embarrassed captain.

As the invisible creator god Khepher, the scarab beetle, pushed the sun to its apex, a cry went out from one of the stern lookouts. A ship was sailing south towards them, and it appeared large enough to help get them off the sand bar. As it approached, the royal barge crew began to hear the faint strains of good-natured jesting float across the river. Crews would never live down the need to be 'rescued' from a sand bar, as long as there was no real danger or emergency. The shouts grew louder, and the barbs more humorously brutal, in good fun. Even the ancestry of the captain, who everyone on the river knew to be flowing with Nile water for many generations, was called into question. At first he blushed deeply, then joined in with his own joking, much at his expense.

The cargo boat pulled alongside and two heavy ropes were tossed to the royal barge. Once secured, the Vizier's crew swam over and joined the other oarsmen, thus doubling the pulling capacity. As the two crews pulled in unison, slowly, slowly the royal vessel was pulled free and floated serenely, ready to resume its proud journey south. The Pharaoh's emissary obtained the name of the rescuing captain, and promised some sort of reward when both ships docked in Fustat in a couple of days. The Vizier also made it perfectly clear to the chagrined captain that he would not be held responsible for the accident; for, after all, they do happen. For that, the boatman would be eternally grateful – there was no telling how the leader of Egypt might have responded.

By the end of the week, Fustat appeared on the horizon, and the Babylon Fortress rose majestically to great them along the eastern bank of the Nile. The first portion of their odyssey was now over.

Jerusalem, Sinai . . . .
the Negev . . . the present

ONCE WITHIN THE city limits of Jerusalem, we swung a bit south and headed for the area of *Har Herzl* and the Jerusalem forest, the site of *Yad Vashem,* the Museum of the Holocaust. South on Herzl St., we turned onto the small street that led directly to the facility, called *HaZikaron,* 'Remembrance Street'. I sighed as I drank in the lush scenery rolling past the window. The hilly slopes were covered in greenery, it had been a moderately wet spring and the ground had soaked up the moisture in preparation for the incredible panoramic view that would blossom a couple of months after the rain. It was an incredible setting for such a somber destination.

I always felt an unsettling discomfort whenever I got in the vicinity of the vast complex of buildings, gardens, memorials that made up the world's destination for education on humankind's penchant for inflicting horrific agony on fellow humans, simply because of an 'otherness'. Throughout the course of human history, it has been made exceedingly clear that we, as humans, have a built in 'denial' gene. We don't take responsibility, we deflect from culpability, and we scapegoat others to our collective heart's content. Although anthropologists like to state that humankind evolved differently that other animals because of the development of the opposable thumb, I feel that it was the 'pointing finger' that sets us apart psychologically – we point the finger of blame at anyone in the vicinity as long as it doesn't bend back at us. And it's always the minorities that bear the brunt of the blame, no matter where in the world.

The first time that I visited the memorial, with my father when I was a teenager, was also my last for nearly thirty years. In spite of the fact that I had visited Israel at least once a year, and sometimes twice yearly for over two decades, as a field archaeologist and university professor, bringing students of all shapes and sizes, the countrywide tour that was integral to the educational program found me sitting in the coffee shop just outside the entry. After that initial visit, I simply couldn't bring myself to re-enter time and again and be ushered into the world of the darkest moments of human history. It was too overwhelming to me.

It was only in the 90s, with the opening of many new exhibits, such as the Valley of the Lost Communities and the Children's House, that I dared go back inside. And it was clearly only to see those new portions, I still couldn't revisit the horror within the old.

As we entered the car park, Kati saw me visibly stiffen and placed a hand over mine. The squeeze transmitted her concern without words, and told me that strength comes in numbers. At least we only had to go to the administrative building which was a bit removed from the exhibit halls. The educational director of the museum, Varda Sheloni, would be waiting for us in her office. The vast database would be at our disposal.

We were warmly welcomed by Ms. Sheloni, who had worked with Kati a couple of times before. After the prerequisite tea, we got down to business. I outlined the entire story of the Elephantine Papyri, the trace back to Berlin, and the subsequent disappearance of the Aramaic scrolls that had been in their possession for decades. She had no idea what I was going to disclose next.

"The discovery of the missing documents clearly upset your curator counterpart, Conrad Volkmar. Apparently no one had a clue that anything was amiss for a few years. He took the unprecedented action of allowing me and my Egyptian colleague access to the original files in the recesses of the new museum complex. Although we couldn't shed any light on their whereabouts, we did seem to come up with the last remnants of the paper trail from the 1930s. It seems that the last person on record to actually see the scrolls was the official photographer, Kurt Loewe. And that all took place in 1932. Almost immediately following the documentation, the entire museum collection came under the aegis of the Ministry of German Culture, was scrutinized for its 'purity', and within a few more years was transported to underground bunkers to be preserved during the war."

Israelis by nature have learned that one can never be shocked by human nature, but clearly this information was intriguing to Sheloni. She urged me to go on.

"We were able to use the administrative database to try to locate the photographer, to even see if he was still alive, to try to get a handle on where the documents might have been stored after he returned them from the photo studio. Here's where things get really interesting. In the German database, it refers us to Emigdirect."

Varda Sheloni started to pour herself another cup of tea, and when she heard 'Emigdirect' her hand started shaking – tea was spilling all over the table. She suddenly realized that *Yad Vashem's* records could help determine what may have happened to an important part of Jewish history. In addition, Israeli help in this affair could also serve to further repair Israeli-Egyptian relations which had been terribly strained during the Egyptian Spring and subsequent election of a Moslem Brotherhood president, Mohamed Morsi. She took a deep breath and walked over to her computer terminal. Her fingers flew over the keyboard as she sought access to the files involving Jewish refugees from Germany in the post war era. Her hands stopped shaking, her resolve evident.

Kati and I exchanged glances. We smiled, realizing that there may be answers very soon.

"*Mitzuyawn hevrai,* Excellent news my friends", came a quick response as the director looked up from the LCD monitor. "I think that I may have found our *haver,* our friend, Kurt Loewe – provided that there aren't other 'Kurt Lowes' who were aided in coming to Israel immediately following the war." She smiled warmly.

"Apparently Herr Loewe was one of an initial group of German Jews who had the fortune of running and hiding from the Nazis in plain sight as they say. He lived among a group of Berliners who were so poverty-stricken that their neighborhood was totally ignored by Brown Shirts before the outbreak of war, and then was entirely removed from Berlin's infrastructure grid as dwindling utility resources shut down whole sections of the city as the military siphoned off power and water to the more essential parts of the city; namely the Nazi bureaucracy."

We were both a bit mystified. General lore indicated that nearly all of the German Jewish population had been deported long before the outbreak of hostilities. Varda saw and our confusion and elaborated.

"By January 1939, the Gestapo established a *Zentralstelle fuer juedische Auswandeurng,* the 'Central Bureau for Jewish Emigration' in Berlin. However, the Nazis dawdled over getting rid of the city's Jewish community, preferring to exploit it to the fullest and draining it of all value and use before shipping the people out. Berlin became officially *"judenrein"*, clean of Jews, on June 16, 1943. But in various Nazi documents since discovered, there were in fact 6,700 Jews still officially listed as residents of the city. However the authorities were having one hell of a time locating them, and eventually gave up."

"*Oy favoy,* I can't possibly imagine their lives," Kati was shocked to the core. Many of her relatives had lost their lives in the Final Solution, and she was much closer to the subject that I was. "It must have taken an extraordinary individual to survive that."

"According to the database, Kurt Loewe was truly one of the extraordinary. Following the war, as his processing statement goes, he still trusted no one and lived in the shadows. Singlehandedly he made his way to Emigdirect offices many kilometers outside of Berlin. He would leave notes on the door during afterhours, not wishing to show himself, until he ascertained the legitimacy of the agency and the people involved. This went on for a couple of weeks until he finally made contact. From there, they placed him on a convoy to one of the small fishing villages along the Mediterranean coast near Nice. A small, but seaworthy vessel evidently landed him on the Palestinian coast at some time in mid 1946. The British hadn't entirely shut down the coast, limiting emigration as yet so he was one of the lucky ones early on. Within a couple of months, her majesty's navy would create a stranglehold on refugee landings."

"*Ya Allah! Yesh lo mazal!* Was he ever lucky!" I exclaimed. I just couldn't wrap my head around the tribulations that faced this young man seven decades ago.

We sat, somewhat stunned, as Varda printed out the fairly slim file on the German photographer. The last information on his pre-Israel life said that Loewe was shipped to a small *kibbutz* in the northwest *Negev* desert, *Kibbutz Gvulot*. It had been established in 1943 by the JNF, the Jewish National Fund with the majority of founders coming from Romania and Turkey. Its protection came from the group known as *Hashomer Hatzair*, "the Youth Guard". But it was designated a true *kibbutz* only in 1946. Prior to then, it was simply an outpost created to guard JNF land and conduct a bit of soil and climate research to assess the area for suitable agricultural products. Today, the community boasts about 240 members, and, although small and isolated, is self-sufficient.

Apparently Loewe had served in the *Haganah* during the War of Independence, and had been slightly wounded. It was enough to prevent his active involvement in the *Miluim*, the Israeli Defense Forces reserve. At that time, all men were required to serve in the reserves til age 50. Today, the upper age has dropped dramatically. The result for the German was that he could move to a *kibbutz* and live there in relative obscurity for nearly six decades. He apparently didn't want to be bothered too much or take too much responsibility. The eventual informal title that he was given was "everyone's *Saba*, everyone's Grandpa". He was the sort of character that actor Ed Asner always played in his later years – kind, gentle, yet curmudgeonly in a lovable sense. This was just the persona for someone to 'fly under the radar' just enough. Very few were aware of his background details. For survivors of the *Shoah*, Hitler's Final Solution, matters remained personal unless volunteered. But the *kibbutz* kids loved him.

We thanked the museum education director and knew what we had to do next. We needed to drive down south to the agricultural settlement that Kurt Loewe now called home, and see if he would open up just a bit to us. After all, it wasn't necessarily his story that we would focus on, but the missing scrolls that he just might have recollection of in the recesses of a memory that most would choose to forget.

* * *

Meanwhile, just a desert away, Sobhy had just settled back in to the excavation camp situated on the *Serabit* Plateau about 200 m from the New Kingdom Temple complex dedicated to the Goddess *Hathor*. As the foreman, the *qablan,* filled him in on the work that had been done over the week since he had left, he shook his head at the state of the site before him.

The temple was one of the most fascinating sites on the periphery of the Egyptian kingdom during its heyday, when Egypt ruled the east. There was no more powerful a country in the world at that time, the 15th-11th centuries BCE. Her authority spread from Nubia in the south all the way to the midst of modern Syria to the north. She engaged in battle with the Hittites and forged a peace treaty with them that put the frontier within shouting distance of the Euphrates River. Her pharaohs exacted tribute from dozens of peoples under their thumb, and nations trembled whenever they heard the name, *Misr*.

The Temple to the Goddess *Hathor* was situated near the famed turquoise mines of Sinai. Several of them were worked for nearly four centuries, as the semi-precious stone was used for vessels, jewelry and amulets in honor of the gods and goddesses of the Egyptian pantheon. It had started out modestly, as a chapel and shrine on the edge of one of the southern mountain spurs. Each successive pharaoh, according to his wealth, power and prestige, would add rooms, sanctuaries, hypostyle halls or courtyards and their size would depend on how deep the pharaoh's 'pockets' were. The building then took on a linear footprint; with one chamber in front of the previous, on axis, with a minor exception. Due to the topography of the plateau, the latest additions to the temple were forced to 'bend' a bit off the straight line so the surface could accommodate it. All in all, it was an extraordinary feat.

After its abandonment at the end of the New Kingdom, the site wasn't disturbed. It wasn't destroyed by humans, nor by natural disaster. Rather, it ever so slowly eroded, at the mercy of the constantly blowing desert winds. Since they blew in only one direction, the Red Nubian Sandstone stelae were perpetually bombarded by effects similar to sand-blasting; with desert particles serving as mini-windborn projectiles. As a result, the back sides of all the stelae were deeply pitted and hollowed out, while the fronts remained almost pristine for 34 centuries or so. No one bothered to try to preserve this monument. Travelers like David Roberts would visit in the mid-19th century, sketch and water color painting its ruins, and then move on.

As Sobhy surveyed his surroundings, he couldn't help but be reminded of yet another Israeli 'triumph' of sorts. Following the 1967 War, Israeli archaeologists achieved within six years what the Egyptians had failed to do for decades – survey and plot the entire Sinai Peninsula and plot its numerous archaeological remains, including *Serabit.*

There was really something to be said about a nation-state that was truly obsessed with its past, and the links to the ancient civilizations that shaped it. He recalled his university days, when the professor constantly reminded the class of the unwritten axiom in archaeology that everything old finds its way to the surface, while modern stuff works its way into in the soil. It seemed that it was even more so the case in Israel. As Sobhy had learned from his newfound American and Israeli friends over the past few months, every Israeli was taught to go on hikes and keep his or her eye to the ground; you could never tell when you might spot a potsherd of the ancient world that had popped up onto the surface. He fondly thought back to the story his American archaeologist friend told about how he got into 'the business', as he had put it.

"I was a senior in high school. I had already been accepted into university, as had most others, and we all 'cruised' through the second semester. My parents had asked if I'd like an early graduation present. My eyes lit up the entire neighborhood! A '69 Mustang Fastback! I dreamt of being the big man on campus the next year. 'How would you like a trip to Israel?' my father asked. I deflated like a three day old helium balloon. But at least I would get out of school for a couple of weeks.

I knew that I was in deep doo-doo when we got to the airport. The second youngest person in the group, sponsored by my parent's synagogue, WAS MY FATHER! I had always heard the Yiddish term, 'Altekocker' thrown around but never really understood it. (my parents used Yiddish when I wasn't to know what they were saying, so I never really learned it). Now I did.

We got to Ben Gurion Airport in Israel and I was all set for a really miserable time. The third day into the journey, we visited the archaeological site of Masada, overlooking the Dead Sea. The guide knew the horrific time I was having, and walked over to me. He handed me a rocky clump of clay and told me to put it in my pocket and see him after dinner.

We were at a brand new motel-style accommodation called the Nof Arad, in the small development town of Arad, population 11,000 at that time. You walked out the door of your bungalow and the entire Judean Desert was on your doorstep. But at that time I didn't see the beauty, the mystery, the excitement of the desert environment. Well, I met him and we walked over to a sink. He ran the 'rock' under the faucet. As the dirt melted away, the charred spout of a 2000 year old Herodian Roman oil lamp filled my eyes. I was stunned, I was 'hooked'. From that point on, I didn't see a single 'person' on the rest of the trip. My eyes were glued to the ground, hoping to find another clue to the past. That was my start. I still have the oil lamp fragment; but, sitting next to it on a shelf, is a complete oil lamp that was one of a small cache discovered on an excavation that I served as American co-director of 20 years later from a site in the Negev about 50 km west of Masada."

Sobhy smiled and wondered where his colleague was in Israel, and whether or not he was having luck in tracking down the evidence so sorely needed to recover the Aramaic documents from Elephantine Island – that just so happened to have disappeared in Germany.

"Ya Rais! Kif halek?" He was shaken from his reverie when several of the workmen saw that he had returned and came over to greet him.

"*Qwayeis ahwi shukran*" he answered. "I'm great, thank you." He quickly got back to the matters at hand, and, remembering the Israelis who had been there decades before, outlined his plan. He had brought with him a scholarly journal article on restoration and preservation of stone artifacts. Thankfully, he had an English translation with him, leaving the original Hebrew back in Cairo. With the new government and its Muslim Brotherhood leanings, there was a renewed fervor in Egypt, and many of the *fellahin*, the peasants, felt that renewed Moslem spirituality could naturally be likened to anti-Israeli sentiment. Fortunately, the majority of the better educated Egyptians realized that there was no connection. However, in the Sinai, the *Bedouin* had ideas of their own that needed to be watched. After all, with the Egyptian government having a full plate in Cairo and the Nile Valley, Sinai was all but forgotten and the *Bedouin* enjoyed a modicum of independence that they hadn't felt since the Sadat days. Their boldness shocked some, as they kidnapped tourists seemingly at will in exchange for funds – in other words, it was purely financial piracy with no ideology involved. Sobhy felt lucky that the SCA guards came from Luxor, and were not *Bedouin.*

He opened the document, scanned it briefly to make sure that he had the data correct, and began to explain how the Egyptians were ready to more fully preserve this wonderful site. He made it clear to the workers that this idea came directly from Cairo, and nowhere else. As a result, they beamed with pride at the glorious scientific breakthrough of the Supreme Council of Antiquities. Sobhy had them, they were fully on his side and he had no more worries.

Following the lead of the Israeli archaeologists years earlier, Sobhy had his men mix a silicon solution. Rather than 'paint on' the solution and cover the exterior of the Red Nubian Sandstone monuments, he had the workmen inject the liquid, using industrial strength syringes that he had brought from Cairo. This fluid then bonded the stone from within, and would prevent any further deterioration from the harsh winds. Nothing could be done to the *stelae* in their damaged states, but the erosion process was arrested. As the work progressed for a few days, the workmen began to look at Sobhy as if he were a pharaoh himself; and they were proud to be a part of this extraordinary undertaking in the southern desert of Sinai.

Soon he could return to Cairo, in triumph, and persuade the SCA director to give him a few days off so that he could continue to help the others and, in the process, get more Elephantine Papyri returned to the Cairo Museum.

* * *

Kati and I packed a couple of small rucksacks with basic necessities in case we had to spend the night in *Kibbutz Gvulot*. We threw a couple of *'jerrycanim'*, large styrofoam-insulated water jugs, in the back seat, along with a cooler containing *pita, hummus*, tomatoes, cucumbers, onions and a plastic bag of olives and headed out the parking lot of the *Supersol* to the road south. We opted to travel south "old school", utilizing the older highways that traversed Israel, rather than the newer express toll road. This allowed us to 'slow down and smell the cacti' along the way, and see the Israel of the 1970s and 80s – a kinder, gentler world to be sure.

We left Jerusalem and headed south and slightly west along Route 40, passing through *Kiryat Gat*. Off to the side, we saw the enormous Intel industrial area, where they made computer chips. From there, the road bended a bit to the east but continued south; through the border of the *Shephelah* and the *Judean Hills*, approaching the Western *Negev*. As we passed *Kibbutz Beit Kama*, I remarked about a young *kibbutznik* that I had made the acquaintance of many years earlier. At that point, Kati, apparently tired of driving, turned and punched me on the arm; obviously to get her blood flowing again. What else could it have been? I rubbed my arm and shut up; a smug smile was emblazoned across her face.

This was the beginning of the land allocated to Israel's *Bedouin* population back in the 70s, when the government attempted to bring the semi nomads into the grid so to speak; integrating them into the healthcare and educational network. But it could only be done if they were sedentized to a degree.

The only *Bedouin* community to have the 'city' designation is *Rahat*. By the end of the first decade of the 21st century, it was the largest settlement in the world, with a population approaching 54,000. It was the 'poster child' for all that was wrong, and right, with the way that the Israeli government dealt with its *Bedouin* citizens. The process of changing your pattern of living is rife with difficulties, and the transition from semi nomadic to sedentary living is a brutal change. The troubles that were rampant in *Bedouin* society came about primarily because of integration into Israeli society. Rapid, and poorly prepared for, change often leads to seeking a means of escape; and alcohol and drug abuse are the most common least expensive mechanisms out there. Throughout the 70s, 80s and early 90s, the young *Bedouin* were trapped in the no-person's land of tradition and change – and they dealt with it poorly. In addition, the westernized Israelis couldn't understand for the life of them why the *Bedouin* so strongly resisted the quantum leap into the new era. Only at the turn of the 21st century did both sides begin to see the light, and benefits provided by the government began to be balanced with traditional values.

However, as they say in this part of the world, change comes 'slowly, slowly'. The unemployment level remains high, as does an inordinate amount of crime. But, with the integration of health care and infrastructure reform, there has been a slow turnabout. The ramshackle shacks of *Rahat* have begun to be replaced by beautiful concrete villas, and schools and clinics dot the community. And even though some traditional *Bedouin* values are being replaced by modern realities, the kindheartedness and warmth of the people still shines through. As *Rahat* receded in our rear-view mirror, I fondly remembered noting various lifestyle benchmarks with my *Bedouin* friends; going from *hafla* to *hafla* in celebration of their lives. I remembered that I felt that I couldn't look another lamb in the face after all the meals that I was at as a special guest. The only course worthy of visitors was the *mensef.* It consisted of fresh-baked *pita* bread lining an enormous tray that was laden with boiled rice, roasted vegetables, and grilled lamb. You tore off a piece of bread and rolled up in it the lamb-rice-veggie mixture and ate it as a hand-held morsel. But of course, you *had* to eat it with your right hand because, well, the left hand was reserved for other bodily functions. Woe is the left-hander who forgot this essential bit of *Bedouin* etiquette.

I was proud to sponsor the first *Bedouin* to come to the US and earn a doctoral degree in child psychology, and then see him return to his community of *Tel Sheva* to help the children cope with change in their society. President Shimon Peres of Israel would also note with a great sense of pride the first *Bedouin* woman from the same village and same clan, that of *Abu Reqaiq*, who became Israel's first female *Bedouin* entrepreneur and create her own line of Dead Sea cosmetics, now, know worldwide. Progress was coming, slowly, slowly, but it was coming.

At *Mishmar HaNegev* we turned off at a roadside stand. We stretched our legs, got a couple of glasses of cold, fresh-squeezed *eshkoliot*, grapefruit juice, and *falafel*, and topped up the tank. From there, we would be entering the *Eshkol* Regional Council District. We swung onto the narrower-laned Road 241 and headed towards the community of *Ofakim.* Founded in the mid 1950s as the regional center for all of the agricultural communities, it never grew beyond around 24,000 people. Although we were only twenty km or so due west of *Beersheva*, it was well over 45 minutes by road away. As we passed the small *moshav* of *Tze'elim*, we were within a few more minutes of *Kibbutz Gvulot.* The couple of hours drive had passed smoothly, but the inherent tension I always had when driving in Israel had given me the literal pain in the neck. I was glad to see the hand-carved sign that was adjacent to the gate and guard tower outpost of the small farming community.

As we approached, the swirl of dust that I had seen out of the corner of my eye grew closer. At first, I thought that it was a small dust devil, that random whirlwind that picked up dirt and debris as it blew across the desert landscape. As it neared the road, I saw that it wasn't a creation of nature, but humankind.

A *Bedouin* youth was guiding his flock of sheep and goats from one pasturage to another. Or perhaps I should more accurately have thought that it was driving him. Those animals always seemed to have minds of their own, and were right more of the time than the humans who shepherded them. We were forced to wait about fifteen minutes until they crossed the asphalt path to the *kibbutz.*

"*Azeh ma'shehu*", murmured Kati. "Isn't it something; to see such a sight? An Israeli *kibbutz* is just ahead, and a *Bedouin* shepherd is passing by within spitting distance, and nobody cares, feels threatened, or raises an alarm. *This* is exactly the way it should be, don't you think? It's our dream, to live in peace and friendship. We've always had a good relationship with the *bedu,* and they have begun to prosper in many ways as part of the Israeli model . . ."

I stopped her there. "Ah, but that's part of the problem . . . the Israeli model. Yes, the *Bedouin* have Israeli citizenship, and yes, the majority see themselves as a part of the State. But in the eyes of many on both sides, they are second-class citizens who often are forced to choose sides politically, societally, economically . . ."

"But if you consider the other Arab countries that they live in, Israel offers them much more in spite of the fact that it's a Jewish State and they are in the minority. Where else in the world would you consider *voluntarily,* happily, serving your state military? You do know that nearly three-quarters of the *Bedouin* males serve in the IDF even though they are exempt. This shows some kind of appreciation for your nation, I think".

Kati was right on these points. This issue was becoming clearer throughout the region, especially in Sinai in the year following the Egyptian Spring of 2011. As the newly elected government of the Moslem Brotherhood's Mohamed Morsi tried to cope with matters of rebuilding the country, the Sinai *Bedouin* saw an opportunity to assert their power in that region far-removed from the Cairo political machine. The *Bedouin,* long abused by the previous Mubarak regime, threw off the weakened shackles of the central government, taking the law into their own hands, wreaking havoc. Tourists were kidnapped for ransom money, pipelines were sabotaged, and a 'wild west' air of lawlessness prevailed.

It certainly didn't help matters that Islamic terror movements now found a weak link in the area's security and began to flood the Sinai with arms and personnel in their fight with both Israel and moderate Arab states. One of the most recent events had occurred just a few dozen kilometers from where we were. *Bedouin* shot up an Egyptian border outpost, killing several Egyptian soldiers, and attempted to cross into Israel on a terrorist mission. Although thwarted by the Israelis, and then mopped up by the Egyptians, it still served as a wake-up call to the new Egyptian government. Their own citizens were seeking some sort of autonomy at Egypt's expense. And in addition, threatened to de-stabilize the peace with Israel – something that Morsi and his government sorely needed in spite of Moslem Brotherhood rhetoric.

Meanwhile, the flock had moved far enough along to be nothing more than a dust devil in the distance, and we continued on into *Kibbutz Gvulot.* We hadn't called ahead, and we both felt a bit bad about that, but were certain that it was better to come unannounced and gently ask the questions, rather than allow an old man to get worked up in anticipation of a pending visit where ghosts might painfully intrude well in advance.

We parked the car in a dusty lot adjacent to the *kibbutz* manager's office and got out, glad to stretch our legs. Energy saving cars might get great kilometerage but they were notoriously short on luxury and interior space. Although the manager was out taking a tour of the fields, the community secretary filled us in on where to go to find Kurt Loewe. As was the case on the majority of *kibbutzim*, there was a small cadre of managerial staff. They were the paid personnel who professionally ran things. The *kibbutz* executive committee were members who were voted into serving on a fixed term; being relieved of their traditional duties in the communal environment in order to attend to the business of ensuring smooth operations. After serving, they would return to the usual tasks that they were involved in previously, and a newly council would take their place. I had spent some time on a *kibbutz* not far from *Gvulot*, and was familiar with the protocol.

Gvulot was a traditional *kibbutz*, firmly rooted in the soil. Although agricultural settlements were the backbone of the movement from its inception in the late 19th century, by the 1980s things had radically changed in Israel and many were shifting gears to survive in new economic times. Industry, tourism, spirituality were all carving out their niches; but *Gvulot* remained true to its origins. We walked down a stone-lined path out of the inner courtyard that served as the original heart of the settlement. This community was organized in the traditional 1930s 'stockade style' of architecture. Everything was laid out in concentric squares, with safety and security of prime concern. The central courtyard surrounded the original water tower. The first tier of buildings included dormitory-style sleeping quarters, the children's house, dining room/kitchen and offices. The next level of buildings included barns and storage facilities. All of this was then surrounded by a stockade-like enclosure that was fronted with a barbed-wire fence. From there, all that lay beyond as far as the eye could see were the fields of the *kibbutz*. This system provided the best security imaginable at that time. In the settlement core not much had changed in several decades, with the exception of a bomb shelter network that was constructed in the 1960s beneath the children's house. However, in the optimistic years during the mid 1990s, a ring of small bungalows, each called a *tserif*, was built for those 'elder statespeople' of the community – those who were rewarded for their loyalty and longevity by having small, private quarters. That was the area that we were directed to.

As we walked past the barn, the 'aroma' of the *kibbutz* made its presence known to Kati and me. "*Ya'allah! Azeh rayach!* What a smell!" Kati, the city girl all the way, wrinkled her nose as the steamy manure's odor wafted out into the compound. I laughed, and mentioned to her that this was where everyone got their start in the *kibbutz* world, including me. It was called the *refet*, the cowshed. From there, you could only work your way up.

"I can't for the life of me see you shoveling shit!" She was laughing so hard the tears were flowing.

"Clearly you've never dealt with academic deans and provosts!" I was laughing too.

We approached the ring of small huts, like little Cape Cod style houses, and looked for the one marked "*gimel*", G. It was a neat, whitewashed building no bigger than a double garage back in the states, with a concrete-tiled roof. Unassuming, plain and simple – it apparently was a reflection of the man who dwelt within. We walked up the crushed gravel path and rapped on the door.

A short, sun-weathered old man with a startling shock of thick, white hair opened the door as if expecting friends. The safety of the close-knit *kibbutz* community allowed for such simple, yet honest actions.

"Baruch ha-ba!" Welcome to my home". The strength of the voice, tinged with the faintest central European accented Hebrew, belied any physical frailties there might have been in this gentleman. But one glance made it clear that years of physical labor in the desert had hardened this individual, and no advance of years could deny the rock solid nature of the man. He greeted us as if we were the next door neighbors coming over for coffee.

"*B'vakasha.* Please, come around to the back '*marpeset*', patio, where we can sit and have coffee. The view is *hetzi*-fifty." He smiled. It was common to mix idioms and expressions in Hebrew and other languages, given the international flavor of Israel's citizens. In this case, his first take of us was to use English. In other words, the view was 50-50, so-so.

Kurt Loewe clearly made an impression on all who met him. As Kati charmed him, and he verbally flirted with her as well, the setting became more and more natural. There was a disarming ease about him that we noted. No small wonder that everyone at *Kibbutz Gvulot* felt that he was their universal grandfather. We almost forgot our purpose, so comfortable were we in the back yard overlooking the transition from the *Shephelah*, the gently rolling hills, into the Western *Negev* desert. I established a link with him, as I told him briefly of my work in the desert around *Beersheva*, first at the *tel*, then other sites just a few kliks away from there northeast of the modern city. This link got stronger as he mentioned that he had served as a photographer for several excavations under the auspices of *Ben Gurion* University of the *Negev* in *Beersheva*. These had included projects at *Gerar* and *Tel Muqanna*, literally a stone's throw from his backyard. He became quite animated, as he described the work, and I sat, enthralled.

But it was up to Kati to gently pull us away from that thread and segue into his earlier work as a photographer in Germany. When she broached the subject, he didn't seem all that surprised, but resigned to the fact that finally after all these decades he had to tell his story. A far off gaze, clouded in the haze of nearly 70 years, allowed him to gather his thoughts. He excused himself from the patio, and went inside for a few moments. We both sat there, silently, afraid that we had opened a long scabbed-over wound.

Kurt Loewe returned moments later, with a tattered leather architect's portfolio. It looked every bit as old as the German Jew. He had a faint smile on his face, as he opened the straps that secured it.

"You know, I haven't spoken of Germany since Israel's War of Independence so many years ago. It was as if, when I felt the State and the Jewish people would survive . . . as if I could then bury the past of uncertainty and death, relegating it to a distant memory. So no one on the *kibbutz* knows of my past, I'm the sort of mysterious *saba,* the unknown grandfather, who just sort of appeared one day with the founding fathers of the community. No one pressed me, as everyone who survived the 'Paperhanger from Bavaria' had their own private hells to deal with in their own fashion. But recently, as my generation neared death, everyone felt that the stories needed to be preserved, for when oral history dies without being recorded . . . well . . . it's like that tree that falls in the forest with no one around. *Fahr-shtay*?"

We both shook our heads 'yes' when he asked in Yiddish, "Do you understand?" He was referring to the philosopher George Berkeley's 1710 rumination. To our generation, it was of the essence to record the most horrific episode in the history of humankind when it came to mass murder. Not only would Holocaust deniers have their day, but the fraudulent historical revisionists would be able to present a 'valid' second opinion about the Final Solution. Loewe apparently felt that this opportunity that availed itself through our visit was his moment to tell part of his incredible story.

"But first, *kinder,* a *glazzela tay, b'vakasha*." His mixture of 'Heb-lish' and 'Yid-brew' Kati found endearing. So off she went with him to the kitchen for tea in tall glasses before the story began to be told.

As I waited, I texted my colleague and friend, Sobhy; to find out how things were in Sinai. I was a bit cryptic about Kati and me visiting Kurt Loewe, because you never knew when someone was 'eavesdropping' on texts or cell calls. In this youtube video age, everything seemed to be fair game in the cyber world. All we needed was for an intercept to allow black helicopters to sweep out of the sky and land in a small *kibbutz* back yard! OKOKOK, so I'm just kidding, a bit. Dark Nazi secrets were right up the alley of conspiracy-mongerers, or is it *conspiracy mongrels?* To me, they were one and the same. Anyway, I was more concerned with how his excavation/restoration project was going, since it was of vital interest to the archaeologist in me as well. Before he could respond, the two other 'conspirators' returned with the refreshments.

"You know, I just did what I had to do back then. No one thought of danger, or ramifications of our actions, we just did and hoped for the best. The brown-shirted thugs were everywhere and were determined to fill the coffers of the likes of Goering at the expense of all Germany. Of course, how did they say it . . . 'we're only following orders . . .' "A steely flare of anger flitted across his face, but only for a moment. He went on while opening the tattered valise.

"The idiots sent by Goering to the museum didn't know a damn thing about art, archaeology or artifacts. They only had to do the biding of that beast, that *mamzer*, that pig . . ." He caught himself. "Sorry, I sometimes get carried away." Kati smiled at him that melting trademark smile of hers, and it reassured the *kibbutznik*.

"Not to worry, *haver*, friend, although we never experienced it, your sentiments are shared. Please, go on," she gently prodded.

"*B'seder*, okay, I appreciate it. You have no idea – or maybe you actually do. Regardless, when I was assigned to complete photographing many of the collections that would either be stolen by the Nazis or placed in remote storage; it was at the same time that some plumbing renovations were to take place. You know how it is; old pipes either spring leaks and then damage collections, or, when seen, old pipes should be replaced as a preventative measure. I can't remember exactly which it was, but it was underway. As I began to photograph some of the papyrus scrolls that German excavations had uncovered earlier in the century in Egypt, and then had illegally taken back to the Fatherland, I noticed that many were written in what looked like poor Hebrew. I later learned that it was the derivative, Aramaic. Remember, at that time, although we were Jewish, we also thought that if we assimilated to a high degree, and acted as good German citizens, we could be included. Little did we know . . ."

He began to drift off again. And once, more, Kati steered him back with her kind demeanor.

"Sorry, sometimes I digress", he said, a bit sheepishly. He was embarrassed at what 'older age' could do to the mind.

"Yes, you certainly do!" I said laughingly. He looked at me a moment, then looked at Kati, and suddenly any ice build-up had broken as we all broke down in comic tears.

"So, as I was saying, I thought that, at that moment, I had a unique chance to save a bit of my heritage. I didn't know for how long, or if it would work, but I seized an opportunity. But first, I did my duty and continued to photograph the items as assigned to me. I then printed the black and whites, and wrote on the back the corresponding registration numbers, etc. and filed the pictures and the negatives in the appropriate cabinets in the offices. However, I also printed a set of pictures for myself."

He then pulled a worn manila folder from the portfolio case. Out tumbled several beautifully rendered photographs of the papyrus scrolls from the German museum collection. I looked at them, awestruck. The photographic artistry was unbelievable. Their clarity was phenomenal. I had seen images of this quality only once before. The photographs of the Dead Sea Scrolls that John Trevor had taken just before 1949 are still regarded today as the finest photographic collection of those incredible documents ever taken. That included the modern digital imagery of the early 21st century. I was stunned.

"These are incredible, priceless . . ." I suddenly was caught without words.

Loewe simply said, "Thank you". It was a testament to the talents that the much younger man possessed all those decades ago. He acknowledged his skill with grace, and appreciation.

Once again, the gentle Kati gently prodded. "*Nu*, so what happened then?"

Loewe suddenly was himself caught up in the emotional moment. The words flowed freely, rapidly. He described the final hours before he felt it was time to flee his dear homeland, and city of his birth. He had a canister that contained photo prints and blank paper. The guards were well aware of it, and its use, so thought nothing of it and it wasn't searched after the first couple of times he entered and left the museum. So he took the scrolls that he felt were the most pertinent to the task at hand, and gently rolled them in felt and inserted them in the tube – and proceeded to walk out the door with his paraphernalia as he had done dozens of times before.

For several days, a bathroom had been undergoing repairs in the synagogue. As he made preparations a couple of days earlier, he non-chalantly poked his head in the bath and innocently inquired of the plumbers what they were doing. He discovered that a couple of the waste pipes were so badly corroded that they couldn't be repaired, so the workmen were installing new pipes. However, as he found out, it was too labor intensive and costly to remove the pipes from floor to floor down to the basement. Too many walls would have to be broken and replastered. So what the plumbers were doing was capping off the old pipes and installing new ones adjacent in the same cavity space.

Loewe saw the opportunity. He took the tube with him to the restroom and pried the cap of that sealed, unused waste stack. He inserted the tube with the scrolls in the abandoned pipe, glued the cap on, and then proceeded to smear it with plaster dust – giving it the appearance of not having been touched for days. He then walked out of the synagogue and never looked back.

We all took a collective deep breath. I could see the light bulbs going off in rapid fire above all of our heads. I took the set of photos, flipped them over, and began to look at registration numbers. You don't need to know German to translate those. As I scanned them, one number suddenly jumped out at me. It was #12737. I flipped it over. It was the missing Aramaic parchment scroll from Elephantine Island that was the target of our intercontinental search. Loewe's crystal-clear photo on the other side was stunning.

We knew what needed to be done now. We had to get to the *Rykestrasse* Synagogue in Berlin and find a way to get into the wall of the restroom to see if the unused waste stack was still there. If so, would we find the canister still inside after so many decades.

Kurt Loewe was now also caught up in the moment. It was as if, given a renewed reason to go on, he regained his youth. A glimmer was now in his eye, and he projected an animated sense of purpose. He opened a drawer and grabbed a couple of sheets of writing paper. He thought a bit, and then started to sketch. Photographers aren't just equipment technicians who were masters with cameras and light. They also had to be skilled observers, and oftentimes artists in their own right. With a keen sense of mind's eye-hand coordination, he drew the layout of the building where the restroom was. He also sketched an isometric view of the bathroom as he remembered it, and which wall had the plumbing work done. That accomplished, he also noted where on the wall he reckoned the sealed pipe to be located.

By that time, it was very late in the day. Any thought of driving back to Tel Aviv was put on the back-burner. This was confirmed when the *kibbutznik* insisted that we use his spare bedroom and set out first light.

"Go with God", he said, as we prepared to leave the *kibbutz* the next morning. "Find the scrolls of our history, retrieve them, and stick it to the Nazis again after all these years. They're no longer here . . . but we clearly are. So who won in the long run . . . ."

He clasped our hands, then hugged and kissed us both with a fierce embrace, and we were off.

XXI

Tingis, 417 BCE

AFTER A FORTNIGHT of travel, the Vizier and his family saw the towers of the Tingis city walls rising majestically on the western horizon. The ordeal of the journey had come to an end, but now the ordeal of transition became a reality. While everyone else breathed a sigh of relief and their excitement was evident, underlying it all was an atmosphere of uncertainty. What was in store for them and how would their return actually be seen by those in power?

A messenger rode ahead for a few dozen stadia to present the caravan's letters of introduction to the guards. After all, it wouldn't do to simply approach the gated city with no advance notice in this age of unrest and instability. Brazen, head-on attacks were more commonplace than ever, and caution was essential. Trigger-happy archers on the parapets could unleash a deadly barrage – and apologies afterwards were useless to the dead. The group halted in a small copse of trees that had a small stream running through it. Relief from the growing day's heat came in the form of shade and cool liquid refreshment. In addition, they were still hidden from view and could rest comfortably while awaiting the return of the envoy.

Inside the port city, controlled chaos reigned. For around a century, after the last great political and military upheaval, Maroc had enjoyed relative peace and prosperity. The Carthaginians had disappeared once again into the desert on the other side of the High Atlas Mountains, and all seemed right with the world . . . maybe.

For several years, the stresses of running the city-state that encompassed the northern part of the land, from the Great Sea to the mountains, became more and difficult. A new threat, coming out of the desert, was not Carthaginian in nature now. It was the Berber.

Their ancient kingdom, which at one time had preferred uneasy co-existence with the northerners, now desired to make inroads in the lowlands and control more of the caravan routes. Their forays across the mountain passes threatened Fez and Volubilis. Lulled into a certain complacency for decades, the current Agella's advisors were caught unaware and unprepared for the turmoil caused by the marauders.

However, he knew his country's history from the copious archives. He read the annals that described the smooth running of the government several generations ago, and it was all due to the chief advisor's acumen politically and economically. He had also learned of the events leading up to the outbreak of war with the Carthaginian Empire based to the east. In the weeks of uncertainty prior to the eventual victory over them, there was a major evacuation of the civilian population. If the land was to fall to the enemy, the Agella wanted to make sure that no slaughter of innocents would take place. One of the documents alluded to the fact that the Agella, with great appreciation, had outfitted a caravan and sent it away to Misr, far on the other side of the continent. In it, as a measure of gratitude for services well done was his 'Judean' and his family. He knew that they had come from that faraway land, and that perhaps a modicum of safety, security and kinship might be found along the banks of the great river. He also knew from the archives that his predecessors had kept a distant eye on that family for generations, taking pride in the fact that they had continued their tradition of serving the nation that protected them in the most noble of ways – as advisors. Their success was quietly heralded across the Levantine coast.

With similar threats abounding, the Agella had sent for the descendant of the advisor, with the hope of righting his ship of the desert and ensuring the survival of his kingdom. Now the moment had arrived. Word had gotten to him that a long-awaited caravan from Misr was now situated only a couple of kilometers from the southeast gate. A messenger was making his way to the palace with a sealed scroll of introduction. He fervently hoped that it was the descendant of the Judean advisor to his grandfather. In addition, he prayed that the man was only half as capable as his ancestor. If this was the case, he rationalized, that the kingdom would still be spared and order returned to the land around Tingis. He paced quickly from door to window and back, awaiting the messenger.

* * *

About half an hour's walk away, another man paced to and fro, also awaiting news. The former vizier of Egypt watched his family with a mixture of pride and unsettled uncertainty. They had conducted themselves well, accepting their patriarch's decision without question. If the land of Egypt trusted his judgment for so many years, then so could they. The hardest part of the journey was the initial cruise down the Nile. They had still been in Misr, and everything was so familiar, still tugging at their sleeves as if reluctant to let them go. But once they left the Nile Valley and struck out into the Great Western Desert, it became an adventure of extraordinary proportion and hardship. At times they felt like insisting that they turn back, but carried on along the coast of the Great Sea, always marching toward the setting sun. It became easier, as the rhythm of the desert regularized the pace. They adjusted to the two-a-day segments of travel. The first, early in the morning, was designed to make good progress before the heat of midday. At that time, the escorts would try to find an oasis with shade and water, so the hottest time of day could be spent resting and rehydrating themselves. Then, as the sun fully entered the downward arc to the horizon, the group would gather itself up and continue on for a few more hours til sundown. At that point, they would camp again, unpack for the night, cook a meal and settle in until sunrise. The whole cycle would start afresh at dawn.

Major breaks in the routine came every so often, as the group approached a large community. They would still encamp away from the community, but send a couple of scouts to see if the town was approachable. If so, then the group would stay for a few days, re-provision themselves, and then get ready to move on. These respites were essential for the well-being of all and, as a result, the long trek was made bearable and, in the long run, a great success.

And now, as they sat in a small copse of cork trees, the sentinels that had been posted saw a sole traveler approach on foot. Once they were certain that none followed or were hiding, ready to pounce, they made themselves visible and escorted the man into the camp. Without guile, he greeted the Egyptians and wordlessly handed the elder statesman a wood-encased scroll. As he unrolled the document, he noted that, as a courtesy, the language that it was written in was Aramaic, the 'lingua franca' of the ancient eastern Mediterranean basin. He read it, and a warmth suffused his entire being. The family was being welcomed in to the community with a feast planned for that very evening. They were to bring the entire entourage in order for them to be accommodated in a setting luxurious enough for the noblest of nobility. The Egyptian profusely thanked the envoy, who then stepped back to wait and serve as an escort into Tingis.

XXII

Volubilis, 1348 CE

IBN BATTUTA WAS fully refreshed after a couple of days, and his audience with the Caliph, the title bestowed on Morocco's leader since the advent of Islam nearly seven centuries earlier, was scheduled for later that afternoon. As he wandered the streets of Volubilis, the orchestrated chaos that was the hallmark of the public areas of any Arabic city, was apparent. Vendors shouted good-naturedly at prospective clients, who in turn happily shouted back. The narrow streets rang with the bellowed chant, 'Balak! Balak!' – a not-so-subtle warning for pedestrians to get out of the way of donkeys laden with all sorts of good. The chronicler felt right at home, even though the Arabic accent that he heard was distinctive from the more familiar guttural variation of the Arabian Peninsula and points farther east that he had explored for several years Yet there were slight differences in this city as well. For all intents and purposes, it was part of an Islamic fiefdom, under Sharia, or Islamic, Law. The Caliph ruled with a firm, yet unbiased, hand and all of his subjects seemed to be comfortable with the ways that things were in every way. But underlying it all were little quirks in the society that he simply couldn't put a finger on. And it nagged him a wee bit.

As he passed food stalls and other merchants associated with the culinary art, he noted that the strict dietary laws of Islam were enforced as to what could or could not be sold to eat. These laws, referred to as Halal, were universal throughout North Africa and the Mideast, wherever Arab states prevailed.

However, there were several strange mutations to this law found in public dining halls and inns where food was served. When he entered these establishments, he noted that they were very surreptitiously divided in two dining areas. As he sat in one, he noted that no one had ordered any meat dishes; while in the other there was no cheese or dairy product served on the table alongside the lamb or chicken. He also noted a small sign requesting guests not to move from one side to the other with their food once they were served. He observed that all the occupants of the dining establishments had absolutely no problem with this as well. This perplexed him a bit, and he racked his brain to figure out an explanation, but could find none.

Throughout the community, he also noted that there seemed to be a greater respect for women, treating them more as equals in the town than in any other Arab city outside of this district. For centuries, both the Koran and Hadith of Mohammed has stressed certain levels of equality between men and women, but an underlying current of sexism still created a formidable barrier. Here, it seemed that many of these barriers were being broken down.

As for the cultural and spiritual nature of Walili, it appeared that Islam as both religion and way of life was slightly expanded in some ways. Many of the public and private buildings had small, decorative boxes affixed to doorposts – some seemed to be hundreds of years old. They were abraded, burnished with an ancient patina that gave a polished, smoothed look. Any writing or indication of what they were had long since vanished. A final idiosyncrasy that he saw came from the masjid, or religious building, adjacent to the inn, the riad, that he stayed at. One morning, after prayers, he idly browsed some of the written material on a table near the door. He noted a calendar of events and upcoming holidays. Most of the entries were typical of an Islamic religious institution, with study sessions, times of sunrise and sunset. These were essential for the Islamic day began at sundown and ended at sunset about twenty-four hours later. Yet, in Islam, all of the holidays were human-related and none dealt with life-cycle events. But here, for instance, there was reference to an upcoming festival oriented toward the fall harvest, alluding to impermanent huts built in the fields for the farmers to utilize in order to get in the crop before it spoiled. Ibn Battuta was more and more fascinated with his part of his homeland that he returned to after so many years.

As he strolled through the streets, he also noted that he felt more cosmopolitan in many ways than in the usual Arab city. An atmosphere of great tolerance prevailed, and he was truly enamored with this openness. It felt liberating, almost joyous in approach. Then it hit him, and his wonderment increased. The city felt like an environment that he had read about in some ancient journals – a city whose feel was similar to those written about just prior to the Arab conquest of the region, when ethnicities and religions were all treated with a greater dignity and respect. It was a time before the Caliphate, when either Christian or Jewish rulers wore the mantle of authority.

At times, it almost seemed as if the current caliph here based on Walili was more Jewish than Moslem. 'Could that be?' he mused as he continued his daily constitutional.

XXIII

Berlin . . . the present

IT TOOK A few days of hasty preparation, but finally Kati and I were ready to head back to Berlin and see if we could turn back the clock on 'plumbing repairs' in the old synagogue. She got permission from the Department of Antiquities and Museums to follow up this lead. In addition, they actually paid for her ticket and time, since the Israel Museum had a stake in this matter. For several years, there had been a good working relationship with the Cairo Museum, especially regarding repatriation of Sinai antiquities, and an inquiry to Cairo made it clear that, should missing documents be recovered, an arrangement might be made for a transfer of one or two scrolls to the Jerusalem museum's permanent collection. Of course it didn't hurt that Sobhy, now in extremely good graces in both organizations, helped to pave the way.

We made travel arrangements for two days hence, and began to plan our visit. I had emailed Volkmar to give him the courtesy of advance notice, and he had responded warmly. In fact, he said that a car and driver would meet us at Tegel and take us to a hotel nearby that the museum would pay for, extending the hospitality one step further. It really was the VIP treatment.

The day came, and with it the expectation that many questions could finally be resolved regarding the missing scrolls. Travel was uneventful, in fact, really boring. We were mentally and, to an extent, physically exhausted from all the recent activity. But we were both too wired, beyond the stage, to readily snooze on the four hour flight. So I started talking. We both had been part of excavations in the *Negev* centered around *Beersheva*, so I reminisced a bit about the 'good old days' of the *Tel Sheva* project directed by Yohanon Aharoni in the 70s. Those were my earliest field archaeology experiences, and were mixed with an incredible amount of frivolous fun as the first couple of seasons, as a student, I had no real responsibility. I fondly recalled adventures that were on the edge, verging on outrageous – but that's what youth is for I suppose.

There were four of us who were taken under the wing of Fred Annison, professor of languages, geography and God-forbid, an excellent archaeologist in his own right. But you could *never* call him that to his face! It would be, in his mind, the ultimate insult. He would always say, "Some of my best friends are archaeologists, but I'd never let my daughter marry one!" Fortunately, he had a son, so the potentiality never arose. We four were called *Ahim shel Mohamed,* 'the brothers of Mohamed'. No, it didn't refer to the Prophet, but rather the administrative camp foreman of the expedition, *Mohamed abu Reqaiq.* He and his family took us in and extended their hospitality to us. As I have said before, there is absolutely nothing like *Bedouin* hospitality. As we learned their ways, we were made honorary members of the *Abu Reqaiq* clan. We even took five of the hard hats used in deep trenches and etched on them in Hebrew the phrase; gave one to Mo, as we sometimes called him, and had our picture taken together.

This gang of four supplied the anecdotes for several years. One fellow, Big Ira, was as imposing as a Redwood, well over 6 and a half feet tall, weighing in at 300 or so pounds – nobody actually asked him his weight. He really didn't care too much about studying archaeology, he was just there for the experience. So whenever rocks, or I guess, boulders, needed to be moved, there was Ira. Yet for all his imposing presence, he was a kind and gentle soul. The expedition director, Yohanon Aharoni, would walk around the site, and have his small *pastish,* or handpick, hanging from a belt loop, ready to use at a moment's notice. One day Ira asked to have his photo taken with Aharoni. As we got out the camera, he tied a rope around his waist, and slung a full-sized pick through it, put his arm around the director, and had the photo taken. The most hilarious thing was that, given their two sizes, the full pick looked to be just as proportional on Ira's belt as the small handpick did with Aharoni!

And then there was Hesh. A transplanted American, he had that kind of personality that had girls flocking to him even without trying. It was a curse rather than a blessing, and he tried to deal with it as best as he could. I recalled one particular young lady who became enamored with him, yet he did absolutely nothing to lead her on. She took the four of us under her wing (so to speak) and every night she would come into our cabin, kiss us very chastely goodnight, and blow out the candle on the table in the middle of the room as she left. I need to explain this. Because there was only one overhead light that filled every corner very brightly, we opted to use a candle in the evening because the ceiling light would disrupt people's sleep. So the candle would be blown out by the last to turn in. Until this particular young lady, named Leora. She began the habit, and none of us objected because it was innocent. Until one evening. She came in as usual, gave us a peck on the cheek as usual, but then lingered at Hesh's cot. She then left.

Hesh suddenly sat up and stated with anguish, "What have I done?" We all groused a bit because he had taken us out of a pre-sleep calm, and asked what had he done. He told us that he told Leora to come back in half an hour when we were all supposed to be asleep. Apparently the kiss was more than a kiss. He bemoaned the fact and said that he needed a way out. The fourth member of our group was a fellow we called Mississippi John. A charming southerner, he physically was as far-removed from the swarthy Hesh as one could imagine, with thinning blond hair and a somewhat Pillsbury dough-boyish figure. We had all known that Leora had it in for Hesh, and had protected him up til now. So Mississippi said the he and Hesh should exchange beds, and that should take care of the problem for good.

About 40 minutes later, the screen door squealed and protested a bit as it was gently opened. A figure came in and got under the cover of Hesh's bed. Ira was chewing on his pillow to keep from laughing out loud, I stuffed a corner of my sheet in my mouth. We all waited for what seemed like an eternity. Finally, after a couple of excruciatingly long minutes, a high-pitched scream split the air as a rush of wind accompanied a form that literally flew out the door. The laughter erupted. When we asked John what happened, and why it took so long for Leora to discover the prank, he simply said, "A southern gentleman nevuh tails!" And to this day, he never has.

As I finished the story, I felt a slight weight on my shoulder, and heard a gentle snuffle. Kati was out like a light. I closed my eyes and smiled the rest of the way to Berlin.

* * *

As promised, a car and small boutique hotel awaited us after landing. Within the hour we were able to scrub 'airplane air' away and make our way to Museum Island. The driver was kind enough to wait for us, and I left him a good tip. Apparently he had called Volkmar while we freshened up and he was waiting, armed with a broad smile, at the entrance of the museum.

"*Willkommen mein dame und herr*!" He embraced me with a peck on each cheek, and vigorously pumped Kati's hand. He seemed very glad to see us. He gave us each academic visitor badges on lanyards after we sat for a moment to have digital ID photos taken and embossed. We then headed up to his suite of offices. His receptionist remembered me and greeted me with warm professionalism as we entered the inner office.

Of course, there was an urn of thick, rich coffee and pastry waiting on the 17th century sideboard. Once again, I was amazed with the casual use of priceless antique furniture. To Kati, it was all 'modern history' so to speak, and her neutral look said that it didn't affect her at all. After a couple of minutes of background chatter, in essence presenting Kati's *bona fides* as an unofficial, 'official' representative of the Israel Museum and the Israeli government, I began to outline the research and subsequent results surrounding the missing Egyptian documents. In addition, I presented to Volkmar the letter from the Egyptian Supreme Council of Antiquities, co-signed by Sobhy, that stated that I was authorized to accept and transmit any and all correspondence that would help to clarify the situation. Yes, it was a bit unusual, but Sobhy's high rank afforded him some *protkesia* in this matter. Plus, it had saved the struggling Egyptian government considerable money since they didn't have to pay to send him to Berlin again.

Kati, Sobhy and I decided to play it close to the vest, and not tell too much until we had a chance to confirm Kurt Loewe's strange tale. Only after we had further investigated at the synagogue would Volkmar and the German government be brought up to speed. If any documents were recovered, we needed to ascertain if in fact the full details should be given to the Germans; after all, generations ago they *had* archaeologically robbed Egypt blind and then ravaged Europe mercilessly in the 1930s and 40s as a result of personal greed and ethnic cleansing. So, in spite of the warmth of the meeting, we were circumspect.

As we told the bare bones of the narrative, leaving out many crucial details of the *kibbutznik's* recollection, a dark look fleetingly crossed the museologist's face. It lasted just a second, but I caught it clearly. I was uneasy, it seemed that underneath it all was a sense of mistrust and skepticism. I wasn't quite sure what to make of it, so kept my game face as Kati and I made apologies and feigned a bit of weariness and expressed a desire to return to the hotel to rest a bit. She then turned on the thousand watt smile and charmed the socks off Volkmar, promising to return in a couple of days after we explored the options available to us.

The 'look' gone, Volkmar was once again the gracious, amiable host. As we left, this time Kati got the dual peck on the cheeks. She accepted graciously and, if I saw correctly, actually batted an eyelash! She wasn't laying it on too thick, but flirted just a touch in order to disarm the German, who seemed to fall for it 110%. Of course, as I had known for quite some time, Kati had that effect on men. Perhaps he would let his guard down just a little as well.

As we left the museum, I waved off the driver who was still waiting and took Kati's elbow, steering her toward one of the several sidewalk cafes on the island. We took a table that was out of earshot from any other diners and ordered a couple of coffees.

"So, what were your initial thoughts?" I asked as I sipped. I kept glancing around, nervously.

"And why are you glancing around nervously?" she first asked. Nothing got past this extraordinary woman. "Don't answer that, I think that I know. My first impression of Volkmar, once past the charming and friendly part, is that he's very, ummm, *German*, if you know what I mean. Something just doesn't seem right in Denmark, as the bard once said."

"So you got it too?" I felt much better, paranoia wasn't one of my usual qualities; but these were unusual times. "I was afraid that I was reading things into the situation, but apparently not. You saw the break in his mask for just a second as well."

"I think that we need to be on our toes, and keep a keen eye." She thought a minute and snapped her fingers. "Now I understand something that had been tugging at me in a distant corner, but I had sort of ignored."

"Such as . . . ?" I sipped again.

"Why was he so eager to supply a car and driver, why would the museum, as an arm of the German government, put out the expense of accommodation, for someone who had just been met recently, and, in a roundabout way, might threaten the *de facto* ownership of some potentially quite valuable antiquities – all the while exposing another aspect of Nazi Germany's sordid past?"

I sat back, everything that I suspected seemed to now be confirmed. We'd have to be really cautious, take extraordinary measures, and protect ourselves in ways that would be innovative in order to achieve our goals.

"Well now, the game's afoot" I said as we got up to leave. We needed to channel Sherlock in more ways than one now.

* * *

We walked back to the hotel, just a few minutes away. We went right to the room and did a quick check. I felt sort of silly for all the cloak and dagger stuff, but a couple of simple precautions sure as hell beat 'the dagger' part of the saying. Nothing seemed amiss so we planned the rest of the day. We'd take a brief stroll around, do a bit of the sightseeing routine, and see if we saw anything out of the ordinary.

As we left both of us scanned the street. We saw no one that looked really suspicious, but again, wouldn't that be the sign of a good surveillance? Forget the black SUVs with tinted windows, the dark suits with sunglasses, even on a cloud-filled day. Forget the men lounging in front of store-fronts or sitting on park benches reading newspaper and occasionally talking into their sleeves. We were such *kleiner fisch* as the Germans would say, "small fry". As we strolled along the embankment we ambled toward the *Petersburger Strasse* which inexplicably turned into *Danziger Strasse* and continued northwest through a pleasant neighborhood. After a mile or so, we passed the massive new sports complex and turned left on *Prenslauer Allees.* I suggested that we stop for a coffee and sat outdoors to people watch at a small place called the CK Café. We were now only a couple of blocks from *Rykestrasse* and our ultimate destination. For all intents and purposes, we were only a couple of tourists with lots of time on our hands.

After the refreshment, we made a leisurely circuit of the area, approaching our destination from the north, the opposite side of where we had come from. We proceeded up *Wortherstrasse,* to *Kollwitzstrasse,* and then south again on *Knaackstrasse.* At the Pasternak Restaurant we turned once more and suddenly, on our left, was the complex.

The *Rykestrasse* Synagogue had been restored to all its pre-war grandeur. The building had suffered severe damage in the Second World War in a series of massive bomb blasts. In the forty years that followed, the war ruins were left exposed to the harmful effects of the weather and exigency measures to safeguard the structure were only undertaken for the first time in the 1980s. But the preservation was haphazard and the building continued to deteriorate, although at a slower speed. It was only during the first years of the new millennium did the world's Jewish community, in concert with the German government, begin to seriously make plans for the rehabilitation of such a wonderful house of worship.

After a couple of years of work, the *Rykstrasse* Synagogue was finally rededicated in August of 2007. The re-sanctified *shul* also underwent a spiritual change of sorts as well. The new congregation was designed to be a more right of center, Orthodox synagogue; complete with a *mehitza,* a partition for separate seating. Several rabbis from around the world brought *Torah* scrolls that had been rescued from communities during the war. The ceremony of rededication, full of emotion, was attended by political leaders from Central Europe and Israel as well as survivors of the Final Solution. "It is now the most beautiful synagogue in Germany," according to the community's cultural director.

It was now up to us to see if Herr Loewe's memory was as sharp as he made it out to be.

We saw a Romaneque style building adjacent to the street, built in a row-technique abutting the other structures. This was the school for the Jewish community. We walked through the gated entry into a large courtyard removed from the noise of the street and faced the incredible Gothic-style façade, with an extraordinary rose window. Kati let out a small gasp, the beauty was overwhelming. We stood in silence for a few moments then entered after reading the dedicatory plaque next to the doorway. The elegantly restored prayer hall was stunning. The potential of a cavern-like central aisle, soaring into the heavens, dwarfing congregants, leaving them with a sense of remoteness, was removed by the dropped, flat, wooden beamed ceiling. This lent an air of intimacy that otherwise would have been lost. The upper women's gallery that rose above the side aisles was gracefully framed by plastered arched that rose above the supporting columns of the first floor.

Beneath the apse, the *bamah,* or prayer platform, rose nearly a storey above the main floor. Its grandeur was designed to reflect the glory of God, and accomplished it in a monumental, yet somewhat subdued, fashion. It was painted a deep cobalt blue, with yellow-gold stars designed to represent the heavens. The

Ark of the Law, the *Aron Kodesh*, was flanked by two bronze *menorot*, candelabras, affixed high on the wall on either side of the Eternal Flame, the *Ner Tamid*, said to be the 'eternal spark of the creation of the world.'

After taking it all in, we sat in a small alcove for a moment to get our bearings.

"According to Kurt, the restroom that was in the process of being remodeled was located on the second floor", I said. "That seems to rule out the sanctuary since the only thing up there that I see is the gallery. There are only facilities on the main floor just off the vestibule entry. The only restrooms that may be upstairs we should find in the school building that we walked through."

Kati thought for a moment and agreed. We wandered around the sanctuary for a few more minutes, giving the impression to anyone who might see us that we were tourists. Then after picking up a brochure and leaving a few DM in the *pushke*, the charity box, we headed out into the courtyard and back to the school building. We were still surprised at the emptiness, the silence of the place. Save for the sole security guard at the street level entry, we didn't encounter another person.

We went upstairs and entered the narrow hall, flanked by classrooms. I closed my eyes, and suddenly I 'heard' the laughter and running feet of kids as they scurried into their Sunday school classes. For the briefest of moments I sensed the vibrancy of the *Rykstrasse* Jewish community prior to the catastrophe of the Final Solution. And instantaneously it was gone. I felt Kati's hand on my arm, gripping me tightly.

"You were swaying a bit with your eyes closed, I thought you were going to faint or something" she said.

"Perhaps it was too much coffee and not enough water," I smiled, and we went on.

It was going to be really hard to ascertain anything, given the length of time that had passed, and the more recent renovation work. I wasn't at all sure that we were going to find even the slightest indication of what Loewe had described. Down the hall were a set of restroom facilities. We explored both, since there was no one around to object to opposite-sex entries. The gleaming white subway-tiled facilities indicated nothing to us. Gentle tapping on the walls simply got us nowhere. I thought that unless we had x-ray vision or infrared scanners we were up a creek. We went back downstairs and sat a moment in the lobby. I had an idea.

We crossed to the administrative office of the school, and entered the reception. Inside, there was a bit of life. Two school administrators were working as they prepared for the upcoming school year. "Follow my lead" I told Kati in a whisper.

"Guten tag . . . spreksen zie Englisch, bitte?" I asked. The younger of the two looked up, smiled and said, "Of course, *ein bissel*, a little. I proceeded to explain

that we were tourists, and, with professions directly related to the world of architecture, we were fascinated by the restoration process involved in the synagogue. (I made no mention of Judaism, Israel, or the Final Solution). I further explained, ad-libbing freely, that traffic flow and building facilities were of interest to us. Kati nodded vigorously, and chimed in that we all could learn a great deal about how older structures accommodated the needs of their clientele. May we spoke a bit too rapidly, but a glazed-over look told us that the school staffer appeared lost. I quickly picked up the thread.

"One of the major issues of public buildings is time/facility management." (I was now really 'winging' it) We saw the restrooms for congregants in the sanctuary, but they were all at the rear far from the pulpit area (No sense in tipping our knowledge of Jewish architectural terms) Are there any other facilities in the main building that we didn't see?"

A look of comprehension passed across his face, and he smiled. Now he understood what we meant, and supplied us with an answer. There *was* another, private restroom that was hidden behind the apse, behind a secret paneled door. Inside, up a small flight of stairs, was a washroom facility that could be used by the rabbi, cantor and choir 'on the sly' should the need arise during services. Not that it was a secret actually, but rather a convenience that wouldn't disrupt the service.

I glanced at Kati, and suddenly something just felt right. It would be the perfect location since it was already somewhat off the radar even when the *Rykestrasse* Synagogue was in full swing. It might not have even been included in the original plans. We both profusely thanked the administrator and went back to the outer lobby . . . and discovered another problem.

As I looked out the window toward the street, I saw something, or rather someone, that caused me to do a double-take.

"Look out the window at the street, and tell me what *you* see." Kati glanced at me with a quizzical look, but then eyed the street scene. Her eyes widened perceptibly, and she got up to go to the window.

I grabbed her wrist. "Don't do that!" I said perhaps a bit too sharply, and pulled her back to the bench.

"It looks like the driver who met us at the airport!" she exclaimed. "That's quite a coincidence!" From the dark recesses in the hall, a few feet back from the window, no one could possibly see us. But it seemed suddenly as if the wild fantasy I had a few hours earlier about Volkmar's 'gracious' behavior was coming to fruition. "We have been followed, it seems. But to what end? If he had suspicions about where the documents might be, why not go through proper channels governmentally? Or does he have something more sinister in mind?"

I certainly had no idea, having completely trusted the man from the beginning. But if he was trying to recover missing scrolls for his own gain, then

Sobhy and I had been used from the outset, and now, with Kati, unwittingly did the dirty work for him.

I motioned for her to wait, and quickly returned to the office. "One last question, if I may. We have certain fire codes in our country, and wondered about the number of exits for a complex this size". After securing my answer, I returned to Kati.

"Follow me," I said. "We're going through a secondary door into the courtyard and then into the synagogue. That way our watcher won't see us exit the school and return to the sanctuary. In addition, after we're done, there is a small fire exit only at the rear of the synagogue that opens to a series of small courtyards and alleys that make their way to *Knaackstrasse.* We can leave however things end up without being seen by our driver buddy."

We returned to the synagogue. It was still empty. So we made our way up to the *Bamah* and around the seats reserved for congregation president, rabbi and cantor. Sure enough, behind the wainscoted panel was a very narrow staircase. Another quick look into the sanctuary, and we ascended the narrow flight to a very small landing in what seemed to be immediately behind the *Torah* Shrine. A small door, no higher than five feet or so, opened into a tiny half-bath. Our spirits lifted, it seemed that this was a place that time had forgotten. The fixtures looked exactly how one would imagine seventy year old plumbing to look, down to the ceramic inserts in the handles that were labeled *Heis* and *Kalte,* 'hot' and 'cold'. In addition, a badly worn rubber stopper on a chain was wrapped around one of the posts.

We looked at each other with anticipatory grins on our faces. A very small, wire-mesh window let in a miniscule amount of light. I found the switch and a single bare bulb lit the speckled mirror above the pedestal sink. Old, chipped, faded green ceramic tile faced the wall behind the sink and toilet; the other three were painted plaster. At first glance the ceramic wall looked whole. I decided to run my hand over it, to see if I felt any anomalies or unevenness in it. Unfortunately it felt perfectly straight, as if tiled at one time with no repair work done. I was beginning to feel that Kurt Loewe's memory wasn't as sharp as he may have thought or, with stranger things occurring all around us, he lied to us.

I began to turn to Kati and tell her that it was a bust, when she started to run her hand along the wall as well. "You're feeling for the wrong things here," she whispered. Her hands were tracing the grout lines, not the entire surface of the wall. Brilliant.

"Here!" she exclaimed. "Run your finger across these lines. See how the texture and the depth are inconsistent!" She was right. The pattern that we followed surrounded a set of four by four tiles. Each tile was ten centimeters square, so the area measured off the equivalent of about sixteen square inches – just the right size for fixing a leak!

I took out a pen and 'worried it' along one of the seams. The old grout was flakey and readily turned to powder with just a bit of pressure. It was relatively easy to remove. In addition, the adhesive quality of the mastic used to secure the tiles themselves was less than perfect. I soon discovered why. Within a few minutes the replacement set of tiles were out. There wasn't a solid surface behind them, but a couple of lath strips. After all, it was a somewhat hasty patch job I assumed. The meager light from the single bulb didn't get very far into the cavity, so we had to feel with our hands. I immediately felt two pipes, and ran my fingers up and down them. They were solid, and joined the lav faucet fixture. I muttered something that any censor would have a field day with and withdrew my hand.

My frustration showed, I was afraid that we had come this far, discovered that Kurt Loewe's memory had been correct; but that we had been too late. It seemed that at some point in time the photo tube that he had said that he placed had been removed. I leaned against the opposite wall and slowly slid down it to the floor.

But Kati wasn't about to give up. She stuck her slender arm into the hole that we made, and inserted it all the way to her elbow.

"It stands to reason that the supply line pipes would be centered in the hole and that . . ." she exhaled loudly and wiggled her arm a bit more. ". . . that the sealed off waste stack would be off . . . to . . . the . . . side!" she said triumphantly. I could see in arm muscles that she was rotating her hand in a limited fashion. She withdrew her arm and triumphantly held up a threaded black cast-iron cap. She set it on the floor and stuck her hand and arm back into the hole. "Aha! Help me out here! I've got something! Get ready to grab and pull, because I'm slowly inching a piece up with only two fingers. That's all the room I have here!"

Slowly, slowly, a thin, dusty cardboard tube peeked up and out the hole. I firmly grasped it and gently worked it out of the wall. The old *kibbutznik's* memory was intact! As was the tube that he had inserted so many decades ago! It came free and we both sat back, cradling it. We dusted off our arms, covered in plaster and grout dust.

"You open it."

"No, *you* open it!"

"What if it's empty?"

She grabbed the cylinder and started to twist the cap. After an initial sharp twist, it turned smoothly, freely. A very dry layer of plumber's putty had given way. We both held our breaths as it came free. A slightly stale odor wafted up at us. Inside we saw a tightly rolled coil black felt, exactly like the type used as backdrop material for photo shoots even today.

As she pulled the felt roll out of the tube, a faint shower of dust fell to the floor. Only about a foot and a half high, the felt was lined with white linen. We began to unroll it, and it turned out to be two feet long. I grabbed the wall tiles and placed one on each corner, to anchor it. We then gently peeled back the linen backing. Looking back at us suddenly were four parchment documents. Yellowed, cracked but rather flexible, their Aramaic writing still jumped off the documents in a bold and clear fashion. We were stunned.

* * *

We weren't quite sure what to do. After all, assumed protocol would be to return the documents to the *Neues* Museum and then have Sobhy as representative of the Egyptian government return to negotiate. On the other hand, didn't Aramaic parchments have a place in Jewish history, and therefore in the Israel Museum. On the third hand, why were there so many indicators that pointed to illicit, or at least suspicious, activity on the part of Herr Volkmar. My head was reeling. The first thing that we needed to do was find a way out of the complex and the watchful eyes of our previous 'driver', who was waiting patiently to tail us on *Rykestrasse*.

As we aware from the earlier conversations with the synagogue administrative staff, there were exit doors discretely positioned around the buildings. I slid the tube into the small rucksack that Kati used as a carryall/purse, and it barely showed outside the top flap. We then hurried down the stairs and out into the main sanctuary. As the sun faded, the hall was cast in a myriad of shadows. We left, staying in dark recesses of the courtyard, and then took one of the small exits. They weren't alarmed, because they were self-locking to the outside. After all, that's what emergency exits do. We found ourselves around the corner from the main façade, on *Knaackstrasse*. I took a small gamble, indicating that Kati should stay there a moment, and slowly walked to the intersection. There, a couple of hundred meters away, the driver sent by Volkmar paced impatiently on the sidewalk side of his vehicle. In the space of one minute, I saw him glance irritably at his watch. He clearly wasn't having a good day.

I returned to my companion, and we hailed a cab back to our hotel. We needed to check out, find other accommodations and leave Berlin as soon as possible.

* * *

Back at the *Neues* Museum, Volkmar paced his elegant office, anxious to hear something from his security agent-turned-driver. He needed to know if the American and Israeli had found out anything about the missing scrolls. Ever since he had discovered that they might be located, he worked the phones and email with his many contacts in the illicit antiquities business. Since these items had fallen off the grid decades ago, they weren't on anyone's modern radar, until now. And at best, they were 'an interesting tidbit' as Americans would say; but nothing earth-shattering. Whether they weren't re-discovered, or he grabbed them for himself if they were, their public profile wouldn't make a splash. However, if they *were* found by the pair, the publicity would be enormous and, for Volkmar, an opportunity of a lifetime would be lost.

For a couple of years now, he had felt that his role at the museum was becoming the 'deadest' of dead-ends. The Executive Director was his age, and therefore would retire at the same time as he did. There was no chance of moving up. Rising costs and a cost of living increase that simply didn't cover it in the current European economy meant that he needed to find an alternate source of income. He had discovered that the broad market for illegal antiquities was becoming more far flung; as both the *uber-rich* and those looking for a bit of added security found this avenue to their liking. And, to a museum associate director who also felt that he needed more income, it was a shot-gun marriage made in heaven.

The end result was that a few, not-so-rare items in dusty storeroom bins made their way on occasion into the netherworld of private collectors. Volkmar had made a small, but tidy sum in dealing with these folks who took great pleasure in owning things. At times, he simply couldn't understand them. After all, they would illegally obtain objects d'art but couldn't display them in their homes. One of them had invited him to their home on the outskirts of Berlin. After a sumptuous dinner, the 'client' escorted him into a basement beneath the house. It turned out that the opulent building was constructed in the post-war era over an old bunker. The industrialist who built the house incorporated it into his cellar, behind a swinging bookshelf panel wall. Humidity and temperature controlled, it was a state-of-the-art gallery that would make any museum staff drool over. In it were scores of antiquities from Europe and the MidEast.

Over snifters of 25 year old brandy, the collector said that his passion for art collection took a major turn during the first Bush Gulf War of 1991. Thousands of antiquities were smuggled out of Iraq in the chaos of the summer of that year; and this man took advantage of the situation. There were no fewer than fifteen cuneiform clay tablets in hermetically sealed cases, scores of ceramic vessels on display stands, and even a couple of stone-carved panels that had originally lined the walls of Sennacherib's Palace in Nineveh.

At first, Volkmar was appalled. What good were these items displayed in a private museum. He asked the man that exact question. His reply was that he simply enjoyed owning them; coming down from time to time with a good glass of wine sitting in his leather chair, and eyeing the pieces. He also said that he even loved *smelling* the world of the past.

Then the museum officer's business side kicked into full swing. He knew that he had a client now that could ensure his financial future at the expense of a few items that never saw the light of day in his museum anyway. But now, sitting in his office on Museum Island, he could feel it all draining away if the foreigners were successful.

There was a knock at the door.

"*Geben sie bitte.* Enter".

The hulking security-guard-turned-driver came into the office with a contrite look on his face. Volkmar knew instantly that something was wrong. The man related how he spent a good deal of the day, following and watching the archaeologist and Israeli museum representative as they made their way through the city. At one point, he lost them in the crowds on the street. He then used his initiative and went to the *Rykestrasse* Synagogue, based on everything that Volkmar had told him earlier. He was more than excited to try to capture possible 'museum thieves' as Vokmar had put it. The man then sat outside the temple for a couple of hours, but saw no one who matched the description. After a while, he entered the school building that fronted the street, and politely enquired as to whether two of his 'friends' that he was supposed to meet here had arrived. Apparently, one of the staff said that a couple that vaguely matched the description had been here earlier, but they assumed that they had left for the building was now closed to the public.

A look of exasperation crossed Volkmar's face as the guard continued his story. From the synagogue, he hurriedly made his way back to the hotel that they had booked for the two. He found out that they had checked out a few hours earlier. That was when he returned to the museum. Conrad dismissed him with a wave of the hand and sat back. *What to do now?* He mused. At least he wasn't complicit in any crimes *this time.*

* * *

As we took a cab to the vicinity of Berlin-Tegel Airport, Kati got on the phone and made a couple of calls. She got in touch with the Israel Museum director and very briefly and somewhat cryptically explained the bare bones of what had transpired in Berlin. He in turn made a couple of phone calls of his own to other governmental offices and the corporate headquarters of *El Al* Israel Airlines. When she told me, I reminded her of something.

"You know what *El Al* really stands for don't you?" I took a stab at lightening the mood a bit. "*Every Landing Always Late*".

She laughed and took my hand. By that time, we found ourselves in front of the Dorint Hotel Berlin-Tegel on *Gotthardstrasse.* Only five minutes from the terminal, with a shuttle service, we were ideally situated. I paid the equivalent of $140 in cash just in case anyone was really looking for us hard. We'd only be there for a few short overnight hours til our flight in mid-morning.

Once settled in, I went out and made a call to the *Neues* Museum. Boy was I nervous, and I hoped that it didn't sound that way in my voice. I used a public phone (yes, there are still a few coin-operated machines in Berlin) a couple of blocks from the hotel. As I was transferred to Volkmar's office, I started sweating.

It's a good thing that the phone 'egg' didn't have a long cord, as I would have been pacing back and forth relentlessly. Suddenly, I breathed a sigh of relief. I was being routed to voice mail. It made it very easy. I left a hurried message apologizing in advance. We had discovered nothing of interest at the synagogue. But in the meantime, Kati had gotten a phone call from her boss in the Israel Museum about a mini-crisis regarding one of the collection installations that she had been overseeing. She needed to get back as soon as possible so we had booked a flight later that evening. I again apologized profusely, hope that he had better luck in ascertaining what happened to the missing scrolls, and hoped to see him again in the near future. I hung up and leaned heavily for a couple of moments on the ledge beneath the phone. At least that was over and done with, and, hopefully, in a convincing manner. At least convincing enough for a few hours.

When I returned to the room, I took a series of photos of the four documents with my cell phone, and uploaded them to both the director of the Israel Museum and my Egyptian colleague, Sobhy. We were formulating a plan as to how to proceed with the artifacts that would sit well with both the Egyptian Supreme Council of Antiquities and the Israel Department of Antiquities and Museums. But first, we needed to get out of Germany with the scrolls. I felt fairly certain that Volkmar didn't have the clearance to check hotel records other than simply calling the reception and asking for a client. There were a couple of dozen hotels in the airport area, and the Dorint wasn't high on the list of the type of hotel that the majority of middle class travelers would stay in – in spite of its cost. I also felt secure in the notion that he couldn't access any passport control/exit records as well. Kati and I both believed that we were dealing with personal greed here, and not any German governmental collusion.

After a light dinner, Kati got a call from Israel. The museum director informed her that all of his contacts had agreed to work with her. The tacit understanding was that he had called in a number of favors, and that she had better return with something extraordinarily worthwhile. Apparently he hadn't seen the emailed photos yet.

The next morning we checked out and took the short shuttle ride to Tegel. Since we only had carry-ons the initial check-in went very smoothly. When we got to security, we didn't know what was in store for us. The museum director had said not to worry, so we didn't . . . too much. One thing that is tremendously reassuring when flying *El Al* is that, by mutual consent, all security arrangements for their flights are run by former Israeli military. It allows for extraordinary security, but also allows host countries to be 'off the hook' should any security breaches pertaining to an Israeli aircraft occur.

We approached the first checkpoint that led to a short concourse designated for the airline, and presented our passports. The agent scanned them, glanced at us, and ushered us over to a private screening booth. We looked at each other blankly, but our hearts were racing. Another pair of security guards were there;

male and female. We each went into the booth separately. I had nothing to worry about; I didn't carry in my rollerbag a cardboard tube with priceless antiquities in it. I passed through and waited somewhat impatiently on the other side. Within a few moments, Kati emerged, smiling, as well.

"*Nu? Ma koray*? What happened?" I quickly asked.

"*Shum devar, habibi!* Not a damn thing!" She breathed a sigh of relief. "Apparently the security team was informed that I might be bringing a piece of Israel's stolen history back to the Israel Museum, and that they should look the other way. With no German security around, it was easy. When they looked at the x-ray, they simply asked what was in the tube. For the record, I told them that they were posters. Since everything is recorded, they went by protocol and had the proper answers, and here we are!"

We walked down the concourse. It would be here that we would part ways for a while. The six gates were all designated for *El Al* flights. Kati would take one to *Ben Gurion* Airport. I would head back to Tangiers to see if there was any further information that could validate the incredible information on one particular scroll.

XXIV

Back to Tangier, Jerusalem, Cairo

KATI AND I hugged and boarded our respective flights. I had to undergo another security check, since this particular *El Al* flight was headed for Tangiers. I was anxious to see if there was a tangible connection remaining to the mysterious contents of P. Berlin 13737, now miraculously retrieved from the *Rykestrasse* Synagogue. Was there really an ancestral, priestly family for the elusive Yohanon ben Yakoub? Did he eventually return as the document indicated? *Why* was he asked to return? All of these questions ran through my mind as the 757 winged its way southwest across the Pyrenees toward the far end of Africa.

Some 3 hours later, the overhead lights dimmed and a 'ping' signaled the flight attendant announcement that we had descended through ten thousand feet, and all electronic devices needed to be turned off. With seatbelts fastened and tray tables in their upright and locked position, we broke through a midlevel line of clouds and could see the Mediterranean coastline of Morocco come into view. From here, I could imagine, almost see, the fictitious 'dotted line' that demarcated the Atlantic's waters from those of the Med.

A couple of minor bumps and the craft settled onto the tarmac. I thought that it was a whole lot smoother than any landing from a Delta captain – they were notorious hotshots who constantly thought that they were landing on a short aircraft carrier and their landing was captured by arresting cables. However, I also remembered that this reputation wasn't reserved for former Northwest Airlines pilots – long considered to be the finest in the world before the hostile takeover of their airline.

I had texted my dear friend Omar that I was returning to *Maroc*, via Tangier-Boukhalef Airport. I didn't expect a quick response as I had absolutely no idea where he was in the country. So when we touched down, and the double-ping announced that we had parked, and I turned on my phone, I wasn't surprised that there was no text or voicemail. However, I was delighted to get a brief "landed TLV on to J" from Kati.

I emerged from Passport Control and headed through baggage claim for the taxi stand. The pneumatic doors 'whooshed' open and the bright warmth of the Mediterranean zone was welcome from the gloom of Germany. I rummaged around and pulled out my sunglasses to shield me from the glare, and just before I was enveloped by large arms I smelled the aroma of a smoldering *Gitane*.

"*Bonjour mon ami! Ca va?* "How in the world did he find me, I laughed out loud. Two quick pecks on each cheek, and the grip was loosened enough so that I could see my pal. "I have a tour group and the timing has been perfect. I'm here in Tangiers for another day, you're here for who knows how long, *c'est bien, oui?*"

I couldn't argue the basic facts. At least we could have dinner and I could retell the story up to this time, get some ideas from Omar, and continue to explore while he left for Fez in another day's time. Perfect in all ways. We got in the old Peugeot and headed toward town, about 20 minutes away. I told him that I had booked a room at the *El Minzah* on *Rue del la Liberte*. Omar remarked at my good taste and, as any good tour guide, proceeded to fill me in on the history.

"You know, *habibi*, this hotel was opened by an Englander name John Crichton-Stuart back in 1930. This man was one of those aristocratic types, with all sorts of fingers in the pie."

"Don't you mean 'with fingers in all sorts of pies?" I innocently (or not) asked.

"Whatever . . . anyway, some of the most incredible celebrities to ever come to *Maroc* have stayed here – Sir Rex Harrison, Rita Hayworth, Rock Hudson and even Jean Claude van Damme. By the way, how can *you* afford it?" I cranked down the car window a bit further to see if the *Gitane*'s smoke would follow the slipstream away from me. No such luck.

We pulled into the short circular drive and Omar deposited me with little fanfare. "I'm off to meet the group at the toy museum of Malcolm Forbes. I'll find you later in the day or at breakfast tomorrow." With that he was off. I entered the hotel and took in the elegant lobby. The *El Minzah's* architecture, her fountains, and interior court gardens with its orange trees created an unreal atmosphere both by day and by night. I checked in, found my room and flopped down on the bed. There were more pillows than one could imagine. One of the difficulties of hotel stays was the 'three bears syndrome" of pillows – one was always too firm, one was always to soft, but if you were lucky one could be just right. All too often 'just right" never found its way onto beds in my rooms. But here, in Tangiers, a bit of luxury guaranteed *4*, yes, I said 4, varieties of pillow comfort. I really wanted to stay up until dinner and beyond and be totally refreshed for the coming day, so I grabbed a magazine that was strategically placed on the low table facing the sofa in the large room.

I began to browse through the several-year old copy of *Saudi Aramco World.* Although over a decade old, the main article leaped off the page at me. It was as if another omen fell into my lap, literally. The article was 'The Longest *Hajj*: The Journeys of *Ibn Battuta*" by Douglas Bullis. In it, he described the journeys of the 14th century Muslim scholar and world traveler.

Suddenly I felt as if I had drunk a dozen cups of Turkish coffee. I sat up and the drowsiness fell away like a snake's shedded skin. I grabbed a bottle of water and started to pore over the article, picking up the phone and hastily calling Omar. My eyes were opened to a new world, that of the 14th century, and a world of apparent religious harmony and interaction.

Ibn Battuta's works had been relatively obscure, even within the Muslim world, for several centuries. According to historians, at the instigation of the Sultan of Morocco, *Abu Inan Faris, Ibn Battuta* dictated an account of his journeys to *Ibn Juzayy,* a scholar whom he had previously met in Granada. The account is the only source for *Ibn Battuta's* adventures. Apparently a couple of manuscripts had been discovered in the Middle East in the early 19th century. Extracts were published in both German and English, with abridged versions of the text.

During the French Occupation of Algeria in the 1830s, 5 manuscripts were discovered with more complete versions of the text. These were brought back to the *Biblioteque National de Paris* and studied by French scholars. The result was a set of four volumes published starting in 1853 that fully translated the Arabic text and included extensive notes.

With the phone rolling over into voicemail, I left him a message telling him to meet me at a restaurant near the ancient *medina,* just up the hill from the hotel; Restaurant *El Korsan.* It was noted for its Moroccan specialties such as *couscous* and *tangines.* I hoped that he wouldn't be late, as I was bursting with excitement.

* * *

Meanwhile, in Israel, Kati was greeted unexpectedly outside the *Ben Gurion* Airport. The Director of IDAM himself, Dror Amnon, was holding a paper cup of coffee and leaning against his beige Mitsubishi Pajero in a 'no-parking official vehicles' spot just off the exit. He reached back into the vehicle to place the cup in its holder, and walked toward her, beaming.

"*Ahlen, ahlen giveret! Manishma*? Hi my dear, how's things?" He was truly delighted to see her. After all, it wasn't every day that a significant portion of Jewish history was returned home – no matter how it occurred. To Amnon, the fact that it was stolen to begin with was justification for whatever means were necessary to right a wrong. No matter that the objects were stolen from *an entirely different country* – they were still items crucial to Jewish history and deserved a place in its national archives; meaning the Israel Museum. However, he understood the need for compromise and discretion, so he had directly communicated with his counterpart at the SCA, Egypt's Supreme Council of Antiquities. He in turn had notified his liaison with Israel on a couple of previous matters, Sobhy. The end result would be a Solomonic splitting of the scrolls that were recovered so both countries could be satisfied.

At first, Kati stretched out her hand in greeting, and suddenly found herself drawn into a bear hug of warm embrace. Their relationship was both professional and personal. She had known Amnon for nearly two decades and oftentimes he was more like a father to her than her boss.

As they approached the SUV, he reached in and grabbed a second cup of coffee and handed it to her as he took her backpack and gently placed it in the rear compartment. She was grateful, as events of the past few days had started to catch up on the flight, and her energy was starting to wane. There was nothing like Israeli coffee to get one moving full speed again. The German brew was just, well, too *foo foo* for her. They got onto Highway 1 to Jerusalem before she started describing what was in the backpack.

* * *

I arrived at the *El Korsan* a few minutes after appointed time, fashionably late. However, Omar, ever the Moroccan, or French Moroccan, or whatever he really was, was fashionably, fashionably later. *Was it intentional, to try and one-up anyone, or simply a quirk in his nature*, I thought. I gave it no more thought and suddenly he flew in, out of breath, as a human tornado might.

"You know, I would have been a touch early if it wasn't for the damn traffic. You'd think that you were in Casa or Marrakesh, not a ville like Tangiers." He was good at relieving tension, I'll say that.

"*Excusez-moi, min fadlak!*" I've heard of mixed metaphors before, but *mixed tongues*? Ah well, that was Omar. "*Pardon, mon ami!* I'm so sorry I'm late, but you know the *Anglisi* tourists, they're not so much interested in the sites but the tastes! *Show me . . . the way . . . to the next whiskey bar . . .*" He started to sing, surprisingly well, a line from Jim Morrison and the Doors from back in the early 70s. I laughed.

"*How, don't ask why . . . .*" And by now both of us were laughing. After a bottle of water came to us at the bar, we ordered a couple of different *tagines* to share while waiting for our table. Then we got down to it. I recounted the tale of Germany, and what had transpired, leaving out only the most felonious of details. After all, international thievery, to a certain degree, was still international thievery. It gave a whole new meaning to 'don't ask, don't tell.'

I smiled also, and with a tap on the shoulder, the host escorted us to our table. We were being led toward the dance floor, to be nearer the entertainment and evening belly dance show, but I steered the hostess toward a quieter, farther back area. Omar frowned, and then abruptly turned on his famous grin.

"You're right *mon ami*, we have lots to discuss and need to do it with clear heads and a quieter spot. The show must go on . . . for us . . . later!" Now, he laughed, and I joined him.

To his credit, Omar only asked a couple of pertinent questions regarding content, and not provenance. I felt that he didn't want to get involved in the 'pre-Tangiers' part of this adventure. The aroma of the *tagines* preceded the waiter by only a few seconds, and I quickly discovered how ravenous I was. We both ate in relative silence, punctuated only by the occasional 'pass the *pita*'. Like the *tagines*, our thoughts were stewing a bit before being served up. Finally, with small demi-tasses of Turkish coffee on the mostly cleared table, I resumed the story with the *Aramco World* article.

"What do you know about *Ibn Battuta*, and can you get us into the Archaeological Museum Library? I need to see the originals and ask you to translate the Arabic as precisely as you can. I want to get your spin regarding the nuance of language." I was keenly aware of how to place the hook in my friend and companion. He still smarted a bit from the notion that he could make more money as a tour guide than university professor. Where did I hear that before? Sobhy had the same situation in Egypt. As a matter of fact, it was sadly the case actually all over the world for academics in the liberal arts. Yes, professors in the science world moonlighted as consultants to big business and industry, and were able to earn more than their keep in that way; but for the arts there was little consultancy out there. Salaries remained a pittance, and one had to be extraordinarily creative. Hence, the tourism industry connection.

Omar was delighted to show off his expertise. However, with me it was like 'preaching to the choir'. Nevertheless, he was pleased. He arranged to pick me up the next morning and we would discover firsthand what *Ibn Battuta* said to the world.

Things were looking up. It was a bright, cloudless day in Tangiers and I took a stroll around the hotel grounds before the appointed pick up time – and then deliberately came to the *porte cochere* a few minutes late. After all, 'fashion' was 'fashion', wasn't it? Once again, I was trumped! The rattling Peugeot pulled up just a minute after I arrived. *Was he watching from the street in order to get there last?* The thought did cross my mind.

I waved as if nothing was amiss and got in the car. Thankfully, the windows were all down, so the *Gitane*-injected air wasn't all that bad. Nonetheless, I kept my head close to the passenger's window, not unlike humankind's best friend. It was only a few minute drive to *Dar El Makhzen* palace, on *Place de la Kasbah*. Omar maneuvered into the car park and set the emergency brake. From there, we then headed inside and he flashed his credentials at the security guard, who then telephoned the administrative office.

A few moments later a bespectacled, short, 'well-fed' man came to the entry and effusively shook his colleague's hand. Omar took on an air of academic importance, drawing himself up to his full height. He 'towered' above the man. Of course, *anyone* over five foot eight would 'tower' above this fellow. I thought to myself, *Remember why Moroccans are so short? It's so they can fit under the Equator!* I smiled to myself, and caught the museum agent looking at me curiously.

"It's nothing, really. I was merely thinking of seeing *Ibn Battuta's* works and the pleasure that it would give me." Whew.

In return, the man beamed. For obvious reasons, he was very proud of the collection that he oversaw, yet apparently was not very well thanked by his government for it. I sensed this, and now knew how to keep on his good side – through flattery.

He led us down one of the high-ceilinged galleries to the wing that housed manuscripts. It had its own climate controlled environment, apart from the rest of the museum; however, there was no added security. We passed through a double air-lock into the wing. Although open to the public, it was rarely visited by tourists. The scholarly atmosphere was apparent here. The entire area was chronologically arranged, and we were taken back to the area that housed the collection of the Middle Ages. You could smell the antiquity, almost taste the historical significance of the documents stored here. This small museum's collection of literature rivaled that of the finest museums in the world. And, thankfully, it knew how to preserve them.

He stopped at a sealed case that had a small, framed drawing on its top – the traveler and scholar, *Ibn Battuta.* Omar peered down at the contents through the glass vitrine. Lying open, about one-third of the way through the text, was an illustrated copy of the *Rihla,* 'The Journey', of *Ibn Battuta's* travels, that had been dictated to *Ibn Juzayy* so many centuries ago.

"*Ya Allah!*" whispered Omar. "It's exquisite!"

"*Iywa,* yes indeed." The curator was positively giddy with pride. "Of course, you know that the entire name of the volume is *"A Gift to Those Who Contemplate the Wonders of Cities and the Marvels of Travelling"* he went on. Apparently he felt the need to deliver in a subtle manner his own *bona fides.* I smiled, and thanked him profusely for his presence in assisting us. Remember about the 'greased wheel', *bakshish.* Well, this was intellectual *bakshish-ing* at its finest.

"Would it be at all possible to, carefully, examine the text outside of the case," I asked. A long explanation followed about protocol, and curatorial caution, warnings and admonitions. But at the end of it all, the museum official walked to a cabinet to procure a couple of pairs of latex gloves and key. He then proceeded, with great pomp (I could almost hear a twenty-one gun salute and the Moroccan national anthem playing in the background), handed us the gloves to put on and then unlocked the case. He then placed the book on a felt covered table a couple of feet away and told us in no uncertain terms that we had half an hour with the priceless manuscript before it needed to be returned. He trusted us fully, he said, so he would leave us to our task and return later. His parting words admonished us to any use of photography. But in passing made it clear that, for a small fee, official photos could be made available to us for whatever we needed. I smiled at his back as he left; the bottom line was always the bottom line no matter where you were in the world.

Omar was speechless. He had never been this close to such a document. For that matter, neither had I. This complete version of *Ibn Battuta's* monumental work was considered by some to be a 'bible' for the historical geography of North Africa and the Middle East. It eloquently described a world six centuries long dead, and with a clarity that gave the reader a 'you are here' glimpse. I shook my friend out of his reverie, noting that we had a half an hour to try to discover a link to the Elephantine scroll's message and meaning.

He surreptitiously pulled out his IPhone.

"What are you doing?" I asked, fearful that the curator might return early.

"PLEASE!" he begged, "Just take one photo of me with the book. I swear on my mother that noting will come of it except that I have it. It's so important, so incredible, so . . . ."

I cut him off. I agreed to one quick pic. Since there was no flash as long as I positioned myself just so no one knew anything. And suddenly it was done. Omar beamed and got down to the task at hand. He almost immediately found the section that related to the traveler's journeys in Morocco, and then after another moment found a reference to *Walili*, or *Volubilis* as we know it now. He read it aloud and we both were stunned.

As I stroll through the streets, I feel more cosmopolitan in many ways than in the usual Arab city. An atmosphere of great tolerance prevails, this openness is heartwarming to me. It seems liberating, almost joyous in its approach. The city feels like an environment that I had read about in some ancient journals – a city whose feel was similar to those written about just prior to the Arab conquest of the region, when ethnicities and religions were all treated with a greater dignity and respect. It was a time before the Caliphate, when either Christian or Jewish rulers wore the mantle of authority.

At times, it seems as if the current caliph here based on Walili is more Jewish than Moslem. 'Could that be?'

Now I was speechless. Things were certainly rolling about in my head now. We had confirmation, of sorts, that there was a major Jewish presence that seemed at least to be heavily involved in ruling the land; or, at best, a ruler with Jewish origins indeed *did* rule the land.

The curator returned, precisely on time, to our regret. It meant that we had to return the priceless book to its case, and leave it behind. I decided that, regardless of cost, it would be good to 'purchase' a photo of the two pages in question, so that we could reference them again. I said 'purchase' because I felt that the money given to the small, self-important man would indeed go to a 'good' cause, his, rather than the museum. Once again, the notion of *bakshish* came back to haunt us. But all in all it would be worth it considering what we had learned.

We left *Dar el Makhzen* with a photo and a renewed sense of purpose. I barely smelled the *Gitane* already between Omar's lips as we drove away.

* * *

The frenetic pace that marked the administrative wing of the Rockefeller Museum in eastern Jerusalem was like a gust of refreshing air to Kati. She loved the energy that flowed here. Coordinating the many excavations in Israel, and administering the great museums and antiquities sites was both a calling and challenge to the Israelis and foreign scholars-in-residence there. To the average Israeli, the tie to the land was at the core of their being. They saw thousands of years of dwelling in the area between the Jordan River and the Mediterranean as proof positive of their right to live there. And it really had nothing to do with the spiritual message of the biblical narrative, but the social and historical one. To them, it lent considerable strength to their position when modern politics came into play.

The two made their way into the inner core of offices, and directly to Dror Amnon's small study. His time in the military, along with the general Israeli consensus of equity, made him choose this small office. Everything he needed was there, including the coffee maker. As soon as he opened the door he headed directly for it. He drew water from the ensuite bath (the *only* perk that he allowed for) and filled the reservoir. Two heaping scoops of a blend that only he knew the recipe for began to bubble and fill the pot. The aroma was seductive.

Fortified with the thick, sweet brew, Kati opened the bag and withdrew the photo tube. Dror had taken everything off of his worktable, and wiped it down with a disinfectant. He then unrolled white craft paper to ensure a clean surface. On it, Kati unrolled the felt backing and gently removed the cover sheet. A slightly musty smell arose as the four documents came to light on the office table. The director of IDAM looked at the documents with a mixture of awe, respect and, truth be told, joy; as a part of the Jewish community's past was revealed. He had seen the photos that were sent to him; but in person, well, it was overwhelming.

"*Oy favoy! Azeh ma shehu. Be'emet!* It's really something unbelievable isn't it!" He spoke in a hushed voice, as if no one was to hear, as if it was a secret to be cherished. "Now, what to do with these scrolls, and, I know, which ones do we share with our Egyptian colleagues; for after all, they *are* Elephantine scrolls, regardless of who stole them!"

Kati smiled, perhaps there really was a thaw in Israeli-Egyptian relations.

* * *

As soon as he received the text message with the embedded photos, Sobhy packed his things and gave orders as to how to continue the preservation work at *Serabit.* He placed a call to the SCA office, and, of course, was routed to voice mail. He left a message for the director that indicated that he was returning from Sinai earlier than expected because of some information that he had gotten. Would the director be available the next day as soon as he arrived in the city, so they could discuss it.

He threw the phone down on the seat and started the return trip to *Um el Dunya,* the Mother of the World, Cairo. If he drove nonstop, resting only at benzene stations and grabbing a *falafel* and soft drink for the road, it might take 7 or 8 hours. That wasn't terrible, given the driving conditions. Thankfully, he had tanked up the day before. In addition, he had loaded the vehicle with bottled water at the same time, so the first leg of the journey could pass fairly quickly.

Thank goodness the old UN road along the coast of the Reed Sea was in splendid condition. *Those Norwegians really knew how to build a road in the desert,* he thought. From there, as he sped north, it merged with the even older Israeli-built road that ran along the old *Bar-Lev* Line from after the 1967 War. At least now there were a couple of rest stops that remained open. This part of the trip worried him the most, as in recent months the lawlessness of the Sinai became more and more evident.

Mohamed Morsi had such a full plate in Cairo, dealing with the revolution and recent elections, he had no time for the desert fringe. As a result, the *Bedouin* in Sinai were more and more brazen in their attacks – ambushing and kidnapping simply for financial gain. With no military to speak of, it was 'quite fashionable'. But Sobhy would have none of it. He literally flew through encampments, and practically ran around the car when he did stop for petrol. He even relieved himself nearby the pumps rather than walk around back to the toilet. He didn't care; there really wasn't anyone around to see him anyway. And truth be told, he probably found the desert cleaner than the ancient facilities.

Finally, signs announced the tunnels that ran under the Suez Canal, meaning that, once through them, he only had a little over 100 km to go to the Ring Road that ran around the periphery of Cairo. One more stop should do it, and on the other side of the Canal, it would be safer.

He now was flying with 'the pedal to the metal' as they say. He was approaching 140 kmh, which translated to nearly 85 mph. Of course, in this part of Egypt speed limits meant nothing, so he had no police to worry about. It was the more typical desert road traffic that he had to contend with – oxcarts and camels which moved at a considerably slower pace. But he was able to weave his way around with minimal slowdowns.

At KM 101 he passed the faded green and white sign that doubled as an historical marker as well. For it was here that the Israeli army penetrated to its deepest in Egyptian soil before the cease fire of 1973 took place. Although that war played a major role in shaping Sobhy's world view, and his now very positive view of Jews and Israelis, he barely gave the sign a second thought. Funny, he noted, every other time he passed this spot he would run the memories through his head, giving him something to focus on as he passed the time either to or from Sinai. Today, it was all he could do to focus on the road and other traffic that was flashing by at an extraordinary rate of speed.

* * *

The next day Omar knew what our next step should be. He mentioned a reference book that alluded to *Ibn Battuta's* connection with the Sephardic Jewish community of the *Maghreb*, North Africa and the Levant. Apparently Nehemia Levtzion, in *Corpus of Early Arabic Sources for West Africa,* had made allusions to this but, at least to Omar's knowledge, had never followed up. It was now up to us. He drove us to a regional campus of the *Abdelmalek Essaâdi* University that was located in Tangiers, only a few minutes away. Although it was what we in the states would call a 'satellite' campus, its library was one of the best in all of the city. Omar had called ahead first thing in the morning.

"You know, when I called the school to inquire about the library, after I had identified myself, I was put on hold for a moment. They then set up the appointment for this morning. However, that wasn't all. I got a call back a few minutes later. It was from the president's office of the university. Boy was I confused. Were they going to rescind the invite?" He now grinned enigmatically and paused.

Okay, the suspense was killing me, sort of. So I forced myself to play into scenario and asked what it was all about.

"*Mon ami*, the secretary said to me, 'will you please hold for President Dr. *Houdaifa Ameziane*?"

"So?" I asked.

"We went to school together! I couldn't believe it. 'HooDoo' was a president now! And he was the greatest prankster in our class. Why I remember the time in osteology class that he took a disarticulated skeleton and . . . ."

I cut him off, telling him I didn't care where this story was going, but it would go without me!

"*Tayib*, okay, but he said that he would be happy to meet us at the library." At least we had an 'in' in the school to grease any wheels. We would arrive at the school in a few moments time so we roughly outlined a plan. Things were moving faster.

When we entered the library, a man about our age came forward to greet Omar. He was distinguished looking, in an Islamic scholarly way. Salt-and-pepper hair matched his full beard, without moustache. He wore a plain, white *kufi*, or skullcap. He walked over to Omar, and cast an appraising gaze up and down.

He then smiled and embraced his college-days companion warmly. Omar was delighted to see him as well.

"*Ahlen, rais*! Greetings Mr. President" he said with all the ceremony that he could muster. He still saw the twenty-something student rabble rouser from his past. Of course, the same could be said for all of us when being re-introduced to old friends who hadn't seen each other in decades. "Allow me to introduce my friend and colleague".

I came forward and shook hands with President *Ameziane*. He ushered us into a small study room and shut the door. Inside was a tray with coffee and a plate of *Kab El Ghazal*, Moroccan almond cookies. As always, food takes precedence to all else in North Africa and the Middle East. I munched and Omar talked. First, for a couple of minutes, they caught up on the last dozen years. Then, as I was wiping the last crumbles from my mouth, he started to talk about *Ibn Battuta*, and the history of the Moroccan Jewish Community. Then, he interjected where applicable the documents from Elephantine that linked the two countries on opposite ends of Africa. As he described the connection, Omar also referenced the book by Levtzion that also alluded to a connection.

President *Ameziane* was intrigued. He pulled out his small tablet and did some scrolling. It took a minute or two, but he looked up and smiled. "The entire library catalog was put online just a couple of months ago." The pride in his voice was evident. "It was my initiative that got the government funding for it."

Both of us murmured congratulatory responses as we waited anxiously for him to continue. He had found that the library did indeed have a copy of *The Corpus*. He called one of the librarians to assist and retrieve the text. While we waited, he carried on with Omar, fondly remembering the college days.

With the arrival of the book, and our skimming through its contents, it was becoming clearer by the minute what so many people today miss – that Jews, Christians and North Africans got along famously in the generations preceding the Arabic/Islamic conquest of the late 7th Century of this era. In fact, based on the research of scores of scholars of all backgrounds, they took turns ruling; based on talent and ability rather than ethnicity or spiritual orientation. In other words, they had a lot more common sense for the greater good of their land than most of us do today.

None of us was surprised at learning this, especially the university president. He had spent nearly all of his academic life studying the history of Morocco, and was very familiar its pre-Islamic backdrop. Every so often he would drop a gem on Omar and me regarding the nature of pre-Roman society in the *Maghreb*. He would point us to this book or that article that supported his notions.

But the real kicker to me was his offhand remark about how *Volubilis* (he preferred the Roman name to the city and region) was said to have Jewish tribal leaders assume control of the city's defenses as the Phoenicians approached in the

500s BCE. Then, when things got to be overwhelming, the *agella*, or king, agreed to send his Jewish advisors and their families to seek protection elsewhere.

My mind started shift into overdrive. Was it possible that they had journeyed thousands of miles east to the Nile Valley, and then south to *Syene*. Could they have been a large part of the nucleus of the Jewish community on the island of *Yeb*, in the Nile; today known as Elephantine. And then, a century later, when the area around *Tingis* became safe, the community sent an 'all-clear' message to Egypt that requested that the descendants of the advisors to the Moroccan kings return in honor to their homeland to once again serve with dignity. Wow. It was the only word that I could think of.

I needed to assimilate all this, and then tell Omar my hypothesis. But I certainly didn't want to do it at the library of *Abdelmalek Essaâdi* University – with its president as a witness.

I thanked *Ameziane* and walked out to the car. This gave Omar a few minutes alone with his friend to say his goodbye, assuredly with promises to stay in touch in a much closer fashion the previous decades. And, if I knew Omar, he would indeed follow up on this promise in a timely way.

I sat, daydreaming a bit, and a few minutes later I smelled the *Gitane* before I saw my colleague. Without opening my eyes I called a greeting through the open window.

"How do you do it?" he asked. "You looked like you were sleeping."

"I was, until the cancer-stick's indelicate aroma filled my nostrils. You need to get a less smelly vice, *habib*." I laughed. He laughed. But we knew the truth, his addiction would catch up with him. But I certainly hoped that it was later rather than sooner.

I started to speak, but he cautioned me not to; just yet. We drove to a small café and settled down in the patio, out of earshot. Then I told him exactly what I thought. He agreed with me fully, but warned against too much exposure at this time.

"You know, this could be precisely the reason that *Maroc* has had strong relations with its Jews. In addition, remember back to the 90s. After 1994, with the first inklings of any movement between the Israelis and Palestinians, who was it that took the initiative? Our own beloved King, Mohamed V. Ignoring all external Arab world pressure, he set up a clandestine meeting between Arafat and Itzhak Rabin in his mountain retreat above *Ifrane* in the Atlas Mountains. No one knew of it until much later – after it was successful in its dialog. After all, no one wanted to be optimistic and then see things fall flat. *That* would not look good on a king's resume – trust me on that. But once the seeds were sown, Morocco embarked on low level diplomatic relations with Israel in spite of the entire Arab world, and the fact that the two countries had not even entered into negotiations for a comprehensive peace treat-yet. The diplomatic brilliance of the king's moves would serve as a model for a few other Arab states that would allow them the same latitude without the perception of a 'peace treaty'".

I couldn't have summed it up any better. But, in light of the general atmosphere that was prevalent in the Arab world following its 'Spring' and subsequent upheaval, I agreed that the timing wasn't right. But we could catalog all of our findings, prepare them, and wait for the right moment. The quest that I had initially started a couple of months ago seemed to be coming to successful closure.

XXV

Cairo to Jerusalem, and Tangier

AS SOON AS Sobhy hit the ring road around Cairo, he headed east and north to *Heliopolis* where his flat was. It wasn't so much that he needed to get home, but to take a quick shower and change clothes for what might be one of the most important meetings of his career.

As he approach Cairo, exiting out of the dead zone of mobile reception that was all too common in the deserts of Egypt, he called the switchboard of the Supreme Council of Antiquities. He hurriedly explained, although a bit cryptically, that he needed to have an emergency meeting with the director and that he had urgent information that needed to be addressed, but in person. The receptionist, a somewhat lethargic cousin of a colleague's university friend who 'needed a job and could they pleasepleaseplease find something in the government in Cairo since they were from Upper Egypt and it would impress the villagers to no end and earn a great deal of *bakshish* credit etcetcetc . . .' stonewalled a bit. After all, she *was* supposed to be the gate-keeper for the director. But she certainly couldn't tell a legitimate sense of urgency if she was hit over the head with it.

The phone call eventually was put through, but with Sobhy fuming all the while at Egyptian bureaucracy. *That's exactly what's wrong with this country*, he thought to himself. He got his audience with the director for later that afternoon. He knew that he had to be cautious since the director didn't 'just see' any of his regional directors on a moment's notice. Once again, generations of Egyptian posturing shaped the nation even though it was the 21st century. So he needed to be fresh, not someone just out of a desert excavation. He also needed to have all of his *spiel* in order to convince the mainly traditional head of all antiquities for the country. Plus, there was always the political side. Ever since the new regime of the Brotherhood with the new president, Mohamed Morsi, things had been chilly regarding Israel.

So the Egyptian archaeologist was thankful that he had a couple of hours to consider his presentation, and make himself presentable as well. Once in his flat, after a long, hot, shower (praise *Allah* that the hot water was on!) he sat down at his computer. The images sent to him on his cell via email could now be accessed in a larger format, with higher resolution.

Immediately, as he viewed the pictures, he was overwhelmed with pride for his Egyptian heritage. These scrolls were a priceless part of his nation's history, and to get at least some of it back in the homeland was an incredible joy. At the same time, he felt an immeasurable sense of gratitude for his American and now, Israeli, friends who had made this happen. Although a small piece of him tugged at his nationalistic tendency to demand that all the scrolls be returned to *Misr*, the majority portion of his psyche insisted that no one should ever take the stance than that insufferable, pompous former director, Zahi Hawass, had toward the world.

No, the realities of the 19th and early 20th century and Egyptology were an unfortunate part of the past, and as Paul Williams, the songwriter, once said that 'you can get back to the place, but not the time'; adverse possession after a century becomes the rule rather than exception. It is up to the nation states to negotiate in good faith and do what is right in the world of compromise to move forward. So he needed to craft an argument that would be of benefit to Israel and the Jewish world as well as Egypt. The emotions that he felt for both sides, fueled by love of country and personal friendship, would guide him, he was sure.

* * *

Meanwhile, across the continent, early that morning I was preparing to leave Morocco with the information at hand. As I prepared to check out of the *El Minzah*, with Omar patiently waiting for me by his car (apparently the *Gitane* had a greater impact than I did) and having a smoke, I got a phone call on my mobile. I debated whether or not to answer as I had a flight to catch, but the caller ID came up *Moroccan Ministry of Culture*. No longer a debate, I pressed 'accept' and got the surprise of my life.

On the line was the direct secretary to the Minister of Culture, *Mohamed Sbihi*. I knew very little about the current Moroccan government, and even less about those who headed the governmental ministries. The secretary asked if I could hold for the Minister. I stuttered an 'Of course' and proceeded to listen to canned Arabic music.

I quickly leaned over and asked Omar who this man was, questioning why on earth he would call me.

"*Habibi*, this man is one of the closest ministers to Prime Minister *Abdellilah Benkirane*. Apparently they had gone to university together. *Benkirane* chose politics as life after school, while *Sbihi* chose academia. For many years he has served on the faculty of two of our more prestigious schools – *Mohamed V* University in *Rabat* and *al-Akhawayn* in *Ifrane*." Omar seemed duly impressed, until a frown crossed his face.

"*Mon ami*, what in *Allah's* name have you done to get the government on you?" The look showed that he really was concerned.

I was perplexed as well. "I haven't the slightest . . ." The secretary came back on the line before I could finish and announced Minister of Culture *Sbihi*. I listened intently for a few moments, proffered my thanks at the call, and a guarantee that I would do as he said. Somewhat shocked, I slumped against the car and rubbed my eyes. Omar looked at me with an expectant expression.

I told him that the minister requested that I meet with him before leaving the country. He suggested a place that was almost neutral, the American Legation Complex in the *medina*. He said that I could bring a colleague as witness if I so chose. Well, I so chose, and Omar became my 'second'. We had an hour until the appointed time.

The American Legation in Tangiers is one of the oldest and most significant outposts of American diplomacy. As a matter of fact, it is *the* oldest American public property outside of the United States. It commemorates the historic cultural and diplomatic relations between the United States and the Kingdom of Morocco. It is representative of the 1786 Moroccan – American Treaty of Friendship, which is still in force today. This was the first international accord of the fledgling United States. This complex was presented to the United States in 1821 by *Sultan Moulay Suliman*. The first property acquired abroad by the United States government, it housed the United States Legation and Consulate for 140 years, the longest period any building abroad has been occupied as a United States diplomatic post. Over the years, as its mission grew, surrounding houses adjacent to the original structure would be bought and halls blown open to link the buildings. During World War II, the American intelligence community would use it as a base of operations in the neutral territory.

When I told this to Omar as we waited at a café for our appointment, he smiled and began to 'channel' Rick as he addressed Dooley Wilson. Who? Well, how about the piano-playing Sam in *Casablanca*.

"Play it, play it again *Sham*!" Now he was laughing. But I had to correct him.

"He *never* said that, it's a cinemagraphic myth!"

"*Tayib*, then what did he say, *mon ami*?"

"You played it for her, and you can play it for me. And this time, play it right!"

"Well, I was close, wasn't I?" he stated as a matter of course.

As the named time grew close, we walked into the medina via the entry near the Grand Mosque by *Avenue Mohamed V* and on to the *Rue de Portugal.* From there, a few minutes farther took us to *Rue d'Amerique* and the famous #8. To our surprise, a sign on the door stated that the Legation Museum was closed for restoration. My perplexed look gave way to understanding as the door beneath the seal of the United States swung partway open. Our names were called and we were ushered in, the door closing quickly behind us. Now it dawned on us why the spot was chosen. No one would be around, especially tourists, if the building had been shut down for a while for desperately needed work.

We were led upstairs to one of the sitting rooms, and found the President of *Abdelmalek Essaâdi* University, President Dr. *Houdaifa Ameziane* waiting for us, in the company of a couple of other gentlemen.

"*Marhaba*, welcome my friends." He greeted us effusively. "I would like to introduce you to Minister *Mohamed Sbihi.* I thought it better to have a known go-between for this meeting". He acknowledged us with a smile and traditional three-peck kiss on the cheeks. He was a very informal person for such a formal role in government – something that both Omar and I were pleasantly surprised at. It immediately set us both at ease, in an uneasy situation.

As soon as we were seated, the other man present, clearly a staff member of the minister, brought out a silver service and poured the rich, minty tea that was the signature drink of the country. There were only a couple of moments of small talk, as the minister got right down the matter at hand.

He acknowledged the enormous role that Jewish Moroccans had over the centuries. They would serve as advisors to the *caliphate,* ministers in various governmental positions. Their loyalty was never in doubt. As a matter of fact, he even referred to the Ambassador at Large in the end of the 20th and early part of the 21st century, *Serge Verdugo,* a Jew from *Meknes.* President *Benkirane* thought so highly of him that he was appointed Minister of Tourism in 2011.

"I recall an event that I attended a couple of years back. Mr. *Verdugo* spoke very eloquently about the Moroccan Jewish Community and its role in the Kingdom. It was in a speech delivered in New York at an event entitled "*Two Thousand Years Of Jewish Life in Morocco: An Epic Journey*." He said, 'Although life for the Jews in Morocco was not always one of 'wine and roses', it was always better than what other Jews experienced in most parts of the world. The Kingdom of Morocco bears witness to the viability of a Jewish community living peacefully in Arab country for centuries.'"

Sbihi was grateful that others were familiar with the tolerant attitude that Morocco shared with its minority communities, recognizing their value. However, he stressed the tightrope that his country was walking in the Arab World, especially with regard to Israel and Iran. Morocco had always been seen as the mediator in backroom negotiations. Under the leadership of the relatively new king, *Mohamed VI*, the policy of his father, *Hassan II*, would continue in this vein. However, with regard to the information from the annals of *Ibn Battuta*, and documentation from Egypt, the monarchy would not publicly acknowledge the most major of roles that a Jew seems to have played as a leader of the country.

I found this stance exasperating, to say the least. The pressure from the royal household was oppressive. I told *Sbihi* that in so many words. How could he attempt to censure intellectual property that truly belonged to the world. He pondered this for a moment. He excused himself and wandered into the next room, punching the keypad on his mobile as he left.

We sat back, perplexed and nervous, as we awaited his return. Omar, always the unflappable presence, proceeded to pour more mint tea and pull a couple of *Ghoriba* almond and walnut cookies from the plate. I looked at him, he returned the look a bit sheepishly, and admitted that when he became nervous, he ate . . . a lot. I smiled and reached over for one of the delicacies myself.

A couple of cups of tea and several cookies later, the minister returned to the sitting room. He asked for the fax number of the Legation, and excused himself once more. However, this time it lasted only a couple of minutes. By now, Omar and I were really confused over what was going on. The minister requested that we all go to the office where the fax machine was located, and wait to see what popped out.

* * *

In Cairo, Sobhy's meeting with the director of the SCA went better than expected. The powerpoint that he created about the Elephantine scrolls was a little longer than he wanted, but he felt it imperative to outline the history and importance of the documents because they were of an historical age that the director had not studied in as great detail as he had of Pharaonic Egypt, millennia ago.

After about 10 minutes, the first image of the 4 scrolls that had been in the hands of the Germans for nearly a century hit the screen. Needless to say, the director was extremely impressed by the rediscovery and recovery of an important part of Egypt's past. He thought out loud that it was just the thing that the fledgling government needed for the population to restore its pride in its nation. Every little bit helped was his view.

Sobhy agreed with him wholeheartedly. However, he felt incumbent to remind the director that his American and Israeli friends were instrumental in this endeavor and they were the ones who actually, at great risk, 'liberated' the scrolls from the Germans. He also needed to remind the director that the only way that the scrolls could be gotten out of Germany was with the aid and planning carried out by the Israelis. He also, in a quieter voice, reminded him that the scrolls were currently in Israel.

The director sighed. He knew deep down that Sobhy was right. But he also knew of the frailties of the modern political scene. Should word of the actual facts leak out, the Islamists in government would have a fit and things could easily spiral out of control. The only way that things could work out to everyone's benefit was quiet diplomacy.

Now it was Sobhy's turn to sigh – but in relief. The bigger picture was seen by all now and things could proceed. The head of the Supreme Council of Antiquities gave the younger man full authority to do as he saw fit for all; and make the director look very good in the meantime. Handshakes all around, pecks on cheeks, and a letter of authorization concluded the meeting. He would travel to the Israel Museum and negotiate the return of a couple of the scrolls, which he considered to be a fair, Solomonic division. The tricky part would be the delicate task of how to keep the Israelis from broadcasting around the world the return coupled with what was discovered in the text. Now it was up to Sobhy to get in touch with his friends in Jerusalem and work on details that everyone could live with, and take pride in at the same time.

He packed a small bag and paid some bills that he'd been neglecting since a couple of weeks before he had left for Sinai. They were a bit overdue. *Ma'alesh,* he thought. Since the revolution nobody paid bills on time anyway. The recipients should be delighted that they were getting paid, no matter when. As soon as he completed his tasks, and informed the building super that he'd be gone a few days, he went downstairs to hail a taxi. Given the state of affairs in Sinai, driving in his private car was more than dangerous. Buses were safe, with security on board. Even the Sinai *Bedouin* wouldn't be so brazen.

He hit the street and hailed a black and white *Lada* taxi. As he got in, he noted that it was a 'newer' model, dated to 1990! He sat back on the cracked vinyl seat as the vehicle pulled away from his flat, belching a noxious black plume of oily smoke.

"*Ezzayak, rais, il bassat min fadluk,* please, sir, to the bus station." *Let the journey begin,* he thought as he texted his companions about his pending arrival at the Tel Aviv Bus Station.

In the American Legation office, the atmosphere was charged. The machine gave out the electronic 'squeal' associated with an incoming fax, and what began to come out of the machine both surprised and astounded us.

••

من مكتب صاحب السمو الملكي والسادس من جلالة الملك محمد

Royal Majesty King Mohamed VI

It was a personal letter from the King of Morocco himself! The letter was an eloquent statement affirming the major role that the Jewish community of Morocco had played in the success and longevity of independent rule over the centuries. It went on to describe how the monarchy had discovered that there MAY have been a Jewish-led Caliphate in the land hundreds of years ago. The letter also stated without a doubt that *Ibn Battuta* was correct in his assumptions in the 14th century; yet no one outside the monarchy had found it out until now.

The king then went on to make an unusually brave claim in light of the current world situation. He felt that the discovery could be politically 'spun' to show an extraordinary strength within the Moroccan Arab nation – that these were *Arab Jews* who helped rule the country. As a result, this was the basis for the lack of discrimination against the Jewish community that usually was seen throughout the general Arab world. It revealed an Arabic Morocco that showed great tolerance in matters of spirituality as it exhibited cultural unity.

We all were stunned into silence as the letter was read to us. The impact was profound, with the potential of being a regional game-changer. But the question was, *which way would the game be changed, for the positive or the calamitous?*

The final paragraph before the King's signature stated that, in spite of all the evidence, the discovery need remain quiet for the time. The King argued that, although Morocco may be ready to accept this part of its history, the rest of the Arab world, in the current climate, would react harshly and with an impulsively violent answer. The Kingdom of Morocco would be in jeopardy at the hands of its Arab brethren and the radical right wing Islamist movements that were enjoying their greatest power since the Golden Age of Islam in the 13th century.

The King would send by official courier a copy of the letter to the heads of state of the major superpowers and Israel, for their eyes only at this time. With these leaders 'in the loop' so to speak, privy to this material, they all could begin to work together in quiet, unassuming ways for the betterment of the region. Then, at a given point in time, agree to release the information when all felt that the time was right. When would that be? Only God knew and God's greatness would be recognized when humankind had the timing revealed. This was how the King of Morocco ended his letter.

* * *

Sobhy made it to the *Tourgoman* Bus Terminal in time to catch the #100 Bus to *Tel Aviv* via north Sinai and the *Rafah* border crossing. It would be over eight grueling hours on a bus that was suspect at best, and a rattletrap at worst. However, it had ample security and this was all that mattered. At the kiosk just outside the station, he stocked up on water and snacks. There was one stop near *El Arish*, but that was nearly six hours into the trip.

Once on board, he was reminded of the story that his American archaeologist colleague told about a bus ride to *Eilat*, in the *Arabah*, on the Gulf of *Aqaba*. In that story, the oversold bus was chaotic, as passengers almost revolted because of seating. With several people standing on what was a four hour bus ride, a brouhaha was brewing was over a dog, sitting quietly on one of the seats next to its owner. People were cursing, shouting, pushing and shoving because the dog was sitting – taking a seat away from one of the human passengers. The dog's owner was adamant that the dog stay. Why? Because he had bought the dog a ticket! The bus driver was so unnerved by the commotion that he pulled off the road, in the midst of the *Negev* desert. He ordered everyone out to try to sort through this madness. When he found out what was going on, he decided that the only way to solve the problem was put it to a vote. They did. The dog won! Sobhy thought that in spite of the differences in cultures, you *had* to admire the Israeli democratic point of view. As the story concluded, everyone filed back on the bus quietly, respectfully. A vote had been taken, the results announced, and you accepted it no matter what.

That would never happen on an Egyptian bus, with its peasants all vying for a seat. They didn't even get up for the elderly here. So he hunkered down in his numbered seat, put his small daypack behind his head, and hoped to get some rest during the journey.

If all went well, and there were no concerns at the border crossing where they would change to an Israeli bus, he should arrive at the *Tahana Mercazit Tel Aviv*, the Central Bus Station, around 9:30 pm. He had texted *Kati Ben Yair* from the museum that he would call when he got settled on the Israeli bus. With a closer handle on the actual arrival time at that point, they would know when to be at the station to pick him up. Apparently, to save time, they would drive to *Tel Aviv* in late afternoon, have dinner, and await his call. Since it was only another hour and a half to Jerusalem, they would all go to her flat and spend the night – heading to the museum the following morning.

* * *

Kati called me in Tangiers, but the phone was turned off. I was still in the meeting with Omar and the minister when it came in. After the meeting was concluded, and the letter from the Moroccan King himself was sent via diplomatic pouch to the heads of state who had a stake in all this, we left the Legation. We exited the *medina* and as I turned on the phone I saw the missed call. There was such poor reception in the close quarters of the old city that it was only outside the city walls that I got a couple of bars. There was no voicemail message, but instead a text message that was beeping incessantly. I opened it and read about Sobhy's pending journey to Israel.

It was indeed great news; apparently the Egyptians and Israelis had reached some sort of framework to divide the scrolls (not literally, I hoped!) and each have a share in their nation's archives. She was waiting to hear from the Egyptian when he reached the border, and would meet him and take him to Tel Aviv. When could I be expected, she asked in the text, so that I could 'mediate' if that became necessary. The director of IDAM, Israeli Department of Antiquities and Museums, Dror Amnon, would be present. I knew from past experience that, as a former IDF general, he could be as hard-headed as they came and firmly entrenched in his own philosophy. Sometimes, no, *oftentimes*, it was at odds with much of the traditional perspective. However, *most* of the time, it was spot-on at the end of the day. We all could only hope that he would be a bit flexible in this instance, should the need arise.

I relayed all of this to Omar as we walked to his car. He was delighted at the news, but saddened at the prospect that he knew I'd be flying back to Israel as soon as possible. I too was a bit sad, but the excitement of the scroll transfer and a successful resolution to all this overrode the feeling. Things now were moving rapidly. The ride was quiet as we went to the *El Minzah* to pick up my bag, and check flights out to *Ben Gurion* Airport.

As it turned out, there were travel complications that arose. There were no nonstop flights out in the late afternoon. I had a couple of choices. I could fly out of Tangier, make a stop in Barcelona, and make it to Tel Aviv by two in the morning. Or, if we hurried, get to Casablanca and fly via Brussels to Tel Aviv, arriving by around midnight. Provided that we could get to the main international airport of the country in time, it was the best option. I would arrive just around the time that Kati and Sobhy were passing by on the way to Jerusalem. I asked Omar when was the last time that he had the Peugeot serviced. Indignantly, he replied that he always maintained his vehicle in top shape. And then, somewhat apologetically, said that he needed to have the oil changed since it had been 6,000 km ago.

But he assured me that it could get to Casa speedily and safely. Did I see his fingers crossed as his hand lay on the driver's side window sill? As they say, *Ma'alesh*, so be it. Within a few minutes we were on the N1 and speeding towards the Mohamed V Airport on the southern side of Casablanca.

XXVI

"This is the end, beautiful friend, the end . . ."

MY HEAD ACHED, my back ached, my 'aches' even ached. I still couldn't believe the speed with which Omar maneuvered his ancient Peugeot through Moroccan traffic on the way to the airport. The Atlantic coast around *Larache* and *Asileh* was a blur. *Rabat* flew by as if it were a village, rather than political capitol of the country. The constant beeping of the horns (his and all others) blended into one continuous soundtrack. Where was the traffic patrol arm of *Le Sûreté Nationale* when you either needed them (to protect from the road rage that Omar was inciting) or when you didn't (allowing Omar to 'fly' me to the airport with a new land speed record).

I was wired, tired and dehydrated as we approached journey's end. Every time that I tried to drink the water sloshed all over me-it was that kind of road trip. I've been on amusement park rides that were safer. But at least I was still in one piece as he turned into the terminal driveway. He pulled up with a not so subtle application of the brakes, and the car stopped at one of the entries leading to the departure counters.

I sat back for a moment to gather my thoughts and he was the first to speak.

"You know, *mon ami*, your researches have opened many people's eyes in this land, including my own. We have been 'slapped in the face' by our own insensitive, skewed view of our own glorious heritage. We never appreciated, nor, I guess, cared for the great contribution our Jewish cousins made to Morocco century after century. *Oui,* we sort of tolerated the *Sephardic* community better than other Arab countries, but it still wasn't 100%. You showed us how truly important it is to recognize everyone's contributions to the national good, and how essential it is to support all citizens in the same way that they support the nation."

He seemed to suddenly grow pensive and quieted down. Outside of his tour guide lectures, I hadn't ever recalled that many words at one breathe. I felt humbled, and a bit embarrassed. All I'd done was follow the leads of history, and I as much told him so. He told me to shut up and take the honor he saw fit to bestow – and said that I'd be lucky if he ever did so to me again! We both laughed and I got my bag and left the car.

He started singing, "This is the end, byoo-ti-ful friend, the end . . . my only friend, the end . . ." I recognized it.

"The Doors, 1967", I said and smiled. I countered with "When the music's over, turn out the lights . . ." and waved as I entered the terminal. Omar gave a small French Foreign Legion salute and pulled away from the curb, humming to himself "The music is your special friend, dance on fire as it intends, music is your special friend . . . . Until the end'. Rolling down the window, he pulled a *Gitane* from his pocket and pushed the lighter button on the dashboard. He would await that phone call that told him the outcome.

* * *

The dusty, smeared window prevented a clean view of a magnificent scene. The attendants who worked in the bus garage back in Cairo had a lackadaisical approach to cleaning and maintenance. They hosed down the bus with water, turning dust to mud. Then, as much out of laziness than anything else, simply grabbed some old newspaper and tried to dry off the glass. All this did was to smear the mud around rather than remove it. The result was a translucent film that let a minimum of light into the compartment.

On the left was the Mediterranean Sea; sparkling a green-blue in the sunlight. To the right, just south, was the vast expanse of the Northern Sandy Desert of Sinai. The gently rolling dunes extended as far as the eye could see. So, with no view available, Sobhy shut his eyes and envisioned the region, starting to remember a more distant time. He recalled his role in the 1973 War with Israel, the *Yom Kippur* War, as the other side had called it. Funny, he thought, he no longer called them 'the enemy' but simply 'the other side' of the war. Because of the last couple of years, and the unique relationships that were forged since his travel there, something he never would have thought of just a half-decade ago, the Israelis were real people to him. He was proud of the fact that that he played a major role in the re-discovery of an ancient granite statue that had gone missing in the Cairo Museum. He took pleasure in his commitment to understanding the past through the use of archaeology, no matter where it led. He embraced the notion that, regardless of how things played out, knowing the truth and accepting it and then 'running with' for a greater understanding of the world was all that really mattered to him. So, he could accept the notion that one of the great kings of the New Kingdom of ancient Egypt could actually have been Israel's Pharaoh as well.

He valued the friendships forged through common loves of archaeology and history, and common hates that involved senseless violence and terror. The ready acceptance by the archaeological community, from the director of the Israeli Department of Antiquities and Museums, Dror Amnon, down to everyday field technicians that he met in the labs of the Israel Museum, had a deep impact on him. Throw in the personal friendships developed with people such as Kati and Eitan, and Sobhy sometimes felt more at home in the *Negev* than his own country. This inspired him all the more to work tirelessly at resolving national differences and continue his efforts at conciliation. He smiled at that and began to doze.

He dreamt of the Sinai operations that he had been involved with. He remembered the jubilant crossing of *Suez* and the surge through the sand barrier, known as the *Bar-Lev* Line by the Israelis for the general who designed it. Everyone was caught up in the moment of surprise, as each and every Egyptian soldier shouted out '*Allah Akbar*, God is great!' even if they were not Moslem; as was the case with the young archaeologist, himself a Coptic Christian. At that instant, all were unified as Egyptian citizens regardless of spirituality or ethnicity. Nubian fought alongside Alexandrian; *fellah,* or peasant, next to city dweller.

He sighed aloud, causing the seat neighbor adjacent to slightly nudge his shoulder to get him to shut up. With a small snort, he roused himself and shifted his position slightly. As he settled back in, on one hand, he lamented the unity felt in the heat of battle. Yet on the other hand, he silently celebrated the fact that the end result of the war was the eventual peace treaty with Israel, and Egypt would regain its role as leader of the Arab world.

These were the positive memories. He tried to repress the more painful ones – painful on both national and personal levels. In the greater scheme of things, the pain of defeat at the hands of the Israelis, in part due to the inept leadership of Egypt's battle and supply officers, in part due to the passion and fervor that the Israeli soldier demonstrated as he or she was faced with the potential of a 'first defeat' at the hands of Arab states, weighed heavily on him.

He wondered, how could you possibly imagine that you could defeat an enemy who felt that they were faced with extinction should they lose. That 'tooth and nail' ferocity demonstration when you had your back to the wall caused him to admire the Israelis back then, no matter how grudgingly. In fact, on the opposite side of the coin, Sobhy was repulsed by the Egyptian soldiers' response to the Israeli counterattack as they themselves re-crossed the *Suez* with their own Gazelle pontoon bridges, trapping over 40,000 Egyptian soldiers of the Third Army Corps. Brigadier General *Yusuf Affifi*, his officers and men, were clearly no match for General *Avram Adnan* and tank battalion commander *Arik Sharon.* His daring raid would be the straw that broke the Egyptian camel's back, as he positioned his troops within 100 km of Cairo, with literally no one but third string reserves in the way. There wasn't the same sense of urgency on the part of the Egyptian conscripts, most of them illiterates who had no idea of the consequences.

Yes, there was a tremendous amount of respect for the Israeli soldier. They knew how to fight, and why they had to fight. In addition, they didn't let the rigid protocols that were found in so many armies get in the way of their capabilities. In fact, a certain sense of informality between officers and men reinforced the familial feel to the military, imparting a sense of 'we're all family and need to stick together'. Officers and men called each other by first names. Israeli officers led the way, rather than fight from positions at the rear. The sad result was that there were inordinate numbers of casualties among the officers, and regrettably battlefield commissions were often fast and furious.

But on the other hand, Sobhy recognized that there were shining examples of Egyptian military prowess and heroism. He saw that in his own unit in battles that raged near the Chinese Farm. As the scene of the world's greatest, and largest, tank battle to that date, the heavy pall of smoke that surrounded the battlefield for days broke down all semblance of order and sanity. It was up to individual units to show their mettle against the re-armed and reinforced Israeli troops. His small detachment would fight almost to the last man, and his respect for his comrades was unflagging. It was here, in 1973, that he got his 'permanent watch face' as he preferred to call it; a round scar on his wrist, from an Israeli bullet that shattered flesh and bone. His anger and hatred for the Israelis and everything they represented was at times overwhelming. But when he met the American professor and archaeologist, an entirely new world was opened up to him and friends were made 'from the other side'. These became permanent, strong friendships with bonds that now seemed to be unbreakable, and for this he was grateful.

As he drifted off in this dream world, Sobhy realized how lucky he was to know what Joni Mitchell meant when she wrote the lyrics to *Both Sides Now* back in 1967.

* * *

Back in Jerusalem, Kati had called the director of *Masada* National Park, Eitan, to ask if he would come up and join her when she picked everyone up at the various locations. She told him that she felt like a *Sherut,* the shared taxi system that was so popular in Israel. It was the best-of-all-worlds public transportation.

Financially, for riders, it was in between the fares on public buses and private taxis. That made far more affordable for Israelis to travel. In addition, it was quicker and more private than a motor coach. This allowed for a bit of luxury, as they held only around seven people or so. The drawback versus the private cab was that, unless you wanted to be dropped off at a spot directly on the route, you ended up at the private taxi station at the end of the line and would need to find your way to your final destination.

Eitan was more than happy to accommodate his friends. He had just completed a major renovation project with the Swiss built cable car system that ascended the mountain. After the major excavation project of 1963-65 by Yigal Yadin of the Hebrew University, the site was opened up to tourists by the National Parks Authority. Initially, the only access came via a somewhat strenuous hike. The much more difficult one was on the east side of "The Mountain" as everyone associated with it called it. It was the famous Snake Path that twisted and turned its way nearly 1400 ft down to the Dead Sea Valley floor. This was the only access to Herod's mountain-top monolith; thus allowing for extraordinary safety and security. A handful of men at the summit could hold off thousands. The path itself was rather steep, and at places only wide enough for two people at a time. On one side was the mountain cliff, on the other it was "good night Irene" down to the base.

The 'easier' access was on the western side, and used the Roman Ramp to ascend to the acropolis of *Masada.* Non-existent at the time that Herod constructed his citadel, this ramp was built during the siege of the fortress by the Roman General *Flavius Silva* and the chief engineer, *Rubrius Gallos.* The ramp is only about 375 m high itself, and comes to within a few dozen feet of the summit. It is still in use for those who desire to ascend on foot, but not with the risks and difficulty of the Snake Path.

The original cable car was built in 1971 by the Karl Brandle Co. of Switzerland. It was 900 m long with an elevation of 290 m. There was one support pillar that was needed to aid in the suspension of the cables. However, because of this, the pulley system was open and had the potential for derailment. The new system was built by the Van Roll Co. with no support pillar necessary. This allowed the pulleys on the two cars to be fully enclosed around the cable, making it much safer. However, it needed to be noted that there was never an major accident with injury or death due to the design of the first system.

As she met Eitan at the *Tahana Mercazit Yerushalyim*, the Central Bus Station, she recalled some of the '*Masada*' stories that her American friend had relayed over the years. Her favorite involved someone that they had nicknamed, 'the nut', because of his weird ideas. He got the notion that he could run down the Snake Path from the top of the mountain as fast as he could. While doing this, with everyone yelling at him to take it easy, he descended with one had raised high in the air, balled up into a fist. At the bottom, while being berated by the tour guide, the *Masada* personnel, and just about anyone else who thought that they could influence him, he merely smiled. When asked, he simply stated, "I was just holding on to the hand of God. Nothing could possibly go wrong". Enough said, hence the term, 'the nut'.

Eitan laughed at hearing the story told through another voice. After all, he had heard it from his American archaeologist buddy often enough.

But his thoughts turned serious for a moment. For some reason, he also suddenly recalled the dangers of working on The Mountain as well. A few of the National Parks Authority personnel had come down with cardiac and respiratory problems over the years and two had died; yet no one could ascertain why. Finally, a few years ago, one of the doctors put two and two together. He compiled the data from each shift that the employees had on working the cable car. The analysis shocked him. With a nearly 1100 ft change in elevation, going from the lowest dry spot on earth, the atmospheric pressure changes took a debilitating toll on the cable car operators. They began to suffer coronary difficulties, as well as pulmonary ones.

It was a surprisingly simple 'fix'. Cable car operators were limited to only four round trips per day, rotating with other employees. This prevented a build-up of something akin to the 'bends' for a deep-sea diver. Ever since, there had been no medical problems among staff.

"You know, I totally understand all that," Kati said. "Every time that I travel either on the road from Jerusalem to the Dead Sea, or *Arad* to *Masada*, I can feel it too. You know the blue and white sign that says," *Pnai Yam, Niveau de la Mer*, Sea Level"? Well, I swear that once I pass it, within a hundred meters or so, I can feel the oppressive, heavy, low pressure atmosphere of the lowest land anywhere on earth. It takes a couple of hours to adjust. I'm just glad that they figured it all out."

By the time that they had finished their conversation, they were passing the small community of *Shoham* and were only a few minutes from the Tel Aviv city limits. They were right on time. They only hoped that Sobhy's bus was also. From there, a short wait and then they would swing by *Sde Tufa Ben Gurion*, Israel's main international airport, to get everyone reunited and headed back to Jerusalem.

* * *

A commotion in the bus caused Sobhy to stir from his deep sleep. He shifted in the seat and opened his eyes. He stared at the rucksack that he was clutching to his chest. *Where is my dubi, my bear?* he thought. Suddenly he remembered, he wasn't in his parents' flat in the Cairo neighborhood of Garden City, and he didn't have his stuffed toy with him. He was on a bus pulling into the Tel Aviv bus station. Typical of all middle easterners, Israeli and Arab alike, they were all getting up out of their seats and rummaging about the overhead racks to get their belongings and exit the bus before it had come to a complete stop in the bay that it was assigned. Of course, when the air brakes were engaged at the end, and the bus sharply stopped, several of the passengers stumbled against each other or fell back into their seats. Sobhy smiled at this, as he felt these peasants deserved their just rewards for impatience. While waiting, he texted the museum curator, Kati, that the bus had arrived and he was just about to enter the terminal.

He slowly gathered up his things and shuffled his way to the door along the others. As soon as he hit the bottom stair, the sights and sounds of "the city that never sleeps" assaulted his senses.

"*Allo! Begela! Begela! Begela! Felafel hahm! Bagels! Hot Felafel!*"

The smells were overwhelmingly wonderful. You couldn't even catch a whiff of diesel exhaust here, like back in Cairo. Street vendors lined the sidewalks just opposite the terminal exit and its shops. Although in the oldest part of the city, it still hustled and bustled and teemed with life in spite of the late hour. He hated to admit it, but Sobhy *missed* this incredibly vibrant life that was the hallmark of Israel in general, and Tel Aviv in particular.

People swarmed around him as he stood in line to purchase a *falafel*, the uibiquitous Middle East fast food sandwich. Stuffed in a *pita* pocketbread, deep-fried balls of crushed chickpeas, whole wheat, cumin, olive oil, garlic and salt and pepper nestled in a bed of shredded lettuce. A hot sauce of jalapenos, garlic, cilantro and red pepper, called *Harif*, can burn your insides. The other option, *Tahina*, a garlicky sesame sauce, were his two options. Sobhy pulled the 'Solomonic split', and spooned a little of both before topping it off with a slice of dill pickle. He thought a moment, and ordered a couple more. He wasn't sure if Kati had yet eaten, or if everyone else would be hungry as well, A litre of orange Kinley soda rounded out the take-away. As the vendor handed him the plastic sack, it was lucky that he still had some Israeli *Shekels* in his wallet from his last visit. He still remembered with pride the way that he and the others had tracked down and identified the provenance of the granite statue from the Cairo Museum storeroom, that they had dubbed "Israel's Pharaoh". That adventure had led to the development of incredible friendships, not just in the professional world of archaeology either – but deep, long lasting relationships with people that he now held dear and would do anything for them.

He smiled at the thought, and looked forward with excitement to seeing the Israelis again. A couple of people looked at him as if he was a bit crazy, with that wide grin on his face, as he hit the street outside the station. Funny, he thought, *El Majnoon*, 'the crazy one', is what he nicknamed his American colleague and friend. He hoped that he made his flight out of Morocco.

"Ya Sobhy! *Habibi*! Over here!" Both Kati and Eitan jumped out of the car and embraced the Egyptian. Eitan grabbed the carry-on and slid it into the boot of the car. Sobhy held on to the plastic bag of take-away as if his life depended on it.

The reunion was almost complete. The band of friends that had solved the mystery of the granite statue fragment hidden in the Cairo Museum were almost all together again. Now it was time to hit the road and wait for the final member at *Ben Gurion* Airport.

"*Azeh re-akh!* What an aroma!" said Eitan as they rolled out of the car park on the way to the Highway 1 that would lead them to the airport and then on to Jerusalem.

"I figured that an early evening snack might be in order before the flight arrived from Maroc", Sobhy said. "I also know that *everyone* that I know loves *ta'amiya*, or as you say here, *falafel*. The vendor inside the bus station is perfectly positioned, you know. I couldn't resist, so I got enough for all of us, including *El Majnoon*." He was referring to his American friend en route.

They all laughed at this, but Eitan kept eyeing the bag covetously.

"I think that maybe I'll keep that bag up here in front with me, away from the hands of the esteemed director of *Masada* National Park." She smiled and then winked over her shoulder at Eitan. As always, whoever was the recipient of that patented smile always melted and acquiesced to anything she said. But, as her friends knew, behind that smile was a strong, sharp, person who could match wits and hold her own with anyone, on any level. The Israeli and the Egyptian both knew this, and appreciated it tremendously.

They climbed the gentle hills of the *Shephelah* as they road made its way to the vicinity of the ancient town of *Lydda*, known as modern day *Lod*. The small community played a major role in the history of the biblical world. Located about fifteen km southeast of Tel Aviv, it is in the heart of the central district of Israel today. A modern community of nearly 80,000 people, it is as old as the land itself. The archaeological record shows evidence that dates to the Early Bronze Age, around 3200 BCE.

Sobhy remarked that this town is one of many mentioned on the list of Canaanite towns described in the annals of *Thutmose III*; engraved on the walls of his chapel at the marvelous *Karnak* Temple in *Luxor* – dated to around 1468 BCE. You could see the pride on his face.

By the time of the Israelite Conquest of the land at the beginning of the Iron Age, the name appeared as a town occupied by the tribe of Benjamin in 3 biblical texts; *Chronicles, Ezra and Nehemiah.*

Until the Romans destroyed it in 70 CE, the town served as a center for Jewish thought. After that, it was made a Roman city. The Arab conquest in the 7th century by *Amr Ibn al-As* renamed it *al-Lud*, creating a capitol of the Military District of Palestine. Salvage excavations carried out in the late 1990s by the Israel Antiquities Authority discovered well preserved Roman mosaic floors. However, part of the tragedy of salvage excavation is that there is no additional money for preservation or restoration – the floors were covered over until a later time with added funds.

Both Eitan and Sobhy chafed at hearing this from Kati, that font of archaeological knowledge. They both knew firsthand about the lack of funds for archaeological research and restoration. They sat, fuming, for a while, and all remained silent for the duration. Within a few minutes, the exit for the airport came into view, and they proceeded to the mobile phone parking lot to wait to hear from their friend.

As Kati called the automated arrivals hotline, both Sobhy and Eitan got out of the car and spread the contents of the 'lunchbox' bag on the boot lid of the car. They then leaned against the car and ate the sandwiches while watching planes arrive and depart from the airport, a handful of km away. At most airports, the phone lot was relatively near. However, given the realities of the MidEast, it needed to be situated outside of handheld rocket launcher range. In addition, the IDF routinely patrolled the lot and constantly asked for ID. In Israel, security was *never* considered to be overkill.

As she punched the button to end the call, she remarked that the flight from Casablanca was on time, and due to arrive, according to the recorded message, within thirty minutes or so 'Mideast standard time'; which meant at any time in the next, say century! They all laughed at this as Eitan handed her a *falafel* and plastic cup of Kinley. She sat on the bonnet of the car while the other two sat on the concrete curb by the front bumper.

Soon, her cell phone chimed with a text. The flight had arrived but not yet gotten to the gate. I texted her that it would probably take a bit of time, as there were a couple of families of Moroccan Jews who were making *aliyah*, emigration to Israel.

She texted back, "So . . . ?"

My response, "Prob 15 fam mem ea pty . . ." "Probably means 15 family members in each party", for those of us who can be quite clueless when it comes to 'txt abbrv'. I smiled (LOL) and envisioned her response.

She started to laugh, and the two companions looked up quizzically. She showed them the text, and they too joined in. They then sat back and waited for the final call indicating that I was walking out of the terminal.

The call soon followed, and the three friends packed up and headed for the arrivals terminal drive. The traffic was nightmarish, as Israelis and tourists alike queued up on the sidewalk for their rides. Since a majority of them had ample, if not overwhelming, amounts of baggage, the approach was bumper to bumper, cars sitting as family members greeted each other, weeping and laughing at the same time. There was a total disregard for anyone outside each passenger's immediate circle of friends and relatives, and horns blared and tempers ran a bit short. *'Welcome to Israel'* was the only thought that crossed my mind as I fought my way to the curb with my carry-on. The nature of the crowd brought a cartoon to mind. A vulture was approaching the security counter at an airport, and the screener on duty reminded the bird of prey that he was limited to 'one *carrion* per person'. That's how it felt.

I got to the first layer of people by the curb and saw Kati's car waiting two rows farther out from the sidewalk. She had the perfect spot, with no other cars sandwiching her in and blocking her. I waved, and three hands popped out of the windows and waved back. Because of security measures and constantly patrolling soldiers, no one was supposed to sit and wait more than a couple of minutes. Well, rules were meant to be broken. The officers had absolutely no desire to go up against a Jewish mother's wrath while waiting for a son or daughter to return from their after-army *tiyul shehroor*, their global adventure to let off steam and explore before settling down to the 'real world'. Actually, no one *ever* wanted to go up against any Jewish mother *at any time*!

She popped the boot lid remotely and I threw my stuff in and slammed the lid home. I then got into the back seat with Eitan, hugging and fist-bumping all around the front seat occupants, then leaning over and giving Kati a kiss on the cheek. As was always the case with ex-IDF soldiers, Eitan immediately fell into a deep sleep. They could sleep anywhere, anytime. Sobhy and I caught up on the last few days, while Kati drove on in the dark, commenting when she could. She drove out of the airport area and hit the on-ramp to Jerusalem and the flat on *Bnei Batira* Street.

We found a parking spot a half block from her home after the forty minute drive. We roused Eitan from his beauty sleep (not that he needed it) and dragged the bags into Kati's flat. Although we were all a bit 'wired' (except for Eitan) we needed to get some sleep because the following day was a big one for all.

Apparently our Egyptian friend was too wired to sleep. He told them he'd just watch a bit of television and probably nod off while doing so. A couple of murmured 'whatevers' and the rest of us retreated to the bedrooms.

Sobhy picked up the remote. He was constantly amazed at Israeli television. Cable and satellite systems offered a plethora of viewing opportunities. Since the 'Egyptian Spring', things had been a bit tightened up by the Morsi government. In fact, some networks were even blocked from being received due to 'questionable content' by the Ministers of Media, *Salah Medwali*, Culture, *Mohamed Arab*, and Religious Endowment, *Taalat Salem*. Although labeled as 'Independent' political party members, they clearly were towing the line of the Moslem Brotherhood backed coalition of the president. Sobhy felt that the writing was on the wall if things continued in this way. As a matter of fact, he was appalled that even Big Bird on *Share'a Simsim*, Sesame Street, was taken off the air. He had to smile inwardly though. The attitude even trickled down to politics in the last American election. Didn't Romney say that he too would end endowments to the American educational network. *What is the world coming to?* He thought.

Another thing that amazed him was the airing of Arabic networks without censorship. Some of the most virulent material came across the airways from dictatorial regimes in the region hellbent on destroying Israel; if not with their rhetoric and loosely veiled threats, then with the actual threat of violence. Even Ahmadinejad of Iran got seen by Israel. He guessed that the concept of 'knowing your enemy' was essential in Israel. The citizenry of Israel was head and shoulders above the average Egyptian when it came to viewing the world and understanding it. He only hoped that the current trends in Egyptian politics didn't blunt the slowly growing notion that taking an interest in the world by all her citizens was for the eventual benefit of Egypt on the whole.

As he was surfing the channels, he was shocked to discover an Egyptian station that was broadcasting re-runs of the Egyptian Premier League, the national league for soccer. The reason for re-broadcasts was that the government had suspended play for a while, due to the increasing cases of fan violence. Many people in the world had no idea as to the frenzied levels of violence that was on the rise globally among the rabid fans. It seemed as if all of their frustrations politically, socially, economically, were now being played out in the stands and parking lots and public transportation venues rather than in peaceful political demonstration.

Sadly, several months after the event, riots were still commonplace in Suez City. Some people wanted *any* pretext for demonstrating against the government.

The match that was being aired was from last season, between 'his' team, *Al Ahly*, and *Zamalek SC*. They were bitter rivals. He sat back and watched. He sighed, as he remembered the most incredible year for *any* professional football club in the world. Back in 2005, *Al Ahly* did the almost unimaginable feat of going undefeated in forty-six matches! He sat back, and watched as international star *Moustafa Kamel Mansour* scored two goals for his team within five minutes. *Ah, for the good old days . . . .* as he drifted off to sleep.

* * *

Sunrises in the Mideast are quite spectacular. And sunrise over Jerusalem, well, it can be stunning. The "City of Gold" as honored by the Israeli songstress, *Shuly Natan*, gleams in the sunlight, as it plays off the yellow-hued *Nari* limestone that accounts for the vast majority of the buildings. As my body clock has always been geared to the sun, no matter what time, no matter where in the world, I found myself rising before the others. I found Sobhy snoring on the couch, and the television on. I turned it off and he snuffled and rolled over, still sound asleep. I crept out of the flat on tiptoe and padded up the stairs to the rooftop. There, amid the solar hot water panels and tanks, called *Dod Shemesh*, I sat down with a hot tea and *bagela* and prepared to watch 'the show'. A low bank of clouds enveloped the crest of the Mt. of Olives, *Har Zitim*, on the eastern horizon. They picked up the first rays of light and turned grey, then a shade of purple. Within a few moments they seemed to dissipate and the yellow-gold beams of light began to warm the earth.

As I watched the climb, the Old City, just off to the left, a bit northeast of me, started to come awake with the bathing rays of warmth. The bells of the Church of the *Pater Noster*, also known as *Eleona*, began to peel; summoning the faithful to morning prayer. At the same time, the plaintive call of the *muezzin* reminded the Moslem community of its obligation that "prayer is better than sleep". What an incredible city.

Slowly, as the sunlight rose over the city and embraced me with its warmth as well, I was joined by the others. Apparently, the pull of this wonderful city awakened them as well. Sobhy was first, followed by Kati. It always amazed him that he, as an Egyptian, was actually standing *in Al Quds*, The Holy City. Although, as a Coptic Christian, the role of Jerusalem didn't have the impact that it did for other branches of his faith, or for Jews or Moslems as its third holiest location, he was still in awe to be here.

"Think of it," he said. "we are standing at the crossroads of western religious thought. Where else in the world can this kind of convergence occur."

We murmured our agreement, nursed our drinks, and watched some more. When the entire ball of yellow-white rose to its full diameter above the horizon, we retreated back to the apartment to plan the day. As we approached the door, Eitan stumbled out, rubbing his eyes. We ushered him back in and made a typical Israeli *kibbutz* breakfast; mixed salad of tomatoes, cucumbers, onions and olives, hardboiled eggs, thick-sliced bread, and equally 'thick' coffee.

After breakfast, I ushered them all into the salon and cleared off the coffee table. I then grabbed the cylinder that Kati had been keeping safe. True to her word, she hadn't said a thing to anyone in the Israel Antiquities Authority, or her close friends. The only thing that *mekhes*, customs, knew was that she had a tube of *posterim*, posters, that she was bringing back from Germany. Nobody had even asked about the contents as she left the airport terminal. If they had asked, she would have supplied them with a letter that she had worked up. While the German curator, Conrad, had been showing me around the facility for a few minutes, she had purloined a couple of sheets of writing paper with the museum logo from his desk. She then had word processed and printed a generic letter with no signature that described a number of poster reproductions that she was taking back to the Israel Museum. But things went so smoothly that it wasn't needed.

I twisted the plastic cap off of the cardboard tube and gently slid the rolled felt out and on to the table. Eitan and Sobhy placed coffee cups and plates on the corners. I then began to remove the topmost layer of material, revealing what was below. Sobhy and Kati had already seen the scrolls, but nevertheless still let out collective gasps. Eitan was seeing them for the first time, and clearly was stunned speechless. He looked in awe at documents that outlined historical events dated to well over twenty-five centuries ago. The lettering was so crisp even after all the centuries, that he could make out a few words here and there. After all, *Aramaic* is the first-cousin to both biblical and modern Hebrew. Where he stumbled, Kati helped out with translation. He glanced at her admiringly; then resumed staring at the four documents.

Sobhy was still overwhelmed at the coup that we had pulled off, and now had to work our way through a suitable arrangement for both Israel and Egypt via back-channels and secrecy. We also needed to figure a plausible way to explain how Israel and Egypt would wind up with four scrolls that German archaeologists had dug up decades ago. And then there was the matter of the documents 'disappearing' before World War Two. How were we to ever explain them 'magically reappearing' in two other countries.

We headed out to our meeting with the IAA director, who preferred offices in the steeped-in-history grounds of the Rockefeller Museum, originally known at the Palestine Archaeological Museum, located just north of the Old City in the eastern side of the city.

In 1925, one of the world's great Near Eastern archaeologists, James Henry Breasted of the Oriental Institute of the University of Chicago, noted that Jerusalem had no museum to showcase archaeology of the biblical world. As a result, he would lobby the Rockefeller family for funds to help build a regional center. A site would be chosen on the eastern side of the city, near the northeast corner of the Old City, on a hill known as *Karm al-Sheikh*. It was named after *Sheikh Muhammad al-Halili*, the *Mufti*, or religious leader, of Jerusalem in the 17th century. Although the dedication ceremony and setting of the cornerstone took place on 19 June, 1930, the building itself wouldn't be opened for over eight years, in 1938.

Today, with the reunification of the city, it serves as the second most important archaeological museum in Jerusalem. Its library is unsurpassed in its depth and scope, and scholars from around the world make use of the facility.

* * *

We waited patiently in the small outer chamber for Dror Amnon. Small demitasses of *'ahwah masboot'*, thick sweet Turkish coffee, had been drained in the twenty minutes that it took for the Director to wrap up some business. When he came out to greet us, he was effusive in his praise for the international relationships that we had forged in the previous several months. He gave Sobhy an enormous bear-hug of greeting, lifting him a few cm off the ground. Sobhy roared with laughter as he broke free and kissed Amnon on both cheeks and then again for a third peck.

Not one to waste undo time, after the initial greetings, he asked what was so important. Kati pulled the cardboard cylinder from her rucksack and slowly slid the rolled documents out of the container. While the rest of us grinned in anticipation, Dror Amnon's look of bemusement quickly morphed into one of amazement. He gazed at scrolls that hadn't been 'home' in 6 decades; or 2,400 years, depending on how you counted.

He took a deep breath, and simply stared in awe. No one spoke, no one broke the magic of the moment. Israeli, American Jew and Coptic Egyptian all stood in the presence of pieces of history thought lost during World War II.

"I have to think this through a bit. Let me get this straight, *I* am the one who needs to break the news to the Minister of Education in Germany, and Director of the Supreme Council of Antiquities in Egypt, that some Elephantine Papyri that had been appropriated by German archaeologists nearly 80 years ago in Aswan suddenly have reappeared in Israel? *Ov favoy!Azeh balagan yesh li!* Holy #(*&$*#, what a mess!)

We all laughed, the tension broken.

"I'm up for any ideas" the Director said. Suddenly, true to MidEast culture in any language, we all started talking at once. Then, again, as part of the polite side of MidEast culture in any language, we all profusely apologized for breaking into to each other's thoughts at the same time. A second of silence . . . and we all started in unison presenting our points again!

It reminded me of that bus ride in the *Arava* a few years ago, the overflowing busload of passengers, and the dog who sat next to his master, oblivious to the human clamor for his seat that disrupted even the usually unflappable *Egged* driver nearly seven m forward in the bus. It got to be so bad, that he pulled over in the midst of the desert and ordered everyone off the bus. Having done that, he proceeded to ask what the commotion at the rear was all about. The passenger with the dog said that he had purchased a ticket (and seat) for the dog; and, even though there were nearly a dozen people standing, he felt that the dog deserved the seat!

The uproar continued amongst the passengers, until the driver did what he felt was in the best interest of Israeli-style democracy. He took a vote. Believe it or not, *the dog won!* And, true to Israeli form, the rest of the three hour journey to *Beersheva* was completed in relative silence, although a few standees groused quietly under their breath.

Finally, a plan was hashed out. Amnon would call Germany, and explain that, with the passing of a German-born Israeli citizen who had emigrated to Palestine in 1946 as a survivor immediately after the war, his possessions had been gone through by his descendants. These included a safe deposit box in *Bank HaPoalim.* In cataloging the contents, they discovered the tube that contained the scrolls, previously unbeknownst to any family member. With the 'thief' now dead, after six decades, and the statute of limitations (of a crime that no one even knew about) expired, it would serve neither country's best interests to dredge up the past. In essence, with the new approach to archaeology and artifact ownership, certainly the Germans didn't want to insist on having material 'stolen' from Egypt in the 1920s returned to them. After all, they were still being obstinate when it came to the Ludwig Borchardt theft of the stunningly beautiful Nefertiti bust in 1913. In addition, they certainly didn't want to revisit anything that took place during the era of the Third Reich and the Nazis . . . .

The IAA Director was absolutely certain that the German government would agree to 'his take' on the re-discovery. In addition, he would draft a letter that Sobhy would take back to the Supreme Council, along with the one scroll whose connection to the Elephantine Jewish community was more tenuous. Its historic significance as part of the vast Elephantine collection was of greater import to the history of Egypt at that time, rather than the Elephantine Jewish community. Plus, the reference made to the Jews living on the island, and Egypt's recognition of its 2,500 year old Jewish community, would help the current government in its international relations as well. Pres. Morsi could put a feather in his *keffiyeh* over this one, showing the world the ready acceptance of its Jewish citizenry then, and now.

Sobhy thought that it was a brilliant idea. Although he was unsure as to its potential success, he was certain that its plausibility offered an olive branch, and a face-saving approach for all three countries. The rest of us agreed with his analysis. We left the Director to carefully word his statement, send it out, and anxiously wait for the replies.

* * *

We left the Rockefeller and headed toward the Old City's Damascus Gate. For several months now, the situation in Jerusalem between its eastern Arab residents and its Jewish western inhabitants had calmed a bit.

Ever since the incredible, energetic and imaginative Teddy Kollek left office in 1993, the mayoral post had been a contentious one to say the least. Kollek's successor, Ehud Olmert, served two terms; the first *Likud* member to hold the position. He had a wonderful vision for the city, enlisting great minds to create major building projects that would enhance its image in the world. These included millions of *shekels* for revamping the educational system, developing a road infrastructure, including the 'ring road', and beginning construction of a city light rail system. Perhaps little known, but still of major importance, was the respect that he gained when he addressed an international conference on conflict resolution in Derry, N. Ireland in 1995. He spoke about how political leaders can address the fears between people that prevents their relationships to grow. His closing remark was a powerful one.

"How are fears born? They are born because of differences in tradition and history; they are born because of differences in emotional, political and national circumstances. Because of such differences, people fear they cannot live together. If we are to overcome such fear, a credible and healthy political process must be carefully and painfully

developed. A political process that does not aim to change the other or to overcome differences, but that allows each side to live peacefully in spite of their differences."

It's sad that his legacy would be tainted with scandal and corruption during his tenure at Prime Minister of Israel from 2006-09, ending with his resignation; facing a conviction for breach of trust in a couple of major political corruption cases.

However, the city would suffer under its next mayor, Uri Lupolianski. A *Haredi*, or extremely Orthodox Jew, he ran for mayor as a member of United Torah Judaism. He made a considerable effort to serve the city in an unbiased way. To attract students to Jerusalem's institutions of higher education, Lupolianski inaugurated the "Lupolianski Package" which offers special tuition and housing subsidies to university students renting apartments in the city center. Hi-tech workers who choose to live and work in Jerusalem were also eligible for a monthly grant to cover part of their living expenses. In addition, earlier in his career, he founded the *Yad Sarah*, designed to help the elderly and disabled. It lends out medical equipment and supplies a variety of services to the sick, elderly and lonely. However, this all was eclipsed by his deeply religious position on many issues. Lupolianski was accused of preferring Jews for civil service over Arabs, and of basing municipal decisions on his religious views. He also clashed with the Israeli gay and lesbian community for trying to stop their annual Gay pride parade in Jerusalem. But no matter how 'religious' one might be, the specter of graft and political corruption still looms heavily over the office. In 2011, a couple of years after leaving office, he was indicted with 17 others for allegedly giving or receiving bribes to advance various real estate ventures.

The current mayor, Nir Barkat, is a secular politician, contrasting with both his predecessor Lupoliansky and his rival in the election, Meir Porush, both described as *Haredi* Jews. Barkat started his career in the hi-tech industry by founding a software company called BRM in 1988, which specialized in antivirus software. He then entered the political arena by serving on Jerusalem's city council before winning the mayoral election in 2008. His visions for Jerusalem seem to be more conciliatory, stressing the secular over the spiritual. As a result, the calmer face of the city seems to be prevailing.

So, as we wandered through the Damascus Gate, it was more reminiscent of the heady days of cooperation in the 1970s. There was a sense of friendship and hospitality, albeit somewhat guarded. Kati led us down the cobbled street, past the canopied fruit and vegetable stalls, to *Sheikh Rahman* street, branching off to the left. We proceeded about fifty m, then we approached a small café with a couple of round tables fronting it, jutting out into the passers-by way. The hand-painted sign that lazily swung above us read, *Uncle Moustache.*

I immediately was drawn back to the past. This was *the* hangout for young travelers in the 70s. It had phenomenally good coffee, and, for a price, a limited variety of other 'stimulants' that were trendy during that time. No, no, no . . .

there was nothing hard or addictive, it was limited to weed and hash. 'Uncle's' moustache was now all grey, but the gleam in his eye was still evident. Of course, Eitan and I recognized him immediately, but we were simply two of perhaps thousands who stopped by his small restaurant. His staff simply smiled and took our orders. There was only one significant difference that I noticed – a small sign hung in the window that announced the location as a wi-fi hotspot. How times have changed.

This was what grabbed Sobhy's attention much more quickly than the rest of us. He immediately pulled out his tablet and began to surf, while the rest of us drank in the view . . . and extremely good coffee. We chatted quietly among ourselves, when he suddenly became animated.

"You've got to see this!" he exclaimed. "There's amazing news out of Morocco. I've checked several websites, like *Le Soir Echos* and *La Gazette du Maroc* in French, *Morocco Mirror* in English, and *Al Anbaa,* the official newspaper of the government of King Mohamed VI; and they all say basically the same thing. The Moroccan government is in the process of officially sponsoring the creation of a new exhibit that will tour the country, and eventually many locales throughout the world, that highlights the contribution of its Moroccan Jewish community throughout the ages. It goes on to say this new endeavor is in part the result of the recent discovery of ancient documents that attest to the *significant* Jewish contributions to establishing Moroccan independence and economic security centuries ago. The king is even quoted as saying that its time that not only Moroccans, but all Arabs, recognize the significance of their Sephardic brethren. Wow! He's really going on to the branch for this one."

"You mean, 'out on a limb' don't you?"

I smiled. Once again, the Egyptian, trying his best, butchered another idiom in the English language. But I also smiled at remembering the parting words that I had with Omar just a few short days earlier. It seemed as if things were coming full circle again.

We were all feeling good about the situation as we relaxed and waited for word from the Israeli Director of IDAM.

Meanwhile, both Kati's and Eitan's smartphones buzzed with incoming text messages. Both said the same thing; 'Come back to the office as soon as possible. Amnon'. We finished our coffees and hurried back to the Rockefeller.

As soon as we entered the administrative wing, we were ushered into the Director's office. We found Dror Amnon sitting at his desk, with his back to us, gazing out the window at the museum courtyard below. He swiveled around and faced us, all smiles.

"I have good news, *Hevrai*, my friends. I not only got an email from the Director of the Supreme Council of Antiquities in Cairo, but got a phone call just a few minutes ago. We have a resolution that's good for both countries, respects both people, and acknowledges our joint efforts in furthering relationships for the two. It seems that there is a glimmer of perfection in an otherwise imperfect world."

We all looked at each other, then at him, in anticipation.

"Ya Sobhy, *habibi*! My dear Egyptian friend and colleague. You are to take one of the four Elephantine Papyri back to Cairo with you. Your director and I have mutually agreed as to which one. I'm sure that you should find an email waiting for you."

Sobhy immediately began to pull out his tablet.

"Not NOW, *Ya Hamar*! Wait til after the meeting," I hissed to him. He grinned sheepishly and surreptitiously slid the device back into his bag. Fortunately the IDAM director missed the sequence.

"We will be issuing a joint statement that describes 'a unique discovery' in a safety deposit box found in Israel of some Elephantine Papyri that describe in detail the role of the Jewish community in Aswan nearly 24 centuries ago. We will go on to say that, in a sign of extraordinary cooperation between Israel and Egypt, one of the documents would be immediately returned to the Supreme Council of Antiquities. But, as a sign of gratitude in the pursuit of historical accuracy, the Egyptian government has put the three documents on 'permanent loan' to the Israeli Department of Antiquities and Museums to serve as the core of a new exhibit that revolves around Jewish Egyptian life in the Persian and Hellenistic Ages. This exhibit may eventually even tour Egypt, provided that the political timing is right."

We sat back, incredulous looks on our faces. Then, typical of the Mid East, we all started yammering in concert, laughing all the while. Dror Amnon served us all coffee, but then, amazingly, opened a desk drawer and pulled out a bottle of 777 Israeli brandy. He then poured generous measures in each of our cups as well "*L'haim! Sakhten!* Congratulations to us all in the pursuit of our collective pasts!"

* * *

We all couldn't wait to get started on implementing the arrangement. Sobhy eventually got his email confirming from Egypt's end the initiation of the deal. He was escorted by Israeli security to the airport with a new, stainless steel, airtight cylinder that housed the papyrus scroll. A small Israeli Gulfstream was waiting for him at Ben Gurion Airport, along with a member of the Egyptian Consular Office in Jerusalem. Together, they flew back to Cairo as guests of the State of Israel. However, their arrival at Heliopolis was subdued, security tight; until they were able to get into the confines of the Egyptian Museum. After all, the square fronting the museum, *Tahrir*, was still the site of daily demonstrations both for, and against, the current government. The 'Egyptian Spring' was still blossoming, and on occasion violently.

There, Sobhy was greeted as a hero, bringing back an Egyptian treasure that had been missing for decades. It was then announced that he would serve as the curator for the development of a new exhibit that focused on the Elephantine Papyri, prominently featuring the significant role that the Jewish community played on the island of *Yeb*, twenty-four centuries earlier. It would open in several months, and eventually tour in Alexandria and Aswan, before (hopefully) going on to Israel and Morocco.

No mention was ever made of Berlin, and that tragic connection.

* * *

Eitan returned to *Arad*, and his direction of *Masada* National Park. It seemed that there were rumors about re-making the movie of the same name, given new archaeological discoveries that may have tweaked the story just a bit from the Josephus-based mini-series of the early 1980s. There was even a bit of talk about dedicating it Ehud Netzer, the recently deceased Israel archaeologist who dedicated his whole career to King Herod and discovered his royal tomb – only to die on the site in a tragic fall. But as Eitan would say, 'what a way to go!'

And for me, it was the same refrain, as always.

* * *

Kati and I left Jerusalem and also went south to *Arad;* once more heading out to *Nahal Tzipporah* a few kliks to the east. A *bedouin* friend had a family camp there, but the season for them at that locale had yet to begin, and I felt it to be just the ticket. Due to a plentiful winter rain, this part of the desert continued its riot of colorful desert flora well into late Spring. We left our jeep under a rock overhang near the entry, and hiked the rest of the way. The twists and turns of the *wadi* yielded surprises at every bend. The loudest sounds that we heard were our heartbeats, the absence of other people a blessing. It was the time of *Pesach*, the Passover – when thoughts naturally turn to the *Midbar*, and another, earlier wilderness encounter in the desert. For after all, *we too* were slaves of a Pharaoh in Egypt . . . . as the liturgy tells us. So too were the Jews of Elephantine, and in many ways, their descendants in Morocco.

"Does not wisdom call out? Does not understanding raise her voice? On the heights along the way, where the paths meet, she takes her stand;"
(Prov 8:1-2)

Edwards Brothers Malloy
Thorofare, NJ USA
March 7, 2014